"Charming, messy, and achingly relatable, *Mighty Millie Novak* nails that tender time of finding your footing and claiming your space in a daunting world. A fantastic reminder of the power of sports, teammates, and believing in yourself, this is a book I am definitely cheering for!"
—Dahlia Adler, award-winning author of *Cool for the Summer* and *Home Field Advantage*

"*Mighty Millie Novak* is a roller-derby-filled sapphic coming-of-age novel about falling in love, coming into your own, and what it means to be part of a team. A delight of a read."
—Rachael Lippincott, *New York Times* best-selling author of *She Gets the Girl*

"Full of heart and with a pace faster than a derby bout, this charming sapphic story is perfect for the roller derby girlies, the queer kids looking for their place and their people, and anyone curious about derby life and the fierce players behind it. An absolute treat!"
—Jamie Pacton, award-winning, best-selling author of *The Absinthe Underground, The Vermilion Emporium, Furious, Lucky Girl,* and *The Life and (Medieval) Times of Kit Sweetly*

"*Mighty Millie Novak* is a delight of a debut that'll have you cheering for Mighty as she navigates complex relationships—familial, platonic, and romantic—all while exploring what it means to be authentic to herself, both on and off the roller derby rink. With authentic social anxiety rep, pun-tastic derby nicknames, and relatable teenage mishaps, Mighty will steal your heart, one lap at a time."
—Amelia Diane Coombs, author of *Keep My Heart in San Francisco* and *Exactly Where You Need to Be*

"Set against the thrilling, fast-paced backdrop of roller derby, *Mighty Millie Novak* checks every box for what a YA should be. The perfectly imperfect Mighty's struggles with social anxiety, navigation of loneliness and divorce, and sweet sapphic romance came together for a satisfying and authentic conclusion. A vibrant and poignant debut in contemporary YA."

—Serena Kaylor, author of *The Calculation of You and Me*

"Sincere and big-hearted, with a hero that truly lives up to her name. You'll want to cheer for Mighty Millie both on and off the track as she navigates changing friendships and complicated family dynamics along the rough-and-tumble road to self-discovery. Holden shines an authentic and loving spotlight on the roller derby community. Grab a bookmark and helmet and strap yourself in for the ride!"

—Kit Rosewater, author of The Derby Daredevils series

"*Mighty Millie Novak* explores the parts of ourselves we often keep hidden from the outside world. The parts that are unsure, confused, deeply insecure, and afraid. The parts that wonder if this is just another stage or will we always feel like this. Holden doesn't avoid tackling the sometimes uncomfortable truths and thoughts that come with being a teenager, but she also shows how wonderfully fun, surprising, messy, and exciting it all can be. Especially on roller skates! A charmingly cute, honest, and raw debut!"

—Jackie Khalilieh, author of *Something More*

"A heartfelt story full of feelings, messiness, and roller derby! *Mighty Millie Novak* shows how life's shake-ups can quickly put everything in perspective and help us see what makes us mighty. Millie's derby family rolled their way into my heart!"

—Jenna Miller, author of *We Got the Beat*

"You'll fall hard for Mighty Millie Novak on her journey from rookie member of the Prairie Skate Juniors team, feeling like a loner fraud, to living up to her Mighty name, as she's forced to find the courage to learn who she really is, what she wants, and how to stand up for her dreams, against the fast, fun backdrop of roller derby drama with a wonderful cast of colorful characters, and the sweetest sapphic love story! *Mighty Millie Novak* is a dazzling debut!"

—Keely Parrack, author of *10 Hours to Go*

MIGHTY MILLIE NOVAK

BY ELIZABETH HOLDEN

Mendota Heights, Minnesota

First Edition
First Printing, 2024

Book design by Karli Kruse
Cover design by Karli Kruse
Cover illustration by Chloe Friedlein

Flux, an imprint of North Star Editions, Inc.

This is a work of fiction. Names, characters, places, and incidents are either the product of the author's imagination or are used fictitiously, and any resemblance to actual persons living or dead, business establishments, events, or locales is entirely coincidental.

Library of Congress Cataloging-in-Publication Data
Names: Holden, Elizabeth, 1981- author.
Title: Mighty Millie Novak / Elizabeth Holden.
Description: First edition. | Mendota Heights, Minnesota: Flux, 2024. |
    Audience: Grades 10–12.
Identifiers: LCCN 2024004348 (print) | LCCN 2024004349 (ebook) | ISBN
    9781635831030 (paperback) | ISBN 9781635831047 (ebook)
Subjects: CYAC: Roller derby--Fiction. | Roller skating--Fiction. |
    Self-esteem--Fiction. | Family problems--Fiction. | Crushes--Fiction. |
    Lesbians--Fiction.
Classification: LCC PZ7.1.H64574 Mi 2024 (print) | LCC PZ7.1.H64574
    (ebook) | DDC [Fic]--dc23
LC record available at https://lccn.loc.gov/2024004348
LC ebook record available at https://lccn.loc.gov/2024004349

Flux
North Star Editions, Inc.
2297 Waters Drive
Mendota Heights, MN 55120
www.fluxnow.com

Printed in Canada

For Mom and Buff, for absolutely everything.

CHAPTER 1

The next five minutes were going to determine everything about my future—or at least, my future in roller derby, which was all that mattered.

I wiped the sweat off my face with the hem of my T-shirt, took one more puff from my inhaler, and skated back onto the track. My muscles were warm from the previous hour of drills and skills, and my mind—well, it was as clear as it was going to be, all things considered. The only thing left? The dreaded 27 in 5.

"Get it, Mighty!" Pumpkin shouted from the sidelines. She'd already done hers, skating 29 easy laps in five minutes, and was now sitting on the edge of the rink, unlacing her skates. I smiled at her weakly, glad for the encouragement but at the same time wishing she wouldn't watch. The fewer witnesses, the better.

I'd gotten the required 27 laps a few times in practice, but that was practice, when the pressure was off. And it had always been close. Today it seemed less likely, given my nerves, my exhaustion from the rest of the assessment, and the effort it took to push away thoughts of my parents' announcement this morning.

Stork rolled onto the track and lined up behind me. Great. Stork was tall and angular, like her namesake, and her legs devoured the track effortlessly. She would blow past me immediately.

The white of Stork's mouthguard flashed as she smiled at me. "Don't be nervous, Mighty."

I smiled back half-heartedly, not replying, vaguely offended. In what universe would I not be nervous? If I got even 26.5 laps, it meant no real roller derby for me, just more time with the Skatertots, practicing and hoping and dreaming.

"Everybody ready?" The powerful voice of Coach Ann boomed through the rink.

I braced my toe stops on the ground and bent my knees, ready to sprint at the whistle blast. I could do this. I didn't need to compete with Stork. Everyone was always talking about her speed, complimenting her, saying what potential she had as a jammer . . . wouldn't they all be surprised if it were me, Millie Novak, a.k.a. Dino Might, who was the fastest? I could be more than just the goofy one, the comic relief. I could be an actual threat on the track. I could—

The whistle blew, startling me. Instead of a perfect sprint on my toe stops to accelerate, I stumbled, slipped, and flung my arms out for balance. Stork smacked into my flailing right arm as she blasted past me, and I tumbled onto my knees. Oh God, there went my chance.

I picked myself up as fast as I could, trying not to panic, and started to skate. Before I could even reach the first turn, Stork was coming around again.

"Sorry about hitting you!" she called over her shoulder as she passed me.

Predictably, Ann and our other coach, Cleo, immediately shouted, "No sorries in derby!" in unison at Stork. But I was glad she'd apologized.

I'd done the math yesterday: I needed to average 5.4 laps per minute. I kept count in my head, though Ann's count would be my official score. When Cleo called out the end of the first minute, I had barely done five laps. Not enough. I needed to speed up. Despair crept in, and I tried to outskate it.

Two minutes in. My lungs burned, my thighs burned, and I'd only done a little more than ten laps. Had I used my inhaler before I started? Suddenly I wasn't sure. What if I had an asthma attack right now? What if—

I nearly collided with A. Dora Bell, a skinny, wobbly girl with enormous glasses.

"Sorry!" I shouted to Dora.

"No sorries in derby!" the coaches yelled.

Three minutes down. Sweat dripped from under my helmet and stung my eyes. My legs quivered.

"Keep doing your crossovers, Mighty!" Ann shouted. "You need to pick up the pace a little."

I crossed right leg over left, right leg over left, again, again, again. My legs trembled. I kept moving. I tried to ignore the fear rattling in my brain, tried to ignore the sound of Stork's lap counter yelling, "Twenty laps already? You're crushing it, Stork!"

Oh, it was hopeless. I'd never wanted anything as badly as I wanted to be an official member of the Prairie Skate Juniors, but how could it happen, given my speed today? Maybe I could beg Ann to let me redo it. Maybe I could even tell her about my morning, that my parents had announced their long-time-coming divorce just two hours before I hit the rink. How could Ann not take pity on me then?

There was a shout from the opposite end of the track.

"Dora!" Ann's voice was high and panicked. "Are you okay?"

I risked a glance to see what had happened. A. Dora Bell was lying on her back, a few feet off the track. She must have fallen and slid out of bounds. I started coasting to a stop, but Dora raised her arm and gave us a thumbs-up, then rolled over and clambered to her feet.

Thank God. I didn't want Dora to be seriously hurt, even if—the sneaky, selfish part of my mind noted—the coaches would surely have called off the 27 in 5 and I'd get a redo another day.

I brought my focus back to my laps. I could at least finish with dignity and get as close as I could. With one minute left, I was just shy of 21 laps. I wasn't fast enough to get six more laps in a minute, but I'd hustle, get the best score I could.

"Twenty-two laps, Mighty!" Ann yelled. "Only five to go! You can do it!"

What? She must have counted wrong! I was at 21, with six left. But the excitement in her words fueled a new fire in me. So what if my thighs quivered and my calves ached, so what if every breath in my lungs burned like fire, so what if my vision was blurred with sweat? There was only a minute left! I pushed harder, harder, harder.

When the whistle blew, I was immediately crushed in hugs from all sides. Ann, Pumpkin, and Dora—now in shoes—were cheering and jumping and squeezing me.

"Twenty-seven and a half laps!" Ann said in my ear. "Oh, Mighty, I'm so proud of you! You've come so far since May!"

Now was the time to tell her she'd miscounted, that I was only at 26.5 when the whistle blew. Dora's accident must have distracted Ann and made her lose count. My heart sinking, I guided Ann away from Dora and Pumpkin, so I could confess privately.

"The thing is . . ." I sighed.

Someone behind me caught Ann's eye. "And you! How many laps did you get?"

Stork skated up, executing a neat little hockey stop next to me. "Thirty-one. It felt pretty good." Her face was flushed red, but otherwise she didn't look tired at all. "How about you, Mighty?"

I bit my lip. Now or never. Time to confess. I shrugged, then grinned. "Twenty-seven and a half! Success!"

What really was the difference? Was I less safe on the track because I was a little slow? No. It was arbitrary, really. A lot of derby leagues didn't even require the 27 in 5 anymore, I'd heard. So how much could it really matter?

I followed Stork off the track, then sat on the ground next to my gear bag to take off my skates. Pumpkin dropped down and sat cross-legged next to me, chattering about the earlier part of the assessment and how she felt Cleo, the coach who'd assessed her, hadn't been fair.

"I mean, half-plows? We were told full-plow stops were on the assessment, not half-plows!"

I was grateful for her rush of words, and nodded along, agreeing at all points.

Every practice, all summer, there had been a constant tightness in my chest that had nothing to do with my asthma. So many girls, and it seemed all of them were more athletic and confident and normal than I was. But for some reason, in the last two weeks of Skatertots, Pumpkin had decided we were friends.

Pumpkin—Pumpkin Slice Latte—was a self-proclaimed rink rat who'd grown up skating every Friday night. She was new to contact drills, but her skating was smooth and confident. I'd made her laugh during the increasingly challenging practices—cracking jokes at my own unathletic expense, imitating Cleo's drill sergeant barking and Stork's earnest perfection—and that had been enough to earn me her friendship, apparently. Having someone to stand next to during warm-ups, someone to roll my eyes to during a particularly tough drill or a show-off move from Stork, someone to whisper and joke with during long, boring announcements from the coaches—it made that tightness in my chest ease.

"I thought your half-plows looked fine," I said, yanking my elbow pads down my arms and shoving them into my bag. Some girls had complicated methods of keeping their gear clean: spritzing sprays, clipping pads to the outside of the bag so they could air dry, shoving scented sachets inside. It seemed like too much trouble, so I'd ignore the issue until my dad would eventually offer to throw my gear in the washer for me.

Maybe I'd need to start washing it myself. My dad was planning to move out, my parents had said this morning during the eerily calm joint announcement of their divorce.

My brother, Ben, and I had suspected it was coming—they'd fought constantly our whole lives, and yet, this past summer, a quiet had fallen over the house, an unsettling sense of otherwise-inexplicable peace. But it was one thing to sense it and another thing for it to actually happen.

"Don't feel bad, your half-plows were okay, too!" Pumpkin said cheerily, misreading the look on my face.

"Anyway"—I tore my mind away from the mess of my family—"if you're a jammer, you won't even need to do plow stops, you'll just have to skate fast." Jammers were the ones who scored the points and, frankly, got all the glory.

"Me? Are you kidding?" Pumpkin laughed. "No thanks. Jamming sucks."

"All right, fair." Any time I'd tried jamming during Skatertots practices, I'd been instantly exhausted and demoralized. Pumpkin was right. Not that that stopped my fantasies of glory and adoration and screaming fans.

I shoved the last of my pads into my gear bag, zipped it shut, then sat on the carpet with my knees tucked to my chest. A noise from the back of the rink drew my attention—one girl, a halfway decent skater I didn't know by name, was crying. Another skater, Seitan Worshipper, put an arm around her. Their voices carried over to us.

"Hey, you did your best. It was a tough assessment."

It was clear the crying girl thought she wouldn't make the team. How many laps had she gotten? I looked away from the scene.

Pumpkin caught my eye, winced, and leaned in close to whisper.

"If I don't make the team, I'm not doing another session of Skatertots. Screw it. I'll just have fun at the rink with my friends, where no one is judging me."

What would I do if I didn't make it? Would I stay in Skatertots if my only friend was gone? Imagining it made my stomach hurt.

"Hey." Pumpkin jerked her chin to the left, drawing my attention to the two people approaching us.

Ann and Cleo were still holding their clipboards, faces carefully neutral. Ann spoke quietly. "Can you both stick around for a few minutes?"

We nodded. My dad was probably already outside in the car, waiting for me, but I wasn't feeling especially charitable toward either of my parents at the moment. He could wait.

"Meet us in the side room in ten." The coaches moved on.

Pumpkin grabbed my arm, her nails digging in. "Oh my God, this is it, isn't it? We made the team!"

I grinned, her enthusiasm contagious. "I think so!" It was official, then: I'd take that 26.5 to my grave, even if it gave me an ulcer to have to live a lie.

CHAPTER 2

Pumpkin was right! We were rookie members of the Prairie Skate Juniors! I half-skipped, half-ran through the rink's breezeway and out the door, swinging my gear bag.

Then I spotted my dad waiting for me in the car, his eyes looking down at his phone, and reality drenched me like a wave. Ugh, the divorce. There was so much more coming. Awkward conversations, custody decisions, my dad packing and sorting and moving—all perfect opportunities for my parents to argue and for me to be thrown in the middle of it. For the millionth time today, I wished Ben weren't away at college.

"How'd it go?" my dad asked as I collapsed into the passenger seat.

"Intense. But amazing."

"Yeah?"

"I made the team!" I couldn't help but grin, despite my trepidation at the inevitable divorce garbage.

"Congrats!" He held out one hand for a half-hearted high five, keeping his eyes on the road as he pulled away from the rink. I indulged him and smacked his hand. "When's your first practice?"

"In a week. And the Juniors practices are supposedly way tougher than Skatertots. So we'll see if I survive."

"I know your mom has had concerns about safety, but that's just her being irrational. I'm sure you'll be fine."

I ignored the random dig at my mom. It barely fazed me at this point.

"There were only five open spots, from girls who went off to college or were old enough to leave Juniors and try out for charter." Prairie Skate's 18-and-up charter team players were the real rockstars of the league. I could barely bring myself to look at them when they occasionally wandered into the rink during Skatertots practices, in case I did something embarrassing and drew their attention. "I can't believe I got one of the spots."

"Well, I'm sure you earned it."

I swallowed, thinking, *26.5, 26.5, only 26.5.* How many other skaters deserved this spot more than I did? The memory of the crying skater popped in my head.

"I hope I do okay. I hope . . ." I trailed off. I didn't know how to articulate all the things I hoped.

My dad paused. I could see the shift in his face the moment he decided it was okay to change the subject. "When we get home, we have some household things to do. I'm going to start packing. And you really need to clean your room."

"Ah." I fiddled with the seat-belt strap, pulling it loose and then tightening it again. "If you're moving out, isn't my messy room Mom's problem now?"

He tilted his head and looked at me, his eyes stern.

"Kidding."

We rode in silence for a few minutes, until nerves made me break it. "So . . . yeah. I'm on the team. For real." I'd seen the Juniors skaters around the rink this summer, occasionally helping at Skatertot practices. They were confident, fearless, wild. Their sheer badassery on the track took my breath away. Becoming a member of the Prairie Skate Juniors was like getting a new, better identity.

"It really is great, honey. Nice job."

Unbidden, the memory of Ben making the varsity baseball team when he was my age rose to my mind. My dad had whooped loudly, immediately called a bunch of our relatives to share the news, and insisted we go out to dinner to celebrate.

I shifted in my seat, wishing I could open the car door and jump out.

Of my parents, my dad supported my participation in roller derby more than my mom did. But he still didn't take it seriously. I wasn't sure if he was expecting me to eventually give up and retreat to my bedroom with my laptop and my headphones and my zero real friends, or if he just didn't think of derby as a real enough sport to be worth caring about.

"So Mom thinks I'm going to get hurt?" Yes, I had the self-awareness to know I was deliberately pitting him against my mom so he would further praise my accomplishment today. I just didn't have the self-control to stop myself. "Does she want me to quit or something?"

A deep breath from my dad, then a sudden silence. Censoring himself. "Your mother might think that, but I don't. Don't let her nonsense get in your head. Keep playing."

I debated responding with "No kidding, I just made the team, of course I'm going to keep playing."

I debated telling him how transparent it was that he was only being supportive to gain points against my mom.

I debated telling him about the 27 in 5, how I couldn't stop thinking about my false result and worrying I didn't really belong on the team.

Finally, I sighed, said nothing, propped my feet heavily on the dashboard, and shut my eyes.

That night, my mom sequestered herself in the bedroom to talk on the phone with her sister, and my dad retreated to his home office to pack boxes of boring legal books. The house maintained its silence, still unnerving after an entire lifetime of my parents' constant arguing.

I curled up burrito-style in a blanket on the couch and watched *Whip It!* The roller derby in the 2009 movie was way different from what we did at practice—they played on a banked track, sloping upward from the inside of the track to the outside, for starters—but it was still derby. I'd watched the movie a million times since I'd joined Skatertots four months ago. Tonight, I half-watched while searching my phone for pictures of dyed green hair. My hair was currently a faded orangey pink, brown roots starting to show. It might be fun to switch to green, one of our team colors.

Guess what? I texted Ben. *I made the Prairie Skate Juniors! You're going to have to come watch my games, like I did for you. You know what an enthusiastic fan I was.*

I smiled as I sent it. I had famously once fallen asleep at a baseball game of Ben's.

Anyway, loser, text me back. I'm bored.

I scrolled through more photos of gorgeous green hair, idly noting things I liked, imagining how they'd look on me. Waiting. A few minutes later, a notification buzzed, and my heart leapt. Ben! But no, just an automated email reminding me of some late schoolwork. Deflated, I deleted it and went back to scrolling.

Ben and I were very different, and he always gave me a hard time about, well, everything, but he accepted me, let me hang out with him and his friends, and made me a part of his life. It wasn't fair, really, that he was away at college. He should have stayed nearby and gone to school in the Chicago suburbs instead of down in Champaign, so I could still hang out with him. Okay, I hadn't actually expected that, but I certainly would have appreciated it.

I eventually dozed off, then woke up at 1 a.m. with drool on my face. A quick look at my phone—no reply from Ben. My insides twisted.

The week before he'd moved out, in a rare burst of sincerity, Ben had pulled me aside and promised we'd still talk a lot. He'd assured me that I wouldn't be alone just because he was living far away. I'd been outwardly nonchalant when he said it, but in my heart, I'd been relying on that promise. And now he couldn't even find thirty seconds to return a text?

I staggered upstairs, a dull, lonely ache in my chest. There was a line of light under my dad's office door. Maybe he'd dozed off in there, since I'd been on the couch. The ache intensified.

Once I climbed into bed, my brain started running a highlight reel of awkward things I'd said during assessments and visions of Ben deleting my texts unread. I tried to force myself to imagine successfully playing derby, but as I dozed off, the vision morphed into one of Ann and Cleo yelling at me over hiding my 27 in 5 result.

CHAPTER 3

My mom drove me to my first official team practice a few days later. I hated being stuck relying on my parents for rides, as I was now that Ben was away at college. My requests were often wielded passive-aggressively by one parent against the other ("I can't continue this conversation, Millie *needs me*."), and always made me aware that, fundamentally, I had no more independence at nearly sixteen than I'd had at, say, eleven.

"Be safe, Millie," my mom said as she pulled up to the rink's entrance. Her face had the pinched, lemony look it always had when she talked about derby. She'd spent the spring pushing me to find a club or sport to join, then reacted with horror when I'd chosen roller derby. Whatever my dad's motivations had been when he'd brought up her fears about derby the other day, he'd been right.

"Yeah, yeah. It's just another practice, nothing to worry about." I unbuckled my seat belt, keeping my eyes off her and my nerves hidden. It *wasn't* just another practice. This was the real deal. "Besides, you never worried about Ben when he went to baseball practice."

"That's different—"

I cut her off, stepping out of the car and shutting the door. It made her mad, that sort of thing, but she'd been tentative around me lately, not calling out rudeness like she normally would.

It was the impending divorce. My dad was apartment hunting and sleeping on the couch, and both parents tiptoed around each other, and around me, everything in a delicate stasis that felt like it could erupt back into yelling at the slightest provocation. Ugh, was Ben ever lucky to have moved out.

Stork was already at the rink, waiting outside for the doors to open. She had made the team, too, of course. Stork Raving Mad was fast and fit and worked harder than the rest of us put together. There'd been no doubt she'd make it.

She was standing in a grassy patch outside the building, hopping back and forth. Her shaggy blonde hair whipped across her face in rhythm with her jumps, and her pale skin was red with exertion.

"Hey, Mighty." She didn't look up at me or break her rhythm. "The doors are still locked. We're the first ones here."

"Ready for this?"

She smiled, continuing to hop. "We'll see. I'm going to make sure I'm good and warmed up, anyway."

I wondered if I should start jumping, too, or if it would look obviously copycat-ish. Stretching seemed like a good compromise, so I set my bag on the ground and sank into a lunge.

"So, what do you think," I asked, "are you going to be a jammer?" Jammers scored points by lapping the opposing team's blockers. They were the ones announcers talked about the most, the ones who skated the fastest, the ones who did the most dramatic jumps and took the biggest hits. "Me, I'd love to be a jammer—all that fame!—but I don't see it as likely, given my lack of speed and overall just-barely-adequateness." I raised my arms above my head, then tugged my tank top down when it rose up. I was short and roundish, solidly built, like a fire hydrant, not exactly made for speed or grace.

Stork laughed, not denying my description of myself, and switched her hops from front-to-back to left-to-right. "I'll just do whatever the coaches think is best."

Which would be jamming. Come on. She didn't need the false modesty.

A few veteran skaters arrived, all piling out of the same car, talking loudly and laughing. I was instantly self-conscious. They'd be assessing the new rookies—how could they not?—deciding if we were better or worse than their former teammates, the girls who'd moved on to college and/or the charter team, their absences creating the spots we rookies had taken. If the vet skaters were going to love me, it wouldn't be because of my skill on the track, that was for sure. At least I could try to be friendly and amusing.

Aware of their eyes on me, my heart pounding, I smiled and said, "Hi! I'm Mighty! I'm one of the new rookies! I'm not very good, but my full name is Dino Might, and I swear I'm better on the track than actual dinosaurs that have been dead for millions of years, so at least there's that." God, that barely made any sense. I sounded like a nerdy little kid. But still, best to make sure they knew I wasn't unaware of my lack of talent.

There were four of them, three of whom murmured hello. The one closest to me, who had huge muscles and a barbed-wire tattoo on her thigh, rolled her eyes. "Spare me your rookie self-deprecation."

My cheeks burned. Could I walk home from here? It couldn't be worse than living through a practice with these people, right?

More skaters were arriving. Pay and Bee, the other new rookies, showed up together. Impaylor Swift and Stings Like Abbee were best friends outside of derby, inseparable during practices, always partnering together during drills, never seeming especially interested in socializing or working with anyone else. They both wore sleek black yoga pants and matching sports bras, had long, beautiful hair—Pay's in tiny braids, Bee's a mass of dark curls—and smooth, flawless skin—Pay's warm, russet brown, Bee's milky and freckle dusted.

They never appeared fazed by even the toughest drill or most brutal critique. Basically, they were cool.

I'd been too intimidated to try to befriend them during Skatertots practices. Today, though, their familiar faces were way less scary than those of the vets, and I was delighted to see them.

"Hey, Mighty." Pay set her gear bag down on the ground. "Congrats on making the team."

"You, too." I pulled one knee to my chest, then wobbled and dropped it. I lowered my voice. "You want to bet on if I'll survive practice? I'm giving 2-to-1 odds that I'll die of an asthma attack and 3-to-1 odds that the vet skater with the muscles will decide to murder me."

Pay and Bee gave each other raised-eyebrow looks.

"Just kidding." I blushed. "I mean, obviously. Probably."

"You'll be fine, Mighty." Bee turned to Pay. "Did you hear what Tai said in geometry today?"

I'd been dismissed from the conversation. That was fine. I was jittery as hell, all sweat and social anxiety.

A pair of hands clapped down on my shoulders from behind. "Mighty! We did it!"

I spun around and saw *Pumpkin*. That ease, that relief, flooded through me as it always did when I was with her, like my brain was singing, *I have a friend, see, I know how to have friends!* I wished she'd been here a second earlier; she would have laughed at my death-odds joke. I gave her a hug. "We made it! The big time! You ready for this?"

"Ha! I'm probably going to break my ankle immediately when some vet flattens me. I heard that happened to a girl a few years ago. That will totally be me." She cracked open an energy drink and took a swig, then pulled off her hoodie, revealing a chicly threadbare vintage Sex Pistols T-shirt beneath it.

"Ohhh, no way, we'll be glorious." I spun around dramatically, a burst of optimism flooding me now that I could reassure her.

"You won't break your ankle. You won't even break . . . a nail. Stork probably won't even break a sweat."

Stork half-smiled, without looking at us. "I'm going to jog a few laps around the parking lot."

Pumpkin wrinkled her nose. "Running sucks. That's why I skate, for God's sake, so I don't have to ever run again." Oh, I was so, so glad that Pumpkin had made the team with me.

"I run track at school," Stork said, "but it's only in the spring, and I wanted to do something new."

"Wow, so you're, what, a jock?" Pumpkin laughed. "The jocks at my school would never play roller derby. I assume, anyway. I don't think I've ever spoken to them. My friends and I are basically, like, the punks. South High must be different than St. Mary's."

Stork just shrugged in response. Pumpkin continued chattering at her about the differences between their schools. I watched, trying to think of something to say that would keep me in the conversation.

After thinking hard: "How do you like Catholic school, Pumpkin?" An unimpressive showing, but at least it wasn't as bizarre as my earlier dinosaur comment.

"Eh, it's fine. Fifteen hundred students and everyone knows who I am, because I'm one of, like, ten Latinas in the whole damn school, and I'm the only one who ever had a buzz cut." She ran a hand over her dark hair, now fluffy and a few inches long. "Anyway, as far as schools go, it could be worse."

One of the vets, a rainbow-haired girl with a round face and a friendly smile, turned toward us. "My cousin is going to St. Mary's next year. She's so nervous about high school, she'll be glad to hear that."

Pumpkin shrugged. "I mean, it's school. It still basically sucks, let's be clear."

The vet turned her attention to me, still smiling. "Do you go there, too?"

The crushing sensation in my chest returned. "No, I'm

homeschooled. Online-schooled, really. I do classes through an online high school."

"Do you get lonely or bored? I know I would."

"Eh, it's better than dealing with all the random assholes I'd have to see if I went to a normal high school." I meant it—I could only imagine what sorts of things I'd have to put up with in a typical public school—but also, yes, obviously I was lonely and bored. It was just better than the alternative.

"Have you been homeschooled your whole life? Or, like, since Covid?" Pay asked. She and Bee were listening now, and Stork was hanging back from starting her jog, too.

This was too much focus on the wrong sort of thing about me. I'd managed to only mention being homeschooled once during Skatertots, and had then quickly changed the subject. Now a quicksand feeling began in my brain, like I was going to get sucked into the ground, held in place in everyone's minds as "too weird to befriend."

"Neither—it wasn't after Covid or for my whole life. I've been doing online school since sixth grade. Bullies, right? Ugh. But really I left because of pneumonia, and I never went back." Once again, upon review, my sentences were barely coherent.

I'd been bullied for lots of uninventive reasons all throughout fifth and sixth grades. The random cruelty of preteen girls had left me convinced any friendly conversation was a trap, and any disdain was inevitable. After I got sick, I convinced my parents to switch me to online school.

Thinking of my bout with pneumonia, which had messed up my lungs permanently, I turned away from the other rookies' curious looks and began digging through my gear bag to find my inhaler.

"I get it," Pumpkin said. "Like I said, the jocks at my school would never play derby, or even see it as a real sport."

That wasn't what I'd meant, but I was still glad she'd backed me up.

Stork took a few steps closer to Pumpkin. "You might not

think of yourself as a jock, but you *are* an athlete. You need to see yourself as one if you want to do well." She looked over at me. "You too, Mighty."

Me, an athlete. Ha. I couldn't wait to text Ben after practice and tell him that. He'd have to respond to that, if for no other reason than to make fun of me. He'd probably pee his pants laughing. Ben was the athlete in the family. He'd played baseball all through high school, and I knew he was planning to play in college. Meanwhile, my lack of coordination and disdain for sports had been a family joke my whole life. I was uncoordinated, uninterested in watching either of the ursine-based Chicago teams my parents and brother supported, and uneasy in any situation where a ball could potentially hit me. Last time I'd agreed to play catch with Ben, I'd ended up with a black eye.

"Athlete is *not* the right word for us, Stork. It makes us sound so boring!" Pumpkin laughed. "Derby girls are the weird ones, all dyed hair and pierced and queer, and whatever."

"Yeah!" I piped up. "I'm all three of those things." I had dyed my hair bright pink at the beginning of summer and had talked my parents into letting me get a discreet sparkly stud in my left nostril.

Stork shook her head. "We play a competitive sport. I'm an athlete, and you're my teammates, so I sure as hell hope you are, too." With that, she took off into the parking lot for her jog.

With Stork gone, Pay and Bee returned to their private conversation, and the rainbow-haired vet got pulled away by her friends. Pumpkin turned to me. "So you're queer? There are so many queer girls in derby I almost feel weird being straight!"

She had just mentioned, like two minutes ago, that she went to St. Mary's, the Catholic high school. What if she was super religious and judgy?

"Yes indeed," I said. "I ... like girls, guys—anyone willing to have me, really. I mean, that came out wrong. You know what I mean." My face burned.

"I think Spineapple likes girls. You should go out with her. She just left Juniors and made charter this summer."

Relief. She wasn't judgy, just doing that thing straight girls did where, if they knew two girls who liked girls, they thought they must be made for each other.

There was certainly no actual reason to think Spineapple would be a good match for me. If Spineapple was on the charter team, that meant she was one of the rockstar skaters competing for our league's ranking, playing other teams around the country. Spineapple, therefore, was both older than me and a way better derby player. It wasn't likely she was looking for a young, awkward, unathletic girlfriend—or a woefully inexperienced one.

"Hello there!" Ann's voice carried across the parking lot. She and Cleo were getting out of a minivan. "Your coaches have arrived! We'll have the doors open for you in just a second."

Ann's appearance, with her wide smile and friendly mom energy, was a relief. I hadn't wanted to continue the current vein of my conversation with Pumpkin. I was embarrassingly inexperienced—there'd been only a few fairly chaste kisses in my past. I didn't even have enough of a social life to have crushes on anyone I knew, so I was stuck fantasizing about being with hot fictional characters. Harley Quinn, for example, got me through eighth grade, and more recently I'd imagined being the girlfriend of nearly every character on *Heartstopper*.

So, obviously, talking about dating was yet another minefield where I might say something weird. Best to avoid it.

I picked up my gear bag with one hand and clapped the other around Pumpkin's shoulders. "Time to go crush it at practice, right?"

"Ha! I love your confidence."

"Oh, it's complete b.s." I grinned. "Let's go."

"Lower, Mighty. Lower!"

I grunted. "I can't. I'll fall."

"Stop talking and just do it." Gables, the tattooed girl who'd been snarky with me before practice, was watching critically as I pressed against the side wall and attempted to do a wall-sit in roller skates.

Ann's whistle blew just as I lost my stance. My wheels rolled forward and I slid to the ground, landing on my butt with a thump. Blushing furiously, I clambered to my feet and swapped spots with Gables. She immediately dropped into a low stance, her back pressed against the wall, her wheels making constant minute adjustments. "See? Like this."

I sighed. "I'm not as strong as you, that's why I can't do it."

She rolled her eyes. "How do you think you get stronger?"

I glanced around, looking for a compassionate face, and luckily caught Pumpkin's eye. She was partnered with Stork, a few people down the line, and was currently the one on the wall. She grimaced, then made a "just shoot me" motion with her hand. I stifled a laugh.

After the minute was up, Ann blew four sharp whistle blasts. "Come on back to the middle, everyone! Grab a quick drink, and then it's time to really get to work!"

Pumpkin and I immediately skated to each other before joining the rest of the group.

"This is brutal," she hissed.

"I know! And Gables is so scary!"

We sat down on the cement floor, close enough that our knee pads were touching. Cleo began explaining the next drill, and Pumpkin leaned in even closer to whisper, "Do you know Gables's full derby name?"

I shook my head.

"Anne of Mean Gables!"

"That badass? With that name? And she goes by Gables?"

My shoulders shook as I tried to hold back laughter. "Do you think it's because she identifies more with the house in *Anne of Green Gables* than with any of the characters? I mean, no one expects houses to be friendly." It was such a ridiculous joke, but it got Pumpkin going, too. When she accidentally snorted, I lost it and burst out laughing. Everyone's eyes swiveled to us.

Both coaches glared. Ann had an "I'm not mad, just disappointed" look on her face. Cleo's face said "Yes, I'm actually mad."

"Pumpkin? Mighty? Did you have something to say?" Cleo's voice was ice.

I coughed. "Just, uh . . . you know . . ."

"Girlish high spirits," Pumpkin chimed in.

This set me off again.

"All right, time for the drill," Ann said brusquely. "Pumpkin, you work with this group up front. Mighty, you work with Luna and Dex back here."

We split up regretfully, still giggling.

After practice, Cleo and Ann handed out a few forms.

"Don't forget to have your parents sign these and return them, or do it through the link we emailed," Ann said.

"We need them back by the end of the month," Cleo added. "Or sooner."

I couldn't tell if our coaches were best friends or a couple, but either way, they couldn't have been a more mismatched pair. Ann Archy, short and round and cheerful, wore sweatpants, bright-colored bandanas over bushy auburn hair, and high-tops in Prairie Skate green. She was always there with a hug or a word of encouragement. Cleo—full derby name Cleo-smack-ya—looked just like her namesake Cleopatra, gorgeous and bronze-skinned with shiny black hair. She was powerful and shrewd like Cleopatra, too. She cut through people's bullshit, tolerated no dissent, and prized hard work above everything. Obviously, I was terrified of her. Thank God it had been Ann counting my 27 in 5 that day, and not her.

"The Winter Showcase is only three months away," Cleo continued, "and that's coming up sooner than you'd think. I want you blocking it off on your calendars now."

"What's the Winter Showcase?" Bee asked. I was glad she'd spoken up; I'd been afraid it was something I'd already been told and had forgotten.

"It's a small public scrimmage. You'll all divide into two teams and play each other. This will be the first time the rookies are in front of a crowd, and it's a nice, low-key way to start. It's not advertised. Mostly just friends and families attend."

A public scrimmage! Oh, I couldn't wait, I couldn't wait. A chance to feel like an actual derby girl, in front of an audience! Instead of cheering for the impossibly cool girls on the track, I would be one of them. Me, out there on the track! Wildly confident and strong! Me.

Suddenly I wasn't sure if it was excitement or terror roiling through my stomach.

"Then in January, we start playing other teams. Most important?" Cleo waved one of the sheets of paper she was holding. "Soy Anything. Last weekend in March."

A few vets groaned.

She glared at them with laser eyes. "We are not the same team we were last season. We're going to show them what the Prairie Skate Juniors can do in a year."

The person standing closest to me was Luna, a slim girl with a magnificent mane of hair dyed in stripes of light blue, light pink, and white, to perfectly match the trans flag. Normally a vet skater with fantastic hair would intimidate me into silence, but Luna had been friendly during practice. She'd helped me with my turn-around stops, cheering when I finally did a decent one. I nervously shuffled closer to her and whispered, "What's Soy Anything?"

"It's a tournament in Central Illinois. That '80s movie, *Say Anything*, plus it's in soybean country, get it?"

I nodded. "More Illinois puns, sure." Our league's name came from Illinois's nickname, the Prairie State. And though it was still in-state, a tournament in Central Illinois sounded like a world away. I barely left the Chicago suburbs. Maybe it would be near Champaign, and I could combine it with a visit with Ben. Then I imagined actually playing in the tournament and felt nearly sick with fear. What if I let everyone down? What if I screwed up so monumentally that I cost us a win? The horrible quicksand feeling started sucking at my brain again.

"We went last season," Luna continued, "and were utterly destroyed. We lost all three of our games."

Cleo paused in whatever she was saying, and her eyes found Luna and me in the back of the group. "Dino Might? Stellar-Luna? Am I not entertaining enough for you girls?"

I shook my head rapidly, eyes wide. Luna shook her head, too. She gave me a quick glance that might have been a glare, then took a few steps away. Great, now the one vet who'd been friendly was annoyed I'd gotten her in trouble. My face burned.

"No more side chatter." Cleo sighed, then turned back to the group as a whole. "If those other teams think they can underestimate us this year, it will be their mistake. Because we're going to win the Juniors division. That trophy is coming home with us." And her glare turned into the world's most intense, scary smile.

I shivered. Practice today had been brutal; my interactions with teammates iffy. It was hard to imagine ever feeling like I belonged here, like I deserved this. But I could think of one surefire way: crush it at Soy Anything, playing so well I single-handedly win us the tournament.

I shivered again.

CHAPTER 4

time until Soy Anything: 6 months, 9 days

I found Ben online a few days later.

"What's up?" He was sitting at his dorm room desk. His roommate's desk was visible over his shoulder, a tall stack of textbooks piled on the chair.

"Nothing. I'm bored." I'd been lounging in bed all morning, mentally replaying our last practice—especially a sprinting drill where I'd come in dead last—and massaging my aching calves.

"Aren't you supposed to be in 'school' right now?" Ben asked, leaning back in his chair, his fingers bending into air quotes around the word *school.*

"You can 'go to hell,'" I said, doing air quotes back. "My schedule is flexible, and I have freedom to arrange things as I like, not that it's any of your business."

Ben had been critical of my choice to continue online school, which was unfair since he had been an unnaturally confident high school freshman at the time I'd switched, and I had been a friendless, miserable sixth grader. I couldn't admit to him now that I was bored and lonely most days, with Pumpkin my only friend. And did Pumpkin even count as a real friend if we hadn't hung out outside of practice?

"How's college?"

"Tough. There are three hundred students in my calc class. It's ridiculous." He ran his hand through his mop of brown hair, a familiar gesture, then rubbed his face and yawned. "Last night, me and Kev had a genius idea."

"What?" Kevin was his roommate, who I'd met for all of two seconds when we helped Ben move in last month. I knew nothing about the guy besides his name.

"There was a deal on pizzas if you got multiple XLs late at night, so we ordered two XL pizzas at midnight so we each had our own to eat, then stayed up till three playing *Madden*."

"Genius. I'm jealous. You get to stay up eating pizza with friends, I get to watch Mom and Dad awkwardly avoid each other while trying to be all sensitive to me." I shuddered. "Mom, especially. She keeps just watching me, like she's sure I'm about to burst into tears any moment."

The day after the divorce announcement had been the last time Ben and I had video chatted, and we'd both agreed that we preferred the divorce to the constant arguing of the past few years. I still would've chosen a third option, one where they got along and stayed married and didn't disrupt my life, but no one had offered me that one.

"Has Dad found an apartment yet?"

I nodded. "Supposedly he's taking me over there this weekend so I can see it. Because—and I was given no choice in the matter—I'm going to be there every other weekend."

Ben looked away from me, first offscreen and then down at his lap. "Sorry you have to deal with all this by yourself. I swear, I'll have you come down for a visit soon."

"You better." I wanted to pin it down further—*let's choose a date, get it scheduled, please!*—but since I already worried I was a clingy little sister, I kept it to myself.

"Are you still doing roller derby? That'll get you out of the house sometimes at least, right?"

"Of course, I'm still doing it! Last night was our second team practice." I scowled. "And I'm not going to quit."

Yes, I'd only joined derby because my mom was pressuring me to find something social to do—a move I now suspected had been motivated by her knowledge of the impending divorce. But my love for it was instant and real. At my very first practice with the Skatertots, I'd felt a sense of a secret door opening, like, *Oh, this is where my actual life is.* Cool, interesting girls with the confidence and attitude I'd always wished for? I was devoted immediately.

But Ben, like my parents, apparently didn't take it seriously. Did he think he could be the only one in the family to play a sport? As in so many interactions with my brother, I swung from adoration to aggravation in an instant.

"No black eyes or broken ankles yet, huh?" He took a swig from a bottle of Gatorade, either oblivious to my irritation or knowing but not caring.

"I'm doing great. I'm totally an athlete now." I thought of Stork's remark that we were all athletes. It didn't feel true, but I could pretend it did when talking to Ben.

He smirked. "Ah yes, it makes sense. I remember all those long runs we'd take together."

Ben had invited me to join him on a jog from time to time, but I'd always laughed at him, the idea absurd. Now I thought about Pumpkin's reply to Stork. "I don't need to love running. I'm playing roller derby, that's my workout."

He raised his eyebrows. "I ran because our coach had us running for fitness and cross-training, not because I loved it."

A shout from the background interrupted him, and Ben twisted around in his chair.

"What was that?" I asked.

"Hey, Novak!" The voice of the guy in the background was clearer now, and a second later he stepped into frame. He was tall and muscular, with nice brown eyes and a scattering of acne across his cheeks. Cute. A baseball teammate, I imagined. When he spotted me on the screen, he faltered. "Oh, sorry. We're going to grab breakfast before chem lab. We wanted to see if you were coming."

Ben nodded, then turned back to me. "Sorry, Millie. Gotta run."

"See you later. Have a good chem lab!" I said, blushing as I realized he was already gone.

Fine. Well. In a fit of enthusiasm laced with spite toward Ben, I decided to begin my day with some cross-training of my own.

I started with one hundred sit-ups. At first, I felt like I was in a montage at the beginning of a sports movie, but somewhere around thirty it lost its novelty. I finished, somehow, and collapsed onto my back, my nightshirt sticking to me. God, you could really tell how gross my bedroom was at this level. I was making close-up eye contact with potato chip crumbs and some matted teal hair. My hair hadn't been teal for months. *Ew.*

Maybe I should vacuum. On the other hand, sit-ups alone weren't enough for me to brag to Ben. If I wanted to prove he wasn't the only one in the family who could cross-train for the sport they loved, I needed to do more. Besides, getting fitter was the first step in my quest for glory at the tournament in March. It was time to go for a jog.

I tugged a tight sports bra down over my boobs—they were big, which I generally liked, but not if they were going to flop all over or, like, smack me in the face as I ran. Then, before I lost momentum, I finished getting dressed, laced up my sneakers, and pounded down the stairs. I was getting that sports-movie-montage feeling again. Maybe this scene would be set to the old Beyoncé song "Run the World (Girls)," something illustrating I was tough, and also a nice pun. I was going to run so fast, so far. That'd show Ben.

Jogging shouldn't be that bad, theoretically. I'd made it through the 27 in 5—okay, maybe not at quite the speed I was supposed to, but close enough. If I could skate hard for five minutes, I could certainly jog for longer. Right? I took two puffs from my inhaler and stepped out the front door, prepared to tackle the challenge.

The first block felt amazing. I was bounding down the

sidewalk in the crisp autumn air, feeling every bit the athlete I'd told Ben I was. My legs were strong, pounding hard on the sidewalk, propelling me forward. My arms pumped in rhythm. This was fantastic! *Why hadn't I started sooner?*

Then, as I began the second block, I realized why: because jogging was horrible. My lungs couldn't handle the pace; I was unable to take a full breath before I was sucking in another. I panted, my mouth hanging open. Soon the energy was sapped from my legs, too. I slowed to a shuffle, sweat creeping down the sides of my face.

It was boring, too! How could anyone keep this up for miles? It was the same action the whole time, and there was nothing to see but a bunch of boring, near-identical suburban houses. I hated running. I *hated* it.

My mood plummeted. I was going to be such a big disappointment to Stork, to the vet skaters, to the whole team. The idea of me as an athlete had never seemed more ridiculous. Suddenly my mind was back in sixth-grade gym class, being picked dead last whenever we were divided into teams, apologizing to anyone who had to partner with me. I'd never been sporty. Just because derby girls were, as Pumpkin had said, pierced and queer with dyed hair, it didn't mean I'd automatically fit in. My teammates had to be able to tell I joined derby because I wanted friends and confidence and a cooler personality; I was no athlete, and never would be. This jog was proof that I had no chance in hell of leading my team to victory at Soy Anything.

I struggled my way around the next block, shuffling and panting, hoping none of my neighbors would see me. When I finally reached home, I collapsed dramatically in my front yard. No one would hear about this—not Ben, not Pumpkin, and certainly no one else on the team.

After a cold shower mixed with hot tears, I wrapped up in a towel and climbed back into bed. The blood of a squashed mosquito stained the ceiling directly above me. It had been there for three summers now, a tiny brown splat that looked kind of like a stick-figure ballerina. I wondered how long it would stay up there. Another three years?

A shivery, trapped-in-time feeling ran through me. How many times in the last three years had I lay on my bed, lonely, aimless, and staring at the ceiling just like this? How many times would I do this in the future? Was this what my life would always be?

My phone vibrated. Thank God, a distraction from my thoughts. Maybe Ben apologizing for his quick exit?

Nope. It was Stork, sending a message to all of us rookies.

Can you get to our next practice early? We have things to discuss.

CHAPTER 5

time until Soy Anything: 6 months, 6 days

I didn't want to ask my parents to bring me to practice early. My dad was still ostensibly living at our house, but he was rarely spotted, like Bigfoot or something. If I asked my mom, she'd say yes, but her face would show all her suppressed thoughts about a sport she clearly found weird and dangerous. So, with a little trepidation, I asked Pumpkin for a ride. She said yes immediately.

My mom snagged me as I stepped out the door. "Where are you going?"

"Derby. A teammate is driving me. We have to get there early today."

She pursed her lips. "Do you have your inhaler?"

"Of course, I'm not gonna forget it." Halfway through my defensive reply, I realized that my inhaler was on top of my dresser. Oops. But I couldn't back down now. "Did you send my coaches back those forms about the Winter Showcase and Soy Anything?"

She nodded. "I need you to—"

"That's Pumpkin's car, gotta go!" I hopped off the porch, glad to interrupt wherever that sentence was going.

"Sorry about the mess," Pumpkin said as I opened the car door. She grabbed an empty water bottle and a sweater off the passenger seat, tossing them into the back. The spikes on the chunky black bracelet she was wearing came within inches of my face.

"No problem. You should see my bedroom." I sat down

gingerly, resting my feet on some papers I hoped weren't important.

"What do you think Stork wants?"

"No idea." I wanted to complain about Stork, or admit that she intimidated me, but I didn't know Pumpkin well enough to let it all out yet. "I guess we'll find out."

"It's not going to be anything fun, I guarantee it."

When we pulled up to the rink, we saw the other rookies in a huddle beneath the awning over the entrance. Stork was looking at her phone. Pay and Bee were next to her, shivering together, a single blanket wrapped around their shoulders. It was starting to drizzle, and even though they were technically covered, the wind was blowing the rain right at them. I wished I'd brought my jacket. My favorite thrift store find, the oversized and faded denim jacket would have kept me warm physically and emotionally.

Stork looked up from her phone as Pumpkin and I walked up. "Okay, I want to talk about Soy Anything. We've all heard the vets talk about how rough the tournament is. We have a long way to go if we want to do well—the whole team, and us five rookies specifically. So I think we should really kick up our cross-training."

God, what awful timing. It was as if she knew about the disaster of my attempt the other day. I picked at the leftover nail polish on my fingernails and let my shoulders roll inward.

"What do you all currently do?" Stork asked.

"I lift weights," Bee said, "and Pay comes with me to the gym sometimes."

Pay nodded and shivered, wrapping the blanket tighter around herself. "I also do HIIT workouts with my sister."

"What about you two?" Stork looked at Pumpkin and me.

I opened my mouth, like I was going to speak, which was absurd, because what could I say? I jogged once and wanted to die? I didn't even know what a HIIT workout was, and if I tried to lift weights, I'd probably drop one on my head and kill myself. I shut my mouth again and looked at Pumpkin.

She zipped her hoodie, not bothering to look up at Stork. "Not much. Does moshing at punk shows count? Or walking all over Chicago on the weekends?"

Stork didn't respond to this. "I think the five of us should commit to a dedicated cross-training program. Because," and now she addressed Pumpkin directly, "we're athletes, remember?"

Pumpkin muttered something inaudibly, crossing her arms over her chest.

"What do you have in mind?" Pay's eyes quickly darted over to Bee's. She sounded skeptical, which I appreciated.

"Well, that's what I thought we could discuss. I think weights and HIIT, doing both, could be good. Do all of you have a gym membership?"

Pumpkin and I both shook our heads no.

"Weights at home?"

Again no.

Stork chewed on her lower lip. She didn't look irritated, just like she was thinking hard. "All right. My uncle owns a little gym not too far from here. I bet I can convince him to let us all work out there together. That might be even better, actually, than working out separately and reporting it to each other." She nodded, like she'd convinced herself. "Yeah, this could be good. I'll talk to him about creating some sort of training plan for us all."

If my thoughts were visible, they would be a big red X drawn over this whole scene. Yes, I wanted to get better at derby, but surely there was another option besides Stork's uncle's gym. I didn't want to humiliate myself doing inevitably impossible workouts in front of the other rookies, and I didn't want to get bossed around by Stork. That jog in my neighborhood had been bad enough. How much worse would I have felt if Stork had been there, sprinting into the distance and leaving me in the dust?

There was a bit of loose gravel on the ground, and I drew an X in it with the toe of my sneaker. "I'm not sure," I said, without looking up. "I want to think about it."

"How do you expect to get better at derby if you don't cross-train?" *Now* Stork sounded irritated.

I tried and it sucked, I wanted to scream, but I stayed quiet.

"Um, derby practice? The reason we're here right now." Pumpkin glared at Stork, her big brown eyes narrowed and furious.

"You know we need more than that if we want to win games."

"Actually, I don't know that," Pumpkin retorted. "You just declared it, like we're supposed to believe you."

"Cross-training helps performance! You think I came up with that myself?"

"No, I think I don't want to give up my free time just because another rookie says so."

Stork and Pumpkin squared off to face each other, both with their hands on their hips.

Okay, okay, I didn't want to cross-train any more than Pumpkin did, but I also didn't want to witness a fight between the two of them. Pay and Bee were staying quiet, watching the scene from under their blanket, so apparently I needed to make peace between them myself.

"Hey, Stork? Pumpkin? How about this? Let's think about it." My stomach ached as I spoke. Making peace and diffusing tension was, unfortunately, a skill I'd practiced way too often with my parents. "We don't need to decide right now. Stork can talk to her uncle and get more information, and we can think about our schedules and our lives and what we want to do."

"Fine," Stork and Pumpkin said in unison, both still salty.

A slamming car door broke the tension. It was Cleo,

carrying not only her gear bag but a big net bag filled with what looked like karate belts.

"Nice to see you here early, rookies! Ann can't make it today, so I'm wrangling you solo. We're gonna have some fun." Cleo's grin made it clear her definition of 'fun' would be brutal. "Move over and let me unlock the door, and you can get inside and start warming up."

Half an hour into practice, I raised my hand and waved it desperately, trying to get Cleo's attention. "Can I say something?" I gasped.

She nodded for me to continue.

"Does anyone . . . have an albuterol . . . inhaler? I forgot mine." Though my asthma was generally mild, intense exercise aggravated it. This whole practice had indeed been miserable, as I'd imagined, and we still had over an hour left. Ann had led the last practice, and it had been tough but fun. Cleo, I was pretty sure, wanted us to improve badly enough that she was willing to kill for it—kill me, anyway. Right now, my lungs felt like someone had wrapped a belt around them and pulled it tight.

Speaking of belts, I was currently tethered to Gables by two karate belts knotted together. We were taking turns running sprints on our toe stops back and forth across the rink, with our partners dropped into low plow stops behind us to provide resistance. Gables, of course, was ferociously strong. When I plowed and Gables sprinted, I was dragged forward at terrifyingly high speeds, barely slowing her down at all. When it was my turn to sprint, I could barely pull her ten feet before Cleo blew the whistle.

"I've got an inhaler, Mighty," said Pay, taking off the belt attaching her to Bee and skating off the rink. "Back in a sec."

After a couple puffs from Pay's inhaler and a few minutes watching Gables sprint back and forth by herself, I felt good enough to jump back in. The imaginary belt around my lungs had loosened, so I slipped the real one back on and settled it around my hips.

"This time," Gables said, "get lower, and get your feet out in front of you, and really push your heels out. Drop your butt. And engage your core."

That was too many instructions. Gables took off on her toe stops, and I zoomed away again.

Before it was my turn to sprint, Cleo blew four short whistle blasts. "Come back together, get some water, and let's talk about the next drill. Yes, it's more endurance. I know you all passed your 27 in 5, but that doesn't mean you don't need faster laps and better crossovers."

My cheeks burned, and not just from exertion. I hadn't thought about Ann's miscount today. What if Cleo was going to make us do the 27 in 5 again right now? What would happen if I couldn't pass? I imagined the shame of being demoted back to the Skatertots. Could they do that? Could they send me back?

"Come on," Gables said, using the karate belt to pull me onto the track. "Ready for this?"

I'd been so absorbed in my anxious vision of demotion that I'd missed Cleo's explanation of the drill. "What are we doing?"

Gables grinned. "Taking turns skating laps with the belts, towing our partner, so we can really lean into the turns without being afraid of falling down. I'll go first. You stand to my right and get in a good low stance, to provide resistance."

Being towed around by Gables was surprisingly fun. I yelled "Whee!" a few times, waving to Pumpkin when she was near. My wheels rolled smoothly along the concrete floor. The cheesy, dated posters along the rink's walls blurred into streaks of bright colors as I zoomed by.

But then time was up, and it was my turn to skate. If I'd

thought my thighs had burned during the 27 in 5, that was nothing compared to skating laps while pulling Gables.

"Lean, Mighty!" Cleo shouted at me. "Lean in, and push with that inside leg. Use it to get more power."

My legs were quivering Jell-O incapable of providing power. I wanted to protest that I couldn't do it, but I didn't have the wind available to speak. When the whistle finally blew, I pulled the belt over my head, pulled off my tank top, and collapsed, sweat-soaked, onto the floor.

"Get a drink, everyone. Take a breather." Cleo was speaking somewhere above my head. I couldn't bring myself to sit up to look at her. "Now, what did that feel like? What did you learn?"

People talked, but I barely listened. I could only feel the cool concrete floor under my sweaty body, and the ease in my legs, finally at rest.

"All right." Cleo clapped her hands. "Now that you've had a quick break, we'll do it again."

An hour later, we staggered off the rink and de-geared. I'd survived, barely. Even the effort of pulling off my pads and my skates was overwhelming.

Pay was pulling her braids back into a thick ponytail at the nape of her neck, quietly chatting with Bee, when I approached.

"Thanks for the inhaler." I tossed it back to her. "You're a lifesaver. Like, literally."

She zipped it into a pocket on the front of her gear bag. "Anytime, teammate."

I smiled as I walked away. I was a teammate. It felt good, but scary. If people depended on me, that meant I could let them down.

Cleo got our attention for one last talk as we packed up our gear. "Today, we focused on conditioning and on basic skills, the building blocks of good derby," she said. "As we go forward, we'll keep this sort of conditioning integrated into practices, but add in more hitting drills and then in-practice scrimmages. I want you exhausted when you're doing this, so that when it comes time for actual games, it feels easy. Practice is supposed to be harder than games."

Everyone nodded, most of us too worn out to speak.

"Soy Anything is six months away. That's long enough to be transformative, but short enough that we can't waste time. What does this mean for all of you?" She paused for emphasis. "Work. Lots and lots of work. Hard work."

Ugh. In my heart, the idea of hard work scared me not because I was lazy but because . . . what if it didn't make a difference? What if I tried my absolute best and still sucked? I wished I could just do the fun stuff, have the fishnets-and-bruises aesthetic, and magically improve.

I glanced around, hoping to catch the eye of someone—anyone—who felt as intimidated by Cleo's pronouncement as I did. Instead, I saw Stork nodding seriously, scribbling notes in a tiny notebook. Oh God. If Stork was intense before, what would she be like after hearing this?

"We'll use the Winter Showcase and other games to refine our strategy and practice operating cohesively," Cleo said. "This is a team sport, and you need to practice together enough that you'll anticipate each other's moves on the track on a subconscious level, on pure instinct."

"Hey, Cleo?" Luna pulled her fabulous trans-flag-colored hair, now sweaty, into a messy bun on top of her head as she spoke. "Do we know which other Juniors teams will be at Soy Anything?"

"Not yet. I'll let you know when I find out."

Gables snickered. "I know who we're all thinking of, and don't worry, we're going to fucking destroy them."

I had no idea what she was referring to, and based on the shiver that ran through the other vet skaters, I didn't want to know.

Cleo's jaw tightened. "Gables, remind me what could happen if you use language like that during a game."

"A penalty." Gables rolled her eyes. "We will *gosh darn* destroy the Sonics, okay?"

Luna spoke up again. "How are you going to make roster decisions?" A derby game could only have fifteen skaters per team, so not all of us would be able to skate in any given game.

"If you want to be rostered, you know what I recommend?" Cleo looked out at us expectantly, waiting for a response.

"Work," I murmured queasily. "Lots and lots of work."

"I'll see you all next week." She gave us her scary grin. "Time to head out, give the charter skaters some room."

For the first time, I noticed more people had been filtering into the rink as she spoke. Charter skaters were wandering in, chatting and laughing and beginning to unpack their gear bags.

"Come on," Gables said. "Let's get out of here, everyone. The charter skaters think we're too obnoxious and annoying. We don't want to distract them with our immaturity while they're practicing." She said it loudly, her voice thick with sarcasm.

One of the nearest charter skaters, a heavy girl with full-sleeve tattoos, snickered. "I miss you, too, Gables."

"Oooh, yeah, charter practice." Pumpkin came up behind me and leaned her elbows on my shoulders. "Look, Mighty. The charter team." She gave me a nudge, pointing to the stream of skaters flowing in the doors. "The. Charter. Team."

Ah. Okay. I figured it out after a second. Spineapple, the eighteen-year-old who'd left Juniors for charter over the summer, the one Pumpkin thought I should date, had walked in. I looked at her, trying not to be obvious. She had short, bleached hair, a septum piercing, and a denim vest with the Prairie Skate Rollers logo printed on the back. She looked really cool, obviously, but also really intimidating.

"Come on, grab your bag and let's head out to the parking

lot. *Now.*" Pumpkin pulled on my arm. Luna gave us a quizzical look, and I shrugged, trying to look as mystified as she did.

I scurried along with Pumpkin, laughing, trying to look anywhere but at Spineapple. But I should've paid more attention to Pumpkin's path. She planted us right in front of Spineapple and her friends.

"Spineapple? Me and Mighty saw you in that exhibition game at the county fair last summer. The way you knocked that one jammer literally into the crowd? Amazing. Mighty and I just wanted to say it was *amazing.*"

"Oh." Spineapple looked slightly stunned. "Okay, uh, thank you." She turned back to her friends to finish her conversation.

Outside, I grabbed Pumpkin in an only somewhat-playful headlock. "I swear to God, Pumpkin, you are the least subtle person ever. I'm going to have to kill you; it's my only option."

Pumpkin tried to shout something back at me but was laughing too hard. We scuffled around a bit, then I started laughing while she twisted away from me. "You'll thank me someday. Like, at your wedding."

I wanted to be indignant, but I was still laughing too hard.

"Now come on." Pumpkin tugged at my elbow. "Let's get going. I need to shower before I see my boyfriend tonight."

Pumpkin had a boyfriend? That left a weird feeling in my stomach. Not because I was attracted to her. No, pangs of jealousy were twisting my insides because she had a thriving social life outside of derby. I wasn't the life raft for her that she was for me.

As we headed to her car, we passed Stork, sitting in her own car, fiddling with her skate and examining one of the wheels.

"One second," I said to Pumpkin, then knocked on Stork's car window.

She set her skate in her lap and rolled down the window. "What is it?" Her voice was cool.

"You were right." It hurt to say it. I bit my lip. "Today

basically destroyed me. I need to get way better if I want to do well at Soy Anything."

I had my own personal reasons for needing success at the March tournament, ones that I definitely wouldn't try to explain to Stork. It was the shiver of fear I'd felt when Pay called me "teammate," and the praise everyone heaped on Stork because she was so good, and the way no one in my family expected me to keep taking roller derby seriously. It was all those things and more. Soy Anything was my chance to prove I really deserved this spot on the team, this derby-girl image, this new life. I had to give it my best shot.

Stork looked at me expectantly. I bit my lip again.

"So, yeah, let me know what your uncle says about us training at his gym. I'm in. Let's do your cross-training thing."

Spending extra time with Stork was still the last thing I wanted to do—I couldn't forget how many times I'd heard Cleo say "Great job, Stork" in the past two hours. Why give myself another avenue to falter in comparison to her? But Stork's face had split into a delighted smile, and I couldn't help but feel a little bit excited, too.

CHAPTER 6

time until Soy Anything: 5 months, 27 days

My dad had officially moved out, but movers still needed to get some big furniture items, like his desk and office shelves. They were scheduled for a weekday, so I planned to hole up in my bedroom until they were gone. It wasn't that I couldn't bear to watch, exactly. It just felt uncomfortable. Wrong.

Shortly before they arrived, I had an idea. Maybe it was the plan for cross-training with Stork that gave me the idea, or at least put me in the right mindset to come up with it. I was feeling slightly, minorly, cautiously optimistic.

Online school gave me freedom, as I'd told Ben, and really, why didn't I take more advantage of it? All day every day I padded around the house, bored and restless. But no longer! It was time to take advantage of it. Because I not only had freedom, I had wheels.

Ha, not a car. Even though I'd be sixteen soon, I still needed quite a few supervised driving hours with my parents before I could take the driver's test. Even then, I didn't expect to get a car.

But I did have skates.

I put together an outfit that was my best approximation of the sorts I'd seen Lady Trample, a famous jammer from Australia, wearing in her skatepark videos: white knee socks with two teal stripes at the top, dark purple denim shorts with a super-high waist, and a cropped sweatshirt with a badass-looking unicorn on it. Then I threw my books and laptop in my backpack, strapped on my various pieces of protective gear—knee pads, elbow pads, wrist guards, mouthguard, helmet—and pulled on my skates. Time to go! It was morning, the sun was out, the air was crisp, and I wasn't going to waste a minute of this day.

There were three small stairs leading from my porch down to the sidewalk. I had not considered stairs. Carefully, I turned around, knelt down, and crawled backward down the steps, like a toddler. Then, feeling significantly less cool, I struggled to my feet and started skating.

There was a diner not quite two miles from my house, and I could stay on quiet subdivision roads almost the whole way. I would skate to the diner, have breakfast, spend a few hours on my homework, and skate home. It would be wonderful.

The sidewalk, though, was bumpier than I'd imagined. Every twig, every acorn, every crack shook my skates and made my whole body reverberate. Was I doing something wrong? At the next intersection, I leaned on the street sign and examined my wheels. Everything looked fine, not that I really knew what I was looking at. My skates were standard beginner's derby skates, and I hadn't altered them beyond trading out black laces for sparkly green ones. Maybe I just needed to get used to the road. It was bound to feel different than skating on a derby track—I should've expected it.

A few blocks from my house, the houses got bigger and fancier, and the sidewalks disappeared. I stepped carefully into the street, positive that as soon as I got my bearings, a sports car would come squealing around a corner and flatten me. But all that happened was a tiny dog on a porch began barking like mad.

Around the next turn, the trees on either side of the road curved inward toward each other, creating a canopy of foliage. The trees had already lost some of their leaves, but the remaining ones were vivid yellows and reds. A feeling of magic ran through me.

I pushed harder, picking up speed. My feet were still vibrating, and, though it had felt chilly when I'd left the house, my back was starting to sweat underneath my backpack.

One more turn, then two blocks and I'd hit the main road with the diner. I turned right and looked . . . down. I'd never thought of this street as a hill before, but it clearly was. Things looked different in skates than in a car. The street sloped steeply downward until, at a stoplight, it ended in a T-intersection. Cars buzzed past, loud even from two blocks away.

I was going to careen down this hill straight into traffic.

I did a careful T-stop until I wasn't moving, and stared down the hill. What were my options? I could turn around, go back to my house. Or I could skate down the hill fearlessly, trusting myself to stop before the intersection. I didn't like either of those options.

The house next to me had a lush, dark green lawn. All the leaves had been raked into big piles in the middle of the yard, and the grass by the curb was smooth and uniform. Maybe . . . I took a step into the yard, then a few more steps.

This would work. I could just clomp down the hill through everyone's grass. It wouldn't be pretty, and it would leave weird indentations in my wake, but it would work. I started making my way down the hill. Clomp, clomp. clomp.

"Hey!" a voice yelled from an open garage a few houses later. A man stepped onto the driveway, holding a canister of weed killer and glaring at me. "What do you think you're doing on my grass?"

"Sorry!" I shouted back. "The hill was too steep."

"Look what you've done to my lawn!" He took a step toward me, not exactly threateningly, but clearly angry. "Are you going to pay to fix it?"

"But—" It was only some dents in the grass. Good Lord. Well, I was almost at the bottom. I'd be okay. I sighed, stepping back onto the street. "Fine. Jeez. Sorry."

But I'd been right to be afraid of the hill. I picked up speed immediately. I tried to do a T-stop, but I felt my ankle start to bend strangely and had to give up. Maybe the light would change in my favor. Maybe I could grab on to something. Maybe. Oh God. The world was whizzing by, faster each second. Oh God.

I had to bail. I couldn't risk hitting traffic. I aimed for a pile of neatly raked leaves and threw myself forward.

I had been going fast enough that I burst right through the leaves and tumbled onto the grass. My heart was pounding, my breath sharp gasps. Was I okay? I stretched my limbs out, examined them. Only some minor scrapes on my left leg. Crinkled leaves, all gold and brown, were stuck to my clothes. I got unsteadily to my knees and began picking them off me, one at a time. At least no one was home at this house—no witnesses.

Crossing Green Avenue to reach the diner was, thankfully, uneventful. I skated through the parking lot and up to the door.

That's what I'd forgotten. Shoes.

I stuck my head inside. A waitress carrying a coffee pot caught my eye.

"Hi, so yeah, I'm wearing roller skates. Is that okay?"

She laughed. "Roller skates! I love it. Come on in, I'll get you seated."

All eyes were on me as I skated through the diner. My face heated with a mixture of embarrassment and pride. A little boy in a booster seat smacked his mom on the arm to get her attention, then pointed at me. I smiled and waved back, like a beauty queen.

I slid into a vinyl booth, then pulled off my helmet and wrist guards, pulled out my mouthguard, and set them next to me. From a distance, I'd look like a normal customer, albeit one with sweaty pink hair stuck to her head.

I ordered a great big glass of water and a plate of French toast. When it arrived, I pulled *The Scarlet Letter* out of my backpack, the current focus in my English class, and read while I ate. Half my mind was on the book itself, while the other half was narrating to Ben, "See how much better this is than in-person school? I can do assignments anywhere I want!" I hated this book, but I was chipping away at it while eating syrup-covered breakfast food, so that counted as a win.

"Do you go to skateparks like that?" my waitress asked as she refilled my water. "My ten-year-old is always bugging me to take her to one, so she can skateboard. She zips down those ramps like it's nothing. I don't know how."

I thought of my inglorious descent down the hill. "No, I definitely don't go to skateparks. I play roller derby."

Her eyes lit up. "Wow! Elbowing girls in the face, that sort of thing?"

"Well, we're not allowed to elbow people." I hid a smile. It had become a team joke during Skatertots that any time an adult asked about roller derby, they assumed we were constantly throwing elbows. I couldn't wait to share this with everyone.

"I used to watch it on TV when I was a kid." She set the water pitcher back down on my table and shifted her weight to one side. "I loved all the fighting, even though you could tell it was fake."

"Oh, we don't do that now. It's a legit sport." I sounded a little snobby, I knew, but I couldn't help it. To make up for it, I fished a crumpled flier out of my bag. "This is the info on the Juniors program, in case your daughter wants to join once she's older."

"Hey, you never know. I'll tell her about it." She smiled and took the flier, then left me to my French toast.

Once I'd finished eating, I spread my things across the Formica tabletop. I opened my French book, turned on my laptop, and found a clean page in my notebook. French toast, French class—I liked having a theme.

French was worse than English. At least I knew what most of the words meant in *The Scarlet Letter*, even if I didn't care about them. I looked up a few translations, faked my way through an online worksheet, then gave myself another break.

The latest conversation in the rookie group chat had been between Pumpkin, Pay, and Bee, and it concerned the delicious gossip that Gables and a jammer named Toni were secretly hooking up—supposedly someone saw them making out in a bathroom stall after practice last week. I tapped out a quick response (*Do you think it's the thigh tattoo that Toni couldn't resist? Or just Gables's charming personality?*), then added a few quick sentences about my adventures on the way to the diner, sharing the waitress's "elbow to the face" comment and the interaction with the weed-killer jerk on the hill.

When a few minutes had passed with no reply, it hit me: They were all in school right now. Obviously. No wonder they weren't answering. Probably they had to have their phones put away during class or they'd get detentions or something.

Hanging out in this diner was way better than being in high school. Why would Ben think online school was a mistake? The alternative was spending every day in a crowded old building filled with conformists who'd hate my appearance and personality, and homophobes who'd hate my existence. Ben didn't know what he was talking about. Here in this diner, I could relax, be myself, make my own decisions.

I flagged the waitress down and ordered a chocolate shake. When it arrived, in a tall glass and towering with whipped cream, I took a selfie with it and sent it to Ben. *Just another sad and lonely day of online learning*, I wrote.

It was too bad no one had witnessed my ridiculous hill debacle. If Pumpkin had been by my side, it would have been hilarious, instead of terrifying. Too bad she wasn't here with me now, drinking her own chocolate shake. No one in this diner was anywhere near my age. My stomach twisted with faint unease, but I pushed aside the dash of loneliness. As I decided to go back to my French homework, my phone buzzed.

What sort of outdoor wheels did you buy? It was Stork.

I didn't. These are just the ones that came with my skates.

Well wasn't it all bumpy? You need lower durometer wheels to skate outside.

Fine, Stork knew more than I did about skating. I didn't know there were different wheels for outdoor skating. I didn't have a clue what *durometer* meant. Maybe I shouldn't have sent that message. Maybe Pumpkin and Pay and Bee were thinking the same thing, wondering what I was doing.

My hands hesitated over my phone as I tried to think of what to write back to Stork. Finally, I wrote "oh" and put my phone away.

My skate home was less eventful but also less fun. I had to go up the big hill, plus it was warmer out, plus I'd spent the previous hours eating, basically, sugar. Regardless, I took another picture of myself once I was outside my house, making sure to include my skates. *Skated about 4 miles today!* I wrote to the rookies, careful not to say anything that Stork might want to correct. *Not bad for a random weekday!*

I was lying on the couch, half-watching TV with my math book open in front of me, when Pumpkin finally replied.

Jealous of your adventures!

I looked at the time. Her school day was over. My mom would be home from work soon; my dad, an hour or two later to grab his final few bags. I was suddenly desperate to escape, to see someone else my age.

I'm so bored right now, I wrote back, hoping it was clear that I was fishing for an invitation to hang out.

I'm at Target with friends now, she wrote, *but let's hang out tonight.*

Victory!

Pumpkin kept writing, now in a private message instead of the rookie group chat.

I have a great idea. It's a surprise. Be outside at 7.

CHAPTER 7

I jumped into Pumpkin's passenger seat as soon as she'd come to a stop. "Tell me, tell me! What are we doing? Where are we going?" I had been waiting on the porch for fifteen minutes. Ready for anything. Also, avoiding my mother.

"Are you sure you want to know? Maybe you should close your eyes and find out when we get there."

I was grinning so hard my face hurt. "Okay."

"Actually..." She reached onto her back seat, which was still overflowing with random junk, and grabbed a brightly colored paisley necktie. "My AP physics teacher gives us extra credit if we wear a tie on the days of exams—ridiculous, right?—so I keep one in the car. But today, it's a blindfold!"

She tied it carefully around my head, covering my eyes, then gave it a yank and pulled it tight.

"So you're in AP classes?" The darkness was immediately disorienting, and we'd only just left my driveway.

"Yeah, I'm a senior. Hopefully I'll pass the AP tests, so I have fewer classes to take in college."

"I'm only a sophomore." It felt like a confession, like admitting I wasn't as cool as her.

Pumpkin wasn't fazed by my sophomore status, at least as far as I could tell beneath the blindfold. "Enjoy it. The workload gets so much worse junior year."

"What's senior year like?"

"Definitely better. At this point, I've got the balance figured out where I can do just enough work to get the grades I need to get into a good college, but nothing beyond that. The main good thing about school is that I get to see my friends and David."

"Your boyfriend?"

"Yeah." Then she snorted. "For now, anyway. I'm pissed at him. He went to see my favorite band at the Metro and didn't invite me. Which, okay, bad enough, right? But I didn't even find out until this girl Angela that I hate shared her photos from the show, and he was in them."

"What a jerk." I wasn't sure exactly what to say, but that seemed safest.

"Right?"

The car shifted as we came to a stop. A moment later, Pumpkin whisked the blindfold off. "Ta-da!"

"Are we at the rink?"

"Yeah! I parked in back, so it's easier to sneak in. The charter team has practice tonight! We can hide in the DJ booth and watch them!"

I laughed. "Genius!"

"Come on," Pumpkin said, climbing out of the car and shutting the door quietly. "I know what to do."

I followed close, stifling nervous laughter. Juniors weren't specifically barred from watching other practices, but we hadn't exactly been invited, either.

"Ann always props open the back door, 'cause it gets so warm in there, even when it's cold out," she said, "so it should be easy enough to slip inside."

But the heavy gray door was locked.

"Huh." Pumpkin paused, hands on her hips. She was wearing a faded band T-shirt thin enough to show the red bra beneath it, and shredded jeans that looked so fantastic on her they made me want an identical pair. I doubted they'd look the same on me, though. Pumpkin and I were both short and curvy, but she looked more like a 1950s pinup than, say, a fire hydrant.

"I have another idea." Pumpkin grabbed my hand. "Come on."

We ran around the side of the building, where the giant garbage and recycling dumpsters were. Pumpkin headed straight for a stack of recycling sitting in front of the bin.

"Find a cardboard box that doesn't look too gross or beat up. We want it to be something we can actually carry stuff in." She held up a specimen. "Something like this."

I looked for my box without asking questions. This was her show; I was just happy to be here and not inside my house. Underneath a pile of flattened cardboard, I found two intact shoe boxes. "How about these?"

She appraised them. "Yes, those will do." She picked up her own box. "Now quick, back to my car!"

We darted to the back of the building, clutching our empty boxes and unsuccessfully fighting laughter.

"All right," Pumpkin said, popping her trunk open. "Find some stuff in here to put in our boxes that looks sort of related to derby, or skating in general. Really, anything. Look in my back seat, too. Then we'll carry the boxes in the front door and say we were told to bring in some stuff for Juniors, to stash in the basement with the rest of our things. And once we're in there for legit reasons, or what they think are legit reasons, we'll just stick around and watch."

I opened up her car's back passenger-side door. "What about this sweatshirt? It could be . . . in case someone forgot a workout shirt to wear to practice."

"Yeah!"

"Oh!" I got on my knees and pulled some things out from under the seat. "Two Gatorades. Perfect. Hydration is important."

She laughed. "Excellent. I'm all set from the trunk. I've got a box of Kleenex, another sweatshirt, and a little shovel."

"Why would Juniors need a shovel?"

She shrugged. "You never know when you might need a shovel."

"Fair enough. I want one more thing for my boxes." I rooted blindly through the papers behind the driver's seat. Then—"Ouch!"

I jerked my hand out. Blood dripped from a jagged line across my palm.

"Mighty!" Pumpkin dropped her box and ran to where I'd been digging.

"What do I do?" I held my hand up above my head, something I was pretty sure I'd seen done in a movie when someone was injured. "It doesn't hurt yet, but . . . okay now it's starting to hurt." I looked up at my hand. Blood was slipping down my palm, past my wrist, and along the side of my arm.

"Oh my God, I'm so sorry." She lifted something from the papers on the floor. "I didn't realize this was still in here." A broken coffee mug. She held it carefully by the handle, as the opposite side was gone, a sharp, dangerous edge in its place.

A fat drop of blood fell from my elbow, plopping onto the seat of Pumpkin's car. "Uh, we need to do something." I looked again at my palm, slick and red.

Pumpkin shook herself. "Sorry. Come on. There's a first aid kit inside the rink. Someone can help us."

I followed her around to the front of the building, watching my arm bemusedly. It looked gruesome but didn't feel real. I started to laugh.

"What?" Pumpkin's face was drawn with fear. "You're laughing. Why are you laughing?"

I began to laugh harder. "You found a legit reason for us to go in the rink!"

She shook her head. "We need to get you help."

As she pushed open the main doors to the rink, I could see beyond her that most of the skaters on the track were watching our entrance. They were standing together in the center of the rink, on a water break. One of them broke away from the pack, skating toward us fast.

"It's a lot of blood, though, that's the one thing. The part you didn't consider." I laughed again, then realized I wasn't feeling quite right. My limbs were tingly, and my vision fuzzy. "I'm woozy," I whispered to Pumpkin, leaning against the wall and then sliding to the ground.

"What's going on?" I heard the charter skater ask Pumpkin as she approached.

"We were trying to drop off some derby stuff, and she cut her hand on a broken cup in my car. Can we use the first aid kit?" Pumpkin sounded worried. I wondered distantly why I wasn't worried.

"Let me take off my skates, and I'll run and grab it." The skater's voice sounded familiar. Was it Ann up there above me? I hoped it was Ann.

"I'm in shoes," Pumpkin replied. "If you stay with her, I can run and get it, instead. That'd be quicker."

"Good idea."

I heard Pumpkin's feet hit the ground as she ran away, then felt someone touch my shoulder. The skater was sitting next to me on the ground. "Your friend will be back in a second, and we'll get you cleaned up." It wasn't Ann; Ann would've known Pumpkin's name. "Just hang tight, okay?"

"Am I gonna die?" I asked weakly. It suddenly felt like a possibility. Would the rink's dirty ceiling tiles be the last thing I ever saw?

"Ha! No. Worst case scenario, we clean it up and decide it's bad enough you need a few stitches. And then you go to the ER and get some stitches. No big deal. You won't even have to miss time on-skates."

"At least I didn't cut my foot," I murmured. The idea of missing time on-skates seemed almost as terrible as dying.

"Right. You skate on the rec team, right?"

Skaters who were both eighteen and out of high school

couldn't skate on the Juniors team. If you were ambitious, you tried out for the charter team. But if you wanted to play derby without the intensity of the charter team, or weren't good enough to make it, you could play on the recreational team. My woozy brain got snagged on the idea that this charter skater had psychically intuited that I'd never be good enough to make charter. Keeping my dully throbbing hand out of my field of vision, I traced the ceiling tiles with my eyes.

"No mosquitos up there," I said after a moment.

The charter skater patted my shoulder again. It was a nice pat, sincere, if you can tell sincerity from such a thing.

"You're very sincere," I continued.

"That . . . is a weird thing to say." But her voice was kind.

I shut my eyes gently. Ah. That was more relaxing.

"Why don't you keep talking to me," the skater said, "while we wait for your friend to come back? What's your name?"

"Mighty. I'm Mighty." I kept my eyes shut. My palm was throbbing harder. Was blood gushing out of it? "Who are you?"

"Okay, I'm back!" Pumpkin was panting. "Sorry, I couldn't find it at first."

The two of them cleaned my hand and arm while I stayed on the carpet with my eyes shut. It was oddly soothing. The mystery charter skater's touch was comforting and firm. After a few minutes, she spoke again. "I think you better go to the hospital, just to be safe. You might need stitches."

"I'll take you," Pumpkin said quickly. Her voice was shaking.

"Thank you." I sighed. I knew I'd have to call my parents when I got to the ER, but that was still better than having to wait for them to come to the rink right now.

"I'm really sorry," Pumpkin continued. "I feel awful. I can't believe my messy car caused this."

"It's okay. Seriously." It was. Pumpkin's concern and the charter skater's tender bandaging of my hand made me feel warm and cared for.

"She'll be just fine, don't worry." The other skater placed her hand on my shoulder one more time and squeezed gently. "Time for me to get back to practice. Let me know how it turns out, okay?"

I fluttered my eyes open and raised my head as she skated away. Her figure was familiar. "Was that . . . Spineapple?" My heartbeat quickened, and it wasn't because of the blood or pain. I could still feel the warm imprint of her hand on my shoulder.

Pumpkin exhaled, then grinned. "If you two fall in love, I won't have to feel so guilty about you getting cut."

CHAPTER 8

time until Soy Anything: 5 months, 26 days

My souvenirs from that night were five stitches and an enormous crush. When I woke up the next morning, Spineapple was waiting for me in my brain. Her bleached hair, her gorgeous strong arms, her soft touch on my injured hand, the way she'd squeezed my shoulder and said, "Just hang tight." And she'd thought I skated for the rec team, which meant she thought I must be eighteen! The same age as her—and therefore dateable!

In reality, I was stuck at not-quite-sixteen. Still. Still. My mind whirred.

Pumpkin had provided information last night that gave me hope. On the drive to the hospital, she told me she'd heard that Spineapple had just turned eighteen in September. A lot of skaters opted to stay on the Juniors team until they finished high school, but Spineapple had immediately tried out for the charter team. Because she was a badass, obviously. But the important thing was that, if she'd only turned eighteen in September, that meant she was indeed a senior in high school. Pumpkin was a senior, and she was my friend. By some sort of transitive property, I could date Spineapple for real.

When I got dressed, I imagined Spineapple seeing my clothes. What would she think? Would she like these high-waisted baggy jeans and this Windy City Rollers T-shirt that I'd cut into a crop top? I thought she would. Imaginary Spineapple kept me company in front of the bathroom mirror while I took my time with my eyeliner, getting perfect wings. I pictured her grinning her crooked grin at me in the mirror—a now-familiar look, because of course I'd been gazing at her photo on the Prairie Skate Rollers website all morning.

I was glad I'd been wearing my Lady Trample outfit when she saw me yesterday—my unicorn sweatshirt, purple shorts, and knee socks—basically the coolest clothes I owned.

I imagined walking down the stairs with Spineapple, as if she'd spent the night. The two of us would make breakfast, flirting and joking around as we flipped pancakes, unable to keep our hands off each other. Her dark eye makeup would be blurry, her bleached hair tousled, her arms strong as she wrapped me in them.

The sight of my mom waiting for me in the kitchen was a bucket of cold water on my brain. She was sitting ramrod straight in a kitchen chair, hands folded together, lips set in a line.

"We need to talk about roller derby."

I froze. "Do we?"

"I don't want you doing something where you get hurt like this."

"Excuse me?" I burst into harsh laughter. "I got hurt because of a *broken coffee cup*, not because of derby."

"Nevertheless."

My heart was racing. If she took this away from me, what would I have? What would my life be? I thought fast. "Dad disagrees. He thinks I should keep playing."

She narrowed her eyes. "He said that?"

I nodded, strode past her, and turned my back to grab a box of cereal. "Yeah, he says it's good for me. We were texting about it this morning. He said he thinks it's excellent for my mental and physical health." If she couldn't see my face, she couldn't see the red flush of my cheeks as I lied. "He's moved out for good now, right?"

"Yes." She sighed, and I knew I'd safely changed the subject. "When you're texting with him, please remind him that there are still several boxes of his things in the basement. He can't use this house as free storage."

"Okay, I'll tell him." I would do no such thing.

"Ben will be here this weekend, by the way."

I spun around. "He will?" I wouldn't have to spend the next two days alone with my mom! Ben would be here! We could stay up late, playing video games and snacking and bantering, just like we had all summer. I poured myself cereal carefully, grinning as I did it. Ben was visiting!

"He's going to the homecoming game with his friends," she continued.

Well. I shoveled a big, frustrated spoonful of cereal into my mouth. That wasn't quite as good. I wished he'd invited me, not that I had any interest in the football team of a high school I didn't go to. But still, any Ben was better than none.

"Is he staying the whole weekend? Like, till Sunday night?"

"I'm not sure." She raised her coffee cup to her lips, the sleeve of her cream-colored blouse sliding down to reveal her delicate wrist. "It's getting late. I'll leave for work in a minute, and you should get started on your schoolwork."

How was she my mom? She was so effortlessly polished all the time, so thin, so, well . . . humorless. And Ben was just a clone of my dad: smart, tall, athletic, driven. I used to occasionally wonder if I'd been adopted, if a family of short, goofy weirdos was missing its daughter. But I'd seen the hospital room pictures. And my mom had the same blue eyes as me.

She was narrowing them again now. "Millie. Schoolwork? Get a move on."

I took a few more bites of cereal, then rinsed the bowl. "Fine. I'll get to work." I headed back upstairs without argument. Oh, I'd get to work: get to work daydreaming more about Spineapple.

"How do you keep everything so clean?" The next afternoon, I parked myself on the nubby blue rug on Ben's bedroom floor, stretched out, relaxed. "My room has never looked this good."

He shrugged. "I just do. It's not some big thing, I just put stuff away." As if to demonstrate, he grabbed an errant book off his dresser and stuck it neatly on the narrow shelf above his bed.

"So you're going to the game tonight?"

"Yeah. Nathan is back in town, and a bunch of us want to see him, so we're all going." His friend Nathan had gone to college far away—Alaska or Arizona or something, I couldn't remember. The setting sun's last rays, shining through Ben's bedroom window, had reached my face, and I shifted onto my side.

"Sounds like fun."

He rolled his eyes. "If you're angling for an invitation, Millie, just say so."

"I'm angling for an invitation."

"Okay, fine, you can come."

I grinned. "Yesss."

"I don't know why you'd want to, anyway. Isn't a high school football game a little mainstream for your tastes these days?" He took a few pairs of neatly folded athletic shorts out of his dresser drawer and set them inside the duffel bag he'd brought home. "I didn't bring nearly enough stuff with me when I moved."

What was it like, being in college? I imagined he already had tons of friends, from the dorm and the baseball team and his classes. Was he going to frat parties and getting wasted on weekends? Was he spending every available hour at baseball practice? Was he meeting up for calculus study dates with girls like his high school girlfriends: pretty, but a little boring?

"Football games *are* too mainstream for me. But I have

nothing to do." *And I miss you.* I didn't say that part out loud. He was leaving tomorrow morning to go back to U of I. This evening was my only chance to spend time with him.

"Don't you have your roller derby friends to hang out with?"

"Pumpkin is out with her boyfriend tonight." I'd told Ben about Pumpkin earlier. I had hoped she'd be free this weekend, and that she and Ben could meet, though I couldn't explain why. They wouldn't have much in common. Pumpkin was nonstop laughter and chatter, she was punk shows in Chicago, she was flares of temper at the slightest whiff of anyone's unearned authority. Ben was baseball, he was deadpan humor, he was boredom as soon as topics outside his own interests were raised. I was sure Pumpkin would find him nauseatingly mainstream, and Ben would find her unnecessarily strange. Still, they were the two most important people to me, so I'd wanted them to meet.

Ben stood up straight and stretched. Had he gotten even taller in the last month and a half? It wasn't fair; he was already tall enough. "I'm leaving for the game now, so if you're coming with me, this is your chance."

I jumped to my feet. "Let's do it."

I'd never been to a high school football game. The lights on the field were bright; the crowd in the stands, loud. The air was smoky and smelled of burning leaves. There were cheerleaders in blue-and-white uniforms kicking and flipping and shouting, a marching band playing loudly and badly, and fans of all ages, from little kids to grandparents, not just teenagers. This was the homecoming game for South High—Ben's high school, and the one I would have gone to if I weren't doing online school. It made me feel a bit weird, weaving my way through the crowd, like a spy or an interloper. But absolutely no one gave me a second glance, of course.

I sat with Ben and his friends in the stands, trying to get

into the game but not brave enough to ask questions about it. It was more compelling than I'd expected it to be. My eyes tracked the feet of the guy with the ball, watching his quick footwork with envy. A moment later, an opposing player dove on him and they both crashed to the ground.

"Was that allowed? The way he grabbed him with his arms to bring him down?" I half-whispered to Ben.

"Yeah, of course," he answered distractedly, still watching the field.

"Oh. We can't do that in derby. It would be a penalty. We can only use our hips or our shoulders or whatever when we hit people, not our arms."

He didn't reply, but I still felt a little bit cool. I played a contact sport, something Ben had never done.

At halftime, I climbed down from the bleachers and headed for the bathroom and the concession stand. The line for the bathroom was long. By the time I was through it, the second half of the game had started. I decided to get my snacks anyway, rather than rush back to watch.

I made my way across the grass to the concession stand, enjoying the lack of crowds now that everyone was back in the stands. A gust of cool autumn air blew in, and I pulled my hoodie tighter around myself. Then I heard my name. My derby name.

"Mighty?"

I turned around. It was Stork, in leggings and sneakers and a navy-blue fleece. Her shaggy blonde hair was whipping across her face in the wind.

"Hey!" I waved. It was weird to see her in the real world, away from the rink.

"What are you doing here?" she asked, approaching me with her long, loping strides.

"My brother went to South. He's home from college for the night. Is this where you go?" As I asked, I remembered that yes, it was. What if she knew Ben? Weird.

She nodded. "I have friends in the band."

A pause fell between us now that she was standing next to me. I shrugged. "I'm going to get popcorn and candy. Want to come?"

She did. We got in line together, and immediately Stork began talking about derby.

"Gables told me that the teams that we Juniors need to watch out for this year are Sauk Valley, DeKalb, and maybe Decatur. Sauk Valley apparently destroyed us at Soy Anything last year—the score was something like 250 to 40? That's why I really want us rookies to get ready, you know? I want us to be able to contribute."

She was *so* intense, all the time.

"My other personal goal," she continued, "is to be able to do full push-ups, chest-to-deck. I need better upper body and core strength." She glanced at me—doubting my own core strength, perhaps?—then her eyes fell on my bandaged hand. "What happened?"

I grimaced. "I cut myself on a broken coffee cup in Pumpkin's car."

She winced. "Will you be able to get your wrist guard over that?"

"Oh." I hadn't thought about it. "Probably?"

"I guess you'll figure it out at practice Sunday morning."

I nodded.

"Josh—my uncle—is ready for us, for Sunday afternoon."

I'd forgotten that our private training sessions were starting so soon. I gulped. "Oh yeah?"

She either didn't notice or ignored the trepidation in my voice. "Yeah. He has a really thorough assessment planned, to figure out all our strengths and weaknesses."

"Great . . ." That sounded absolutely hellish, especially since we'd be coming straight from an inevitably exhausting derby practice.

We took a step forward in the concession stand line, now only one person ahead of us.

"He thinks HIIT will be really good for us, in addition to weightlifting."

Okay, so *clearly* I was supposed to know what HIIT meant. I needed to ask. My stomach fluttered. "I'm sorry, I can't remember what HIIT stands for. Can you remind me?"

"High Intensity Interval Training." Was she judging me for not already knowing that? No, I was pretty sure she wasn't. "You know, like, quick rounds of really intense work with short rests in between."

"God, that sounds brutal."

She looked surprised. "No more brutal than derby."

The man in front of us carried away his food, and the cashier waved us forward.

Stepping up to the counter, Stork nodded briskly, decisively. "These workouts will be good. You'll like them."

I couldn't imagine a less likely outcome—I was sure they would just reveal that I was a big lump with no potential as a derby player—but I nodded anyway. I hoped she was right; I needed all the help I could get if I was going to win Soy Anything for us.

Stork helped me carry snacks and drinks back to my place in the stands, since I couldn't juggle it all with my injured hand. As I settled back into my seat next to Ben, she paused, hesitating for just an instant, and I thought perhaps I should invite her to join us. But then she waved and was gone.

CHAPTER 9

time until Soy Anything: 5 months, 22 days

Sunday morning, Pumpkin wrapped me in a tight hug as soon as I saw her. "How's the hand?"

I hugged her back, a little awkwardly. My family was not big into hugging, though I was slowly adapting due to derby. "Fine. I mean, red and gross, but fine." I had it wrapped in a million bandages right now, so I could safely slide my wrist guard on. "You okay?" Her hug had been more intense than I thought my wounded hand called for.

"I fought with David again last night. We started talking about college. He doesn't understand why I won't just agree that we should go to the same school—which is ridiculous, because half the time I think he's about to dump me, anyway."

"Ugh." What should I add? Maybe, *He sucks, dump him first?* "Can you help me with this?" I held out my injured hand, the wrist guard half on, and Pumpkin pulled the Velcro strap taut for me.

"I'm seriously sorry about all that. I cleaned my car yesterday, so it can't claim any other victims."

"It's no big deal, honest." My hand hurt, but really it was the least of my problems. Yesterday morning, I'd said goodbye to Ben, which had been harder than I'd expected. Then I'd spent last night at my dad's apartment, my first time there overnight. It had been weird and quiet and awkward. Time there had ticked so slowly.

"Did you tell Ann and Cleo about the stitches?" Pumpkin

asked. The pair of them were already on the track, setting up some plastic cones.

I shook my head. "I can skate, so why worry them?"

Pumpkin narrowed her big brown eyes at me. "You sure it's not because you're afraid they'll tell you not to skate?"

"Of course not, don't be ridiculous." But I grinned sheepishly. I already worried I was a liability to the team. I didn't want to give anyone further reason to doubt my drive or commitment, which I feared they would if I let my injured hand stop me from skating. "And by the way, I hate that you aren't coming with us to the gym today. I'm totally terrified of what Stork has planned."

"Good luck with that. I'm not jealous." Pumpkin had texted me her regrets yesterday when I'd asked for a ride to practice and to the gym today.

We made our way onto the track. I loved that moment when my feet went from carpet to concrete, and I began to roll freely. Ahhh. I stretched my arms wide and glided forward. In those first moments before drills started, I felt like the best skater in the world.

I did a careful T-stop to slow down, then turned around and began to skate backward. My backward skating was still so slow. I moved my hips back and forth, an awkward exaggeration of a sexy dance, to propel myself.

Pumpkin grabbed my elbows and picked up speed, pushing me, then spinning around so she was the backward one. Her backward skating was quick, elegant, beautiful; she looked like a figure skater even in torn fishnets and a raggedy Misfits T-shirt. She pulled me along behind her.

"Skating is supposed to be fun. That's what Stork doesn't understand. It's not, like, grim and serious business." She spun me around again, quicker, and I shrieked, then giggled.

"I'd have more fun if I'd been skating since birth, like you," I said. "Then I could be all fluid and artful, instead of lurching around like Frankenstein's monster."

She grinned. "You'll get there. We should come here some Friday night at open skate—they play music and dim the lights. It's lots of fun. I mean, the music is terrible, but it's fun to dance to, ironically. And there are cute guys sometimes, too. I think I need to make David jealous, or at least distract myself. But I suppose you're already basically engaged to Spineapple, right?"

Maybe I should've asked her more about David, about their fight about college, and why she thought he wanted to dump her. But instead, given her Spineapple comment, I swatted her arm. "Shut uppp. Or at least be quieter."

"Anyway," she continued, "you're just as good at derby as I am. You and Gables held me back for, like, ever in that drill last practice."

That had been at least 90 percent Gables, but I didn't contradict her. "Well, if I die at Stork's uncle's gym today, don't forget about me."

"Never!" She laughed.

"And you better be there next time."

Now she blinked. "Huh?"

"You said you couldn't make it today because you had other plans."

"Oh." She laughed again. "I just didn't want to go. It sounds miserable. I'll keep making excuses till Stork stops inviting me. Derby is hard enough; I don't need Drill Sergeant Stork bossing me around in my free time."

I ground my teeth against my mouthguard, fighting a surprise wave of tears and visualizing how these gym workouts would go. It was inevitable: Stork and her uncle, being all hardcore. Pay and Bee, laughing and talking together. Me, awkward as ever, alone alone alone. How could I do this every week without Pumpkin?

Four shrill whistle blasts interrupted my thoughts.

"Let's get started!" Cleo yelled. "Spread out, and we'll begin with plow stops on the whistle." Another *tweet*. "Go!"

Plow stops were tough. Pushing your legs out in front of

you, toes in, feet perpendicular to your motion—it wasn't a natural position. I could do decent ones at low speeds, if I had time to focus, but Cleo was shouting for us to sprint between each stop and the whistle blasts were coming faster and faster.

"Mighty!" Cleo's voice was sharp.

I jerked my head around to look at her, abandoning my stop and letting my skates carry me forward.

"These are supposed to be plow stops, not plow 'slowdowns.' You're cheating them. You've got to come to a complete stop, or you aren't getting the full benefit." She beckoned me to her.

My face burned as I skated over. "Sorry."

"Good plow stops mean good body position habits when you're blocking a jammer." She blew the whistle again. "Keep going, everyone! Just because I'm talking to Mighty doesn't mean you're off the hook!" Another whistle. In a quieter voice, she continued, "Watch Stork. Look at how low she drops when she stops."

Stork's face was serious, concentrated. She clearly had no idea we were staring at her. When Cleo blew the whistle, Stork's long, skinny legs pushed out perfectly in front of her and her butt dropped, like, eight inches.

"Stork's a million feet tall," I said. "I can't change my height that much."

Cleo stared at me. "What do I say about excuses?"

I couldn't actually remember Cleo saying anything about excuses, but I could certainly guess. Still, unable to stop myself, I grinned hesitantly and said, "You think they're great, especially coming from me?"

She pushed her long, shiny black hair off her face and looked away. "All right," she called to everyone, "next up are turn-around stops on the whistle." She jerked her head at me. "Go on, Mighty."

I'd been dismissed. Why couldn't she take a joke? And why did she have to single out my plow stops, anyway? Pumpkin was at least as bad at them as I was. Plus, due to a scheduling quirk this week, this was a combined practice with the Skatertots, and their plows were mostly terrible—way worse than mine.

I tried to catch Ann's eye, hoping for a little reassurance, but she was working one-on-one with a Skatertot at the other end of the rink. She gave the skater a high five, her "nice job!" carrying across the rink.

Grimacing, I skated back onto the track, as far away from Cleo as possible.

I was still inwardly fuming when we de-geared an hour and a half later. It had only gotten worse after the first drill. Even Ann looked annoyed with me by the end of practice, when I misunderstood a drill's instructions and skated straight into the back of an unprepared teammate.

Was I kidding myself about my skill level? Had my false 27 in 5 score let me scrape my way onto a team where I didn't belong? Should one of the current Skatertots have this spot instead of me? A couple of them were really good—Seitan Worshipper hit me hard enough today to knock the wind out of me. Were Cleo and Ann wishing they had put Seitan Worshipper on Juniors instead of me?

"What's up? You look mad." Pumpkin was sitting on the ground next to me, in our usual spot in the corner. The carpet—a wild colorful swirly design that looked like it had been installed in the 1990s and never cleaned since—was a little less matted and gross here than in the high-traffic areas.

I pulled my skates off my feet with a jerk, ignoring the wave of pain in my left hand as a wheel pushed into my palm. "Eh. Not a good practice. That's all." Cleo had complimented Pumpkin's backward skating several times, and even though I agreed, it still stung.

"Sorry it was bad. I thought you looked good out there. You knocked down Dora." A. Dora Bell was doing another round of Skatertots and was still a gawky mess of arms and legs.

I shrugged and lowered my voice. "Yeah, but it was Dora. A stiff breeze would knock her down."

Pumpkin pulled a pack of baby wipes out of her gear bag and started wiping down her arms and legs. "I don't want to smell too disgusting when I see my friends," she laughed.

Ah yes, Pumpkin's other friends. Non-derby friends. Of which I had exactly zero. My mood soured further. I tried not to let it show. "God, you're going to hang out with friends, and I'm going to the gym with Stork. I've made poor life choices."

Pumpkin kicked my ankle with her foot, jerked her chin to the left. I looked. Stork was walking up behind us. She was too far away to have heard me. Probably. Right?

"Ready to go?" Stork asked. She had offered to drive me to the gym, since Pumpkin couldn't.

"Just a sec."

She set her bag down and scraped her damp blonde hair into a high ponytail. Her face was lifted, neck long and stork-like, and she didn't meet my or Pumpkin's eyes. Maybe she *had* heard me.

Stork's uncle's gym was a small space located in a strip mall, between a Chinese take-out place and a barbershop. It was only a couple miles from the rink, so I didn't have to make one-on-one conversation with Stork for long. She hadn't brought up my "poor life choices" comment, thank goodness. Pay and Bee arrived a moment after us, and the four of us walked inside as a group.

Stork's uncle looked just like her, except older and male. He was tall, super fit, and had shaggy blond hair. He was currently grouping kettlebells in a small circle.

"Hi, everyone, I'm Josh." He shook each of our hands. "Melanie has told me what you want to work on, and I'm excited to get started."

Melanie? I saw Pay mouth to Bee, grinning. That must have been Stork's real name. She didn't seem like a Melanie. She seemed . . . well, she seemed like a Stork.

"I don't know too much about roller derby," Josh continued, "beyond what Melanie has told me, but I've trained other athletes, and I have a lot of ideas. Today we'll get started with some assessments, and then based on those, I can create individualized plans for you. I'll also be sending you home with some paperwork for your parents to sign, of course." He glanced at Stork. "We're thinking Sundays will work for us to meet as a group, and you'll have some homework to do on your own during the week."

Great, more homework. Maybe Pumpkin had made the right choice, skipping the gym. I reminded myself that I'd chosen this; I'd agreed to Stork's plan so that I'd become a better skater. The thought was hollow, just words.

Josh looked at me. "Is your hand injured?"

I nodded.

"We can do some modifications for you today, then. No push-ups."

Well, that was something. The hand injury was paying off.

We formed a half-circle and began to warm up. Josh led us in stretches and calisthenics. When we did squats, he came around to critique us each in turn. He stared at my legs for a long time, and it would have been creepy in a different situation, but the way Josh looked at us made it clear we were just collections of muscles and bone to him.

"Your weight is over your toes too much," Josh told me, "and you're tilting forward. Keep your chest up and your weight back over your heels. You should be able to pick up your toes when you're squatting."

I tried to lean back but continued to tilt forward. I giggled. "My boobs are just too big. Their gravity is tugging me down."

Pay and Bee both laughed, endearing themselves to me. Stork, without stopping her own squats, spoke up. "Have you seen Ann do squats during warm-ups at practice, Mighty? She's bigger than you, and she has excellent form." Then she addressed Josh. "Maybe Mighty needs to widen her stance?"

Josh peered at me. "Try it."

My face burned. Couldn't she have just laughed at my joke? Begrudgingly, I shifted my feet a few more inches apart.

Josh watched me for a moment longer, then nodded approvingly. "That's a little better. Really focus on drawing your hips back, rather than just bending your knees. You'll get it."

The workout continued like that. We'd do something while Josh watched us and picked apart our form. He had comments for all four of us, but it was me he spoke to the most. Each time, my spirits sank a little lower, and I made jokes to compensate. At least Pay and Bee thought I was funny.

When the other girls did push-ups, or kettlebell swings, or anything else using both hands, I would switch to more squats or lunges or sit-ups. After half an hour, my abs and my thighs were on fire and I wished I had two good hands, after all.

"Let's finish things up outside."

We followed Josh out the back door of the gym. I chugged the last of my water from the bottle as I walked.

The crisp outside air felt amazing on my sweaty skin. I put my hands on my head and took a deep breath. Almost done.

"Time for a short jog." Josh gestured to the dumpsters behind the Chinese restaurant next door. "Once you get past those, you'll see the start of a little path through the trees on your right. Follow the path around, and you'll end up over there"—he pointed in the opposite direction—"about a block away. It's a little over half a mile. Don't push it—this is the start of your cool down."

At Josh's signal, we took off. I let Pay, Bee, and Stork get a head start. It seemed like it would be less demoralizing, so I wouldn't have to watch them pass me. Soon they were out of sight. Embarrassing, but I'd known that would happen. All three of them regularly worked out. I shouldn't be embarrassed. Still.

Once I was in the trees, it was almost peaceful. The sun fell in patches on the path, casting striped shadows from the tree branches above. I knew actual outdoorsy people would laugh at this thin grouping of trees being referred to as the woods, but it was the closest to woods that I, a lifelong suburban inside kid, ever got. Beyond the sound of my breath, I could hear birds chirping to one another, and the faint hum of traffic in the distance.

Yes, I was jogging slowly. Probably a small dog could've walked past me without raising its heart rate. But it wasn't terrible. I was doing it. It felt like a small win, after all my struggles at practice and at the gym.

Then I stepped down on a wet leaf, slipped, and pitched forward. I reached out to catch myself at the last second with, unfortunately, my left hand.

The pain shocked me. Sharp stabs radiated from my palm up my arm. I curled up tightly, right on the path. I'd scraped my knees and my elbow, but all I could feel was the throb of my left hand. It was a red, pulsing pain, sucking my breath away. This time no one was around to help me. Not Spineapple, and not Pumpkin. Not even Stork or Josh.

The tears on my face were hot—that was what I noticed first before I even realized I was crying. Then I noticed it, and the fact of my crying made me cry even harder.

What was my problem?

All I could think about was how much I sucked at derby, was in terrible shape, and had no friends. My brain spiraled further. What if my hand got worse? What if Cleo or Ann noticed it and wouldn't let me skate till it healed? I had nothing but derby. School was sucky and boring and lonely. My dad was distant, my mom was judgy, and Ben was far away. And Pumpkin had a whole mess of other friends. I probably wasn't important to her at all.

I was sitting alone in wet leaves, heaving with sobs, clutching my hand, and feeling sorry for myself. When I'd skated to the diner and gone careening through that pile of leaves on the hill, it had been scary but exciting and kind of funny. Today was so different.

Eventually the pain subsided down to a dull ache. I lifted the hem of my tank top and pressed it to my eyes, willing myself to stop falling apart.

"Mighty!" Stork appeared around the bend, dashing down the path toward me, panic in her voice. "What happened?"

I looked up at her with my red, swollen eyes. She was outlined in gold, the afternoon autumn sun behind her. "I fell."

"Are you hurt?"

I patted my legs gingerly. "Just a little banged up. I slipped on the leaves."

"When you didn't show up, we got worried. Josh is running the path in the opposite direction. Let me text him that I found you." She pulled out her phone. "Are you sure you're all right?"

I hiccupped and wiped my face. "I'm just . . . having a rough day." Then, not wanting her to think I was crying just because I'd done such a bad job at the gym, I added, "Personal stuff. Don't worry about it."

I didn't even consider trying to explain my thoughts to her. Someone who had their life as together as Stork clearly did would not be able to understand the mess in my brain right now. Stork, I was sure, wasted no mental space bemoaning her problems. Any deficiency she noticed in herself was probably recorded in her tiny notebook and then immediately dealt with.

"Well . . . I'm glad you aren't hurt worse. Is your hand okay?"

I took her outstretched arm with my good hand and let her tow me to my feet. "I think so."

"Your stitches didn't rip or anything?"

"Yikes, I don't think so." I glanced over at her and realized her eyes were focused on me, her face drawn and worried. Did I look that awful?

"I'm glad you're okay." She gestured to my legs. "I mean, from the fall. I'm glad it wasn't worse."

I half-smiled, half-grimaced. "Thanks."

We walked the rest of the way back to the gym in silence, but I felt her eyes on me the whole time.

CHAPTER 10

time until Soy Anything: 5 months, 13 days

ey, watch it!" My brother jumped to his feet, and I heard a crash, out of frame. "What the hell, man?"

I shifted position on my bed, unthinkingly, as if by moving to the left I could see more of my brother's room on my laptop screen. This was my first time video chatting with Ben in weeks, and it wasn't off to a great start. "What's going on?"

Ben was still standing up, the Bears logo on his T-shirt the only thing visible. "Kevin just knocked over—"

Kevin, off-screen, interrupted him. "If you hadn't left it on the ground!"

I laughed, a little awkwardly. "Everything okay?"

Ben sat back down, his face flushed and his eyes still distracted. "I had a full beer on the ground, and Kevin just kicked it over and spilled it all over our rug. And now our room smells like beer."

"Won't you get in trouble, if you're caught having beer?" Did I sound like a child? That was always the question when I was talking to him. It was hard to believe that Ben, who had been living in the same house as me my whole life, now lived in a separate world where he could set beers on the floor.

"Not if Kevin gets our rug into the laundry quick enough." Ben looked to his left, glaring.

Kevin popped into the frame, a dripping blue-and-gray rug bundled in his arms. "Hi, Ben's sister."

I waved. "Hi, Ben's roommate."

Ben sighed as Kevin left. "That guy . . ." He shook his head.

"What? Are you starting to get sick of each other?" I asked.

"Nah, we're cool. He's just an idiot." Ben laughed.

"Oh, okay." A tiny part of me was disappointed. If Ben was starting to not like his living situation, his life wouldn't seem so perfect. I could have related to that. But no. Kevin was cool, just an idiot, whatever that meant.

"How's roller derby? Still kicking ass?"

"It's going good! Well, okay, anyway. I'm having fun."

My crying jag on the jogging trail had shaken something loose inside me. The speed with which I'd fallen apart, combined with Pumpkin's words about how derby was supposed to be fun, had made me determined to enjoy myself more. Pumpkin and I were probably enjoying ourselves a little *too* much, honestly. Ann, normally so patient, had snapped at us during the last practice because we'd been making up a goofy little dance instead of doing the drill we were supposed to do.

I outwardly laughed off the scolding but was still feeling guilty today. Dancing and joking with Pumpkin wasn't furthering my goal of dominating at Soy Anything or proving to the team that I was valuable. On the other hand, having fun with my closest friend and teammate *did* make me feel like I belonged.

I pushed away the muddled emotions. "Mom said you'll be home for break in time to see me skate in the Winter Showcase."

"Yeah, I get to see you elbow girls in the face."

I groaned. "We don't elbow people, Ben. If we did, we'd get sent to the penalty box. That's what happens if we do something against the rules. Like in hockey."

Ben rolled his eyes. "I know what a penalty box is, Millie. I am familiar with sports."

"Speaking of, how's baseball?"

"Eh, the Cubs aren't in the playoffs, so who cares?"

I'd meant his own baseball team at U of I, not professional baseball, but I didn't bother to clarify. "How are classes?"

"Fine." He leaned back in his chair, tossed a wadded-up piece of paper in the air, and caught it. My brother was always in motion.

I wondered if his classes were actually fine, or if that was the sort of "fine" that I gave to my parents when they asked me that question. Probably the former.

I shifted so I could lean against the wall, propping the laptop on my knees. "Can I ask you something?"

"About what?" He looked suspicious.

"About sports."

His face cleared. "Yeah, of course."

"How did you ... get good at them? At baseball?"

"You just have to work hard." He shrugged and threw the piece of paper in the air again, not bothering to look at me. "It's not some mystery."

It wasn't that easy, clearly. I worked hard, and I was still struggling. Then I thought of Ann's disappointed, irritated face when she'd spotted Pumpkin and me ignoring the assigned drill and dancing instead. Maybe I wasn't working as hard as I could be.

The fear that lived in my heart, staying mostly hidden, rose into view again: What if no amount of hard work could make me a good skater? At least if I didn't try my absolute hardest, I wouldn't have to learn the answer to that question, because I could always tell myself I could have worked harder.

I did work hard. I did. I mean, I'd been trying harder at derby than I'd ever worked for anything else. But after years of lying around my house doing basically nothing, maybe that bar was set a little too low.

My thoughts went in circles. I couldn't untangle them enough to articulate them to myself, let alone to Ben. Especially since sports, like school, had always come naturally to him.

"This girl Stork, the one I ran into at the football game? She says we need to think of ourselves as athletes. I mean, that's kind of insane—not for her, she's super fit and will definitely be a jammer—but for me." My face flushed as I admitted it.

"She'll be a what?" Ben asked. "A jammer?"

I nodded. "They score the points, one point for each opposing blocker that they lap."

"What will you be?"

The specific guilt over my 26.5 laps flooded back into my brain. "We don't really know our positions yet. We're just practicing, figuring out where we go best. But I'll probably be a blocker. Blockers are the ones who try to stop the opposing jammer, and help our jammer get through. It makes sense, 'cause I'm, like . . . solid."

I had big thighs and a thick layer of fat around my stomach. Looking down at my lap now, I saw a roll of white skin sticking out above the waistband of my sweatpants.

"You know me, I'm like a fire hydrant." My standard line. "Short and squat, hard to knock down, good at getting in the way." I stuck my right arm in the air and made a muscle, then laughed.

"Eh, all positions are important." He said it like it was rote, something he'd been told a million times.

"Right, like how you would have been totally fine being moved from, say, shortstop to first base." I knew enough about baseball to know how Ben had prized his position as shortstop.

"Yeah yeah, whatever, Mils."

We were both quiet for a moment. On my end, the whole house was silent as a tomb. On Ben's end, I heard a girl shriek in the distance, then laugh loudly.

"Family Weekend is coming up," Ben said after a few seconds. "You should come down."

"Yeah?" My heart lifted. "When is it? I'll tell Mom and Dad."

"Or you can just come without them, somehow." He wasn't looking at me, and suddenly I thought it might be deliberate.

He was chewing on his bottom lip, like he did when he was mad but trying not to say anything.

I lowered my voice. "They wouldn't ride together, would they?"

I knew the answer. Since the divorce, they had been stiff and formal with each other. Better than fighting, but I still hated it. My dad stood awkwardly on our porch when he picked me up, instead of walking into the house he'd so recently lived in.

"Let's be honest, would you even want to be trapped in the car with the two of them for several hours?"

I flashed back quickly to a family vacation to Maine when I was ten, the road trip from hell. They'd argued constantly on Day One of the drive, then not spoken on Day Two. "Fair point. How do you think you avoid that sort of thing?"

"Riding in the car with them?"

I shook my head impatiently. "No, a miserable marriage." It was ridiculous that Spineapple popped into my head—right? The way I felt about her was just a crush. On the other hand, didn't all relationships—and therefore all marriages—start with a crush? It wasn't the *most* impossible thing ever to envision, for example, the whole league attending me and Spineapple's raucous wedding reception.

Ben sighed. "I have no idea. I was dating this girl Carly for a few weeks, then she got all weird, and now she's dating some douchey frat bro."

"I'm sorry."

He rolled his eyes. "Don't be. She was kind of boring, anyway."

"I thought that boring was your type." It just slipped out.

"What's your type? Oh wait, you've never dated anyone."

"Oh, piss off, Ben." I pursed my lips.

His phone buzzed on his desk, and he glanced down at it. "All right, Mils, I should probably get going."

"I need to get going, too." Thank goodness he didn't ask

why. My afternoon was an empty corridor, devoid of all plans or fun. But I wasn't going to admit that.

I closed my laptop and sprawled out across my bed, eyes shut.

Why had it been so obvious lately, how much I hated being alone in my house? Was it because the house was quieter with both Ben and my dad gone? Or was it because roller derby had illustrated in stark relief that I had spent the last few years not building a single real friendship, just relying on Ben?

At least I had derby now.

When I first joined, roller derby had looked like the solution to all my problems, the home I didn't know was waiting for me. A brand-new life, a brand-new personality. But making the team hadn't been the instant fix I'd thought it would be. I was still my same anxious, awkward self. What would it take to feel like I really belonged there? Wild success at Soy Anything? Was that even possible? Dating Spineapple? That was even less likely.

Why was it so easy for the other rookies? Pumpkin was happy and funny and well-liked, Pay and Bee were cool and confident—and then there was Stork, darling of the coaches, who'd fit into place on the team as if she'd been there for years. If I was as fast, strong, and agile as Stork, such obvious jammer material, I would never have these doubts.

I lay in bed a while longer, jealous and morose, staring at the ceiling with that ugly squashed mosquito. I wished I could step out of my skin and have a break from my life. From myself.

CHAPTER 11

time until Soy Anything: 4 months, 22 days

Someone must have spilled a Slushie on our patch of carpet recently, as there was now a huge, sticky blue stain where I usually sat. Making faces, Pumpkin and I scooted our gear bags a few feet away.

"Hey," Pumpkin said, giggling. "Guess what? Did you know we're scrimmaging at all our upcoming practices?"

"Shhh." I laughed but smacked her arm. Stork had talked of nothing but scrimmage lately, and she had been sending almost daily messages about it in our rookie group chat. Pumpkin's reference to Stork's over-eagerness was funny, but I also didn't want to be overheard.

"She's way too much, isn't she?" I pulled my pads out of my bag. "Still, I'm kind of glad. All we do are drills. I want to put the pieces together and scrimmage so I know what it's actually like. Figure it out before the Winter Showcase, when there's an audience."

Pumpkin leaned in closer. I could smell her gear, that horrible smell like Doritos from hell. Not that I could judge. Mine smelled just as bad, as did the gear of probably half of the team. I always meant to air it out once I got home after practice, but I could never remember.

"Want to hear something you'll be even more glad about?" Pumpkin whispered.

I nodded.

"I found out where Spineapple works."

"What? How?"

"Um, the internet? It was easy. Once I figured out her real name—Erica Jacobs, by the way—it just took a few minutes before I saw all her social media accounts. She has a part-time job at a coffee shop by the river—Cocoa Café." She waggled her eyebrows at me. "Have any plans after practice?"

"Nope." My mom was going out for drinks with my aunt tonight. I'd planned on reheating leftover pizza and watching old derby games on YouTube.

"Well, then I think I know what we're doing."

I grinned, my heart tripping a little. "Okay, but we have to wash up here in the bathroom before we head over. Make sure I look cute and smell okay."

"Not a problem." She stood up, then extended her hands to me to pull me to my feet. "Let's hit the track."

After a few warm-up drills, Cleo and Ann called us all to sit in the center of the track.

"The Winter Showcase is just over a month away," Ann said. "It's a really good time, and I hope you're all looking forward to it."

"If you're a rookie, your first public game can be scary," Cleo chimed in, "so let it be this one that doesn't matter, rather than one where we're playing another league, or, God forbid, at Soy Anything in March."

Pumpkin nudged me and gestured to Stork. Stork's eyes were trained on Cleo, her face dead serious. I drew my lips into a straight line and widened my eyes to mimic her intense stare. Pumpkin giggled.

Cleo, thankfully oblivious to our side conversation, continued. "Once we get into actual competitive games, we'll have you in more permanent roles for blocker, pivot, and jammer." The pivot was the one blocker who could become a jammer mid-jam, if she was passed the jammer helmet cover. I had enough to think about on the track already; I couldn't imagine the brain power it would take to switch roles. "For the Winter Showcase, though, we'll let you choose. That said, we're going to focus the rest of the day on jammer skills. Get with a partner."

Gables grabbed me before I had the chance to cling to Pumpkin like I usually did when we were asked to pair up. I popped my mouthguard out of place, chewing the corner of it nervously.

"Now grab another pair," Cleo continued. "You should be in a group of four. We'll take turns doing some three-on-one. You'll play for one minute, get thirty seconds to talk about it, and we'll go until each person in your group has jammed three times. Repetition, repetition, repetition. Come grab a jammer helmet cover and then spread out on the track."

Gables and I partnered with Toni and Luna, both experienced skaters.

I liked Luna—she was strong, super-fast, and quick to share snacks after practices. She'd even explained her trans-flag-colored hair-dyeing technique when I'd complimented it after our last practice. But despite her friendliness, I was still intimidated by her, as I was by anyone with confidence.

I didn't know Toni well. She was quiet, with bony hips and shoulders that left bruises on my arms and thighs whenever she hit me during drills. The only thing I knew about her was the rumor that she'd hooked up with Gables. I had seen no evidence of anything between them myself, but I would certainly pay attention today, in case I got any gossip to report back to the rookie group chat.

The four of us grabbed space in the apex of the turn. My heart was already pounding. Jam, against three excellent skaters, three times? I slipped my mouthguard in and out of place with increasing frequency as we waited for the drill to begin. I contemplated pretending I had some sort of dire bathroom emergency and decided that would ultimately be more embarrassing.

"Here, Mighty," Luna said. She passed me a lime green helmet cover. "Why don't you jam first, and we'll block?"

"Ha, all right. Prepare to be dazzled." I laughed ruefully and stretched the cover over my helmet, adjusting it so each big gray jammer star was centered on the sides of my helmet.

Gables, Toni, and Luna formed a tripod—Toni and Luna facing away from me, Gables bracing in front of them, arms extended, facing backward, looking me dead in the eyes. She was as tall as Stork, twice as wide, and all muscle. I was so screwed.

"All you have to do is get past us," she said. "You've got this. You're strong."

"So are Galapagos tortoises, but they aren't good jammers, either."

She rolled her eyes. "Just shut up and skate, Mighty."

Cleo's whistle blasted. Time to move. I skated right and tried to get around Luna, but she moved swiftly in front of me. I moved left, trying the inside, but immediately Toni was there, her butt blocking my path. We weren't allowed to hit people square in the back, so I was stuck.

Right again—there was Luna. Left again—Toni. I aimed for the gap between them, and they quickly closed it, seaming their sides together.

I was gasping for breath, and I'd covered basically no ground, just skated back and forth exhausting myself. Why couldn't my legs move faster? Again, the specter of the failed 27 in 5 floated through my mind.

"Come on," I panted, "can't I just forfeit? Can we be done?"

Gables grinned wickedly. "Shut up and keep skating."

I made another attempt at the seam between Toni and Luna, then, as they closed together, rested for a moment, leaning on their backs. Jamming was horrible. Why would anyone ever jam?

Okay, one more attempt. I hopped on my toe stops and ran left—inside—as fast as I could. I snuck past Toni, squeezing by her hips—yes! I'd done it!—but then Gables planted herself in front of me. I gave a feeble push against her chest, and, without ceding any ground, she turned around, so I was stuck on her back. Toni and Luna rearranged themselves so Toni was on the right and Luna was now the backward-facing brace. They'd created another perfect tripod, lickety-split, and I was trapped again.

Tweet-tweet-tweet-tweet! Cleo's whistle ended this round. I pulled the jammer cover off my helmet and bent forward, hands on my hips, breathing deep. Ohhh, it was so lovely to be done. I wanted to crawl to my water bottle, cradle it like a baby, and drink deep. Instead, after three rounds of blocking, I'd have to do this again.

"Let's talk about why that didn't work," Gables said.

"Thanks," I said, not bothering to straighten from my folded-over posture. "That sounds fun. Let's all relive how much I suck at jamming."

"Seriously. Look at me."

I begrudgingly stood up straight. I was still a little afraid of her.

"You were trying to go fast, right?"

I nodded, deciding I should drop the sarcasm for at least a moment. "But you're all faster than me."

"Right. So speed alone isn't going to work."

"So what do I do?"

She grinned her wicked shark's grin again. "You hit us, Mighty. Hard. You come in like this"—she mimed stepping forward at an angle, leading with her right hip and shoulder—"and you stay low, and then you pop up and drive your hip into us, and you push until there's a space, and then you run like hell. If the brace gets in your way, chest-first, like I did that last time? That's a legal hitting zone. Drive your shoulder into their sternum. Make it hurt."

Hit hard. Make it hurt. I wiped my forehead with the hem of my shirt. It sounded better than just trying to be fast. "Okay," I said. "I'll try next time."

Gables nodded. "That's right."

When it was Gables's turn to jam, I was the brace. I faced backward, extending my arms so they rested on Toni's and Luna's shoulders.

One whistle blast, and immediately Gables took off. No nod or grin or anything to warn me. In a fluid motion, she hit Toni hard enough that she stumbled, drove her shoulder into my chest so that *I* stumbled, and skated away. I rubbed the space between my boobs. "Ow."

Gables reset behind us. This time she gave me a quick look. "Ready?"

I nodded.

She hit Toni again, this time from the other side, knocking her into Luna and creating just enough space on the outside to sneak by her. I shuffled over to cover that gap and was rewarded with another blow to the chest.

I survived the rest of her turn, and Toni's turn and Luna's turn, taking a beating each time. I was hit in the chest, in the hips, in the shoulders. I hit the ground in all sorts of different ways: I fell to my knees, slipped and landed on my butt, and sprawled on my side.

Then Luna was holding the jammer cover out to me again. Now I was even more exhausted. This was going to go worse than the first time.

I stood poised behind the tripod. On my toe stops. I'd get a burst like Gables had. Hit hard. Make it hurt. Run like hell. I could do this. I could do this. Ohhh, I couldn't do this.

The whistle blew. I darted forward, smashing into Toni and taking her by surprise. I hit again. They all stayed in front of me, but their formation was messier, and I kept hitting—Toni again, then Luna, then Toni.

"Watch it!" Pay shouted from the group in front of us.

I looked up. I'd pushed the tripod nearly ten feet, till we'd almost collided with Pay's group. A smile broke across my face.

We moved back to where we'd started. I hit again and

didn't get through, but we were moving and they were more desperate, struggling to re-form.

Another reset. This time I got low, drove my hip into the meat of Luna's thigh. She stumbled, creating just enough space for me to push through. Now I was facing Gables again, chest to chest. I crouched down, shoved my shoulder into her gut, and popped her up. Suddenly Gables was sprawled on her butt, and I was free.

She looked up at me from the ground, grinning. "Yes. Like that."

The sight of Gables on the ground—thrown there by me!—was enough to keep my energy up. I kept pushing and kept hitting hard, mostly failing but still improving each time I tried.

When the practice was done, Cleo called me over. I looked helplessly at Pumpkin—we needed to get to the bathroom and make me cute, or at least less smelly, as soon as possible.

"I was watching you today." Cleo stood perfectly still in front of me, her arms folded, her eyes narrowed.

"Yeah?" I gulped. What had I done? Was she going to tell me I wasn't trying hard enough? Because I actually was, today! What if she was able to tell I wasn't fast enough? Did she know I hadn't really passed my 27 in 5?

She nodded. "I want you to try jamming in the Winter Showcase."

I blinked. "What?"

"You need to get faster, and you goof off with Pumpkin too often, but you have potential." She gestured to my legs. "You're strong. And when you're actually focused, you're fierce. I want to keep seeing that fire, that strength."

"But . . ." But jammers were skinny, and fast, and agile! "But I thought we got to choose what positions we play for the Winter Showcase?"

"You do." Her dark eyes bored into mine. "I'm just telling

you—I want you to jam. So. Keep that in mind when you're choosing."

"Oh." Me, a jammer. I'd die. But also—me, a *jammer.* The one scoring points. Skating laps. The announcer calling my name. Fans cheering. Me waving.

I took a deep breath and opened my mouth to say I wasn't sure, but then I fell silent again. A good jammer was key to a team's success. There were four blockers on the track at any given time, but only one jammer. I would be a critical piece of the team, unremovable, crucial. If I could do it well, I'd be priceless, my place on the team undeniable.

"Okay."

"Okay what?"

"I'll do it. I'll jam."

"Do you need to think about it?"

I paused. Gulped again. "Nope. I'll do it."

She gave me a small, satisfied smile. "Good."

I skated away from her, completely dazed as I de-geared.

"What did Cleo want?" Pumpkin asked as we walked together to the parking lot.

Stork was just a few steps ahead of us. "Uh," I said, "I'll tell you in the car." Somehow I didn't want Stork to know Cleo thought I could jam. Surely Stork would inwardly laugh if she heard that—or worse, be all concerned for our team's fate.

As if she'd sensed me thinking about her, Stork turned around. "Hey, Mighty, good work tonight."

"Oh. Thanks. You, too." Complicated emotions here: I liked hearing I'd done well, but it felt condescending coming from a fellow rookie.

"I saw that nice little hip check you got on Toni, when she got knocked out of bounds," Stork continued. She was wearing a puffy winter coat and gloves, and was struggling to find her car keys in her oversized pockets.

I was cold, and ready to keep walking to Pumpkin's car, but it felt like it might've been rude to end the conversation. "Yeah? Thanks."

"So I'll see you on Sunday, right? Josh is going to start teaching the Olympic lifts to anyone interested. If it doesn't bother your hand, you should try them."

"The cut is mostly healed now, so it shouldn't be an issue." I had no idea what the Olympic lifts were, obviously.

Pumpkin took a few more steps away, aiming for her own car.

"Is Pumpkin giving you a ride home?" Stork asked. She had found her keys, and was just holding them in her hand, looking at me.

"Oh, we're going out to a café, actually."

"Cool." She shifted the strap of her gear bag from her shoulder to her hand. "Well, I guess I'll see you Sunday morning then."

I caught up with Pumpkin and climbed in her car.

"What was all that?" she asked, cranking up the heat and blowing on her hands to warm them. Today was one of the first truly cold days of the season.

"I don't know. I kinda felt like she wanted to be invited to come with us."

"Ha. No thanks. All Stork wants to talk about are sports and fitness. She would absolutely sink this mission."

"Yeah, fair enough." I felt a twinge of guilt that disappeared as we left the rink parking lot. "You really think I look all right?"

"Definitely. The lipstick looks great on you."

I had washed up in the rink's bathroom, so at least I didn't have the stink of derby gear on me. My hair was still damp with sweat, but I scrunched it so at least it wasn't slicked back and helmet shaped. Then Pumpkin remembered she had makeup in her purse. Her skin was a few shades darker than mine so I couldn't use her concealer or foundation, but I put on some mascara and purple lipstick. As a final step, I changed out of my sweaty shirt into a spare clean tank top I'd found tucked away in my gear bag.

We found a parking spot right in front of the café. I turned on the dome light in Pumpkin's car.

"Here, take one more look at me. Good? No smeared mascara, no rogue sweat?" My heart was pounding.

Pumpkin narrowed her eyes, considering me. "One thing." She reached forward and tugged my tank top a little lower, so that I was showing some cleavage. She grinned. "Perfect."

I grinned back. "Let's do this."

CHAPTER 12

Cocoa Café was small and cozy, with quirky decorating, mismatched dishes, and plenty of colorful-looking customers. It smelled strongly of espresso and cookies. There was no sign of Spineapple, so we ordered our drinks from some not-Spineapple woman and waited for them at the counter.

Pumpkin elbowed me. "Look," she whispered, pointing to the back of the espresso machine only somewhat stealthily.

Polaroid photos of the café employees were taped up, with their names written beneath them in glittery silver marker. There was Spineapple, toward the bottom. Her hair was longer in the photo, and she had a lip piercing I didn't recognize. She was grinning crookedly, her arms crossed in front of her. *Erica* was scrawled in a messy hand. I felt dazed with lust and sick with nerves. She was so cool. I was not this cool. And she was older! Eighteen, according to Pumpkin. Surely she was already dating some confident, college-ready girl with a car. I couldn't do this.

Then I thought again about the weight and warmth of her hand on my shoulder the night I cut my palm. Maybe it wasn't impossible.

Our drinks arrived—hot chocolate for me and, appropriately, a pumpkin spice latte for Pumpkin—and we took them to a tiny corner table. It didn't have a good view of the counter, but it was one of the only free spots. There was a mason jar full of Scrabble letters on the table. I pulled a few out and shaped them into a flower with a shaking hand.

"What if she's not working?" I whispered.

"Well," Pumpkin whispered back, "there's no charter practice on Wednesdays, plus I saw a post of her from about a month ago where she mentioned work, and that was on a Wednesday. So I bet she's here."

"You're a good detective," I said. I meant that she was a good friend, but I wasn't the sort of person who gushed like that. Still, I felt comfortable enough to raise a question that had been in the back of my mind. "Why are you helping me so much?"

She tossed her head back and laughed. "You're ridiculous. Why wouldn't I? Who doesn't love romance and drama and intrigue? Come on, Mighty, this is fun."

Okay, maybe I would've preferred if her motivation had been an unerring conviction that Spineapple was my soulmate, but at least she had an answer. I was glad she was entertained by all this.

"You don't think she's too old for me?"

"You mean, am I worried she's going to go to jail for corrupting your innocence?" Pumpkin snorted. "You're both in high school, what's the difference?"

"Okay." I sighed, trying to steady my nerves. What, I wondered, was the current status of Pumpkin's love life? Had she and David broken up? I was forming that question in my head, trying to work out the way to ask politely if she'd been dumped, when the bells at the door jangled. My head swiveled automatically.

It was a middle-aged man with a long, graying ponytail. How disappointing. I returned my eyes to the table.

"Are you and David . . . ?"

Before I could finish my question, another voice carried from the back of the store.

"Hey, Mike, how's your night going?"

My hand shot out, and I dug my nails into Pumpkin's arm. That was Spineapple! She must have been in the back when we'd arrived! All thoughts of Pumpkin and her boyfriend fell promptly out of my head. All thoughts fell out of my head, period.

"What do I do?" I hissed.

Pumpkin hesitated just a second, then smiled. "Go talk to her!" She kicked at the leg of my chair.

"Okay, okay." I grabbed my mug of hot chocolate and walked back up to the counter, forming a plan quickly.

The long-haired man, Mike, was taking his time placing his order, and I had a moment to discreetly look at Spineapple. Her bleached hair was artfully disheveled. She wore no makeup besides thick black eyeliner. Her strong, muscular arms were bare, edges of an intriguing tattoo visible on her shoulders. I looked back at Pumpkin, made an "Eeee! Nervous!" face, then stepped forward. The man had finished ordering. It was my turn. I needed to act natural.

"Hi," I said, examining the countertop and trying to sound a bit distracted. "I was wondering if you have any cinnamon that I could add—" Then I looked up fully at Spineapple and affected surprise. "Oh, hi!"

I saw the wheels turning in her head. After a moment, she smiled warmly. "Hi! You're the one who cut her hand!"

"That's me!" I held up my left palm, showing her the thin red line across it.

"Did you end up needing stitches?"

"Yeah, just a few though. Thanks again for . . . for helping out that night." I'd almost said "for taking care of me" but rerouted at the last second, afraid it sounded too lovestruck.

"Of course! I'm planning to be an EMT, so I'm always up for that sort of thing. Did it heal okay?"

"Yep! I got the stitches out last week." Then, as if it had just occurred to me: "Oh, I'm Dino Might, by the way. Mighty. I don't think I introduced myself that night."

"I think you did, but you were pretty out of it." She grinned, the same crooked grin as in her Polaroid. "Nice to officially meet you, Mighty. I'm Spiny."

Spiny. Of course she went by a nickname, too. I smiled back at her, trying not to let it turn into a full-on dreamy gaze.

She grabbed a damp rag and began to idly wipe down the counter while she spoke. "Are you on the rec team?"

I gave a serious moment's thought to saying yes, but it would've been too hard to maintain the fiction that I was on a team other than my own. "No, I'm on Juniors. I'll be eighteen next month, but I'm not going to try out for the charter team till after this season ends, when I'm done with high school. Get more experience, you know." I nodded, shrugged, tried to look calm. Tried not to look like someone who had just spontaneously told an enormous lie.

"Very cool! We have such a good Juniors program here. That's where I started. I only joined charter this past summer. Isn't Cleo just the best?"

"Yeah! She's great." I wouldn't have described Cleo as the *best*. Way too intense. I far preferred Ann, with her easy smiles and warm encouragement. Cleo scared me. But given her comment tonight on my jamming, I definitely felt warmer toward her than I had previously.

"I learned so much from her. She's the one who encouraged me to go out for charter as soon as I could."

"That's awesome." I took a sip of my hot cocoa. My heart was still fluttering like a hummingbird's. I could barely believe she hadn't spotted my lie. What made me say I was turning eighteen? I hadn't planned to, but it was out there now—no going back.

"Anyway, what do you need?"

What did I need? I stared at her. What a question. So many things. Then, "Oh, yeah. For my hot chocolate! I was wondering if you had some cinnamon I could shake on top."

"Yeah, it's over there by the straws and napkins." She gestured with her chin to a spot right near my table.

"Ah, right, thanks." I walked away, resisting running frantically back to Pumpkin.

Pumpkin and I giggled and chattered and gossiped for another hour. As we put our empty mugs in the dirty dishes bin, Spineapple—Spiny!—glanced up at us from behind the counter.

She grinned at Pumpkin. "Hey, don't let this one"—she jerked a thumb in my direction—"cut herself open on anything else in your car, huh?"

"I'll try to keep her out of trouble." Pumpkin smirked at me.

I held my hands up, laughing. "I'll be careful, I swear!"

"All right, Mighty. Take care," Spiny said. "See you on the track!"

"See you on the track!" we shouted back, and scurried from the café, clutching each other's arms as we ran to the car. We waited till we were inside before we started squealing.

That night, I lay under my covers in bed, wide awake. The day's events kept buzzing around in my brain. Gables's face, grinning at me from the ground after I'd knocked her down. The satisfying ache of the bruises on my chest and arms, proof I'd been working hard. Cleo's voice, serious, believing I could be a jammer. And Spiny! Joking with me, chatting with me, smiling at me. Things were feeling hopeful again. Okay, maybe not school, or my family. But I could ignore that tonight. My life, the things I chose myself—derby and friends and, just maybe, romance—seemed real. Possible. I was making things happen. I grinned into the darkness.

CHAPTER 13

time until Soy Anything: 3 months, 20 days

Cleo and Ann had said, over and over, that the Winter Showcase was coming up fast. It hadn't felt true. The Showcase felt safely, infinitely far away—and then suddenly it was upon us.

I woke up that morning with dread in my heart. I wasn't ready.

While my dream of being a great jammer had grown larger and larger, I'd had no corresponding growth on the track. I had jammed at every mid-practice scrimmage for the last month, and it was as if my initial success had never happened—I rarely got past the opposing blockers, and even when I did, I never scored any points. During drills, whenever I could, I partnered with Pumpkin, who I knew would go easy on me. The only thing I'd made real progress on was the goofy skater dance the two of us had invented.

It was embarrassing, failing over and over in front of my teammates. I knew I should've been unfazed, calm and cool as Stork, and just worked hard, but instead, I let myself slack off. Practicing the dance with Pumpkin. Partnering with Skatertots at any combined practices, since they were easier to hit. Taking more water breaks and bathroom breaks than I actually needed. Fiddling with my skates, relacing them or changing the wheels, to take up time when I should have been jamming.

I wanted to be a great jammer, but the path to get there looked nearly impossible sometimes. Could I be blamed for dodging the embarrassment of getting destroyed by my team's blockers over and over again, for taking the easy way out whenever I could?

Today, I wished I hadn't. I wished my recent-past self had worked her ass off, so that the showcase would feel like an exciting challenge instead of a public humiliation.

Skaters needed to be at the rink earlier than spectators, so Pumpkin picked me up. My mom and Ben would arrive later, as would my dad, in a separate car.

Pumpkin's face bore green lipstick, green zig-zag designs on her temples, and an absolutely panic-stricken look. "I'm so nervous."

"Don't be! This is for fun! We're going to do great." I was comfortable lying for Pumpkin's sake. She didn't need to know I was sick with nerves.

"I don't want to screw up in front of my friends. They've only seen me skate on Friday nights, to music, you know, when I can look cool. Now they're going to see me stand there without a clue, getting my ass kicked. God, why did I join this sport? I should have just stuck with skating for fun on the weekends."

"At least you have friends coming. All my friends are on the team." I'd alluded to this before to Pumpkin but had never said it quite so plainly.

"I'm sure that's not true." She brushed my statement aside. "Everyone likes you."

My face flushed. "You don't have to say that."

"I'm not *just saying it*. Besides, Spiny totally likes you. Focus on that."

We'd been back to Cocoa Café twice since that first time and ran into Spineapple on one of the occasions. She'd been friendly—flirtatious, according to Pumpkin—and my fantasies of dating her had continued unabated.

"In fact," Pumpkin added. "I bet she'll be there today!"

I moaned slightly and put my head in my hands. "That's the

last thing I want." Spiny was an incredible skater. She wasn't going to be attracted to the World's Worst Jammer.

"Anyway, I'm sure you have plenty of friends." She took a left turn a little too fast, and I slid toward the outside of my seat. We were approaching the rink. The butterflies in my stomach increased their fluttering.

"No, I don't. I have my brother and his friends. That's it." I tugged at my shorts. I was wearing lime green booty shorts that were perfect and cute when I was on the track but looked bizarre and way too small in any other context. "My brother's coming to our game, actually. He just got home on his winter break last night."

"Oh, he's in college now?"

Maybe Pumpkin's subtext wasn't *Oh, so you're totally alone now*, but that was how it felt. "Yeah. He is. That was kind of my point before. All my friends are on the team. Like I said, I didn't have a lot of friends at school before I left in sixth grade, and I've pretty much let any of those few friendships wither and die." I twisted my hands in my purse strap. Why was I focusing on this? Maybe because I didn't want to address my pre-game anxiety. "Sooo yeah, your best friend on the team is a total loser."

"Seriously, Mighty? That's bananas. Absolute nonsense. You're smart! Seriously, you get to sleep in, and you don't have to deal with bullshit like detentions and dress codes." Without taking her eyes off the road, she reached across the car and jabbed me with her index finger. "You're smart, and cool, too."

"Thanks," I said automatically, not really feeling it. "You know yesterday was my birthday?"

"What? Why didn't you tell me?"

I wasn't sure. Because I was only turning sixteen, and Pumpkin had been seventeen for months? Because it felt embarrassing to not have any plans for a party? I didn't answer her question. "I had dinner with my mom, then went out for dessert with my dad. They kind of crushed it, as far as gifts, actually."

"Oh yeah?"

If I hadn't been so nervous this morning, this would have been the first thing I'd told her. "My mom got me a gift card to Derby Warehouse, so I can buy new skates. And my dad bought me . . . a car!"

"Holy shit! That's amazing!"

It really was. He'd bought me an old beater, light brown, a little rusty, but who cared? It meant freedom! "I can't use it yet, though. That's the thing—I haven't taken my driver's test yet, and my mom decided I need better grades before I'm allowed to drive, anyway." I kept fiddling with my purse strap. I was pretty sure she'd made this decision in a bit of spite to ruin my appreciation of my dad's gift.

Pumpkin pulled into the rink parking lot, going slowly over the gravel. "I don't want to do this."

I jabbed her in the arm, just as she'd done to me. "You're gonna do great. We both are." I wished I believed it.

Cleo was captaining our team, the green team, and Ann was captaining the gray team. We warmed up separately, off skates, each team taking half of the rink.

Our warm-up turned out to consist of a lot of the same moves that Stork's uncle Josh had us doing at the gym. I noticed Pumpkin watching me curiously as I suffered through the fifteen burpees we'd been told to do.

"What?" I asked, breathing hard.

"You look kind of . . . intense."

I wrinkled my nose, pausing at the top of my motion. "What's that supposed to mean?"

"Mighty, why are you stopping?" Cleo's bark startled me. "Faster. Legs out, keep your hips down, no stopping."

Pumpkin started to laugh as I groaned, getting back to work.

By the time our on-skates warm-ups started, spectators had trickled in. I saw Ben and waved wildly at him. Should I skate over and say hi right now? My parents stood on opposite sides of him, looking stiff and awkward. Nah, I'd finish my warm-up.

Cleo called us over, pulling us into a huddle.

"First rule of today, have fun." The words did not sound natural coming from her mouth. "Second rule, try things. Don't be afraid. Don't hesitate. Just go for it. Remember, all those people out there watching? None of them play roller derby. You're already ahead of them, and everything you do will look great."

Gables grinned and pointed across the rink. "Not exactly true." A small group of charter skaters were sitting together, laughing and talking.

There was Spiny, in the back of the group. My heart pounded. She was here! How did my ass look in the green booty shorts? No, how would I look getting destroyed on the track over and over again? That was the real question.

Cleo rolled her eyes. "Gables, you know what I mean. Your friends and families will be impressed. And all those charter skaters were just like you at one point." She clapped her hands. "Let's talk line-ups. Everyone will get the same amount of play time. You'll rotate through, playing in every three or four jams. No sitting the rookies. This is for experience, not for the win." She looked down at her clipboard. "Let's get a couple rookies in right away. First pack: Mighty, you're jamming. Stork, you're pivot. Blockers are Luna, Rainbow, and Gables."

My eyes darted over to Stork. How would she respond to hearing I was officially a jammer? Was she resentful? Angry? I couldn't tell. She did look a bit queasy. Maybe it was just nerves, the same as Pumpkin and I had.

"Remember," Cleo continued, "Each jam is no more than two minutes, and you can do anything for two minutes. Give it your all today."

I gulped, shivered, reminded myself to breathe. I wasn't even sure what giving it my all looked like.

The whole team gathered on the track for intros. We skated a slow lap all together as music blasted from the sound system and the DJ announced our names.

"Up next, we have Dino Might!" he boomed. This moment should have felt glorious, but I was too terrified of the ensuing scrimmage to enjoy it. Still, I faked it as well as I could. I stood up straight, smiling so hard my cheeks hurt, and waved broadly to the audience. Both my parents and Ben waved back as we passed them. God, let me not completely embarrass myself in front of them. Let me do okay.

Time ticked more slowly than normal. I was at the jam line, toe stops down, my eyes trained on the backs of my opponents just a few feet away. A vet skater named Dex was on my right, wearing the jammer star for the gray team. They smiled at me, and I forced my lips into a return smile, as if I wasn't terrified.

"Five seconds!" The jam timer was loud, her voice projecting clearly over the chatter of the crowd.

Five. I leaned forward, put my weight over my toes. *Four.* Two gray blockers looked at me, scooted closer together. *Three.* Stork, the brace for our blockers' tripod, made eye contact with me. *Two.* I crouched down lower. My heart thudded painfully. *One.*

Tweet!

Dex and I blasted off simultaneously. I smashed against a wall of gray blockers, losing track of Dex immediately. I pushed forward, digging in, making little progress. A step back, then a dart to the inside. They were ready for me; I was trapped again. More pushing, all of it ineffective. Another step back, a dart to the outside. Still stuck.

I saw Dex go flying past me out of the corner of my eye. They must've gotten out of the pack immediately and skated a lap; now they were on their scoring pass, getting points for the gray team. Damn it.

Push, push, push. I was panting, chest heaving. The blockers didn't even seem fazed.

"Good," I heard one tell another, her voice calm, not winded at all. "She's moving in, stay in front of her, get lower ... good, good."

Could I just forfeit? Ugh. Dex was coming around again, on their second scoring pass. I turned and bolted to the outside lane. The hip of an opposing blocker shifted into me as I was unbalanced, and I fell sideways, slamming into the ground, then climbed unsteadily to my feet.

"Mighty! Hey, Mighty!" It was Stork, up ahead of me. She was patting her helmet, then pointing at me, then patting her helmet again.

She wanted me to pass the star. She was the pivot—if I gave her the star helmet cover, she'd become the new jammer, and I'd become a blocker. It was probably a good idea. But I couldn't bear to. What would my family think? What would Spiny think? I leaned on a seam between two gray blockers, trying to breathe, trying to clear my head.

There was Dex coming around again. I was distracted from my own plight for a moment as I watched them barrel up the inside line, nimbly step over Pumpkin's leg, and skate away. Four more points for the gray team.

I backed off again, tried the inside one more time. No luck.

Finally, mercifully, *tweet-tweet-tweet-tweet*. The jam was over. I skated back to our bench, lungs heaving, defeated.

Gables caught up with me as I squirted water from my bottle into my mouth.

"You forgot what we talked about," she said. "Remember? Get low, hit hard, run like hell?"

I held up my hand as I kept drinking. Stop. I couldn't, right now.

She smiled, untroubled. "It's okay. You'll get it."

I didn't, though. The blockers were fiercer today. There was an intensity, a drive, a desperation, that I'd never felt at practice. I jammed seven more times and never made it through the pack. Each time, my spirit sank lower. Why was I doing this? Why was I playing a sport I was so terrible at?

When it wasn't my turn on the track, I watched other skaters jam, and they made it look—well, maybe not easy, but not as unbearably hopeless as it was when I was out there. They did better than me and kept the overall score close.

As we neared the end of the showcase, Stork swapped her pivot stripe for the star, Gables took the pivot cover, and I was put in as a blocker. Thank God. I was equally terrible at blocking, but as a blocker, I was one of four people out there. No matter how badly I did, the whole thing wouldn't be on my shoulders.

I positioned myself close to the inside line. Gables was my brace, and Pumpkin was on my right.

"Gray team is jamming Toni. She's on the outside right now. Just do what I say." Gables gave my shoulder a squeeze. "I'll tell you where she's going."

Oh, it was so nice to see Toni far away, over my right shoulder. She was at the opposite side of the track from me. The pressure was off, and I had Gables to guide me. I was too tired to smile, but some of my fear slipped away.

The jam-starting whistle blew. Just as I'd hoped, Toni ran up the outside line, nowhere near me. Luna, the green blocker closest to her, shifted a foot to the right so her butt was planted right on Toni. Fabric rustled by my left arm. Stork. She'd gotten past the gray blockers, slipped by me, and was lead jammer, the first jammer to pass all the blockers, which meant she had the power to signal the refs to end the jam early if she wanted.

Good. I would be jealous later, but now I felt only relief that something positive had happened for my team. Maybe we could close the gap in the score.

"She's looking in," Gables muttered, her eyes on Toni. "Be ready, Mighty."

Time sped up. Toni sprinted to the inside, there was a gap of about a foot between me and the inside line, I shuffled left to close it, and Toni smacked into my left side—

Gah! I was on my hands and knees, the breath knocked out of me.

Toni hopped over me, sprinted forward, and collided with Gables.

Tweet! A ref's stern shout. "Gray, two-three-two, back block!"

"Power jam!" Gables shouted. "Toni's in the box! Power jam, power jam!"

Toni was in the penalty box! Yes! We had thirty seconds where all we had to focus on was offense. I climbed unsteadily to my feet, trying to follow Gables's lead to hit the gray blockers to clear a path for Stork.

When the jam ended, Stork had scored nineteen points for our team. Everyone on the green bench cheered us as we skated back. We high-fived our teammates as we returned to them, our wrist guards clacking.

The next jam began. I grabbed my water bottle, sat on the bench, and watched. I was glad that last jam had gone so well. I was glad Stork had gotten all those points.

Yep. I was glad.

Oh, I wasn't glad, I was jealous as hell. Damn Stork. I'd spent the last few months training, working harder than I ever had in my life, and I couldn't even get out of the pack once. Her first time jamming, and she gets nineteen points? A rogue sensible thought popped up, reminding me that even if I was working hard, I definitely hadn't been trying my hardest. I pushed the thought away. I was too upset.

Why was I doing this? Why keep playing derby if I was terrible at it? I wrapped my arms around my middle.

"Hey." Gables clapped me on the shoulder. "Stop it."

"What?"

"Stop beating yourself up. It's your first game."

I shrugged. "I'm not beating myself up. I'm just honestly assessing my success, realizing how much I suck."

Gables rolled her eyes. "Your overdone self-deprecation is annoying, Mighty."

My face flushed, and my eyes stung. So not only did I suck at derby, I annoyed people, too.

It got worse after the game. Though we'd won and everyone else on my team was in a buoyant mood, I was doing my best just to fake it. And then Cleo flagged me down.

"Mighty. Hey. Come chat with me for a second."

I padded across the carpet in my socks, following her to an empty side room.

"I know today didn't go how you wanted it to."

I shook my head, not trusting myself to speak.

"Jamming is mentally and physically demanding. Blocking is tough, too, but as a jammer, you're kind of by yourself out there."

Where was she going with this?

She sighed. "If you feel like I pushed you into this, I just want to own up to it, and say I'm sorry."

I nearly choked. She'd brought me over here to apologize? Oh God, this was so much worse than getting a scolding. I'd done so badly that *Cleo* felt guilty about it. "No! I wanted to jam. I still want to!"

"You don't have to do it to please me, Mighty. I'm aware of my reputation as being a little, shall we say, driven. I don't want to bowl you over."

It had been so recently that she'd believed in me. And now she was backing away from her comments after one game?

"It's not because of you. I think jamming is fun!" A lie. It wasn't fun. But I wanted the stardom. More than that, I wanted the chance to prove my worth to the team. A mediocre blocker could be replaced or ignored, but a skilled jammer was crucial to a team's success. If I could actually get out there and score some points, I wouldn't have to worry over whether or not I fit in—it would be a given.

Her deep red lips thinned into a line. "All right."

"Cleo?" My eyes were filled with tears, the drops quivering on my lashes.

"Yes?"

"You don't think I should have stayed in Skatertots another session, do you?" Maybe I'd been wrong to dismiss the 27 in 5 result as meaningless. Maybe it signified my deep unsuitability for this sport.

She batted the question away. "No, of course not. But you need to take training more seriously. Less goofing around with Pumpkin. More hard work."

I tried not to wince. "I'll work hard. I swear." I had to. I couldn't let today's failure be my only outing as a jammer.

"Good." She nodded decisively, but her eyes still looked uncertain.

CHAPTER 14

The afterparty was at a nearby pizza place, where the league had reserved the entire back room. I had never felt so hungry; I couldn't wait to descend on those pizzas, drowning my sorrows in cheese and tomato sauce.

Ben and I rode there with my mom. Ben rode shotgun while I sat in the back seat; the natural order of sibling car spots had immediately returned. It was such a relief to see him there, his long legs propped up on the dashboard in that way my mother hated, his unruly hair draped over the head rest, his left hand tapping against the middle console in rhythm with the music.

"I can't believe you do this," my mom said over and over as she drove, her voice filled with something like awe. "I can't believe you actually go out there on roller skates and hit people."

I had dreaded my family's reactions after how terrible I'd done. But it seemed that Cleo, in her pep talk, had been correct: anything we did on the track looked impressive to people who didn't play derby.

"I just didn't realize what it was like. I can't believe you do this," my mom repeated. She sounded scared, actually, more than impressed. "*Why* do you do this?"

I didn't bother to answer her question seriously. "Because I'm so hardcore, obviously."

Her concern was, conversely, bolstering my mood. If I'd played hard enough to scare my mom, I couldn't have looked *that* useless on the track.

"How about when that girl hit you really hard and knocked

you down?" Ben twisted around to look at me. "That looked like it hurt!"

I grinned. Pain, suffering for your sport, was something Ben respected. "It did!"

"That one girl on your team was really good. The tall one?"

Of course. Sigh. "Stork. Yeah, she's good."

"No, not her. The big one with the tattoo on her thigh, the girl who looks like she could kick my ass." He grinned widely, that familiar smile that looked almost too wide for his face, showing all his teeth, a smile I'd been seeing my entire life when he teased me about something. It was like going back in time, or like relaxing into a hot bath after a long derby practice. I waited a beat for my mom to yell at Ben for swearing, as she would have in the past, but no admonition came.

"That's Gables. And I have no idea how she has a tattoo—she's the same age as me." It had shocked me when I'd learned Gables and I were the same age. With all her confidence and skill, I'd assumed she was older. "Gables is scary, but God, she's an incredible blocker. I'll introduce you to her at the afterparty." Hopefully she would have forgotten her earlier annoyance with me.

My dad had beaten us to the restaurant. He was standing in the lobby, hands shoved in his pockets, awkwardly watching a girl with a bright blue mullet play a crane machine. His face brightened at the sight of us.

I felt bad. Either Ben or I should have ridden with him.

"Let's go find a table," I said quickly, leading the way.

I introduced everyone to Gables, who didn't stop working her way through a slice of deep dish while she spoke to them; to Pay and Bee, who smiled, waved, and immediately returned to their conversation; and to Ann.

Ann gave me a tight hug. "I'm so proud of this one," she said, smiling at my parents. "She has come so far since she started in May."

I blushed. "Yeah, and maybe someday I'll even score a point."

She bopped me on the head with the menu she was holding. "Hey! You worked hard today. You should be pleased."

I hadn't worked nearly as hard as I should have. I'd seen my defeat in the body of every blocker before each jam started. But I was glad Ann hadn't seen it that way.

"I'm going to try harder at practice, Ann. Honest. I want to do better." My words burned with sudden intensity.

Ann grinned at me again. "Yes, you could work harder at practice, I'm not going to disagree. But take a moment to be proud of yourself right now, okay? This is tough stuff. If it were easy, it wouldn't be half as rewarding, would it? So be proud."

Ann was likely not much younger than my parents. Today, like every day, she was wearing a bright bandana over her curly auburn hair, sweatpants, a quippy T-shirt, and lime green high-tops. My parents were both overdressed, standing weirdly far apart from each other, arms straight at their sides. Maybe I could just sneak into the trunk of Ann's car after lunch and then move into her house without anyone noticing.

"It was nice meeting you, Mighty's family." Ann headed across the room to greet someone else.

"Come on, Mils." Ben grabbed my arm, steering me away from our parents and toward the buffet line. "Food."

Pumpkin found us as we shuffled forward in the line. She barreled into me, wrapping her arms around my waist. "We survived!"

I had lost track of her during the scrimmage, developing tunnel vision, focusing only on jamming. Pumpkin could have done great or terrible; I had no idea. Her happy spirit came as a relief.

Ben caught my eye. His raised eyebrows and the line of his lips said *Who is this weirdo?* I ignored him and hugged her back. "We did it!"

She grabbed my shoulders and stared straight into my eyes. "Don't beat yourself up about jamming."

"Ohhh, Pumpkin, please, let's not talk about it." My mood had been improving, in tiny increments, since we'd left the rink. Pumpkin's pity would ruin all my progress.

"Seriously! You fought soooo hard. And we're rookies! It's okay! We're okay!" She started giggling.

Ben caught my eye again, tilted his head toward Pumpkin, and mimed smoking a joint. I rolled my eyes at him, though Pumpkin did seem unnaturally goofy.

"Pumpkin," I said, breaking free from her grip and directing her attention away from me, "this is my brother Ben. Ben, this is my friend and teammate Pumpkin."

"Pumpkin?" he said, a question to us both.

"I'm Sonia, but no one here is going to call me that. Just stick to Pumpkin." Her attention was suddenly caught by someone at the edge of the room. "Hey, Pay! We did it! We survived!" She skipped away.

"She is . . . a lot." Ben ran his hands through his hair, which had gotten even longer and shaggier since I'd seen him when he was here for homecoming.

"She's great," I said defensively, and grabbed a plate from the buffet. "She's just dialed up to eleven today for some reason."

"Everyone here is so . . ." He searched for a word.

I readied my temper, predicting his thought. Weird-looking? Smelly? Strange?

". . . so affectionate," he finished, his tone making it clear that this was not a compliment. "So huggy."

I had been surprised initially, too, but I'd stopped noticing it. "Yeah, they're nice." I decided not to rise to his bait, focusing instead on loading breadsticks onto my plate. "I'm glad you're back for a while. These weekends with just me and Dad, or just me and Mom, are weird. I don't want all that focus on me, you know?"

He sighed. "Why'd they have to do this? Kevin's parents are divorced, too, and they hate each other. They won't even be in the same room. When his dad came to help him move out for winter break, he referred to Kevin's mom as 'that bitch.'"

"Ugh. Charming guy."

"Right? Those are the people who should be divorced. Our parents are just boring, bickering suburbanites who want some excitement in their lives." He rolled his eyes and reached for another slice of pizza, stacking it on top of his already-full plate.

I glanced at my parents. They were talking to each other, arms folded, a couple feet of awkward space between them. "I dunno. They might not be as bad as Kevin's parents, but they've been fighting for years. Who wants to be married to someone you don't like?"

"Oh yeah, and I heard about your birthday gifts." He groaned.

"What? What about them? They're great!"

"Could they be more transparent about trying to curry favor?"

"You think that's why I got a car and skates? To get me on their sides?"

He stayed close to me as we made our way back toward the table. "Either that, or because they feel guilty."

I shrugged. "Well. I'll take that. They should."

Damn Ben. Damn my brother and his insight, tainting my appreciation of my awesome gifts. I walked on ahead of him. The back room had filled up with skaters; my parents were barely visible. I looked around as I maneuvered my way to the table, weaving past people, trying to spot my teammates. Most of them were here.

No Stork, though. Maybe she was running late? She had a lot to celebrate today, after that nineteen-point jam. Surely she'd be here. I'd high-five her when I saw her, tell her congrats on her good work. I'd stuff down my jealousy if it killed me. After all, it would only be more embarrassing if she could tell I was jealous.

I was deep into devouring a slice topped with peppers and mushrooms, my cheeks stuffed like a chipmunk's, when someone tapped me on the shoulder. I turned around. Looked up. Spiny. Oh God.

"Nice job today," she said. She was surrounded by a knot of other charter skaters, none of whom looked especially interested in talking to me.

I shook my head, chewed as fast as I could, my face burning.

She smiled. "I know, jamming is tough. You fought hard, though."

Still frantically chewing.

Spiny looked at the charter skater closest to her and gestured to me. "Kiko, this is Mighty, the one I was telling you about. Mighty, this is Kim Kong."

She had told one of the charter skaters about me? She was talking about me? Thinking about me? My heart nearly stopped.

"Oh yeah," said Kiko. "You're the one who came into our practice that one night covered in blood or whatever."

Oh. Not what I'd imagined.

"All right," Spiny continued. "We better get in line. We're all starving. Take care!"

And she was gone. I took a deep, regretful drink of water, my mouth finally empty. Damn it! Damn this delicious pizza.

"Who was that?" Ben watched Spiny and her friends walk away.

"Spineapple." It came out as a lovelorn sigh. "She's on the charter team."

"Huh. She's hot." He went back to his pizza, oblivious to my death glare.

CHAPTER 15

time until Soy Anything: 3 months, 14 days

Winter break didn't mean much change to my routine, given that I was doing online school, but it was still nice to have the time off. Derby practices were paused till early January, too. Fine by me, as I wasn't quite ready to skate again. If I could have practiced alone, maybe. But it felt too raw to have the team witness more failures.

Mostly I just lay around the house and hung out with my brother. Ben and I stayed up late watching movies or playing video games almost every night. I was terrible at *Madden*—at all sports video games, really—but most of the fun was trash-talking each other, anyway.

The two of us drove to Woodfield Mall the weekend before Christmas to find gifts for our parents, and it was such a crowded nightmare, we gave up before we'd even found a parking spot.

"I could not drive in this," I said, watching Ben try and fail to make it through a light before it changed to red. I still hadn't taken my driver's test. I didn't have enough practice hours. "I'd kill us both."

Ben laughed. "Probably."

"Thanks." I punched him in the arm.

"Watch it, I'm steering. You'll kill us both anyway."

I rolled my eyes, unzipped my coat, and set my feet on the dashboard, relaxing. Woodfield wasn't too far from Dad's apartment—our location this weekend—but in traffic like this, it would be a while before we were back. My winter boots dripped dirty, icy water onto the dash, where it slid onto the floor and my legs.

"What should we buy them?"

Ben shrugged. "Gift cards?"

"Yeah, we could stop at Target, maybe. Oh, and I heard Mom say she needs a new curling iron. Maybe we could get her one." She'd been taking even more care than usual with her appearance lately. Lots of drinks with my aunt, and then "with friends." I had the unsettling feeling that she was going out on dates, and I didn't want to think about it.

"You actually know what type of curling iron Mom wants? I vote we stick with gift cards. Harder to screw up."

"Yeah." I sighed. "I guess so." My mom was notoriously hard to shop for. "Can I come for a visit once you're back at school, since I didn't end up coming for Family Weekend?"

"Sure. I mean, depending on when."

"You have a real busy social life?" I tried to sound sarcastic, but my curiosity was real. Did Ben, like, go to parties and sneak into bars? What did a freshman in college actually do? I knew my brother was cooler than me, in a wholesome, baseball, all-American sort of way—rather than a denim-vest-and-septum-piercing Spineapple sort of way. Would it be weird for him to have me there in the dorm with him?

"Obviously. I'm beloved by all. They're thinking of naming a new engineering building after me, actually."

I socked him in the arm again. "I was thinking of naming Dad's toilet after you, actually."

He ignored the insult. "Dad acts so weird when we're over there."

"Like how?"

"Like he's all nervous, wanting to impress us."

I shrugged. "At least he's barely there." My dad had always been a workaholic, though it was also possible that he felt as awkward as we did and was using work to avoid that awkwardness.

"True."

I set my feet back on the floor. I'd been thinking about something as I lay in bed the past few nights, unable to fall asleep. "Did they ever seem like they liked each other? Maybe when we were little? Like, in between the fights, did they ever seem to actively be happy to see each other, or anything?"

"No. I don't think so." Then, after a pause as he made his way through a slick, slushy intersection: "That's pretty normal, though."

Okay, okay, the reason I'd been thinking about this came from an embarrassing source. But you can't help what paths your mind takes, right? The Spiny fantasies had developed into further detail. I saw us falling in love, getting married when I was twenty-two and she was twenty-four. We'd have a quirky little apartment in Chicago, and we'd both play derby for the Windy City Rollers—Chicago's formidable and highly ranked derby team—and we'd throw parties and play records and have adorable inside jokes and just be the perfect picture of young love.

But I wasn't going to tell Ben that. "My point is, when people get married, they're in love, right? They're crazy about each other. Why else would you get married? And then somehow you end up . . . I don't know, indifferent to each other?" I shuddered.

Ben nodded. "I know. It sucks."

"Yep." The thing was, I was sure my parents had never been crazy about each other, had never had all-consuming crushes before they were together. There was no scenario in which I dated Spiny and it fell apart like this. Okay, okay, I barely knew her, but it was clear: She was wonderful.

Christmas passed awkwardly, if uneventfully. We did indeed give our parents gift cards. Their gifts for us were more restrained than my birthday gifts had been, which had the odd effect of making me feel better. Maybe my birthday gifts really had been just because I'd turned sixteen and it was a big deal, not because they were trying to assuage their guilt or one-up each other.

On New Year's Eve, Ben went to a party with his high school friends, and I went to Pumpkin's house. She'd just broken up with David—her decision, not his, she reported—and she wanted to skip her friend Nora's party because he'd be there. I wished her reason for inviting me had been more about me and less about avoiding someone else, but I was still happy to go. We made sugar cookies with her younger sister, then ran outside at midnight in our pajamas, blowing party horns and cheering.

We went up to her bedroom around 1:30 a.m. Pumpkin tossed me an extra pillow and an afghan off her bed, and I curled up on the surprisingly fancy fainting couch against the opposite wall. It was dark, it was late, and the house was quiet, but I didn't feel ready to fall asleep.

"Let's talk more about derby," I said, punching my pillow and rearranging it under my head.

"I can't wait till our first game." Pumpkin snuggled deeper under the covers. Our first real game of the season was against the Sauk Valley Sonics, one of the Juniors teams we'd likely also face at Soy Anything. "The Winter Showcase was great."

"You really think it was great? You were so scared beforehand!" The fact that she'd had fun at the showcase felt like something of a betrayal.

"Yeah, but afterward, I felt all high almost, from adrenaline. I hit people! I didn't die! I'd imagined it mattering way more than it did. It was just fun—not a big deal at all!"

So it was adrenaline, not weed, that had made her all goofy at the afterparty. I smiled into the darkness. "I want that feeling. Or, like, I want to feel not-miserable. I'll settle for that. But I can't imagine thinking it's not a big deal. Everything I do on the track feels like it's life or death."

"You could just tell Cleo and Ann you don't want to be a jammer, you know."

"I know." My heart sank a little bit just hearing Pumpkin say the words. As soon as Cleo had suggested jamming to me, I'd latched onto it. I wanted the glory. I wanted to be cheered for, to be known, to be a star. I wanted my teammates to love me. "Sometimes I think, why do I keep playing a sport I'm so terrible at?"

"You're not terrible," Pumpkin said automatically.

I sighed. "I'm not great."

"We've only been doing this for seven months."

"Yeah. But so has Stork."

"Ugh. Don't compare yourself to Stork. She doesn't count. She's . . . unnatural." Pumpkin sat up. "Let's go get the rest of the cookies."

I followed her through her darkened house, into the kitchen. We brought the cookies back to her bedroom in a Tupperware container, munching as we talked.

"Why did you decide to join derby, anyway?" Pumpkin asked. "For me, it was the usual: I saw *Whip It* at my older cousin's house. Plus, sometimes derby players would come to the rink on Friday nights when I was there with my friends, and they always looked really cool and tough."

I laughed. "There's a reason I've never told you why I joined. It's ridiculous."

"I can't wait."

I took a big bite of cookie, crumbs spraying out as I laughed harder. "So, okay, my mom told me I needed to join a club. She said she was worried I was alone too much, since I was doing online school."

"Were you? Alone too much, I mean?"

"Definitely." It was painfully obvious in retrospect. "Though I'm pretty sure she just wanted to make sure I'd have something going on in my life when she and my dad announced their divorce. Anyway, I didn't like any of her boring suggestions.

Board game nights at the civic center. A book club for teen girls. Cooking classes. She wouldn't get off my back about it, though, so"—I laughed more—"one day I honestly googled 'badass sports for weird girls' and found an article about roller derby."

Pumpkin collapsed face-first into her pillow, laughing hard. "That should be our team's slogan! 'A badass sport for weird girls.' It's perfect!"

"Hey! I think I forgot to tell you—Spiny went out of her way to talk to me at the Winter Showcase afterparty."

"Ohmygod! Tell me everything right now!"

I filled her in on the brief exchange, leaving out the part where my brother called her hot.

Pumpkin sighed dreamily. "She said 'take care.' Like, she cares about you."

"That's a bit of a stretch." I rolled over onto my back, my cookie finished. That interpretation was clearly coming from Pumpkin's stated love of drama and romance. But still. A decorative throw pillow was wedged uncomfortably under me, and I pulled it out and squeezed it to my chest. I sighed hugely, full of longing. "What do I do next? How do I make this happen?"

"Keep running into her at the café? That's what David did with me. I was working at a grocery store, and he kept going through my checkout line and flirting with me." She sighed now, too. "It was such a cliché. I finally slept with him, and then he dumped me. That was seven months ago, and we got back together two months later. But now that he's my ex again, thinking about it makes me kinda want to murder him."

"Now I want to murder him, too." I said this, but all I was thinking was: Pumpkin had had sex? God, I must've seemed like such a child to her. I'd kissed two people in eighth grade, when I'd briefly joined a library youth group—one boy and one girl. Both times had been extremely chaste and ultimately not that exciting. Then I thought about the math of Pumpkin's statement. "He broke up with you seven months ago? Is *that* why you joined derby?"

She gasped. "Busted! Yeah, it's true. I joined derby as some sort of female empowerment, I-don't-need-a-man thing. Another cliché." She paused. "I really did watch *Whip It*, though."

We both cracked up again.

When we finally calmed down, I said, "I have a new plan to get Spiny's attention. It's... maybe insane."

"Ohmygod, tell me right now!"

"No, not yet. I need to think about it more. But... the wheels are turning. This could be huge."

It involved more lying, which was not my favorite thing. But ohhh, it was such a good idea.

CHAPTER 16

time until Soy Anything: 2 months, 22 days

I wasn't going to enact my plan until Ben was back at school. Not that I wanted him to go, of course. But having my brother in the house when there was a chance, if all went well, of Spiny being there too? That was too nerve-wracking, especially since he'd mentioned he thought she was hot.

We had been getting on each other's nerves over the last few days. I snapped at him because he ate my leftover fries from Portillo's; he snapped at me for leaving wet bath towels all over the floor of our shared bathroom. The charm of playing video games together was dulled by the fact that I lost every single game of *Madden*. But when I woke up on the morning of his departure, I was filled with dread. I didn't want to be alone again.

He packed up his car on a freezing January afternoon. I lingered on the porch, bundled up in my coat, hat, and scarf, glad my face was mostly covered. Ben would never let me hear the end of it if he knew I was crying.

"Well, I'll see you later." he said, leaning his arm on the hood of the car. "Don't let Mom and Dad's bullshit get to you."

"I'll try." I sniffed. "When can I come visit?"

"As soon as you've got your license. Just get your hours, already."

"I will." It was tough to get the required practice hours when the only way to do it was to be in the car with one of my parents, the last thing I ever felt like doing. "I'll still have to pass the test, though. That could be tough."

He waved the idea away. "It's easy."

"That's what you say about everything."

"You'll be fine. If your friend Pumpkin passed, you definitely can."

Pumpkin had picked me up yesterday for another outing to Cocoa Café, and had darted into our house upon arrival, shrieking "I have to pee soooo bad!" as she ran down the hallway and into the bathroom. I sensed that this second encounter had rather cemented Ben's opinion of her.

"Pumpkin is awesome," I said defensively. "You just . . . keep meeting her at weird times. Don't be all judgy." At least my tears had dried up now.

Ben walked closer to me, pausing on the sidewalk in front of the porch. His cheeks and nose were red and raw from the cold. "One last thing before I go, Millie. Never forget this."

"Yeah?" He sounded uncommonly serious.

"You really, really . . ." He paused, looked me straight in the eyes. ". . . suck at *Madden*."

I smacked his arm, grinned, and gave him the finger. "Get out of here before I get my derby friends to beat you up."

He laughed as he got in the car and drove away. I stayed out on the porch, watching his car disappear down the street, then took a deep breath and headed inside.

"Mom," I called, "can you drive me to Sally's?"

Currently my hair was orangey pink, with over an inch of brown roots. I wanted it to look fantastic when I enacted my plan. A trip to Sally Beauty Supply was an absolute necessity.

My mom agreed rather readily, surprising me.

I drove, even though it was only a few minutes away. Every little bit toward my hours helped. She waited in the car while I ran into the shop. I emerged just a few minutes later, my arms clutching a variety of treasures.

Shopping had energized me, taken away some of my natural awkwardness around my mother. I chattered at her about my purchases as I carefully navigated out of the parking lot.

"Okay so I got three different greens, so I can swirl them together and paint them on in different areas and stuff. And I needed bleach, so the dye will show up on my hair. Also, there was a two-for-one lipstick sale, so, you know, how could I not pick up a couple tubes?"

"Well, it looks like you're stocked up. Careful with this car in front of you—they're turning. Slow down." My mom was a nervous passenger, not that I blamed her.

"Do you want me to help you dye your hair?" she continued. "I could get the back for you."

My mom, up to her wrists in green hair dye? Hard to imagine. I'd planned to blast aggressive punk rock and send Pumpkin periodic photo updates. But I couldn't bring myself to turn down her offer. Maybe this was because of last time. I still remembered hearing her swear when she saw what I'd done to the bathroom counter in my carelessness, pink dye splattered across the beige laminate. "Oh. Uh, sure, I guess I'll take help. Thanks."

Once we got home, she changed into an oversized flannel shirt buttoned up to her neck to protect against dye splatters. It had belonged to my dad, and I didn't like seeing her in it.

My mom was far more exacting about the hair transformation process than I was. She snapped on plastic gloves, combed my hair with brisk, aggressive strokes, applied neat layers of bleach with a little brush, covered my hair with a plastic cap, and set an egg timer for twenty minutes.

"Now, let's mix the greens." She adjusted the layer of paper towels on the bathroom counter, then set a plastic bowl down. "Equal amounts of each one?"

"No, keep them separate. I want, like, different areas of color."

She sighed, cut the sigh off, then jogged downstairs to get two more bowls. In the moment I was alone, I wondered again why she had offered to help.

"So. Millie." She carefully poured equal amounts of dye into each plastic bowl. "How's roller derby?"

"We're still on a break, remember? Practices start again next week." I was sick with nerves just thinking about it. I knew Cleo would be watching me closely.

"Are you still enjoying it?"

"Of course! Come on." It was a lot more complicated than my answer made it sound, but I wasn't going to try to explain it. "Did I tell you that at our last Sunday gym thing, I deadlifted 105 pounds?" It had felt amazing. I had immediately tried to deadlift Bee, who probably didn't weigh too much more than that, thinking that if I could do it with a barbell, I could do it with a teammate. She'd giggled and flopped over, falling out of my grip immediately.

"You better be careful. You could screw up your back if you don't know what you're doing."

"Mom." I narrowed my eyes, glared. "Josh makes sure we have good form. I'm not just randomly throwing weights around like an idiot."

"All right, all right." She held up her hands. "I just don't want you to hurt yourself."

"I'm tougher than you think."

She reached out, shifted the cap off my head, and gave my hair a worried look. "It's bright orange."

"That's normal. Brown hair turns orange before it's fully bleached. Just put the cap back."

She stood up and adjusted a row of mason jars on a shelf above the toilet. "I just wish . . ." She trailed off, then went back to stirring the green dye.

"What? You wish what?"

"Oh, nothing."

There was an awkward silence. I didn't know how to explain why some silences felt awkward and some felt natural, but this one was definitely awkward.

She stepped out when I got into the shower to wash the

bleach out of my hair, but came back into the bathroom and kept talking once I was behind the curtain. Why was she so interested in hanging out with me today?

"Are you . . . dating any of these roller derby girls?"

"No, I'm not. *Jesus*, Mom." Not yet, anyway. I would be soon, if my plan worked.

"You can't blame me for asking. It's normal for teenagers to date."

I pursed my lips. "So I'm abnormal?"

"You know that isn't what I meant."

"Do I?" Why had I allowed her to help me dye my hair?

"*Jesus*, Millie." Her voice and intonation sounded exactly like mine. I hated it.

Another awkward silence. With the shower water loud in my ears, I wondered if she'd left the bathroom. "Mom?"

"Yes, Millie?" The tentative note in her voice twisted something inside me.

"Why did you and Dad get married?" I hadn't intended to ask this; the question just spilled out of my mouth.

Her pause was long enough that I wondered again if she had left the bathroom. But eventually she spoke. "It felt like the right thing to do."

"Why? You weren't pregnant with Ben yet or anything, based on the math."

"Oh, Millie, that's not what I meant." Her groan was loud enough I heard it over the roar of the water. "We'd been together for a year and a half, we were graduating college, it was just the natural next step. He asked, and I didn't see any reason not to say yes."

I snorted. I couldn't help myself. "I bet you regret it now, huh?" Again, the reply just slipped out. As soon as I said it, I knew I'd basically invited her to start bitching about my dad.

But I'd predicted her response wrong. "Of course I don't regret it! How could I?"

"Because you two hate each other, obviously. You just spent, what, twenty-ish years living with someone you can't stand. That sucks." Maybe it was the shower curtain between us emboldening me to talk so frankly.

"If I hadn't married your dad," she said slowly, like she was explaining something complex to a child, "then I wouldn't have you and Ben. So how could I regret it?"

The sarcastic, smart-ass response that came to mind was that if she'd married someone else, maybe she could have ended up with a different daughter, one who was sweet and polite and popular, played a normal sport like soccer, and dated, like, some football player dude. I didn't say it. It didn't feel sarcastic, suddenly. It felt obvious.

Unaccountable melancholy slowed my limbs as I washed the shampoo out of my hair. I twisted the shower knob to turn off the water.

"Towel?" my mom asked.

"Towel." I confirmed.

Her arm reached past the curtain, handing me a plush, oversized bath towel the color of sand.

I stuck my head out. "I shouldn't use this one. I'm going to get bleach and green dye all over it."

She shrugged and smiled a little sadly. "It's fine, Millie."

We were both quiet while she helped me apply the dye. It wasn't an awkward silence anymore, but it wasn't a happy one, either.

My hair was nearly done when it occurred to me: I needed to take advantage of her odd mood. The swell of emotions I was feeling was real, but ultimately, I was a hustler, and I was not going to waste this moment.

"Hey, I'm going out with Pumpkin Thursday night, and I'm going to stay at her house really late. Like, midnight. That cool?"

As I knew she would, she hesitated, then said, "Sure. Of course."

Excellent. Everything was in place for my plan.

CHAPTER 17

time until Soy Anything: 2 months, 19 days

Pumpkin whistled when I got in her car. "You look great!"

I grinned. "I do, don't I?"

My hair had turned out fabulous. I had interesting streaks of different shades of green, like a lush forest of hair. I'd styled it carefully, scrunching it with my fingers to create waves. And though it was tough to dress cute during a Midwest cold snap, I felt I'd done well: black boots, fleece-lined black leggings, a black bracelet with silver studs, and a 1980s blue-green sweater dress I'd bought at a thrift shop last winter. A year after buying it, it now clung to me appealingly. My green hair and new bubblegum-pink lipstick contrasted nicely with the dress's bright turquoise color.

"I'm going over to Nora's house to help her make pins for our friend's band, but you better keep me updated," she said. Nora, I took it from context, was one of her mysterious school friends I'd never been introduced to. "If I don't hear anything, I'll pick you up at eleven?"

"Yep. When they close." I checked my reflection in the rearview mirror one more time, pleased. "But I'll message you no matter what."

The frigid air stung my face when I dashed from Pumpkin's car to Cocoa Café. Inside, it was warm and cozy and espresso scented. Ahhhh. I pulled off my coat and looked for an open table, resisting the urge to crane my neck at the counter. Casual. Be casual.

"Hey there, Mighty. New hair?"

I spun around, grinning. "Green for the Prairie Skate Rollers, ready for my first game." I tugged off my hat so Spiny could see it better. "Do you like it?"

"Love it." She winked at me, then went back to cleaning the espresso maker.

She winked! At me! I slung my coat, hat, and scarf onto the table I wanted—near the counter but not suspiciously near it—then gave myself a moment to calm down before I bought my drink.

After a few discreet slow, deep breaths to settle my nerves, I approached the counter.

"What'll it be?" Spiny was still messing with the espresso machine, not looking at me, so I got to stare dreamily at her for a moment without her noticing. She looked especially amazing today. A raggedy cream-colored fisherman's sweater, light-wash jeans, smokey eye makeup, tousled hair. *She is too cool for me!* screamed one half of my brain. *She winked at me!* screamed the other half.

"A large hot chocolate, thanks."

She made it for me without any additional conversation (or winks), and I headed back to my table. Now for my acting job.

Every time the bells at the front door chimed, I'd quickly twist around to see who it was, then look slightly disappointed. Spiny, I knew, looked up at the sound of the bells, too. So she would inevitably catch a glimpse of me, I was sure.

I drummed my fingers on the table. Tapped my foot. Checked my phone. Slowly sipped my hot chocolate with an increasingly frustrated look on my face.

Once I'd finished my drink, it was time for Step Two. I approached the counter with my empty mug.

"Can I get another hot chocolate?" I didn't smile this time.

"You got it." She took the mug from me, her fingertips brushing my knuckles.

I waited a beat to see if she'd ask me what I was up to. Then, when she didn't, I engaged. "Cocoa Café doesn't have any other locations, does it?"

"Nope, we're it. Why?"

There we go. That's what I needed. I sighed, pursed my lips. "Ugh, I was supposed to meet this girl Kristy here on a date, and she should've been here, like, half an hour ago. I think I've been stood up."

Spiny looked up at me, her eyes filled with what looked like genuine concern. "That sucks. I'm so sorry, Mighty."

I shrugged. "It's okay. I knew she was kind of flaky. I should've known this might happen. We met through a friend at my eighteenth birthday party last month and made plans, but she canceled on me once already." My underarms grew damp beneath my sweater dress as I lied, but my face stayed committed to the charade.

Spiny set my finished hot chocolate down in front of me. It was topped with whipped cream and chocolate shavings. A dark chocolate swizzle stick poked crookedly out of the cream. When I got out my wallet, she waved it away. "It's on the house."

I smiled. "Thanks. This helps."

"I thought it might."

Back at my table, I sipped slowly, still watching the door. Heart pounding frantically. Texting Pumpkin with shaking fingers. *This could not be going better!*

Good! Kristy broke your heart and only Spiny can mend it.

I hid a grin and sent Pumpkin a list.

Reasons I am a genius:

1. Now Spiny knows I like girls.

2. Now Spiny knows I'm single.

3. I have a reason to just hang out here by myself.

4. I reminded (aka lied to) Spiny that I'm 18.

By the time I'd finished my second hot chocolate, my stomach was queasy from the combination of nervousness and sugar. I needed real food. I wandered back up to the counter and ordered a sandwich and a glass of water.

"Still no word from this Kristy character?" Spiny asked.

"Nope." I sighed. "The worst thing is that my car isn't working right now. Pumpkin dropped me off, but she can't come and get me till later, so I'm just kind of stuck here." Realizing the obvious answer and trying to address it before Spiny could even think it, I added, "And both my parents are busy, too, so they can't pick me up." I shrugged again. "But it's nice and cozy in here."

"And I'm here, of course," she said matter-of-factly.

I laughed. "Of course."

"If you don't mind waiting another half hour, I could bring you home once we close."

"Oh, really? Gosh, that'd be great."

My next message to Pumpkin was just a bunch of exclamation points.

✶ ✦ ✶

Spiny drove a cool old hotrod car, the sort of car that I was sure I'd recognize, if I knew a single thing about cars.

"It's terrible to drive in the winter." She wrenched the door open. "But what can I say? I love it."

Maybe we would get in a not-very-dangerous-but-still-incapacitating car accident and be stranded together in here overnight. We'd have to huddle together for warmth, and of course it would quickly turn into something more. Did these seats recline? I could dream, right? I buckled up, glancing behind me as I did. Several plastic tubs were shoved into the tiny back seats.

She noticed my glance. "New uniforms for charter that I'm in charge of distributing, T-shirts for sale, big stacks of flyers I need to pass out. Derby stuff. It never ends, right?"

"Right." I gave her directions to my house, wishing it were farther away.

"Oh, that's not far from my girlfriend's place," she said.

Noooooooo. Doooooooom. I nearly clutched my chest, and mentally began composing the distraught message I would send to Pumpkin.

Then she groaned. "Ex-girlfriend, I mean. Ugh. Old habits die hard."

The clouds parted; the heavens sang. There was hope again! "Ah. Sorry."

"It's very . . . on-again, off-again. But it's off for real this time. I'm done with her need for drama. It was just constant fighting. We're wild about each other, but she's an awful person. We couldn't go more than a day or two without being at each other's throats."

"That sounds tiring." How could I compete with this terrible, toxic, alluring, likely incredibly sexy girl?

She laughed. "It's absolutely exhausting."

"When did you two break up?"

"On New Year's Eve. We got into a drunken, screaming fight at a party at Kiko's house. It was like a scene from a bad teen drama."

I thought of when I'd met Spiny's teammate Kiko, my mouth full of pizza at the Winter Showcase afterparty. I suspected I hadn't made a great impression, but at least I hadn't been drunk and screaming. "Wow. I just made cookies and hung out with Pumpkin and her sister on New Year's Eve." Why had I said that? Could I have sounded like any more of a kid? The last thing I wanted was to give her a reason to suspect I'd lied about my age!

But she just laughed again. "You had the right idea."

Two more stoplights, and we'd be turning in to my subdivision. I wished harder for her car to break down. "We have a game against the Sauk Valley Sonics coming up. Did you ever play them when you were in Juniors?"

"The Sonics? Oh, man!" She laughed hard, hitting the steering wheel with her palm. "Their coach is the worst. They're just a whole toxic scene."

"Seriously?"

"One time when we played them, the coach was ejected by the head ref because she kept screaming at her players. When he told her she was being ejected, she got up in his face and screamed at him." Spiny chuckled. "Entertaining, but so toxic."

"That's awful! If Ann or Cleo acted that way, I would've quit a long time ago."

"Ann's so sweet, and I never worked harder than when Cleo was coaching me." She lowered her voice to a conspiratorial whisper. "Even compared to now, for the charter coaches. Don't tell them that, though."

I beamed into the darkness. She was confiding in me!

"Are you coming to our next game?" she asked.

"Of course!" I loved the charter team's games. Lately they'd all been away games, though, so I hadn't seen them play in months.

"We're playing the Dairyland Dolls. They're going to kick our asses, but it'll be fun. And we need our asses kicked if we're going to get any better."

"I bet you'll do well." Was that an embarrassing, fangirlish sort of thing to say?

"Ha! I appreciate your confidence." She smiled.

"Take a right at the next stop sign." Why couldn't this car ride go on forever?

There was my house. The end of the journey, the end of my plan. Anything else that happened would have to be off script. Spiny pulled into the driveway, put the car in park, and pivoted so she was facing me.

My heart was pounding so hard it almost hurt.

"Hey," she said, "I'm sorry you got stood up."

"Yeah," I breathed, trying to sound disappointed. "It sucks, but it's okay."

"Here." She reached her hand out to me. "Hand me your phone. I'll give you my number, in case you ever need to be rescued from some place I don't work at or skate at."

I gulped and fished my phone out of my purse with shaking hands. "Thanks."

"You got it." She entered her number, then kept tapping. "I'm texting myself from your phone, so I'll have your number, too."

"Ah. Cool." An elated grin sprung onto my face. I tried to turn it into a casual smile.

She passed my phone back to me, her gloved fingertips brushing my palm. I bit my lip. For a moment we just looked at each other in the dim light of the nearby streetlamp. Her mouth was bent into that crooked smile. Was she going to kiss me? Oh my God.

"Take care of yourself, Mighty. No dating flakes, and no cutting your hands open." She shook her finger at me, mock-sternly, then reached across the car and gently rested her palm against my cheek, cupping my face. "Have a good night." Her hand slowly returned to the steering wheel.

"Yeah. You, too. Thanks again for the ride."

I climbed out of her hotrod on shaking legs. My brain and stomach were spinning. She'd touched me! I could still feel the raspy knit of her glove on my skin. But what did it mean? It wasn't a kiss. It wasn't anything. Oh, but it was something.

She drove away, and I turned a messy cartwheel in my yard. The ground was icy and slick on my hands. Things were happening. Things were definitely happening.

CHAPTER 18

time until Soy Anything: 2 months, 17 days

The day before derby practices returned was a bright but icy-cold Saturday. I was at my dad's. He was, as usual, at his office for the afternoon. There was nothing to distract my mind from my nerves about tomorrow's practice.

Maybe the weeks off would dull people's memories of my terrible performance at the Winter Showcase. Maybe, since I'd still gone to the gym every Sunday, derby would be easier than I remembered. On the other hand, maybe Cleo would say, "Let's start the year with some conditioning—time for the 27 in 5!"

I texted Pumpkin, looking for an escape, a distraction from my brain. *Can we please hang out today? I am so bored!* Bored felt easier to explain than "terrified." It was just a normal derby practice tomorrow—one that we were sharing with the Skatertots, no less. I shouldn't have been scared.

No immediate reply from Pumpkin. I stretched out on my dad's couch, phone balanced on my stomach, waiting. After half an hour, my phone buzzed. Yes!

It was Stork. *Do you need a ride to the gym after practice tomorrow?*

Sure, I was disappointed it wasn't Pumpkin, but I was oddly pleased to hear from her. Though we'd seen each other at the gym, without practice—or her constant texts about practice—it felt like it had been forever. Also, though I hadn't realized it till this moment, in the back of my mind I'd worried she'd been avoiding talking to me because of my awful performance at the showcase. It was a relief seeing her name pop up on my phone.

Plus, maybe she could be my escape from this apartment.

Yeah, that would be great. But hey, what are you up to today? Want to go to a café and talk about derby strategy?

Surely she wouldn't be able to resist derby talk.

I was right. She replied immediately, and we arranged our plans. She would pick me up in half an hour. We were going to Cocoa Café—my choice, of course. I filled the time until she arrived by getting ready. I hadn't packed any especially cute clothes, so I stole a pinstriped dress shirt from my dad's closet and wore it as a minidress, with tights and boots, the green lace of my bra just barely visible.

I blasted music as I did my makeup, singing along, loudly and badly, to "Closer" by Tegan and Sara, a classic ode to sapphic teenage lust. My heart was pumping, spirits rocketing high, my earlier anxiety suddenly nowhere to be found. Each thought I had ended in an exclamation point: I had plans on a Saturday afternoon! Stork and I were going to have fun! And I might see Spiny there! Spiny had driven me home! She'd given me her number! She'd touched my face! I felt unequivocally *good*, for once.

"Thank you so, so much," I said when Stork arrived, diving into her passenger seat. Her car was different than Pumpkin's— older, clunkier, and way cleaner. There was no way I'd cut my hand open on anything in here.

"Sure, of course. It's a good idea. We spend so much time on the physical aspect of the game, but it's still new to us—of course we need to sit down and talk about it. I brought some paper and markers so we can sketch out scenarios. Have you ever used the NURDS app?" The radio was playing an old rap song, and Stork tapped the steering wheel in time with the beat.

"Uh, no, haven't heard of it."

"It's not what it sounds like—it's an acronym. You can move

people around on a simulation of a track, set up different things. It's a nice reference. It's helping me understand the pack, and the engagement zone."

This was the most I'd ever heard Stork speak at once. I smiled, a bit bowled over, too much so to admit that, despite hearing Ann and Cleo explain the concept of the engagement zone multiple times, I still had no idea what it was. "Cool, I'll have to download it."

We turned onto Route 59, into the heart of terrible Saturday stop-and-go traffic. "So the café we're going to? Spiny works there. You know, Spineapple? From the charter team?"

"Fantastic! If she takes a break or has free time, we can ask her any questions we have."

"Good idea!" As if that hadn't been part of my scheme all along. A few days ago, Spiny had touched my face. Today, who knew what might happen?

When we arrived, Spiny was nowhere to be found. Well, it was midday. Maybe there would be a shift change and she'd come in.

I ordered a hot chocolate, and Stork ordered a plain black coffee. That somehow seemed on-brand for her, and I made a mental note to tell Pumpkin. I shook cinnamon into my hot chocolate, and Stork grabbed us a table.

My phone buzzed in my pocket as I looped back to grab a stack of napkins.

Sorry I missed your message! Still want to get together?

I set down my drink and sent Pumpkin a quick, slightly self-conscious reply. *Actually, I'm hanging out with Stork . . .*

She responded with a few vomit emojis. I replied with a shrugging emoji, shoved my phone in my purse, and headed to the table Stork had chosen.

She had already spread out her paper and markers and was in the process of using a blue marker to draw two concentric ovals shaped like our track. I set my overfull hot chocolate down, careful not to let it slop over the sides onto her paper.

"Before we get into that, can I ask you something?" I asked. I wasn't quite ready to jump into looking at diagrams. "Are you going to jam in the game against the Sonics?"

"Probably a few times. But Ann and Cleo want me to keep being a pivot." She smiled, her eyes still on the paper.

"Why?" Sure, if the jammer passed her helmet cover to the pivot, the pivot would become the jammer—I'd had the chance at the Winter Showcase to pass the star to Stork, and, stubbornly, hadn't done it. But mostly pivots blocked, not jammed. "Why wouldn't they have you jam? It's weird, right?"

Stork sipped her coffee and shrugged. "I'm just going to do what the coaches think is best for the team."

God, her reasonable attitude was frustrating. "You're so fast, though! You should be a jammer! You scored nineteen points in that one jam at the Winter Showcase!"

"Well, thanks—but jamming isn't the only role that takes skill. It'll be fine." Just for a second, on the word *fine*, her eyes dropped to the tabletop and the corners of her mouth turned down. I saw it. She was disappointed. She just didn't want to admit it.

"Whatever position you play, you'll do great." Suddenly I felt warmer toward her. "So, tell me about the app. What's it called? Dorks?"

She laughed. "NURDS. It stands for New Ultimate Roller Derby Simulator. Here, I'll look it up for you." She stretched her arm across the table, and I handed her my phone. Soon she'd brought up the app on both our phones and begun explaining the engagement zone to me.

We stayed at the café for over two hours. Spiny never showed up, but at least I'd gotten away from the empty apartment and distracted myself for a while. I wasn't on quite the high I'd been on when I'd done my makeup, but I still felt buzzy and warm inside, like life was picking up.

When I got back to my dad's, he was already there, laptop open at the kitchen table.

"Is that my shirt?" A reasonable thing for him to ask. He didn't seem pissed, just slightly confused.

"Yeah, I didn't have anything cute enough to wear here, so I borrowed it. I'll change in a second."

He nodded a bit awkwardly. I appreciated him not giving me a hard time about it. "How was your day?"

"Good. I met up with a teammate, and we talked about derby rules the whole time. It was great."

"Does your friend play the same position as you, a . . . what was it, again?"

"A jammer. The ones with the stars on their helmets, who score the points. But no, she's a pivot." Though I still had no idea why.

"Ah, okay." It was clear the information meant nothing to him.

I realized what I had to do, what I should've been doing all along when I spoke to my parents about derby. "Jammers are kind of like the quarterbacks of roller derby. I mean, there are usually three or four jammers who rotate through the position each game, not just one. But it's kind of a quarterback sort of role. That's the best way I can explain it."

"Oh, wow! And that's what you'll keep doing?"

"Yep." He didn't seem to notice the shake in my voice. Saying I was a jammer felt no more real than my so-called 27 in 5 result.

"Do your coaches pay attention to safety? Always make sure you're wearing all your protective gear?"

"Of course." I tried and failed to keep the defensiveness out of my voice.

"I have to admit, after seeing your game, I can't say I blame your mom as much for worrying about you getting hurt. It looked pretty intense." He took a sip from his coffee cup and let his eyes fall back onto the screen of his laptop.

That might be the nicest thing I've heard him say about Mom in . . . ever, maybe. I headed back into the bedroom with a bemused smile on my face.

When I looked at my phone, I saw Pumpkin had sent several Stork-bashing messages. I flopped down on the bed and composed a response.

It was fine, seriously! Although . . . she did drink black coffee and draw derby diagrams. Very Storkish. I smiled as I typed it. I still had the sketches folded in my purse, as Stork had suggested I keep them.

Pumpkin replied right away. *Eyeroll. Sorry I didn't see your text earlier so I could have saved you.*

I wanted to protest again that the afternoon had been good. But it felt weird to insist too hard.

See you at practice in the morn?

Of course!

CHAPTER 19

time until Soy Anything: 2 months, 16 days

But Pumpkin wasn't at practice the next morning. I messaged her with furious speed as I geared up.

Are you running late? Where are you?

I slid my elbow pads up my arms and strapped them in place, buckled my helmet, and looked back at my phone.

Sorry. Stayed out too late, too tired. Have fun!

I shouldn't have been as mad as I was. But I couldn't help it. My body had been churning with a mix of fear and excitement all morning—ready to see my friends and teammates! Ready to prove myself on the track! Also, perhaps, ready to fail spectacularly.

I'd been counting on the sight of Pumpkin to steady my nerves. But she'd abandoned me. Of course there had been practices in the past that she'd skipped, but this one, the first one after the league's winter break? It hurt, even if it shouldn't.

Normally during my warm-up laps, I'd cruise around with Pumpkin, catching up and joking around. Today, I was fueled by fear, anger, and the unsettling feeling that without Pumpkin there, no one would speak to me. My laps were faster, steadier, fiercer than usual.

"Good, Mighty," said Cleo as I passed her. Surprised, I slowed to look at her. She gave me a wry look and waved a hand forward. "Well, don't stop!"

We spent the morning working on basics, since it had been a few weeks and Cleo said she didn't trust any of us to go all-out the first day back. Gradually my anxiety retreated, replaced by general exhaustion. So much repetition, so much sweat. During a quick break, Pay showed me how she used a rubber band to attach her inhaler to her water bottle, and I did the same with mine, glad to have it nearby and at the ready.

Our last drill of the day was a non-contact juking drill. Half of us were scattered about the track, holding a squat. The other half skated fast laps, approached the stationary people as closely as we dared, then hopped to the side and darted away.

My thighs quivered as I held the squat. I'd been wrong when I'd thought practice might be easier than I remembered. It felt harder, if anything.

A breeze blew on my right arm as Gables passed within an inch of me.

"Get lower!" she shouted over her shoulder as she skated away.

I shook out my legs, groaned, and got lower.

When it was my turn to skate and juke, I initially coasted, skating slowly and doing only tiny hops a few feet back from the stationary people. I needed to let my legs recover. It was reasonable; I mean, I'd been practicing for nearly two hours now, I could only do so much. Plus, I was sure if I got any closer, I wouldn't be able to jump away in time, and I'd smash into the person, a mistake no one else had made yet.

Most of the stationary people were facing forward, so we approached their backs when we skated up to them. Gables, however, was facing backward, staring me dead in the eyes as I approached her.

"Closer. Don't bail so early. Load on your leg, like a spring, then jump."

I did a pathetic little hop off my right foot, nowhere near her. She shook her head.

The whistle would blow any second. Maybe I could just skip the last few people. As soon as I had the thought, though, I remembered my conversation with Cleo after the Winter

Showcase. This was a chance to prove that I could work hard, that I wasn't a slacker.

Fine. I'd get closer. I wouldn't chicken out. I took a deep breath, blew it out, and picked up speed.

Stork was the next person I approached. She was facing away from me, holding an impossibly low squat. I kept my eyes on her, did a few more hard strokes to keep my speed up, oh, she was so close, I could reach out and touch her, but I didn't bail, I loaded onto my left leg, I jumped, and—

It was too late. I collided with Stork's back, my speed bringing enough momentum that we both collapsed to the ground, me on top of her.

Cleo blew four drill-ending whistle blasts as we tried to untangle ourselves.

My face burned. "I am *so* sorry. Are you okay?"

"It's fine, don't worry." Stork scooted backward, pulling her long legs from underneath mine. This close to her, I could smell the clean, soapy scents of her deodorant and her gear spray. "Things happen. At least you were trying."

What did that mean? My hackles rose, immediately sure she meant that normally I didn't try. I didn't respond, just climbed to my feet and skated to the center to stretch and cool down while Cleo talked.

"Rosters for the game against the Sauk Valley Sonics will be sent out next week. Since not everyone can make it, all of you with availability will get play time, though some of you will skate more than others. Regardless, give it your all. If you wish you had more play time, remember, a lot can change between now and Soy Anything."

Her words felt ominous. What if she only put me in, like, once? What if she only put me in as a blocker, in a pack with our best blockers, to minimize the damage I could do?

"Before you leave, I need to see a few people one-on-one." She rattled off a few names, finishing with, "Stork and Mighty."

I gulped. I didn't want to be alone with Cleo.

Stork went first. I watched the two of them walk into the empty DJ booth. What could this be about? Cleo hadn't looked angry, just serious . . . but she was Cleo—she always looked serious. I thought back over practice. I had worked hard, but I hadn't done anything to really stand out. I wished now that I'd been braver. Why hadn't I gotten closer to more people on that juking drill? So what if I'd knocked more people down? I should have shown fearlessness.

Ann was sitting at a nearby table, flipping through a notebook. I sidled up.

"Hey Ann."

She looked at me, smiling. "What can I do for you, Mighty?"

"Cleo wanted to talk to a bunch of us, and she's talking to Stork right now, so I was thinking, you could just tell me whatever it is. You know, to save time."

"Ah, no, I'll leave that for Cleo. She's managing the jammers and pivots, since she used to jam."

"Oh, yeah, that makes sense." I tried to sound relaxed.

"It shouldn't take long, though."

I fiddled with the drawstring on my hoodie. "Okay. Cool."

"You did well today, Mighty. I saw your laps—you're getting speedier."

"I think it's more likely it was an optical illusion because someone nearby was skating backwards or something." My heart was suddenly pounding harder. Talking to Ann about my lap speed felt too close to talking about my 27 in 5 result.

"Very funny," she said dryly. "I think the thing you need to work on the most is taking a compliment."

Had she seen through my attempt to avoid the conversation with Cleo? Something about the twinkle of amusement in her eyes as she went back to her notes made me think she had.

Stork found me a minute later, as I was scrolling on my phone, my stomach clenched with anxiety.

"Your turn."

"How was it? Anything wrong?"

"No, nothing's wrong." She smiled at me, but I couldn't tell if it was sincere or not.

When I entered the DJ booth, Cleo's arms were folded across her chest. "Hey, Mighty. I wanted to touch base with you on how our season is going. I'm going to talk to all the potential jammers and pivots this week."

"Sure, okay." Oh God. What if I had to do my 27 in 5 again? Once the thought was in my head, I couldn't get rid of it. I twisted my hands together, tried to look calm.

"Let's talk for a minute about your jamming skills. You struggle to get through the pack, your lap speed is still too slow, and you give up too easily."

My eyes burned. Each one of her words stung. What had been the point of me telling her I wanted to do this, if she was probably going to take it away from me as soon as she had the chance? And Ann's compliment about my speed increasing now felt meaningless and insincere. I bit my bottom lip and tried to breathe.

"But you're a rookie, and no one expects you to look like Scald Eagle or Bonnie Thunders overnight," she continued.

"Okay. Good." I smiled tentatively. Cleo was exaggerating— no one would expect me to look like either of those skaters *ever.* Scald Eagle skated for Denver and Bonnie Thunders for Rose City in Portland; they were two of the most famous jammers in derby. No one in our league was anywhere near that good.

"Still, if you want to get rostered to jam at Soy Anything, I need to see a fair amount of improvement before then. It's tough. Those teams are tough."

My eyes burned again. "Okay." When would she get to the point and tell me my fate?

"I know I've said a lot of things that sound critical, but slow lap speed and giving up too easily are things that are straightforward to fix. I'm telling you because I believe you can improve. I've seen it. You don't look like the same skater you were during Skatertots. And I saw that hit you got on Dex today."

"Yeah, but I was blocking when I did that."

She nodded. "I know. You're more relaxed when you block. You don't get all tense and worried and in your head." She mimed being me, shoulders hunched up around her ears, a look of panic on her face. "If you want to jam, you need to keep working on your fitness, and you need to keep bringing 110 percent ferocity to every single drill in every single practice, but most importantly, you need to get out of your head."

"Okay. I will." I nodded rapidly. As if it was as easy as just declaring it.

"It's tough stuff, I know. I can work with you during practices as much as possible, but there are lots of skaters on this team, and I can't be with you all the time. You'll need to be self-motivated. And if you don't jam at the tournament, that doesn't mean you aren't good at derby. You're, what, sixteen?"

I kept up my rapid nodding.

"You could go far, Mighty, if you don't sabotage yourself. Just keep at it. Do you have any questions for me before we get out of here?"

"What about the Sonics game?" I burst out.

"Yeah, we'll try having you jam a little. We'll mix you into the lineup, even if it isn't quite as often as you'd like."

Oh, thank God, thank God, thank God. It felt like a slippery slope from telling me I couldn't jam to telling me I wouldn't get rostered to the entire team wishing I'd quit. One part of my brain knew that was melodramatic nonsense, but the other part of my brain couldn't shake it.

I turned to leave, but Cleo spoke again.

"You'll have your work cut out for you." She shook her head ruefully. "The Sonics are rough."

CHAPTER 20

During that afternoon's workout with Josh, my mind was adrift, replaying and replaying the conversation with Cleo.

"Keep your knee over your toes, Mighty. Don't go past them." Josh was always watching, always critical.

"I am," I muttered, lowering down into another lunge, grunting as I stood up.

The gym had several floor-to-ceiling mirrors along one wall, and we were doing walking lunges back and forth in front of them. I held a 12-pound dumbbell in each hand. My legs were already Jell-O from practice, and this was just torture. But Cleo's words kept ringing in my ears, and I refused to go easy on myself.

I turned my head to watch myself in the mirror, to make sure my knees weren't going past my toes. That was when I saw them. My jaw dropped in disbelief.

I did another lunge, to be sure. My right knee dropped down and tapped the ground, and as I pushed up on my left leg, indeed, there they were again.

Muscles! My quads were standing out, huge, clearly defined against the rest of my thigh. Setting down my weights, I pushed my knee-length shorts up so my thighs were bare, then lunged again.

"Hey! Everybody! Look at my legs! Can you even believe how strong I am?"

Pay whistled. "You're hot stuff, Mighty." Bee echoed her.

Stork smiled and wrinkled her brow, looking a little

puzzled. "I mean, what did you think was going to happen? You play derby and work out all the time."

I kept moving, a new vigor in my lunges. "I didn't know it would actually work! I still feel like such a . . . I don't know, a big potato on the track, you know?"

Now Stork grinned. "You're not a potato. You're an athlete."

I grinned back, full of wonder. Maybe there was hope for me yet.

Stork sat next to me when we stretched after the workout. "I have a book on mental toughness that I want to lend you."

"Because you think I'm . . . mentally weak?" I scooted slightly away from her as I stretched my hamstrings, remembering her comment during practice about how I was "actually trying."

"Because I read it and thought it was great." She pointed her toes and folded over her left leg. Her scruffy blonde ponytail flipped over the top of her head, and she kept talking from underneath a curtain of hair. "You want to get better. I like that."

I still felt prickly and didn't reply.

"I want to get better, too. Not everyone on our team cares that much." She sat up straight and looked at me. "But I think you get it."

I still didn't reply, but now it was because I was having a hard time gathering my thoughts. I had always seen Stork as in a separate class than me. The idea that she thought of us as similar was surprising, to say the least. My brain was trying to come up with something funny and self-deprecating as a response, but I couldn't think of anything.

"Oh," I finally said. "Thanks."

We stopped at Stork's after we left the gym, so she could lend me the book. She lived at the end of a cul-de-sac in a neighborhood with smaller, older houses packed closely together. She'd grown quieter as we approached her house, quiet enough that I'd begun to wonder if something was wrong.

She parked along the curb.

"I'll be right back." Her voice was clipped. "Wait in the car."

I'd thought everything between us had been fine—good, even—when we left the gym. What had happened?

"Actually, would you mind if I ran inside, so I could use your bathroom? I'll be quick." Maybe it was Stork's sudden mood change making me nervous, or maybe it was the three bottles of water I'd drunk, but I suddenly had a desperate need to pee.

Something weird flashed across her face. "I guess. Yeah, okay." She sighed. "Come on."

I followed her across the lawn, the old and frozen snow crunching under my feet. Did she not want me to come inside? Why? Was she embarrassed by me?

Then I stepped inside, and—oh.

Stork avoided my eyes. "The bathroom is down the hall, first door on the left."

I wound my way carefully through her foyer and into the hall. Stuff, everywhere. My eyes couldn't even sort out individual items. Plastic bins and boxes and bags, stacked on top of one another, balanced precariously. Storage bins filled with a mishmash of unrecognizable objects, cardboard boxes overflowing with clothes, old appliance boxes with worn-out labels, shopping bags thin and stretched to capacity. They made a sort of maze. I could see a path through Stork's living room to the couch, only wide enough for a single person.

The house wasn't dirty or smelly, but it was incredibly, incredibly cluttered.

Actually, I thought as I made my way farther down the hall, *cluttered is an understatement.* I had never watched any of those shows about hoarders on TV, but I knew enough to recognize hoarding when I saw it.

There was space in the bathroom for me to sit on the toilet, but just barely. My knees pushed against a clear plastic dresser with a dozen shoe boxes stacked teetering on top. This was unbelievable. How did Stork live like this? God, no wonder she hadn't wanted me to come inside. I peed hurriedly, washed my hands, and wiped them on my coat to dry them.

"I'm up here," Stork called when I came out. "In my bedroom."

I found the stairs, made my way past stacks of newspapers—newspapers! My parents had read the news online for as long as I could remember—and took a breath at the top. This was just too much. An awful sadness for Stork welled up inside me.

"In here," she called again. "End of the hall."

I slipped into Stork's bedroom, and, wow, what a difference. It was spare, Spartan—a lot like my room at my dad's place, actually. She had a bookcase with neatly arranged books, a slim dresser—its top completely bare—and a single bed covered in a pale blue blanket embroidered with white flowers. The carpet was worn but spotless.

She was facing the bookcase when I entered, and she didn't turn around.

"Hey." I shoved my hands in my pockets, awkward. "Sorry. Uh. Sorry I had to pee."

She spun around. Her face was flushed. "Yeah. No problem. It's just, oh—" She seemed to deflate, sighing hugely and resting both her palms behind her on a shelf. "It's my dad. He's been like this my whole life, but it's gotten worse the past couple of years."

"I'm sorry."

She shrugged. "I didn't know how to warn you."

"It's fine. Seriously." I should have just stayed in the car. I could've held it.

"I just . . ." She trailed off, turning around, her eyes back on her books. Then her tone changed, became more brisk, authoritative; she was back to the Stork I was used to. "I think you'll really like this book. My track coach had us read it freshman year, and it made a big difference in how I saw myself. One of the things I've been thinking about is nervousness before competition, and how we can use that nervous energy to do better, to energize us, rather than letting it sabotage our performance. There's a chapter about that, and I was thinking it might be good to even scan and share with the whole team."

She dragged her fingers along the shelf as she spoke, her eyes scanning each title. I waited quietly, watching her. I was such a jerk, pushing my way into her house. I wanted to apologize again. Probably it wouldn't help, though.

Stork's hand fell to her side. "I can't find it," she muttered. Her shoulders sagged, and her shaggy blonde hair, freed from its ponytail and still damp with sweat from the gym, fell in her face.

"That's okay! No big deal. I could buy my own copy."

"It's just . . . if it's not in here, it's out there." She jerked her thumb behind her, gesturing to the rest of the house.

"Oh." We stood there silently for a moment. "Is it . . . has it always been like this?"

She nodded, eyes downcast. Then, shaking her head, she spoke. "It's always been like this, but it's getting worse. I worry all the time about what will happen when I go away to college. I don't have any brothers or sisters."

"Will your mom help keep it under control?"

Stork laughed harshly. "She totally enables him. I wish . . . I don't know. He keeps saying he's going to sort things, give stuff away, but it just gets worse."

I sat down gingerly on her bed. There was a loose thread in one of the embroidered flowers on her blanket, and I twisted it back and forth between my thumb and middle finger. "That sucks."

She sat down next to me. "Yep."

"At least you've got your own space here."

"Yeah. Though I'm sure as soon as I leave for college, he'll start using it for extra storage, I just know it. By the time I come back for a visit, my room will be gone."

"Is this your senior year?" It made sense to me, worrying about this sort of thing when college was visible on the horizon.

Stork shook her head. "Nah, I'm a sophomore. Same as you, right?"

"Right."

"You do online school, don't you?" I was surprised she'd remembered. "What's that like? I can't imagine staying in my house all the time."

"It's not great." I hadn't admitted it out loud to anyone, not even Pumpkin. "I'm not very self-motivated, and I get really lonely." The embroidery thread had loosened in my hand. I gave it a gentle tug, unraveling it further, then realized what I was doing, felt bad, and smoothed it down with my palm.

"So how come you're doing it?"

I sighed. "I don't really know anymore. I was bullied pretty badly in fifth and sixth grades, so after I missed a bunch of school because of pneumonia, I never went back."

Stork shook her head slowly. "When we were doing online school during Covid, I felt like I forgot how to be a normal person in society. I can't imagine choosing that on purpose, for this many years."

"I definitely don't know how to be a normal person in society, Stork." I laughed, to try to make it a joke, but the words resonated inside of me.

"I need the escape of school, you know?" She paused, and I was sure we were both picturing the chaos surrounding her bedroom. "South High isn't bad. The teachers are decent, for the most part, and they have a really robust sports program."

I wasn't totally sure what robust meant—it sounded like a word straight from a school brochure—and I couldn't imagine caring about the availability of high school sports. "Is it like in the movies, where the football players and cheerleaders are basically gods and goddesses?"

She laughed. "Definitely not. I mean, South isn't perfect, there are some jerks, but mostly it's live and let live. I love our track coach, and I've had a handful of great teachers."

A door slammed downstairs.

"Melanie, you home, hon? I'm back from work!" A man's voice. Her dad.

Stork flinched, then walked to the doorway and yelled down, "I'm upstairs hanging out with one of my teammates! We'll be down soon."

"I'm heading out again in a sec, headed to the grocery store. Anything you need me to pick up?"

They had a whole shouted conversation this way, her dad downstairs and Stork upstairs. Stork requested a specific brand of almonds and a certain style of tampons, he asked follow-up questions, she answered them. Once he was gone again, she came back into the bedroom and flopped down next to me on the bed, lying on her back. A lock of her hair draped across my left palm, curling over the thin red scar that had formed after my injury.

"I love him, you know. He's a good dad." She sounded defensive.

"I can tell." I wasn't just saying it. There had been an ease in their conversation, a casual fondness for each other, that I envied. "He sounds nice."

"He is. It's just . . ." She picked up her arms, let them fall, groaned.

I couldn't remember the last time I'd had a conversation with either of my parents where I felt natural or relaxed. Even when I'd been comparing jammers to quarterbacks for my dad, I'd still felt stilted. "I should probably get going. I've got to drive with my mom for a while this afternoon, so I can finish my hours and finally take my driver's test."

Stork jumped to her feet. "Oh, of course. Sorry I couldn't find the book."

"No prob, seriously." I didn't want her to feel like I was leaving because of her dad, because of weirdness.

Once in the car, I looked at my phone. Several long messages from Pumpkin.

Sorry I missed practice! David came by my house last night! He said he was in the neighborhood and wanted to say hi, but come on, no one just happens to be in the neighborhood.

I grinned and kept reading.

He totally wants me again, it was so obvious. Two weeks ago, he started dating this girl Angela—who I hate, by the way, and who he used to SAY he hated too—and I bet she dumped him.

"Everything okay?" Stork asked.

"Oh, yeah. Just Pumpkin boy drama."

"You know, Pumpkin could be a really good blocker if she tried harder. She's really comfortable in her skates. I wish I was that smooth. She just needs to buckle down, you know?" She paused. "Sorry. I know she's your closest friend on the team."

"No, I know what you mean. I wish she came with us to Josh's gym." I immediately felt a pang of disloyalty. Pumpkin wasn't just my closest friend on the team; she was my best friend, period. I knew the reverse might not be true; she had lots of other friends from school. But still. I shouldn't talk trash about her derby skills. "And let's not pretend I don't goof off with Pumpkin half the time, too."

Stork smiled. "Okay, but half the time is better than all the time."

I smiled too, the words not stinging like they might have a month ago—or even a few hours ago, before Stork had said we both cared about improving, putting us in the same boat.

I wondered what Cleo had said in her private meeting with Stork. Stork hadn't mentioned it on the drive to the gym, so I hadn't brought it up, either. Would she jam against the Sonics? Toni was our team's best jammer, Dex and Rainbow were both experienced jammers, too—and then there was me. Regardless of how jealous I felt, I knew without a doubt that Stork was a way better jammer than me, and our team could definitely use another good jammer. So why was she pivoting so much?

CHAPTER 21

time until Soy Anything: 2 months, 14 days

On Tuesday morning, I woke up sick, head aching, throat raw, nose stuffed. Just a bad cold, but even so, it interfered with my plans. No going to derby practice tomorrow. Argh. Cleo and Ann had both made it clear they didn't want us spreading germs to one another. I wished I could go—partially to keep showing Ann and Cleo that I was working hard, and partially because I didn't want Stork to think I was avoiding her, after seeing her house.

That afternoon, while faking my way through my math homework, I got the shock of my life. A text popped up on my phone screen:

Hey babe, it's Spiny. Are you coming to the charter game against the Dairyland Dolls this Friday? Want to work the merch table? We need someone from 6 to 7.

I couldn't breathe, and it wasn't because of my cold, or even my asthma. Spiny wanted me to come to the game! Sure, she wanted me to volunteer for something, not just be there to cheer, but still. Still! And she'd called me babe! My brain traveled forward in time again to our shared college apartment, to me coming home from class and Spiny wrapping her arms around me the moment I stepped in the door, kissing me deeply as the sounds of retro synth pop music soared around us, me wrapping my legs around her waist as she carried me to the bed, where the fantasy then faded tastefully to black. I couldn't quite picture how things would actually go in the bedroom, but I'd be experienced and confident, for sure.

With shaking hands, I first texted Pumpkin, then replied to Spiny saying *yes, absolutely.*

But on Friday morning, I was, if anything, sicker. There was no way my mom would let me out of the house. Even if she did, I felt cruddy enough I couldn't deny it: I knew I belonged on the couch with a cup of honeyed tea, not at the rink selling T-shirts to a crowd. Low with shame and disappointment, I regretfully updated Spiny. She took it well, said it was no big deal, and told me she hoped I felt better. But I was devastated. What if this would have been the start of our relationship, and now it would never happen?

Nearly all the Juniors were at the game. Pumpkin sent me pictures and updates every few minutes. Stork sent me stats and descriptions of the different lineups and formations used by each team.

I blew my nose, swallowed more Advil, then read Pumpkin's most recent text.

Toni just showed up and she's holding hands with this super-hot girl in thigh-high boots. I think Gables is glaring at them like she's jealous, but that might just be her normal face.

Before I could reply to Pumpkin, another text appeared on the screen, Stork again.

Number 262 on the opposing team is really good—she does these spins to dodge blockers, like a pinball bouncing off them and then skating away! Very cool. You should learn to do that when you jam.

I wasn't sure if all the messages were making me feel better or worse.

Pumpkin snapped a picture of Spiny at the autograph table after the game, bent over, signing a program for a tiny little boy. She looked so cool in her green-and-gray uniform top and matching booty shorts, her arms and legs pale from the winter under her tattoos, but still so visibly muscular. Her quads definitely put mine to shame. It was hard to believe I'd ridden in her car, hard to believe she'd given me her phone number and touched my face.

Pumpkin left the game as soon as it ended to meet up with her school friends, who I had still never met. Stork texted me from the afterparty. It was at a pub-style restaurant near the rink, a place with good nachos, Stork said.

I'm going to stay until I can talk to the coaches, she texted. *I want to ask them strategy questions.*

The whole house was dark except for a single yellow light on the end table. I lay on the couch, drank bottles of blue Gatorade, stared at my phone, and felt sorry for myself. I wanted so badly to be in that restaurant, eating nachos and hanging out with everyone. My eyes were heavy, wanting to shut, but I wasn't ready. I was waiting for a further report from Stork, or even—you never know—another message from Spiny. What was it like in the restaurant? I imagined it was crowded, boisterous and happy even though our team had lost, buzzing with loud conversation and laughter. Had Stork been able to sit with Ann and Cleo? Who else was she talking to? Had anyone mentioned me? Did any of my Juniors teammates miss me?

Eventually, Stork replied. She sent long messages with explanations of different formations I really couldn't visualize, but the tension in my chest eased just at the sight of the words. I hadn't been forgotten. I tossed my empty Gatorade bottles into the recycling bin, then went up to bed.

CHAPTER 22

time until Soy Anything: 2 months, 6 days

In the worst moments of my cold, I'd worried it would cling to me for weeks, stopping me from playing in the Sonics game. I took three Covid tests, full of paranoia, but all came up negative. And by the following week, I felt better—and, unfortunately, good enough to go with my dad on a terrifying errand.

"What if I throw up?" I asked my dad. "Because of nerves, you know? Does the DMV automatically flunk you if you throw up in the car during the test?"

"You are not going to throw up," my dad replied. I watched him carefully, mentally cramming for the test. He signaled, checked his mirror, glanced over his shoulder, merged into the right lane, then turned into the DMV parking lot. So many steps for such a small action.

We had taken my car, but I'd been too scared to drive to the test. It felt like a jinx, like I was bound to get in a fender bender a block away from the testing center. I would drive after I passed—if I passed—when we went to the rink. I was missing the beginning of an evening practice for this, since my dad hadn't been able to get out of work early.

In the lot, my dad aimed the car toward a narrow space between two pickup trucks. I gulped. I wanted my license so badly. The superstitious part of my brain was convinced that made it even less likely I'd actually get it.

"No." I shook my head hard. "Park out there." I pointed to

the row of empty spaces far away from the building. "I need room."

Inside, my dad sat in the bay of plastic chairs at the front of the DMV, reading through some boring lawyer work, while I got in line. Everyone I'd texted today—Ben, Pumpkin, even Stork—had told me they were sure I'd pass, but I still felt nervous. Anything could happen during that driving test. A tree limb could fall on the car. An ice storm could start. An adorable toddler could run into the street. I could, as I'd suggested to my dad, throw up. Like, all over the car. Or the assessor.

At least the written test was a breeze. It had been a delight the last couple days to have a legit reason to neglect my homework and pour over *Rules of the Road* instead. I finished the test with some regret, knowing that all I had left was the scary part.

My assessor for the driving test was an older woman named Wanda with big glasses and long gray hair pulled in a bun. She looked like a witch or a mean librarian, and she carried an intimidating clipboard that reminded me of the ones Ann and Cleo carried during Skatertots evaluations. We were silent on the walk to the car. She watched me carefully as I buckled up with shaking hands.

"Start by heading out of the parking lot and taking your first right into the neighborhood. We'll get parallel parking out of the way first."

I nodded, stone-faced, reversing out of the parking spot. The car had moved only a few inches when I heard Wanda's careful intake of breath. I pressed the brake and looked at her with big eyes.

"I did something wrong, didn't I?"

She regarded me for a moment before she spoke. "Do you think you did something wrong?"

My thoughts raced. Clearly I had, but what? I put the car in park, gripped the steering wheel, and tried to think. "Um."

I tried to take a deep breath, but my chest was tight. "Do you mind if I use my inhaler really quick?"

Face still impassive, she motioned to my purse. "Go ahead."

I took my time using the inhaler—blowing all the air out of my lungs first, carefully sucking in the albuterol, waiting a minute, then doing a second round. Stalling. I kept my eyes on the steering wheel, not daring to look at her.

Finally, with a shaky voice, I spoke. "I didn't check the mirrors' alignment first, to make sure I could see out of all of them." Such a tiny little step, but I had known that was the first thing to do. How had I forgotten?

Wanda nodded. She was smiling slightly. "That's right."

I took a breath, my lungs much more forgiving now. Wanda's shirt, I noticed, was a faded paisley blouse, loose and casual, and her purse was a slouchy denim bag. She suddenly looked less like a witch and more like an old hippie.

"You can relax," she said. "You got your hours, which means you have plenty of experience. You know how to drive. Don't panic."

Her kindness warmed me, and suddenly I was completely relaxed. I knew how to drive. This would be fine. I checked my mirrors and pulled out.

When I came back inside the DMV twenty minutes later, my dad jumped to his feet, his eyes wide, asking without saying it out loud. I sneaked him a smile and quick thumbs-up, then went to get my photo taken. I'd done it! I was getting my driver's license!

I drove us straight to the rink from the DMV. Each practice felt more and more crucial as the game against the Sonics approached. I hated that I was coming to this one late, even though it was for a good reason.

"I'll be back to get you in an hour," my dad said as he got in the driver's seat. He paused for a moment and smiled. "Good work, hon. Not long, and you'll be driving by yourself."

I smiled back, though his words made me prickle. Yeah, yeah, I still wasn't allowed to drive my car alone until I brought my grades up. He didn't need to remind me. "It was Mom who came up with that rule. You don't need to agree with it."

He looked at me levelly. I could see his instinct to fight with Mom struggling to come to the surface. Would he actually side with me on this? But he shook his head. "Nope. Insurance will give you a discount if you're on the honor roll. So that's what we wait for."

"Online school doesn't even have an honor roll!" The idea of my particular online school having anything acknowledging its students, any trappings of a normal high school, was absurd. I watched lecture videos, I submitted work for my classes, I got my grades, I went on my way.

"Above a 3.0, Millie. That's what matters to the insurance company, so that's what matters to us."

It didn't seem fair for him to align himself with Mom now, after fighting with her for my entire life—especially when it meant I couldn't use my own car. I scowled.

Everyone was split off into groups, running some sort of drill on the track, when I arrived.

Ann waved to me. "Nice to have you join us, Mighty!"

If it had been anyone other than Ann, I might have taken the remark as a sarcastic commentary on how late I was to practice. But it was Ann, so it didn't sting. "Sorry I'm late. I just got my license!"

"That's great!" She jogged over to me and gave me a high five. "Were you nervous? I remember when I got mine, I was so scared I was shaking!"

"I was nervous at first, but then it was okay. I just had to remember that I knew what I was doing."

Her smile at me was sneaky. "Think about that if you get nervous before the game against the Sonics. Just remember that you know what you're doing."

"Or, you know, I'll just remember that I am the worst jammer on the team and their blockers are going to flatten me into a pulp."

"Hey." She stepped even closer to me, her eyes warm but serious. "Don't say things like that about my friend Mighty. She's one of my favorite Juniors skaters."

I looked away, uncomfortable with her kindness. "Come on, Ann."

She was smiling patiently. "Yes?"

"I'm not gonna lie. If I was all 'I can do anything! Yay me!' it would be weird and inaccurate."

She held up one finger to me and shouted a few instructions to everyone doing the drill. Then: "Let's go talk for a minute."

I rolled along behind her, following her to the edge of the rink. Once we were far away from everyone, she spoke again.

"This isn't really my business, Mighty, so you're welcome to tell me to butt out, okay? But am I right in thinking that at one point in your life, a person or people said some pretty mean things to you?"

The response on the tip of my tongue was that I must be the first person bad enough at derby to need therapy about it. Somehow, I stopped the words from leaving my mouth. Instead, after a moment, I was honest. Ann was so nice. I owed her that.

"I guess. I mean, yeah, there were a few people who bullied me when I was younger. It was in, like, sixth grade." A handful of kids had ruined public school for me. Their cruelty hadn't been especially creative; it was the relentlessness of it that got to me. Never a break, never a day passing without barbs or jabs knocking me off balance, reminding me of my place. "But it was years ago. I do online school now. It shouldn't matter."

"I'm so sorry, Mighty. It does matter. It's not right, that that happened."

I waved away Ann's words, looking at the ground so she wouldn't see the tears that suddenly stung my eyes.

"Was it scary to join derby, with all these new people?"

I nodded, not trusting my voice. A few deep breaths later, I risked speaking. "Look, I know I'm not that good at derby. I'm not going to pretend I am, just to be all rah-rah positive or whatever. It's better to own it, you know?"

"And maybe it feels safer?" Ann's voice was delicate. "Like, if you say all those sarcastic, self-deprecating things, then you're being mean to yourself first, before anyone else can beat you to it?"

Relief and discomfort hit me in equal measure. Ann saw me too clearly. She'd articulated something about myself I'd never put into words. "Yeah. Maybe." I nudged at the ground with my toe stop.

"I can see how it would feel safer. I get that. But I can also see that by being mean to yourself, you're doing the work of the people in your past, without them even needing to be here. I can't imagine you'd want to do anything for them."

"No." I barked a laugh, then sniffled. "They suck."

"Maybe you should trust your teammates a little bit more. They aren't those jerks from your past. They like you. You don't need to beat anyone to being mean to yourself, because they aren't going to do that."

I wrinkled my nose. "I guess." I couldn't disagree with anything Ann had said. But she made it sound easy, and it wasn't.

"How about this? Would you tell anyone else that they're the worst on the team?"

I wanted to point out that if I was truly the worst, then it wouldn't make sense to say it about anyone else. "I guess not?"

Ann continued. "Even if it were true? Even if someone truly was the worst?"

I sighed begrudgingly. "No, I wouldn't say that to someone else."

"And if you did, I'd be furious. I don't want any of my skaters being mean to each other. That includes you. No more of that. Okay?"

I shrugged. "I'll see what I can do, but no promises."

She looked at me.

"Hey, I'm trying to be honest!" I burst out, and she laughed.

"Fair enough. Why don't you do a few warm-up laps, then join Gables's group?"

I nodded, then sprinted away, trying to shed the moment's intense emotions. My head felt cracked open, all my messed-up thoughts visible to the world, and I wanted to regain control. I looked around for Pumpkin, seeking levity. She was nowhere to be seen. Maybe she was in the bathroom. Or was she skipping practice again?

I skated a few more laps till I felt closer to normal, then joined the group Ann had assigned me to.

Gables filled me in on what I'd missed. "Blockers are practicing sucking back." She nodded at the group. "Let's show her."

Bee, wearing the jammer star on her helmet, stood behind a tripod of blockers: Stork, Luna, and Rainbow. Bee hit the seam between Luna and Stork, got stuck, then shifted back to reset. As soon as Bee reset herself, Luna immediately skated backward to take away the small space that had formed between them, her skates making tight C-cuts on the floor.

"Isn't that a direction penalty?" We could only initiate contact moving in a counterclockwise direction around the track. It was one of the things Stork and I had gone over when we'd had coffee. It was a relief to focus on this, safely far away from the emotions stirred up by my talk with Ann.

Gables shook her head. "Luna didn't hit Bee. She skated back *just* enough to take away the space between them, but she didn't make forceful contact. Crucial difference. Not a penalty, and that way Bee can't get any momentum for her next hit."

They ran it a few more times while I watched. Then Ann blew her whistle, and Bee stepped out.

"Jump in, Mighty," she said. "I need a break." She took a knee, removed her helmet, and shook out her long, curly hair, damp with sweat.

Gables grabbed the jammer helmet cover from Bee and threw it at me. "You jam. You need the practice."

I resisted groaning or making a snarky comment. Gables was right, after all.

Stork was the one closest to me, the one who would have to suck back and take away my space. We tried the drill a few times, then Gables, who had been watching closely, stopped us.

"Stork, get closer to Mighty when you do it. Don't worry so much about hitting her. After she steps back, Mighty is going to be pressing forward, because she's the jammer, so she'll be initiating the motion, not you. Don't think about the penalty." She gestured to both of us. "Try just that one step."

I obligingly hit the seam between Stork and Rainbow, then took a step back. Stork followed me backward, in what, to me, seemed an effective move. But Gables still shook her head. "Really stick on Mighty, Stork. Get your butt right in her lap."

This time when I stepped back, Stork followed immediately. Her whole body pushed against mine; her butt pressed into my lap as Gables had commanded, her back pressed against my chest.

"Nice!" Gables said.

I laughed. "Gosh, Stork, at least buy me dinner first before you do that."

She blushed bright red and turned around to try again.

After practice, I de-geared near the main cluster of skaters rather than in my and Pumpkin's typical corner, as she had never shown up. My feet were aching; a new blister had formed on my left arch, and there was a sharp pain in my right instep. I rubbed my feet while everyone chatted.

Gables caught my eye. "You're working hard lately."

"Thanks." It took all my energy to resist making a joke at my own expense. I wished Ann knew the Herculean effort I was making. "I want to do a good job jamming against the Sonics, you know?"

Gables growled. "I hate the Sonics."

"Spiny—Spineapple—told me their coach is awful, got ejected for screaming at a ref."

"Yep. I was there for that. It was my rookie year. I was terrified."

It was hard to imagine Gables being terrified of anything. Pay tossed me a lacrosse ball from her bag, and I stood up, rolling the ball along the bottoms of my feet for a pseudo-massage. "Did the coach say anything mean to you? Or, I mean, to any of the Prairie Skate Juniors?"

Gables shook her head. "Nah, but some of the Sonics skaters were awful. At one point, I lost my balance and fell in front of a jammer, tripping her, and she yelled 'learn to skate!' at me as I went to the penalty box." She laughed ruefully. "I think I cried."

Gables, losing her balance and falling. Gables, crying. Would wonders never cease?

"How'd you get so good?" I asked her. "How'd you become"—I gestured to her whole body, waving my hands—"this?"

She was spraying her pads with a cleaner that smelled like cloves, not looking up at me. "I didn't quit, Mighty. That's it. That's the secret. I kept showing up."

I wanted to talk more about this concept—was it really that simple?—but Stork, I noticed, was heading out of the rink. I jogged to catch up with her in the breezeway before she could leave.

"Hey," I called. "I wanted to apologize for earlier, joking

around during that sucking-back drill. I hope I didn't make you uncomfortable. I was just kidding around."

She adjusted her duffel bag, which was slung crossways across her chest. "It was fine. I just blush too easily."

"You sure?"

"Definitely. You don't need to apologize."

A tall man with a thick beard walked inside the doors. Stork smiled and waved at him. "Hey, Dad." She gestured to me. "This is my friend Mighty. Mighty, this is my dad. He's picking me up from practice tonight because we're going to the gym together afterward." She poked him in the arm and added bossily, "Right?"

"Right. Melanie—or Stork, as I suppose you call her—has made it her mission to get me to my brother's gym. She's finally got me." He patted his stomach. "I suppose it couldn't hurt."

I smiled. "It's a nice gym. I like it."

He seemed so nice. He didn't seem like a hoarder. What did I even mean, though? How did I know what a hoarder looked like? What, had I thought he'd look unhinged and carry a bunch of shopping bags?

Through the windows, I recognized the outline of my car pulling up. "Gotta go," I said. "Bye, Stork! Bye, Stork's dad."

It was only as I walked away that I realized Stork had called me her friend. I had felt a camaraderie with her as a teammate, but I had never considered whether she was a friend. A small, warm glow rose in my chest as I walked through the parking lot.

CHAPTER 23

time until Soy Anything: 2 months, 3 days

The Sauk Valley Sonics wore orange with blue accents. They warmed up by doing coordinated skating drills: first skating in a curving line like a long snake, then alternating, weaving back and forth across the track, then breaking into partners and hitting each other. All timed perfectly, synchronous.

We watched from our bench. I twisted the hem of my uniform in my hands, back and forth, unable to take my eyes off them.

"Don't let it psych you out," Gables muttered. "That's what they want."

Cleo had crafted a rotation where I would be in every three jams, alternating jamming and blocking, so effectively I'd jam one out of every six jams. When she'd told me the plan at practice last week, I'd felt a little disappointed. That wasn't much. But today, I was relieved. Less pressure.

Pumpkin and I sat next to each other on the bench as the pack for Jam 1 hit the track. Toni was jamming for our team; the Sonics' jammer was a tiny girl with long red hair. I knew she had to be at least fourteen, but she looked young, like an actual kid.

"Gables is gonna crush her," Pumpkin murmured to me. Gables was facing backward, staring daggers at the girl. I grinned.

"She'll eat her alive." I jogged Pumpkin's elbow. "You nervous at all?"

She shrugged. "Eh. Not too bad. You?"

I held out my hand, so she could see it shaking, in response.

The starting whistle blew, and Toni began struggling through the pack of Sonics blockers. She was getting knocked around but still making forward progress. Then—*tweet-tweet*—a referee signaled lead jammer. The tiny redhead had gotten out of the pack and was already halfway around the track!

"My God," I breathed. She was fast! And how on earth had she made it past Gables?

Then she was back into the pack, on her first scoring pass, dodging our blockers. Gables smashed into her, and she wobbled toward the track boundary—yes!—but somehow regained her balance, teetered on one skate, and stayed inside. She was through the pack again, four points for the Sonics, but Toni had gotten past the blockers, too, and was making her way around the track.

The typical strategy, as I understood it, meant that the redhead would now signal that she wanted to call off the jam, ending it before the full two minutes were up. This would prevent Toni from passing any Sonics blockers and scoring points for our team. But the redhead didn't call it off. Instead, she flew past Toni, wove her way past our blockers one more time, and scored another four points. Only then did she call the jam off.

The score was 8–0. Yikes. I stood up. Time for me to go in as a blocker.

Pumpkin smacked me on the butt. "Go get 'em, killer." She stayed on the bench, as she'd be going in the jam after me.

When I first made the team, I'd thought blocking was easier than jamming. But after a few months of experience, I could see how wrong I was. Blocking wasn't easier, just different. It was chaotic. There was so much to think about. At least when I was practicing jamming, I had one goal—skate fast, score points. With blocking, I had to think about stopping the opposing jammer, helping our team's jammer, making sure to stay in the engagement zone, avoiding breaking the pack, not getting peeled off by the opponent's offense, no forearm penalties, no multiplayer penalties—oh, my mind just filled up so fast.

"Five seconds!" bellowed the jam timer. Time to make sure I was in position.

I was covering the outside line. Luna was my brace. She was a great blocker, but not a great communicator like Gables, who would tell me what to do literally every second we were skating. Stork was jamming. I glanced back at her. Her face was serious, focused, but when she caught my eye, she gave me a tiny smile.

The whistle blew, and bam, instantly Stork was gone, sprinting up the inside line. She was lead jammer! Unfortunately, the Sonics jammer was right on her heels. She'd followed right behind Stork—coming nowhere near me—and had gotten out of the pack of blockers just a moment behind her.

Stork completed her first lap, approaching the pack again. Thank God for her long legs, speeding her around. The Sonics jammer was a third of a lap behind her now. Stork hit a seam between two Sonics blockers, shoved her hips between them, then signaled to call off the jam before the other jammer reached us.

Stork had scored two points. The score was now 8–2. I went back to the bench. I'd gotten on the track, gotten my first jam over with, but I hadn't actually *done* anything yet. The opposing jammer had been nowhere near me, and the whole thing was over in less than thirty seconds. My nervousness remained.

The next few jams continued that way: the Sonics would score several points; we'd score a few. When my turn to jam came, the score was 35–13.

Gables was pivoting. "Hey," she whispered to me as we took

the track, "line up in the middle, but look to the outside. I'll play offense for you. I'll hit their blockers toward the inside, so there's a hole for you to run through."

I nodded, my heart pounding in my throat. "What if I can't get there fast enough? What if it doesn't work?"

Gables groaned. "Can you not bring that energy onto the track?"

The little redhead was again jamming for the Sonics. Her name was written large on the back of her jersey: Simply Red. She rolled back and forth next to me behind the jam line, waiting for the jam to start.

I looked over at her. "Hi."

Simply Red kept her eyes straight ahead. "Hi."

"You're really fast." I didn't have it in me to be quiet for more than an instant.

But instead of saying thank you, like any decent human, she rolled her eyes and skated a few feet backward, so I could no longer see her. My blood boiled.

The jam-start whistle blew, and, thank goodness, I remembered to look at Gables. She was so low she could have touched the ground, and she plowed right into the Sonics blockers, knocking one down and holding another behind her. I watched, awed, not moving.

"Go, Mighty! Skate!" she shouted desperately.

Oops. I needed to get through that space! The blockers were already starting to re-form.

I skated as hard as I could, picking my feet up, trying to stay in bounds. A miracle—Gables had caused enough chaos and carnage that I was past the Sonics blockers. A ref blew two short whistles and pointed at me. I paused for a second, my brain not yet recognizing what that meant.

"You're lead jammer, Mighty!" Cleo screamed from the bench, her voice hoarse. "Skate! Faster!"

Oh God. I was lead. I hustled as best I could, but the redhead was already blowing by me. Though I'd gotten past the blockers first, she was the one to hit them first on our second lap. I hit a seam, trying to dig my hip between two Sonics blockers like Stork had done, but it didn't work. I was just pressing ineffectively against them.

I pushed, pushed, pushed, panting. The redhead was gone again, through the pack. She'd scored points, and I was still here, still pushing. I kept pushing. The redhead came around again, she was going to score more. She wove past our formidable blockers like they weren't even there, then came around yet again. Oh God. How could I—

Finally, the voices of my teammates cut through into my consciousness. "Call it, Mighty! Call it off! Call it!"

Hurriedly, I tapped my hips four times, signaling to the ref that I wanted to end the jam.

I looked at the scoreboard as we skated back to our bench. 40–13. The redhead had scored five points, and I'd scored zero. That wouldn't be too big of a deal, except that I'd been lead jammer. I could have ended the jam before she ever scored a point—that was the whole advantage to being lead. And I'd squandred it.

"I'm sorry," I huffed to Ann when I was back at our bench. "I'm not used to being lead."

She smiled and patted my shoulder. "It's okay. Now you'll remember what to do next time."

But I didn't get another chance. Each time I went out to jam, the other jammer got lead, and I struggled and pushed my way through the pack after her. Twice, though, I got past the Sonics blockers fast enough that their jammer called it off before she could score. That, I felt, was as good as I could realistically hope for.

After one of those moments, Cleo caught my eye and gave me a quick nod. "Not bad."

I smiled tightly. A "not bad" from Cleo—I'd cling to that.

The Sonics' lead grew. At the start of the second half, it was 98–45. Depressing. At the same time, I started to relax. It was looking less and less likely that we could win. That meant that if I screwed something up, I couldn't singlehandedly cost Prairie Skate Juniors the game.

As I relaxed, letting some of the pressure off myself, I finally noticed the rest of my team. It was immediately clear that something was wrong with Pumpkin.

She had gotten a lot of penalties in the first half and had taken some hard hits. Now her skating was erratic, messy. She wasn't her usual confident self. Her hits were getting wild and desperate. After Pumpkin made another trip to the penalty box, Cleo took her aside to talk. Though I couldn't hear the full conversation, I caught the word *dangerous*.

We skated onto the track to line up, both blockers in this jam. She looked rattled, wide-eyed.

The redhead, Simply Red, was jamming for the Sonics *again*. Just our luck. After her rudeness to me earlier, Pumpkin and I had talked at halftime and both decided we hated her.

"We're going to destroy her, okay?" I reached out and squeezed Pumpkin's shoulder. "It'll be great."

She smiled weakly. We did a quick, subtle high five, our wrist guards clacking. Gables, our brace, rolled her eyes.

As soon as the jam started, the redhead snuck by Pumpkin on the outside, contorting her body in ways that seemed to defy physics. She was lead jammer. Of course. But Toni was right behind her.

"Green, get to the front!" Gables yelled, her voice hoarse and desperate. She wanted all four of us Prairie Skate blockers in front of the Sonics blockers so Simply Red would have to skate farther to score points. But Pumpkin and I were both stuck behind orange blockers, separated from Gables and Luna, who were already at the front of the pack. We were easy points: Simply Red could slip right by us, grab our two points, then call it off before Toni could score.

"Pumpkin! Mighty! To the front!" Gables yelled, louder.

"I'm trying!" I shifted my weight, trying to step in front of the orange blocker planted in my lap.

In that moment, several things happened simultaneously. Simply Red approached, coming up the inside. Pumpkin glanced over her shoulder, spotted Simply Red, and accelerated backward straight at her, her backward skating as fast and as fluid as ever. Simply Red slowed for an instant, turning to change direction, but she couldn't avoid Pumpkin's incoming hit. Their bodies collided and they both tumbled to the ground, landing in a tangled heap.

"Green one-eight, direction!" A ref gestured at Pumpkin and pointed to the penalty box.

I opened my mouth, indignant. "It wasn't her fault!"

Pumpkin was struggling to get up, clutching her lower back. Simply Red was already up and gone. I sensed Gables and Luna were tangling with her toward the front of the pack, but my attention was focused on Pumpkin. She was finally standing, making her way off the track slowly and hesitantly.

"The jammer hit her in the back! That's a back block penalty!" I shouted at the ref, desperate. How could he not understand this?

The ref whistled. "Green one-two-nine, misconduct!" He looked at me and pointed to the penalty box.

Oh no. I hesitated, wanting to shout more, then finally common sense kicked in and I skated off the track.

Pumpkin and I sat next to each other in the penalty box. She was panting. I was too, but more from anger than from exertion. We watched Simply Red make swift progress around the track, scoring easy points while Toni fought the orange blockers. No matter how good Gables and Luna were, with only two of them on the track, it was hard to hold Simply Red for long.

The jam-ending whistles blew before Pumpkin's and my thirty seconds in the penalty box were over. That meant we'd have to wait here and enter the next jam after our time expired.

But before the next jam could start, the Sonics coach, a short woman with spiky black hair, ran to the middle of the track. She'd called a timeout, or something. Timeouts were still beyond my understanding of how the game worked.

A huddle formed in the middle: the refs, the Sonics coach, and Cleo.

"What's going on?" I whispered to Pumpkin.

"Official review," said a voice right behind me.

I turned around. "Dora! Hey! I didn't know you were officiating." My delight at seeing A. Dora Bell's familiar face, all glasses and braces, overcame some of my anger.

She grinned. "Turned eighteen last week. Signed up to be a ref immediately—turns out that's much more my speed. It'll be a while before I'm allowed to be an on-skates official, but I can do off-skates stuff now." She held up her stopwatch and waved it.

"I didn't even realize that it was you timing my penalty."

"Yep! You have nineteen seconds left once the next jam starts. Pumpkin, you have eleven seconds left."

I stretched my legs out in front of me. "So they're doing an official review? What's that mean?"

"The Sonics coach must have seen something in the last jam that she wants to contest." Dora shrugged. "Normally, I'd assume she was arguing over a penalty on one of her skaters that she thought they didn't deserve, but the Sonics didn't get any penalties in the last jam."

Pumpkin's breath had finally slowed, though she was still gingerly rubbing her back. "So . . . does that mean she's talking about us?"

Dora made a face. "Probably."

I looked at the huddle in the center of the track. The Sonics coach was waving her hands, gesturing at us in the penalty box. My rage rose again. "We already got penalties! What else does she want?"

Dora's voice was apologetic. "She could be asking for an

expulsion, if she thought Pumpkin's direction penalty was dangerous enough, or that your words to the ref were bad enough."

I was momentarily speechless with outrage. How dare she? But Pumpkin looked unconcerned. "Fine with me. I'm exhausted, my back hurts, and I want this to be over. This game sucks. Let them expel me."

Cleo had left the huddle. She was striding toward us, and she looked furious.

The head referee reached the penalty box a second before Cleo did. He stopped in front of Pumpkin. "You're being expelled. Gather your things and leave the track."

"What?" I burst out. "Why?"

The ref was already gone, but Cleo looked at me, her gaze deadly. "You and I will talk later." She then pointed behind her, to where Stork was skating up. "Stork will serve the rest of Pumpkin's penalty for her."

My heart was breaking for Pumpkin. How dare that coach get her expelled? But Pumpkin looked at me quickly before she left the box, smiled wryly, and mimed wiping sweat off her forehead. Why wasn't she angrier?

Stork took Pumpkin's recently vacated seat.

"This is so wrong," I fumed to her.

"She skated backward right into the jammer. It was reckless. And she's been playing dangerously all game—she's had five penalties already. I bet the coach argued it was a safety issue."

I shut my eyes. "I can't right now, Stork."

We finished the rest of the game without incident. We lost, of course. In the high-five line with the Sonics at the end of the game, I tried to rally my spirits, be a gracious host and a good loser.

"Good game," I said as I smacked hands with each Sonic. "Good game, good game."

When I passed Simply Red, she looked away from me and didn't say "good game" in response. Oh, I hated her.

Cleo found me as I was de-gearing. I knew something bad was coming. She didn't even call me away to talk privately, just sat down on the carpet.

"Don't you ever, ever yell at a ref again." Her voice was low and angry.

"But Pumpkin—she got hit square in the back!" How could I just ignore what I'd seen?

"Mighty, you know the rules. Pumpkin initiated a hit while skating opposite the direction of game play. That's dangerous."

"But—"

"Furthermore, it doesn't matter. The ref could make the worst call in the world, and you don't say a thing about it. You play the game. If the call was wrong, you tell me or Ann in between jams, and we'll call a review. You never shout at them."

My eyes burned.

"Penalties happen," Cleo continued. "But penalties for yelling at a ref? There are zero excuses for that. You should never get them."

"I just wanted to defend Pumpkin," I muttered.

She sighed. "This is a team sport, and Pumpkin is not your only teammate. How do you think that felt for Gables and Luna? They were up at the front trying to block that jammer together, just the two of them. You should have been sprinting forward to help, but you were standing still, yelling at a ref." She shook her head, looking disgusted.

I bit my lip. "Oh."

Cleo paused, just looking at me. Finally, she spoke. "If I ever see anything like that in a game from you again, you won't have to wait for the other coach to request you get expelled. I'll pull you myself."

"Wait—the Sonics coach wanted me expelled, too?" This woman was the devil.

Cleo sighed. "Look, the refs weren't going to do it. But she shouldn't have any reason to ask, to begin with."

The tears that had been threatening in my eyes finally spilled. "I'm sorry."

"Good." Cleo stood up, brushing off her legs. "For what it's worth, other than that nonsense, you did all right today. You forced the Sonics jammers to call off the jam four different times." She smiled a small, begrudging smile. "Keep it up."

CHAPTER 24

time until Soy Anything: 2 months, 2 days

Sunday's practice was mellow—lots of stretching, lots of repetition, and lots of discussion of strategy. I'd been nervous Gables and Luna would be mad at me for abandoning them on the track, but they seemed the same: Luna offered me a protein bar while we geared up, and Gables told me to stop chewing so slowly and get my ass on the track. Cleo, too, treated me normally. It was Pumpkin who seemed different. She sat out a few drills, fussing with her skates and taking water breaks way more frequently than usual.

"You okay?" I whispered while Cleo explained the details of our next drill.

She half-shrugged. "Just bored."

The expression on her face as she said it stayed in my mind throughout the rest of practice. What if getting expelled at yesterday's game had ruined derby for Pumpkin? What would I do without her? A small part of my brain reminded me that I'd been just fine without Pumpkin every Sunday at Josh's gym, and that I'd gone to plenty of derby practices that she had skipped, but the knot of anxiety in my stomach remained.

I came up with a plan during the last drill, one where we alternated sprinting around the outside of the track and doing intricate footwork on the inside track. After finishing one of my sprinting laps, I did a quick, messy turn-around stop in front of Pumpkin, where she was doing half-hearted shuffles near the apex.

"Hey." I began shuffling as well, turned backward so I was looking at her.

"Hey." She made an "I-hate-this-drill" face, tongue stuck out, eyes rolling.

"What are you doing after practice today?"

"Nothing. But I'm not going with you to Stork's gym. I told you I don't want to."

I held my palms up, defensive. "I wasn't going to suggest it. Actually, I was thinking of skipping today. Want to go to Cocoa Café and see if Spiny is working?"

"Sure." Pumpkin didn't seem quite as excited about the plan as I'd hoped she'd be, but that was okay. I turned around, facing forward and shuffling next to her. I didn't want to see her face, that look of vague annoyance.

A voice behind me warned "On your outside," and Stork slipped by on my right, speeding past as she began a sprinting lap. I watched till she'd finished her lap and gone to the inside track for footwork, then skated up to her, doing another wobbly turn-around stop. I still struggled with them at high speeds.

"Hey, I'm not going to make it to the gym today." As I said it, I felt a twinge of regret. Maybe I shouldn't have invited Pumpkin to the café. Even though I still hated huffing and puffing through moments of my workouts, I'd started enjoying the routine of the gym. I liked the satisfaction of tight, sore muscles every Monday morning, a tangible sense of progress. I liked the loud music Josh blasted, mostly hardcore stuff from before I was born. I even kind of liked my car rides with Stork on the way there, listening to her dissect the previous practice and talk about plans for improvement.

Now Stork's brows knit together, and her mouth puckered, but just for an instant. Then her face was normal again, smooth and in control. "Oh, okay."

"I have plans with Pumpkin. Sorry. I meant to tell you sooner." Oh Lord, what if she thought I was avoiding her because I'd seen inside her house? I'd missed last week's gym visit, too, because of my cold. But if I tried to tell her that wasn't the case, it would just make it more awkward.

"It's no problem!" Stork said. "I'll let you know what we do today, so you can do an at-home workout focusing on the same muscle groups later."

Oh, Stork, always goal oriented. I smiled at her. "That sounds good. Thanks." I sped off on another fast lap before I could say something awkward.

Pumpkin was quiet on the drive to the café. Her thick black hair had gotten long enough to hang in her face, and it obscured her eyes from my view. Was she okay? I paid for her latte and muffin, to say thanks for agreeing to my plan. She chose our spot—a rickety table with an ornate snow globe on it—and I carried our food and drinks over. I looked around carefully as I walked.

"No sign of Stork yet," I said.

Pumpkin tilted her head. "Stork?"

I laughed. "Spiny. I meant Spiny. They start with the same letter, easy mistake."

She wrinkled her nose. "Still weird, Mighty."

"Was something going on at practice today? I know you said you were just bored, but . . ."

"I just wasn't feeling it." She blew on her latte to cool it. "I mean, we had a game yesterday, for God's sake. I didn't really want to be playing derby again less than 24 hours later."

I nearly responded, "But we need to get better!" What, was I turning into Stork? Instead, I merely took a bite of my chocolate croissant and nodded.

"It was so much fun at the showcase, you know? It was low-key and we knew everyone playing and we were all relaxed. It was no big deal. But yesterday was just so much pressure." Pumpkin shook her head. "It sucked."

"It was horrible, the way you got expelled." My eyes welled

up with tears as I spoke. "Don't let that one ref ruin derby for you!"

Pumpkin sighed. "He didn't ruin derby. I told you. I was totally fine with being expelled. I was glad it was over."

I opened my mouth, shut it, tried to find a way to form my feelings into words. "Well . . . don't let it sour you on playing in future games. Soy Anything is going to be so much fun!"

"I guess." She sipped her drink and looked away.

"It is!"

"Okay, fine."

"Seriously! We'll all be traveling together, staying in a hotel, having fun, playing a ton of different teams . . ." The more desperate I was to convince her, the further away she seemed.

"*Okay*, Mighty."

Her angry tone seemed to surprise us both. We fell silent. Inside, I was panicking. I couldn't fight with Pumpkin. She was my best friend, practically my only friend. Why was I getting on her nerves today?

Finally, Pumpkin shook her head. "Sorry. I'm just crabby." She broke her muffin, an oversized cranberry-orange one dusted with powdered sugar, into a few pieces and gestured to them. "Have some."

I took a piece, offering her some chocolate croissant. "I've come up with a new plan."

"More Spiny plots?"

Did she sound just the slightest bit weary? I was pretty sure she did. But: "Nope! Just me, you, and the road!" I waved my arms, did spirit fingers.

She smiled. "Okay, you've got my attention."

"Want to drive to U of I for the weekend and visit my brother Ben?"

"Yes! That's perfect!" She grinned widely, her big eyes warm again, our mini fight forgotten. "I applied there, but I haven't heard back yet. And I've never actually visited. My sister wants me to go because her best friend's older sister goes there. David doesn't want me to go because he says I'll be bored in some town surrounded by corn, far from Chicago—but actually it's because he's going to Elgin Community College and wants me nearby so he can get me back."

"I keep forgetting you're a senior, leaving me next year! Who am I supposed to talk to at derby practice? Who am I supposed to, like, complain about Stork to?"

She laughed. "You don't need me at derby. You're fine on your own."

Was her tone still weird? I couldn't shake the feeling that something was bothering her about derby. I brushed it aside. She had said she was just being crabby earlier.

"Would you be allowed to drive that far? I have a car, but I'm not allowed to drive it till I get my grades up." I rolled my eyes dramatically.

"Yeah, no prob. I bet my stepdad will let me borrow his car. He has a brand-new Highlander with a great sound system, heated seats, the whole package. We can ride in style."

I had a prescient moment, imagining all the trash and junk Pumpkin and I could fill this nice car with in 48 hours. Well, if he allowed it . . .

"Is your stepdad nice?" My face burned as I said it. What a weird, childish question to ask. But at the same time, it felt good to be on solid ground again, the two of us in sync.

Pumpkin answered around a mouthful of my croissant. "Oh yeah, he's great. Better than my mom, most of the time, honestly. She's always been the strict one."

"When did they get married?"

She swallowed. "When I was six. My sister and I were flower girls." She laughed. "My sister dumped all her petals out right away instead of sprinkling them down the whole aisle, and I started yelling at her for it, right there in front of everyone."

"Was it weird? Like, for you and your dad?"

She shook her head. "I don't think so. But I was little, so what do I know? He watched our dogs the whole wedding weekend, though, so it couldn't have been that weird. I mean, they all get along."

Would my parents get remarried? It turned my stomach, imagining some random man moving into my house, or some random woman in my dad's too-small apartment. Once again, I was frustrated by my parents' inability to keep their lives from messing with mine.

The door chimes rang. It was Spiny, rushing, calling out to the man behind the counter, "Sorry I'm late!" She hadn't seen us yet.

"You gonna talk to her?" Pumpkin asked.

I nodded. "I'll give her a few minutes to get settled." It would also give me a chance to go to the bathroom and make sure I looked and smelled okay. Coming straight from practice was always a hygiene risk.

Spiny was arranging a display of chocolate bars on the counter, forming a neat pyramid, when I approached. Her face lit up when she spotted me, I swear to God.

"Hey there!" she said. "How was that Juniors game yesterday?"

"I mean . . . we lost pretty bad."

She shrugged. "Eh, losing happens. You should've seen what the Dairyland Dolls did to us last weekend. It was brutal."

"Yeah, I'm sorry I missed it!" I laughed nervously. "That came out wrong. I'm not sorry I missed seeing you lose."

"So what have you been up to? Staying out of trouble?" She smiled.

"Trying to." I smiled back. Was I flirting? Was the point getting across?

"No more dates with Kristy?"

I shook my head. This I could answer honestly. "Not one. How about you? No getting back together with your toxic ex?" Did it come out playfully? Oh God, I hoped so.

"Nope. That's over and done." She dusted her hands off, then looked at her chocolate bars critically, moving one a few inches, rotating another. The neat pyramid had become an interesting modernist sort of structure.

Probably this was the moment when I should order another drink or croissant or something. But she was standing next to the counter, not behind it, so did that make it weird? Should I wait to order from the other employee? Except, of course, I didn't actually want anything more to drink, I just wanted an excuse to talk to her. But I wasn't talking, I was just standing here awkwardly. Why did I need to overthink every single social interaction?

"You know," Spiny said, "there's a place not far from here that makes hot chocolate from actual chocolate bars, like this one." She wiggled the bar she was currently holding. "It's next to, I swear, the best Greek restaurant outside of Chicago."

"Oh. I've never had Greek food." I blushed. Why had I admitted that? Now I sounded like a kid, I was sure of it. My lie about my age loomed large in my mind again. How could I expect her to believe I was eighteen?

"You're kidding! You've had baklava, at least, right?" She shifted her weight from one foot to the other, and suddenly seemed a lot closer to me.

I shook my head. "Nope." And I shifted my weight to be closer to her. My heart pounded. I wondered if Pumpkin was watching, so she could tell me later if it looked as significant as it felt.

"Well." Spiny grinned. "We should get Greek food sometime."

My breath fluttered in my chest. "Yeah? Okay. I'd like that."

"Let's make it happen. What evenings are you free?"

A date! A date with Spiny! I tried not to hyperventilate. Oh God, I'd have to figure out how to maintain this ridiculous lie about my age. Could I wait to tell her until I was actually eighteen, and she'd been in love with me for two years? No, no, that was insane. I fought off a hysterical grin.

Unfortunately, given her work schedule, our conflicting

derby practice and game schedules, and me and Pumpkin's upcoming weekend plans for U of I, there weren't a lot of times available. With each moment that passed, each suggestion of a day by one of us and rejection of it by the other, I got more and more worried that she'd change her mind. What if having dinner with me was just too much work? Could I really be worth the effort for her to keep scrolling through her calendar?

Finally, though, we found a date. A Saturday night, way too many weeks away.

She smiled. "Finally! There. Well. Get ready for some of the best roasted potatoes you've ever had in your life." Her eyes twinkled, and she leaned a little closer to me.

"I can't wait." I smiled back, looking straight into her eyes, and dared to lean closer still. Her face was only inches from mine.

"Just wait." She raised her eyebrows. "Garlic. Lemon zest. Parsley. They're life changing." Her breath tickled my skin when she spoke. She pressed a finger against my bare forearm twice, in rhythm with her words. "Life. Changing."

"Sounds fantastic." How could talking about potatoes feel this electric? I took a deep breath, smiled one more time, and walked back to Pumpkin on shaking, ecstatic legs.

We left the café a few minutes later. I was a babbling mess.

"I swear to God," Pumpkin said, "if you say 'garlic, lemon zest, parsley' one more time, I'm going to leave you by the side of the road."

"Should I try Greek food sometime before we go? So I'm prepared? I can still pretend I've never had it when we go out on our date." I laughed, a little hysterically. "Should I do that thing like they do in movies, and not wash the spot on my arm where she touched me?"

"You are ridiculous." Her tone was dry.

"Oh yeah!" I exclaimed as Pumpkin turned into my

neighborhood. Why had it had taken me this long to remember? "Did you say you're talking to David again? Why?"

Pumpkin grimaced. "I don't know. He's been texting me a lot. I'm not sure what I'm going to do. On the one hand, I did confirm that he and Angela broke up. And we have all the same friends, and we've known each other for years. But on the other hand, he's totally self-centered. He never asks me about myself, and when we were dating, he wanted me to come watch his band practice all the time, like I had nothing better to do. Ugh, I don't know."

Maybe that was why she'd seemed crabby today. Maybe it had nothing to do with me, or with derby. I gave her a hug goodbye and waved enthusiastically when I got out of the car. Inside, my head was a churning mess of confusion. A date with Spiny, unexplained distance from Pumpkin: It was a lot of change for one morning.

I pulled my shoelaces tight, pulled my ponytail even tighter, and took a puff of my inhaler and one last gulp of water. Surely, I'd regret this. But I was doing it anyway. I stepped out the front door of my house, winced against the chilly February air on my face, and began to jog.

I'd been going to practice, going to the gym on Sundays, and keeping up with Josh's "homework" workouts—mostly body-weight strength stuff—but I wanted more. Cleo said I needed to work on my endurance. And Stork ran track at school—wouldn't it be awesome if I could tell her I'd started running? She'd be so impressed. Not that I was trying to impress Stork.

I did intervals: 30 seconds running, 30 seconds walking. It was easy at first, harder as I went, but the walking breaks gave me a chance to recover, and, to my surprise, I made it over three miles.

When I got home, I took a sweaty selfie and texted it—well, I started to text it just to Stork, since she was a runner, then realized that was maybe weird. I sent it to the whole rookie group instead.

Nice! Stork texted back. *Want to go with me on a trail run Thursday afternoon? It's finally supposed to be decent weather.*

Sure! What had gotten into me?

Stork wrote more in the group chat. *Anyone else want to come?*

A quick *nope* from Pumpkin. I wasn't surprised. Then, a few minutes later, Pay sent her regrets, saying that she and Bee had plans. So, it would just be Stork and me. I felt a little relieved, a little pleased. After all, Pay and Bee were both much faster runners than I was.

Stork picked me up, and we drove out of town to a county park.

"It's really pretty here once there are leaves on the trees," Stork said, "but it's not too bad now, either."

"I don't suppose there are vending machines along the trail? So I won't starve to death?" I couldn't stop myself from making jokes. It was like a compulsion.

Stork, as usual, took me seriously instead of laughing. "No, but we could get dinner afterward if you want. There's a place with good veggie bowls nearby."

I had planned to make a frozen pizza when I got home, devouring it in a surely desperate hunger. But: "Yeah, let's do it!"

My fitness, it turned out, hadn't made the radical improvement I'd imagined. Once I was jogging next to another person, it was clear I was still slow and ungainly.

Stork had suggested a four-mile loop, and I'd okayed it, since I'd done over three miles the other day. But that had been a mixture of jogging and walking. Once we were about half a mile in, I realized I had no hope of doing the whole loop at this pace. I needed to tell her. But what would she think of me? Maybe I could go back and meet her at the car, and she could run for as long as she wanted, as fast as she wanted.

"Sorry!" I puffed. "I know I'm holding you back."

Stork, sleek in a blue zippered athletic jacket and black running tights, replied in a voice unmarred by exhaustion. "It's no problem. Speed isn't everything, it's just good to get out and move." She jogged a few steps ahead, turned around and jogged backward, smiling at me, then faced forward again and fell back in step with me.

"The thing is . . ." I didn't want to say it. I didn't want her to judge me.

"What?"

"I'm having an off day. I have cramps, first day of my period. I think I need to turn back."

"Oh. Okay." She normally masked any unpleasant emotions so well, but I could hear the note of disappointment in her tone. Damn it. She probably thought I was unathletic and useless, after all.

We turned around and jogged back to the car in silence.

Once we reached the parking lot, I asked, "Is the veggie bowl place expensive? I don't have much cash."

"Oh!" Stork blinked. "You still want to go? You feel good enough?"

"To eat? Yeah, of course!"

"I figured you just needed to go home. But no, the restaurant isn't expensive. And I can spot you cash if you need it." She was smiling now, her mood turning around.

Had she been disappointed not in the workout, but because she thought I was going home? A flush of pleasure blossomed in my chest.

The restaurant was tiny; we shoved into one of just a few closely packed booths. Stork's knees bumped against mine. She'd ordered a bowl teeming with vegetables; kale curled over the edges. Mine had a few roasted veggies but was mostly rice and a tangy, sweet sauce. It was delicious. I wolfed it down.

When the bowl was nearly empty, I wiped my mouth with a napkin and spoke up. "I have something to confess."

"Yeah?" Stork's brows pulled together.

"I don't have my period. I'm not having an off day. I'm just a slow, terrible jogger."

Her face relaxed, and her lips curved into a smile. "You're

not slow and terrible. You're just not as fast as me. But I've been running for years."

"You weren't disappointed or mad?"

"What? No, of course not."

Now I smiled, jogging her elbow with mine. "I totally thought you were judging me."

"Of course not." Her eyes were warm. They were dark brown, a contrast with her light hair. I'd never noticed that before.

Suddenly, the moment felt a bit intense. Could she tell I was staring at her? I looked down at the remains of my meal, then quickly shoved a few more bites of rice in my mouth.

"Speaking of judging"—Stork's gaze was on her own bowl now, too—"thanks. For not being weird about my house. About my dad."

I made a face. "Of course not. I'd never be weird about that. Everybody's families are screwed up. I mean, not that your family is *screwed up*," I stumbled, "it's just, like, the tension in my house is as huge as all the junk in yours. Sometimes I feel like I can barely breathe when I'm at home."

Stork's eyes—her big, expressive, deep brown eyes—were fixed on mine. "Yeah, families are messy." She took a deep breath. "I haven't had a friend inside my house since I was a kid. I've been too embarrassed."

"Really? Not even your school friends? Your track team friends?"

She shook her head.

"Not even anyone else on the derby team?"

At this, her brows drew together again. "You're my best friend on the team, Mighty."

I swallowed. "Oh." My heart was beating faster again. That had never occurred to me. "I didn't think . . . I mean, you're so good at derby, and you're so nice and perfect . . . everyone loves you."

She barked a laugh. "Hardly! I get on people's nerves, with how intense I am."

"No way. I get on people's nerves, with how annoying I am!"

We were both laughing genuinely now. After a moment, when we'd gotten ahold of ourselves, she continued, "I'm not completely un-self-aware. I know I can be a lot to deal with. It's just . . . if I'm going to do something, I'm going to do it right. Go all in."

"That makes sense."

"And it's like . . . sports and fitness are something in my realm of control. I can decide on my workouts, on my health, on my mental training."

Should I say it? "You mean, unlike at home . . . ?" I was immediately scared I'd gone too far.

"Yeah." Her voice lowered. She shook her head, strands of sweat-dampened blonde hair falling in her eyes. "He gets worse every year. I hate it."

"Does he acknowledge that he has a problem?"

"Sort of. The summer before I started high school, he got rid of a bunch of stuff. He swore he was going to get the place totally in shape. He asked my mom and me to go on vacation, said it was going to look great when we came back. We went to Florida to visit my grandma for a week and hung out on the beach. I thought everything was great. Then we came home, and . . ." She covered her eyes with her hands for a moment, then sighed and looked at the ceiling.

"Was it bad?"

"Worse than ever."

I reached out and squeezed her hand. "I'm sorry."

"It's okay." She clasped my hand back, squeezing hard, then picked up her drink. "Thanks for listening to me rant."

I laughed again. "That was *not* a rant, Stork. It was just, like, a conversation."

She smiled wryly. "I wasn't too intense?"

"No. I wasn't too annoying?"

"Ha! No."

We bussed our table and got back in the car. I had the strange sensation of wanting to tell someone about our day, how odd but also oddly enjoyable it had been. But who? Pumpkin would groan, I was sure of it. The only person I felt like telling was Stork, but she'd been the person with me. Strange indeed.

CHAPTER 26

time until Soy Anything: 1 month, 6 days

"Candy?"

"Bag of Hershey's Kisses and bag of Jolly Ranchers. Check!"

"Chips?"

"Potato and tortilla. Check!"

"Cell phone chargers?"

"Check!"

"I-Pass for tolls?"

"Check!"

"Let's hit the road!"

"Wait, wait, wait, I forgot my inhaler!"

Once I was back in the car, inhaler safely in hand, Pumpkin peeled out of the driveway, her stepdad's Highlander's tires screeching.

On the road! Freedom! It was early on a Saturday, a gray late-February morning, but I was wide awake and bouncing with excitement. Just a few hours till we arrived in Champaign-Urbana, home to the University of Illinois. Road trip! We'd stay overnight and return tomorrow. I'd told Ann and Cleo—and Stork—in advance that I'd be missing practice tomorrow morning, so they wouldn't worry. Stork had seemed disappointed, and I'd felt a moment of disappointment then, too.

But that was far from my mind now. Pumpkin navigated us out of the suburbs like a pro, and soon we were on Route 57, cruise control locked in, car aimed straight at U of I. Less than two hours to go.

I unwrapped yet another Hershey's Kiss and popped it in my mouth. "Any news on your U of I application yet?"

"Not yet. I think I have a good shot at getting admitted, but I don't want to count on it till I hear officially."

"What do you think you'll major in?"

She shrugged. "I know I'm supposed to know, and I've been telling my parents I want to major in biology, but I really have no idea."

"Me, neither."

"Well, you've got two more years to figure it out."

Why did I have to be younger than everyone? Younger than Ben, younger than Spiny, younger than Pumpkin? Stork was my age, but she was so . . . Storkish. I no longer thought of that as a bad thing, but she did seem more mature than me.

"Do you want me to take a shift driving?" I asked.

Pumpkin laughed. "It's been half an hour. I'm fine. Also, my stepdad might kill me."

"Well. Just in case you get tired. I'm ready. I'm still not allowed to drive my own car." Having my actual driver's license had really turned out to be a letdown. Nothing felt different since my parents still wouldn't let me have the car until they saw my midterm grades. I was hoping Pumpkin would let me take the car for a spin. Just briefly. Maybe once we were in town and not on the highway anymore.

"Parents, man . . . they can be the worst."

"Right?" Oh, it felt so good to be on the road with Pumpkin, chatting a mile a minute. She didn't seem crabby at all. Everything felt ideal. I was so, so glad she was my friend. "Speaking of parents, did you know Stork's dad is a hoarder? Like real bad?"

Pumpkin's mouth opened into a perfect O. "No way! Ugh, how much would that suck?"

"I know, right? It's like, that's why she's sort of a control freak." That hadn't come out right. I wished I could shove the words back in my mouth. But I wanted Pumpkin to know that Stork didn't need to be her derby nemesis. Stork was human, with her own challenges. "I mean, Stork's got her own issues, and she's not so bad. That's what I meant."

It didn't feel like enough of a course-correct. I shouldn't have brought this up.

But Pumpkin just laughed. "She did extra burpees after practice last week, Mighty, because she wanted to push herself and see what she could do when she was already exhausted. And then Cleo looked at the rest of us like we were lazy. Remember? Don't try to humanize her."

"I know, but . . . she's all right. She is."

"Ha! Yeah, okay, Mighty, whatever you say."

This had gone poorly. I never should have brought up Stork's dad. All I could hope was that Pumpkin would forget this conversation entirely.

Pumpkin's phone vibrated, shaking the cupholder it was resting in. Her eyes flickered over to it.

"Want me to see who it is?" I asked.

She shook her head. "It's David."

"Oh."

"I don't know what's going on with us." She sighed. "He's a jerk, but he's a hot jerk. I miss sleeping with him. And he knows me so well. But I know as soon as I tell him I'll be his girlfriend again, he'll lose interest."

"Want me to tell him to go to hell?" I reached for her phone.

She laughed and swatted my hand away. "I will crash this car if you touch my phone, so help me God." After she was convinced I wouldn't grab the phone, she returned her hand to the steering wheel and continued talking. "He sent me flowers a week ago. Who even does that?" She made a face. "They're roses. It was a few days after Valentine's Day, so they were probably extra cheap leftovers. Still, I can feel myself weakening. And I know he knows that."

"Why are you weakening?"

"Oh, he says how pretty I am, how funny I am, how smart I am. All the stuff you want a guy to say." She gestured to me. "Or a girl, in your case."

"Only one week till my date with Spiny, speaking of!" I bopped around in my seat. "I'm hoping it's warm enough out that I can wear my denim jacket instead of this thing." My giant puffy winter coat was shoved at my feet, unnecessary with the blasting heat and the warmed seats.

"When she becomes your girlfriend, I get all the credit, right?"

"Of course! It was your idea—"

"—and it was my broken mug that you cut your hand on—"

"—and you found out what her real name was—"

"—and where she worked."

"Man, I really do owe it to you."

Pumpkin did a mock bow. "You're welcome."

Ben lived in a residence hall geared toward engineering majors. We weren't staying in his room with him, of course; his roommate, Kevin, had a cousin Marie, who was hosting us at her apartment. We'd meet her later. For now, though, Ben met us in front of his building.

He looked taller, though it had been less than two months since I'd seen him last. His hair was shoved under a Cubs hat. He smiled and waved when he spotted us, and a spot of tension eased in my chest. He'd been pretty agreeable about the visit, but I'd still worried we were intruding.

"Let's get lunch," he said. "We can walk over to one of the better cafeterias. You'll like it. It's got a bunch of different mini restaurants."

"Sounds great!" We followed him. I tried not to look too wide-eyed and overwhelmed by the campus around me, but Pumpkin didn't seem so concerned.

"It's sooo pretty!" she kept exclaiming as we walked. "It feels like a college campus in a movie!"

Ben rolled his eyes at me every time she said it. But she was right. The buildings were tall and, whether beautiful and ornate or rectangular and ugly, all visually interesting. Bare-branched trees lined the streets. Backpack-wearing students flowed everywhere, some head-down and focused on their phones, some shouting to each other, laughing or running.

The third time Ben rolled his eyes at Pumpkin, she caught him. I worried her feelings would be hurt, but instead she hit him on the arm.

"Hey! This is exciting! Don't be a jerk!"

He laughed and rubbed his arm. "You're violent, just like my sister. Must be all that roller derby."

Ben got us guest passes so we could get into the cafeteria, and we found a table. The chairs were brown plastic, the tabletops a little sticky. All the tables were crowded with students eating lunch. I kept expecting Ben to run into friends, to maybe want to ditch us, but he seemed content.

"I guess at a school this big, you don't know everyone," I said thoughtfully, then took a big bite of pizza.

Ben had gotten Chinese food, and he spoke around a big mouthful of egg roll. "Of course not."

"I applied here for fall," Pumpkin told him.

Ben put his hands to his cheeks in mock horror. "You, here? Great, now I have to transfer . . ."

She punched him in the arm again, and he pretended to be wounded. What a dork.

"I think I want to go to school in Chicago," I said. That vision of me and Spiny with our own little apartment drifted back into my mind. I'd live in the dorms for a year or two, then we'd find our place together. Maybe I'd learn to cook, make us Greek food for dinner while Spiny was out doing her EMT job.

"My cousin Lara goes to Columbia College in Chicago. It

is not. This. Nice." Pumpkin pointed at me with her fork for emphasis. "It's just, like, a bunch of buildings scattered in the South Loop. It doesn't feel campus-y at all."

"Besides," Ben said, "aren't you getting ahead of yourself, Mils? You have to actually get decent grades to get into college."

I made a face. "My grades aren't that bad. Mom just wants to spite Dad, I think, and not let me drive the car he gave me."

Pumpkin patted my arm. "You can get your grades up, Mighty. You still have a little time before third quarter grades come out, right?"

"Yes, but can we please change the subject? I don't want you two just sitting here pitying me."

Ben laughed. "No way, people should pity *me*. I'm the one who has to lead you two around all weekend."

Pumpkin hit him in the arm yet again.

After lunch, Ben gave us a quick tour of campus, including only the buildings he deemed important.

"This is the ARC," he said, walking backward down the sidewalk and gesturing to his right. "It's where I usually work out."

"Slow down, I want to look inside!" I ran across the grass and peered through the big glass windows. Inside was a huge fitness area with every machine and weight I could think of. A girl in a navy tracksuit brushed past me and walked through the doors, heading straight for a treadmill.

What would it be like, going to college, making your time your own? I imagined meeting Stork at the gym on a whim, then going for smoothies or hanging out at a café, doing whatever I wanted, not having to report to anyone else. Not that I was going to college with Stork. Not that I was going to U of I. But still. How cool.

"All right, come on." Ben kept walking. "There's more to the tour. Across the street here, you can see the dorm where my lab partner, Mikhail, lives. And up ahead, the corner where Kevin once projectile-vomited into a bush."

"Great tour, great tour." Pumpkin laughed. "I'm sold on this place now."

"Do you actually think you'll go here?" I asked. I hated the idea of Pumpkin moving away, but if she did, U of I wouldn't be a bad place for it. If she were at the same school as Ben, I could visit them both at once. "I mean, I know you said you don't know if you'll get in. But if you do?"

Pumpkin tugged on the strings of the oversized hoodie she was wearing, pulling them back and forth through the hood. "I think so. It's a good school."

We walked a few more steps, pausing so Ben could show us the specific bush Kevin had puked in.

"It's so beautiful. Not the bush, but the whole thing." Pumpkin spread her arms wide. "But also, do I want this sort of stereotypical campus? I'm not sure. I mean, I'm not exactly going to join a sorority, you know?"

"Oh, some of the Greeks are okay," Ben said.

Pumpkin made a face. "Says you. I hardly think I'd fit in." She gestured to her body. Besides the hoodie, she was wearing torn jeans with fishnets showing inside the rips, and beat-up white high-tops covered in pen scribbles.

Ben shrugged. "Whatever. You don't need to join a sorority to go here. Most people don't."

"Now you want me to go?" She grinned. "Yeah, you love me. You can't get enough of me."

"Nah, I just want to keep your bad influence far away from my impressionable little sister." He grinned back at her, and she smacked him with her purse. I rolled my eyes.

"Hey! Novak!" Three guys in the distance waved to us.

"Be right back," Ben said to Pumpkin and me, then trotted over to the group of guys.

Pumpkin hopped onto a short wall bordering an expanse of

brown grass, and walked along it, balancing carefully. "It's so weird that he's your brother."

"Is it?" I'd had that thought myself, many times, but I didn't love hearing it now, not when I was so happy to finally be visiting him.

"He's sort of a bro, isn't he? So ... mainstream." She laughed. "I can't imagine *you* thinking sororities are totally cool."

"Okay, well, obviously we're different people. But he's my brother, you know? He knows me better than anyone. And he's a good guy."

Pumpkin shrugged. "I didn't say otherwise."

"People can be different from each other and still understand each other." Suddenly I wasn't thinking of Ben, but of Stork.

"Okay, okay!" She laughed. "Don't get so defensive."

Ben jogged back to us, and the conversation died. I was glad. It felt like the start of a spat, and that was the last thing I wanted while we were on a road trip.

CHAPTER 27

Marie, Kevin's cousin, had a tiny place in a big old house that had been split into separate apartments. She shared it with three other girls, two girls to each bedroom. Pumpkin and I would be sharing a pull-out couch in the living room.

"Sorry for the mess!" Marie ushered us in cheerfully. She had flaming red hair piled into a topknot and wore highlighter-yellow sweatpants. My brain filed her in the "cool but intimidating" category, where, really, I put most girls older than me.

We cautiously followed her into the apartment. The shades were shut, midday sun peeking in around their edges. It smelled like a mix of thirty different candles with notes of cigarette smoke and weed. There were knickknacks everywhere, a random thong on the couch, and a ping-pong table turned on its side and pushed against the wall.

Marie picked up the thong and tossed it down the hall. "You can throw your bags here, and we'll pull out the bed later."

Pumpkin and I sat down on the couch carefully and simultaneously. Ben stood. He seemed a little awkward, too. I wondered how well he knew Marie.

"Thanks for hosting us," I said, Pumpkin quickly echoing me. The stretch of carpet in my line of sight had three weird stains, each a different color, and one cigarette burn. Oh, why couldn't I stay in a boy's dorm? Would it be so wrong?

"No problem! I have to ask: You're from the suburbs, so does that mean you're Cubs fans like this guy?" She gestured to

Ben with her thumb. "I hope not. This is a diehard Cardinals apartment!" She laughed.

"I don't know anything about baseball beyond, you know, watching Ben play it." I looked up at him. "When does your season start here? I should come watch a game. You saw me play derby, after all."

Ben's face froze. "Oh—Millie, no. I'm not on the team."

"What? Of course you are."

I couldn't decide if he looked mad or just embarrassed. "You know I didn't get a baseball scholarship. So I had to do the open tryouts early last fall. And I was . . ." He took off his hat and ran his fingers through his hair. "*Way* outclassed. I had no shot."

"How come you never told me?" Sadness rose in my throat.

"Hey, Sonia, was it?" Marie was looking at Pumpkin. "Want something to drink? Come see what we have."

Pumpkin hopped up off the couch eagerly and followed Marie into the kitchen. I supposed neither of them wanted to be a part of this conversation.

Ben sat down in Pumpkin's vacated spot. "I didn't say anything because there was nothing to report. I figured if I made the team, then I'd tell you. Otherwise, what? It wouldn't do me any good to have you feel all bad for me."

The tryouts had been early last fall, he'd said. I'd been oblivious. That would've been around the time I did my skills assessment and got on the Juniors team. I thought about how nervous I'd been, how shaken I'd felt after Ann's miscount of my 27 in 5.

"You must miss it," I said.

Ben half-rolled his eyes. "Well, yeah. But what am I gonna do?"

"Can you play with friends, informally or whatever?"

"There's intramural baseball, but it seems sort of pathetic. I mean, I was one of the best players at my high school. I should've been able to make the team."

I groaned. "You're being pathetic *now*. I know how much you love baseball. If you can play it, in any form, you should play it."

He was quiet for a moment. "It's not the same, Mils."

I thought about it, searched for words to make it better. Couldn't find them. What would it be like if, once I turned eighteen, I tried to get on the charter team and failed? How much would that hurt? "Yeah. I know. That sucks."

"It does."

We sat next to each other in silence for a minute.

"I'm sorry, Ben." I didn't look at him. I'd wondered all autumn how Ben's life in college was going, but had I ever actually engaged him in conversation about it? No, I'd just imagined him having fun, and felt bad about my own life in contrast. "I should have asked you in the fall. I was just obsessing about derby and it didn't really occur to me."

He sighed. "It's fine."

"It really does suck. I hate that you aren't on the team."

"Me, too. But what am I gonna do? That's sports." The futon creaked as he stood up. "Let's go in the kitchen and save Marie from Pumpkin."

I saw his attempt at levity and tried to match it. "Whatever, you love Pumpkin. You know she's awesome."

He laughed and walked away. I followed him, thinking again about my earlier conversation with Pumpkin, about how different Ben and I were. Just like I knew Ben understood me on some fundamental level, I understood him, too. I knew how much this must hurt him.

"Hand me that lipstick." Pumpkin pointed to my bubblegum-pink tube, nearly lost in the clutter on Marie's bathroom counter.

I handed it to her. "Trade you for your eyeliner." She passed it over.

We were getting ready to go out because Ben was taking us to a party. A frat party. Not like in the movies, he'd stressed. It was at the engineering frat, so it was mostly nerdy guys, totally nice, he swore. I was equal parts terrified and excited.

Marie peeked into the bathroom. "How's it going?"

"Good!" we chimed.

I was no longer afraid of Marie or her apartment. She and her roommates had been totally friendly all afternoon, coming with us on Part Two of Ben's informal campus tour and taking us to an Indian place for dinner. I'd ordered my curry at the maximum spiciness level and then been unable to eat most of it, so Marie had finished it for me.

I leaned closer to the mirror so I could apply dramatic black wings of eyeliner. My hand was reassuringly steady. A college party? No problem. I could do this.

Pumpkin had borrowed my turquoise sweater dress. Her hair had grown out to chin-length, into a sleek flapper-like bob. I was wearing a tight black top of hers with my best pair of jeans. We looked good. But our hair and makeup were far from done.

"Do you need to get in here?" I asked Marie. "So you can get ready?"

She laughed. "I *am* ready. It's just the engineering frat, not the Oscars." She was still wearing the same yellow sweatpants she'd been in all afternoon.

"This is our first college party," Pumpkin said, "so we have to look good. We have to do this right. Besides, I'm trying to get over my ex, so maybe I can meet someone to distract me." She grinned and raised her eyebrows. "You never know."

I hoped Pumpkin would meet a sweet, nerdy engineering major. Then he'd come up to the suburbs to visit her, and they'd go on a double date with me and Spiny, and . . . oh, I always got ahead of myself.

"Want a drink?" Marie's roommate Kayla had joined her in the doorway, holding a six-pack of beer.

Pumpkin looked at me curiously, as if intuiting that this was the first time I'd ever been offered alcohol.

"Sure..." I said hesitantly, then laughed.

Pumpkin laughed, too, and took a can of beer for each of us from Kayla's hands. "Thanks."

I cracked mine open cautiously. I'd had sips of my parents' wine a few times, but that was it. Would Ben be mad that I was drinking? Well, he wasn't here. He'd had to run back to his dorm room, and he wouldn't be back for a little while. Besides, he wasn't of age, either, and I knew he drank.

I took a sip. Disgusting. Bitter. It tasted the way I imagined urine crossed with garbage would taste. Why did anyone drink this on purpose? I took another sip. Yep, still gross.

Pumpkin was unfazed by the taste, taking drinks in between carefully applying her eye makeup. I took a few more sips, not wanting to look like a child. These weren't quite as bad. Or maybe I was feeling a little fuzzy-headed already? No, not in five minutes. That was ridiculous. I kept drinking.

We finished our makeup and headed into the living room to wait for Ben and Kevin. I kept the beer clutched in my hand. It was mostly empty, now, and warmish. Marie offered me another, and I took it. I drank faster as we sat on the couch, daring myself to be bold, trying to pass the time as we waited. I didn't have much to say, but Marie and her three roommates chattered away, so I didn't need to worry about it. All but one of the girls was going to the party; the one that wasn't going had a paper she needed to write, she said. She didn't seem to mind, just sat on the floor in plaid pajamas and bunny slippers and tapped away at her laptop while we got ready.

When my second beer was empty, I picked up Pumpkin's can and started drinking from it. When I put down it down on the plastic crate they used as a coffee table and the can tumbled over, also empty, Marie brought me another one. I cracked it open, took a long drink. Everyone was acting like this was normal. So, it must have been normal, me drinking.

What would this party be like? Suddenly it sounded so difficult. I'd have to meet all these new people. Really, what I felt like doing was eating chips and staying in with Pumpkin and Ben, talking all night. The two of them had given each other a hard time all day long, fake-arguing and fake-fighting. I was pretty sure it was fake, anyway; I couldn't forget the scornful way Pumpkin had called him mainstream.

I looked at Pumpkin next to me, then leaned against her, weary. "I'm tired. I'm just gonna take a mini nap on you while we wait for the guys."

Ben and Kevin's arrival woke me from a sound sleep. I'd drooled all over Pumpkin's dress. Well, my dress that she was borrowing. So that was good. I patted the spot on her shoulder with my hand.

"Wow," said Ben, looking at us both. "You two look great." He wasn't looking at us both, I realized, even in my sleepy haze. He was looking at Pumpkin.

This somehow made me more tired. "Can I stay home? Here, I mean?" I pointed at the girl with the bunny slippers. "She's staying, too."

Ben furrowed his brow. "You don't want to go?"

"I want to sleep." Sleep pulled on me, tugging me back toward it. "Like a tugboat."

"What?" Ben stared at me.

"She had a couple beers," Marie said. "Just two or three, but I think she's drunk. She barely ate anything at dinner."

Ben groaned. "Are you kidding me, Millie?"

"I'm just gonna sleep." I shooed him with my hands. "Go have fun. Go to the party. I'll be here. Asleep."

He crouched down so his face was only a few inches from mine. "Are you sure?" he asked in a quiet voice. "This is your visit. I don't want to ditch you."

"I'm just gonna sleep, Ben. Seriously. Go." I shooed him away again.

Finally, they all left except Bunny Slippers Girl, who went

back to her bedroom. It was dark and quiet and peaceful. I dozed off, snuggled against the back of the couch, content.

I woke up with a jolt. It was morning, and I was still on the couch. We'd never pulled it out into a bed. Pumpkin? Where was Pumpkin? I sat up, panicked.

There were voices in the hall, right outside the door. That must've been what woke me. I dashed to the door and peered through the peephole.

Oh my God. It was Pumpkin out there with some guy, and they were making out. Her arms were wrapped around him, her face mashed to his. I couldn't believe it. She'd actually found herself a nerdy engineer to help her get over David, just like we'd hoped! And she'd been out all night with him! Good for her!

Then she pulled away from him to say goodbye, and I was able to see his face.

Ben. It was Ben. My brother and Pumpkin had been making out.

I felt dizzy. It wasn't the alcohol.

I dashed back to the couch to feign sleep before she came inside.

CHAPTER 28

time until Soy Anything: 1 month, 5 days

I can't believe it," Pumpkin said for the thousandth time. "I just can't believe it. Your brother! And me! Oh, Mighty, he's so amazing."

We were on the road home. I sat very still in the passenger's seat, arms wrapped around my middle. I'd told Pumpkin I was hungover.

"He was soooo nice at the frat. Did I tell you the bathroom thing? Ohmygod. I had to pee, and I mean, it's a frat house, super nasty and gross. So Ben insisted on going into the bathroom before me and cleaning it up real quick so it wouldn't be that bad when I used it. Isn't that just"—she pressed her hand to her chest and sighed—"just so sweet?"

"Yeah. That's nice." It was! But I hated it. Ben was mine. Pumpkin was mine. Now suddenly they had this connection with each other? Something that cut me right out? He'd kissed her goodbye after our cafeteria breakfast, in full view of me and Kevin. It was just wrong.

"And he said he's going to try to come to Soy Anything, to cheer us on! It's not too far from here! Isn't that so sweet?"

"Yes, yes, he's very sweet, it's been established." I forced my voice to sound jokey rather than bitter.

"I know, he's your brother, it probably sounds weird. But I'm just so happy! We spent the whole night talking. We sat on this crappy little couch and talked and got closer and closer together. And I mean, we actually conversed—it wasn't just him monologuing about how great he is. He was genuinely interested in me, in my life, in everything about me. Eeeee!" She shrieked for what felt like forever, hitting the steering wheel with her palm. "I'm so excited!"

I unwrapped a few Jolly Ranchers and popped them in my mouth, then returned to my slightly-doubled-over posture.

"I'm sorry you missed the party, by the way. I wanted you to go!"

Sure, she did. If I'd gone, this never would have happened. She must have been thrilled that I'd stayed in. "It's okay. The couch was comfy. I slept well." I crunched one of the Jolly Ranchers in half, then quickly added, "I didn't even wake up when you came in."

"We walked from the frat back to his dorm, and it was magical. I wore his coat over mine, to keep warm, and we held hands, and he told me more about the campus and how much he thinks I'd like it if I get to come here in the fall. Then back in his room—"

"I do not want to hear about anything that happened in his room!" I interrupted, faking a laugh.

"No, no, we didn't have sex! We just fooled around."

"I said I didn't want to hear it!" I pressed my hands over my ears.

Pumpkin laughed. "Sorry! I won't say another word about it."

Her phone vibrated. When she glanced at it, her gaze got even gooier. I snuck a look, unsurprised to see my brother's name on the screen.

"You know," I said hesitantly, "he dated a few girls in high school for a while, and this one girl, Sienna? He broke her heart. She was always coming over crying, asking him to take her back."

Pumpkin's voice hardened a little. "So?"

I shrugged. "Just be careful, is all. I'd hate to see you that devastated."

"I know it's new. I know anything could happen. I just feel

so good! It's like, David who? Ha, I can't believe I was ever tempted to go back to him."

"That's great." Should I have been happy, too? Maybe. But I wasn't. Yesterday at lunch we'd been a triangle of friends, and now there was just a circle around the two of them, and I was on the outside. Ben had stolen my best friend. Pumpkin had stolen my brother. I didn't have anyone else. I sighed, and it turned into a groan.

Pumpkin's eyes darted over to me. "You okay?"

"Fine, fine. It's just—"

"What?"

"Nothing."

"*What*, Mighty?"

"Nothing." I paused. "But don't you think you might get bored?"

"You think I'm going to get *bored* of Ben?"

"Yeah. Like, you're the one who said it—he's too normal. Too mainstream."

"I just meant he didn't seem related to you, that's all." She brushed the comment aside. "And also, now I'm realizing that maybe I need someone different from me. Someone a little older and mature, someone with different interests, someone compatible, not identical."

"Whatever you say."

"What's that supposed to mean?"

"Nothing. Jeez."

The car descended into silence.

We were almost home. The stream of conversation Pumpkin and I usually maintained had dried up to a trickle. I'd spent most of the ride imagining how, when Ben was home for the summer, they'd spend every second together and I'd never see either of them. And next fall when Pumpkin was in college? Forget it. It would be like she'd never been my friend; she'd just be Ben's girlfriend. Ben already was too busy at college to talk to me as much as I wanted him to—it would only get worse if Pumpkin were on campus with him. I'd just be lonely in my house with zero friends.

"Hey. I want to say something." Pumpkin's voice was shaky. "It seems like you're almost mad or something that I got together with Ben."

I bit my lip. "I think I am."

"Why can't you just be happy for me? And for him?"

"It's just—I was so excited about this weekend. And now I don't even matter. It's like I'm the third wheel, but he's my brother. You should be the third wheel. Or, like, you're my friend. He should be the third wheel."

I'd sort of thought she'd feel bad for me, but her voice was harsh. "Maybe not everything needs to be about you, Mighty."

"Excuse me?" I crossed my arms in front of my chest and glared at her.

"All we talk about is what you're interested in: your crush on Spiny, your prospects as a jammer, your struggles in school. Any time I've tried to bring up stuff with David, it barely keeps your interest for, like, a second."

"That's because the David thing is pointless!" I erupted.

"You only think that because you're being selfish." Pumpkin's voice was annoyingly firm and calm.

"I can't believe you think I'm selfish. What about at practice last week? I worked with you on hitting for, like, twenty minutes."

"That's because you're obsessed with roller derby! You just want me to be better so the team is better."

"But you love it, too!"

"No, I really don't. I love roller skating, and playing derby is fine. But I'm not obsessed. You act like you're chill about it all, like you just want to have fun, too, but you don't." Her voice was rising in pitch with every word. "You're worse than Stork, because at least Stork is upfront about how single-minded she is. You're fake about it. You try to be everything to everyone, because all you want is for people to like you."

"I am not fake!"

"You are! You pretend like we're the same about derby, but you won't accept that I don't love it like you do."

"Maybe I just want you to care more so our team doesn't lose!" That wasn't true at all. She'd been right—I was mad that she didn't love derby like I did. But right now, I just wanted to hurt her.

"So you're saying I suck? That it will be my fault if we do bad at Soy Anything?" Her voice wasn't calm anymore, not even close.

"I didn't say you suck! That is so not fair!" I briefly put my hands over my face. "I got upset because you had sex with my brother, and somehow now you're yelling at me!"

"I didn't have sex with him!" She was shouting now.

"Oh my God, you know what I meant! You're being so thoughtless!" I was yelling, too, panting hard enough that my lungs hurt. I fished my inhaler out of my purse and took a quick puff.

We'd reached my neighborhood. I tried to slow my breathing. Pumpkin was quiet. She pulled into my driveway.

I muttered "Thanks for driving" and slid out of the car before she had time to respond.

CHAPTER 29

time until Soy Anything: 1 month, 4 days

I was still burning with anger when I woke the next day. I changed hurriedly into workout clothes, said a cursory good morning to my mom, who was working from home for the day, and ran out the door. There was too much fury burning up inside of me with no outlet. I needed to run. I needed to sweat.

I'd kept up the jogging habit I'd started a few weeks ago, tracking my speed and distance, trying to go a little farther or a little faster each time. Today, though, I didn't care how slow I was, or how many walk breaks I needed. I wasn't tracking any stats. I just needed to exhaust myself. *How dare she? How dare she?* My footsteps pounded out the rhythm of the words.

How could Pumpkin not understand how weird this would be for me? How much it would hurt? She'd basically chosen a guy over me and insulted me in the process. I puffed up a hill, my lungs burning.

The tips of my ears and my nose were cold, but the rest of me was radiating heat. I pulled off my jacket and tied it around my waist without breaking my stride. My anger was like a furnace inside of me. I kept running.

When I had no energy left in the tank, I came home. My arms and legs were shaking. My stomach was queasy, not a surprise since yesterday I'd eaten a greasy breakfast, about half a bag of Jolly Ranchers, and nearly nothing else. I'd also run farther than I'd ever gone before: past the nearby Mobil station, past the diner I'd skated to last fall, past our grocery store, up and down hills and in and out of neighborhoods I'd never seen before. I felt terrible and great at once. And I thought of Stork running to escape the chaos of her house. No wonder she was so fast.

"I was just starting to get worried," my mom said when I came in. "You've never been gone this long."

"Needed to run," I huffed, stripping down to my sports bra and shorts right in the foyer, my skin boiling.

She smiled. "You're becoming quite the runner. Maybe I'll come with you sometime."

I narrowed my eyes. "You?"

"I ran track in high school, you know. I really only stopped running when I got pregnant with Ben."

"That jerk," I said, joking but with too much venom in my voice. Then, forcing myself to turn my thoughts away from Ben, "My friend Stork runs track."

"What events?"

"Oh, there are different events? No idea." I used my discarded sweatshirt to sop up the sweat on my face, neck, and chest.

"Tell her I ran middle distance." She smiled, gazing off into, appropriately, the middle distance, as if reliving former glories. "I made it to State when I was a junior."

"Did you win your race, or whatever?"

"No, but it was still a great time. It was in the Quad Cities that year. Remember your Auntie Maggie?"

"Vaguely." She was a fake aunt, one who got to use the title because of a close friendship with my mom. I remembered going to her house a few times when I was little.

"Maggie and I roomed together and had the best time. We snuck out after curfew by climbing out the window. It was only the first floor, but we still felt wild."

My mom, sneaking out? I stared at her, then looked away and stretched my calves on the first stair, not wanting to break her reverie.

"We were supposed to meet these boys from another school

that Maggie had talked to earlier, but they never showed up. So instead, we walked along the Mississippi and stayed up until dawn. It was wonderful." She looked at me wryly. "Don't think this means I approve of you doing anything like that when you go to your tournament."

"I know that, come on." It hurt to picture the tournament. Pumpkin and I could have been sneaking out, having adventures. She probably hated me now.

I headed upstairs to shower, texting Stork as I walked. *What are your track events? My mom just told me she ran track and did middle distance.*

She got right back to me. *I'm a sprinter. But it'd be cool to be a long-distance runner. The steeplechase? How cool!*

I had no idea what a steeplechase was. *When does your season start?* I didn't want to be surprised if she wasn't doing it, like I had been with Ben and baseball.

Next week! But no meets till April.

Well let me know. I'll come cheer for you.

On a whim, I yelled downstairs to my mom. "Can Stork come over for dinner tonight?"

Her footsteps echoed down the hall as she approached, climbing halfway up the stairs before she spoke, apparently unwilling to shout her response. "I was just going to do leftovers, but if she's okay with that, then sure. And if she's going to hang out in your room, please clean it up first. It's getting messy again."

I wanted to protest, but the last thing I needed was for my bedroom to remind Stork of her dad's hoarding problem.

Want to come over for dinner?

Sure! But I have to be home by eight—lots of homework.

That settled, I set about doing a speed-clean of my room before she arrived.

When the doorbell rang several hours later and I opened the door to see Stork on my porch, I knew immediately something looked different about her. But it took me a few moments to figure it out.

"That's it!" I said, staring at her. "This is the first time I've ever seen you wear something besides workout clothes!"

She unwound a wooly scarf from her neck and tucked it in her purse. "It happens sometimes. Like maybe once a month." She smiled. She was wearing a flowered dress layered over a tight long-sleeved T-shirt, and a pair of brown ankle boots. I wouldn't have guessed she was the flowered-dress type. Her blonde hair was loose and flowing over her shoulders, not pulled back in her usual scruffy ponytail.

"You look nice." I smiled back. "Not that there's anything wrong with workout clothes." I had showered after my run, of course, then changed straight back into sweatpants, a sports bra, and a tank top that said *World's Okayest Skater*. I'd stopped wearing that shirt to practices after my talk with Ann, afraid she'd see it as more evidence of me putting myself down, but I still thought it was funny. "Come on in. We're about to eat."

It was actually great to have Stork at the table with my mom and me. My mom asked Stork questions about school and sports. Stork asked questions about my mom's years doing track. I asked them both about how to get better at running. The conversation flowed. I pushed my fight with Pumpkin out of my mind.

"How nice," my mom said, pouring herself a glass of white wine after she finished her food. "We have a sprinter, a middle-distance runner, and a long-distance runner."

I made a face. "I'm not a long-distance runner."

"From what you told me of your route today, you ran over six miles. That's just about the longest distance track event—10,000 meters. Sorry, Millie, you're a long-distance runner."

Stork grinned and nudged my elbow with hers. "Your mom's right. Anyway, if it makes you feel better, the cross-country kids run way farther. You definitely wouldn't be long distance there."

"Come on, Stork. Why would that make me feel better?" I always thought things like this when she spoke; today I said them out loud.

"Good point." She blushed a little, rather charmingly. I thought of when I'd made her blush during practice, when her body had been pressed against mine.

"Well, ladies, I'm off to take a long bath, drink this wine, and read a mystery novel. Melanie, it was lovely to meet you. Millie, please finish loading the dishwasher before you go to bed."

Stork was sitting with her legs twisted up under her, like some sort of yoga bird. My mom had made her a cup of chamomile tea, and she was cupping it with both hands. It was odd to see her in my kitchen, when I thought about it. But I liked it.

"How was your weekend?" she asked.

I got up quickly, putting plates into the dishwasher. The distance I'd gotten from my thoughts about the fight disappeared. My eyes burned with tears. "Fine." I hiccupped, betraying myself. "It's just—I got into a fight with Pumpkin."

"Oh no. I'm so sorry." Stork's voice was gentle.

"I don't want to talk about it, though!"

I was sure she would press me. It's what I would have done in her position. But instead, she said, "Of course. We don't even have to talk about derby at all."

Did she assume the fight had been about roller derby? Well, I supposed it partially was, but only because Pumpkin forced it to be.

"Do you have any board games?" Stork continued. "We could play one, if you want. I don't need to leave for a while yet."

With relief blossoming in my chest, I went to find one.

"Scrabble? Jenga? Scattegories?" I stood on my tiptoes to see the top shelf of our hall closet.

"How about Trivial Pursuit?" Stork was standing behind me, looking over my shoulder.

Trivial Pursuit was at the top of the stack. I struggled to grab it, then felt Stork's arm brush past mine. The hairs on my arm stood up a bit, and I stifled a pleasant shiver.

"Let the tall girl grab it," she said.

I grinned and stepped back.

It turned out to be an old edition, where all the questions were about things that had happened before we were born. We were both terrible at it, eventually giving up when half an hour had passed and neither of us had collected any pie pieces. Scrabble went better. Words were words.

We stayed mostly quiet as we played, talking only a little and not joking around much at all. But it wasn't bad. It was peaceful. Her shaggy blonde hair kept falling in her face as she looked at her tiles, and she would push it back behind her ear with her left hand, the exact same gesture each time, over and over. I wanted to offer her a hair clip but thought that might have been weird, like she'd think I'd been staring at her too much.

Stork stayed till 8:15, only leaving when I pointed out the time and reminded her of her earlier comment about homework. I didn't want her to leave, which made me somehow feel it was even more important to let her know she should go.

I walked her to the door.

"I'm sorry about your fight with Pumpkin," she said. "I know how important she is to you."

My eyes, once again, welled up with tears.

"I'm sure you'll patch things up." Stork dug out her car keys from her purse. "See you at practice on Wednesday?"

I had an odd feeling like I should hug her goodbye, or perhaps cling to her and sob. Instead, wisely, I just waved. "See you at practice."

CHAPTER 30

time until Soy Anything: 1 month, 2 days

Maybe Pumpkin won't be here, I thought as I climbed out of my mom's car at the rink. She'd made it clear she didn't love derby. Maybe she had quit. That would be a relief. Right?

My whole body ached, with both emotion and the strain of having run six miles a couple days prior. I didn't want Pumpkin to quit. I wanted her to apologize dramatically, swear the night with Ben had been a mistake, and, perhaps, promise to go to college in Chicago instead of at U of I.

There she was, pulling on her skates at a table near Toni and Luna rather than in our usual spot. I glanced at her. She caught my eye. I nodded hello, and she gave me a tight-lipped smile. At least she'd acknowledged me.

I was slowly weaving back and forth across the track, warming up my feet, when Cleo appeared in front of me, also in skates.

"Hey," she said briskly, doing stylish backward crossovers across the track as she spoke. "I want to see you blocking a lot today at practice."

My heart sank. "Why?"

"You've been jamming a lot in the past few games, but we need you ready to block, too. You're going to block at least part of the time at Soy Anything, and in Friday's game against DeKalb, too."

She was gone, skating swiftly away, before I could protest.

I took a slow, deep breath and thought about what I'd told Ben. *Play the game for the game's sake.* If I was being honest with myself, it was at least half-ego that made me only want to jam. I liked blocking, too, especially when I was on the track with Gables and I didn't have to think. And in the handful of games we'd played since our disastrous encounter with the Sonics, my mind had reliably descended into panicky chaos each time I jammed.

Stork stood next to me during the coaches' announcements and intros. I was glad.

"Lots of scrimmage-type drills today," Cleo said. "I want to get as much repetition in as we can." She tossed green pinnies to half of us. "Put those on and let's get started."

I struggled into mine. "These smell terrible."

"Well, don't smell them!" Gables said, watching me and making a face. "Jesus, Mighty."

Pumpkin was on the gray team, which just meant the not-green-pinnies team. I was glad it had happened that way, especially since I was going to be blocking. We'd both be in groups of other blockers, focusing on the opposing jammers, not being forced into interactions.

I worked with Gables a lot at first, sticking to her like glue. She was great at communicating and, if that failed, physically shoving me where I needed to go. Then two people on the gray team had to leave early, and Gables moved over there to balance things out.

I went out on the track to block with Stork, Pay, and Luna. Rainbow was jamming for us, and Toni was jamming for gray.

Toni, lined up behind the jam line, was already breathing heavy. "I need a break after this jam," she called to Cleo. "My ankle is bothering me a little."

"Don't believe her," Luna said, shifting into a deeper stance and grinning. "She's just trying to get us to lower our guard. Aren't you, Toni?"

Toni stuck out her tongue at Luna, then crouched down, ready to sprint.

"Five seconds!" Cleo yelled.

I formed a tripod with Luna and Stork. When the whistle blew, Toni aimed at the space between Stork and me, and the two of us quickly closed it. When she moved to the middle, Stork shuffled over quickly, taking up the space. Distantly, I noted the double whistle blast from ahead of us; Rainbow had gotten lead for our team! Toni tried the outside, was caught by Pay and a rapidly moving Stork, then aimed for me again.

I stayed low and swung my hips to the left, smashing into Toni just as she passed me, knocking her out of bounds hard enough that she dropped to her knees.

"Nice," she said as she climbed to her feet.

"Thanks!" I smiled.

In the second it took for me to feel pleased with myself, Toni hit me hard in the ribs and darted past me. I groaned. But Rainbow had come around, scored points, and now called the jam off safely before Toni could score.

All of us blockers high-fived as we skated off the track.

"That was a good hit you got on Toni," Stork said.

I took a gulp of water from my bottle. "Thanks! It felt good."

"Yeah," Luna laughed. "Just don't let her distract you with flattery next time."

I laughed, too. "Sorry."

"Hey, Mighty, cute shorts!" Toni said, coming up behind us and quickly snatching my water bottle. "It works again! Flattery does distract her!"

It became a joke for the rest of practice; people kept complimenting me for random things and then trying to hit me or take my stuff or knock me out of position. It was one of the most fun and funny practices I'd had in a while—as long as I ignored the fact that Pumpkin and I weren't speaking. A few times I caught Pumpkin's eye, and she smiled, but it was tight, guarded, not joining in the joke. There was ice between us.

I ducked out of practice quickly, de-gearing before Pumpkin was even off the track.

Since I was in such a hurry to leave, I didn't even look at my phone until I was in my mom's car. A message from Spiny was waiting for me!

Hey, babe—she called me babe again!—*looking forward to Saturday! Can we meet at the restaurant? I'll be coming in from out of town.*

Damn this fight with Pumpkin. If we'd still been friends, I could have asked her to drop me off. Then I thought about her accusations of selfishness. Had I asked her for too much in my quest to date Spiny? I'd thought she was as excited about it as I was.

I looked covertly at my mom as she drove. There was no way, absolutely no way, I could ask her to drive me. Actually, next weekend I'd be at my dad's. But I wasn't going to ask him, either. Have a parent drop me off on a date? When I was trying to maintain the fiction that I was eighteen? There could be nothing worse.

Maybe I could tell Spiny no, sorry, my car was in the shop, I needed her to pick me up. But I didn't like that idea. I didn't want to be needy, or demanding, or weird; I wasn't sure how it would come across to her, but I doubted it would be good.

I pictured being at my dad's, getting ready for my date, putting on makeup in his bathroom mirror. How bad would it be for him to drive me? It wouldn't be worse than canceling, right? Maybe?

Then I got another idea. My heart pounded as I messaged Spiny back.

No prob! Looking forward to it!

Oh, it was risky, so risky. But also, so good. I wished I could tell Pumpkin. This was going to be scary to plot on my own.

CHAPTER 31

time until Soy Anything: 28 days

I had my license, I had a car, and I was going to drive it. It was that simple.

"I'm going over to Pumpkin's tonight, remember?" I called to my dad as I rummaged through my overnight bag, pulling out my makeup. "She's picking me up soon."

"What time will you be home?"

"By midnight at the latest. That okay?"

"Midnight at the absolute latest."

I got dressed in jeans and my Windy City Rollers T-shirt—nothing flashy, but only because I didn't want to look like I was trying too hard—did my makeup, then stood by his front window, pretending to look for Pumpkin's car. Luckily, it was already dark out. The time change was next weekend, and that would've made my ruse a lot more difficult.

"There she is!" I cried, grabbing my purse and dashing out the door. "See you later!"

My dad kept my car in a parking lot that was on the grounds of his apartment complex but far away from his actual apartment. I'd studied a satellite view of the complex online this morning, making sure I could find my way there. In the dark, on the ground, it was more difficult than I'd envisioned. The streetlights only lit the paths around the actual apartment buildings. I had to veer off into the darkness and cut across a dark expanse of grass before I reached the lot.

But there it was. My car. Brown, four-door, and wonderful.

It wasn't unreasonable for me to drive it; it was mine, after all. I unlocked it and climbed in.

I'd driven it before, with my dad, of course. Tonight, it seemed so much bigger and unfamiliar. The hood loomed in front of me, sticking out what felt like ten feet. When I started the engine, the interior lights glowed yellow in the darkness, too brightly.

"You can do this," I coached myself. "You know how to drive."

I bit my lip in concentration, pulled out of the lot, and wove my way through the apartment complex, careful to steer clear of my dad's building. It was so dark. How had I never realized how dark it was before? Even now that I'd turned onto a bigger road?

Then I saw an oncoming car flash its lights and realized I'd never turned my headlights on. I hastily flipped the switch with shaking hands. That could've been bad.

I'd never driven alone. And even with my lights on, everything looked different: larger, brighter, more aggressive. A truck passed me in the left lane, and I screamed as it barreled by.

But it wasn't far to the restaurant. Fifteen minutes. I'd survive. I had to. If I died, I wouldn't get to go on my date with Spiny.

Spiny was already there when I arrived, sitting in a booth, unwinding a long, striped scarf from around her neck. She beckoned me over, grinning her sexy crooked grin.

I slid into the booth, the vinyl squeaking as I moved. The reality of what I was doing was hitting me. I had to sit across from her for a whole meal? What would we talk about? What if I got parsley in my teeth? Something not unrelated to horror was mixing in with my excitement.

"One more month till your tournament, right?" she asked. "How are practices going? Are you nervous?"

"I am nervous!" I exclaimed, laughing. It felt good to say it, even if she meant about the tournament and I meant about this date. "I've been jamming a lot at practices, but Cleo wants me to practice blocking, too. She's the one making the decisions about jammers, and she says I might not get to jam at Soy Anything. I'm not especially good at it."

It didn't hurt to say this, mostly because I couldn't feel anything beyond a mix of terror and excitement at my proximity to Spiny.

"And I did have fun blocking in our game against DeKalb last night," I continued. The game had been a breath of fresh air. I played well, the other team was friendly, and we won, albeit narrowly. Pumpkin wasn't there; I didn't know if she had chosen to skip it or if she hadn't made the roster. The DeKalb team voted Stork as "Most Valuable Pivot" in the post-game awards, and Stork's eyes had shone with tears when she collected the silly plastic trophy shaped like an ear of corn. It made me smile again now, thinking of it.

"Blocking is underrated. I love being a blocker. You get to crush jammers' souls. There's nothing better than some hot-stuff jammer thinking they're safe, then catching them at the front of the pack and just laying them out!" Spiny waved her arm, implying a big hit. Her nails were painted blue, I noticed, and she had a tattoo of a mermaid snaking up her forearm. Unlike Gables, who I suspected had gotten her tattoo in some shady way, Spiny was a legal adult and had been able to just walk into a tattoo parlor and ask for that tattoo. How was she going to keep believing I was also eighteen?

"That does sound nice, laying out jammers like that. Better than being the one getting constantly laid out, anyway." I laughed, a weird little gasping laugh that didn't sound like my own. "I slid about five feet on my stomach when Gables hit me at practice last week."

The waitress, a woman around my mom's age with a sleek black ponytail, arrived to take our order. Could she tell we were on a date? Could everyone? I hurriedly flipped through the menu, choosing the Vegetarian Mezze Platter almost at random.

Spiny took her time, asking the waitress questions about the specials, about her favorite dish. She was a picture of relaxed confidence. I was sure that I was a picture of teenage anxiety.

"We had an away game in Appleton last night," Spiny said, once the waitress had left. "Want to hear about it?"

"Sure!"

She told me the highlights of the game, not bragging about her performance but not putting herself down, either. I chewed on the straw in my water glass, listening and nodding at appropriate times. Slowly, my heart rate was coming down. This wasn't so bad. It was just two people talking. Well, okay, it was one person talking and one person nodding. Still, it was easy.

When our food arrived, I relaxed further. Something to do. I ripped off a piece of pita bread and dipped it in hummus. "You said you wanted to be an EMT, right? What sort of training do you need?" Was it weird that I remembered this detail? She'd only said it once. Maybe that was weird.

"Oh, I started in January, and it's been great! I finished high school a semester early, and I didn't see any reason to wait. It feels good to be getting a start on real life, you know?"

She dove into an anecdote about her training. I chewed my food, listened, and made appropriate "interested" noises, while mentally preparing for how I'd answer any questions she asked me about school.

But she didn't ask, just told me more details about her EMT classes, eventually segueing into stories of how she'd assisted injured teammates at derby practices.

"So she ended up with a spiral fracture—hey!" Spiny

interrupted herself. "You didn't get any potatoes." She scooted her plate across the table. "Try mine."

I stabbed a potato with my fork and took a bite. It was tender, lemony, and herby, with nice roasted edges. "It's really good!"

"Take more!" Her eyes met mine over the plate. They were deep blue green, long lashed. A lock of bleached hair fell across her face, reminding me, randomly, of Stork's hair when we'd played board games at my house. I smiled reflexively, stabbing another potato.

I hadn't told Stork about my date with Spiny. I'd thought about telling her—surely she'd have questions she'd want me to ask about derby strategy, if nothing else—but I hadn't. It felt weird, somehow.

When the check came, Spiny snatched it before I could look at it, and handed the waitress her credit card.

"It's not too late. Want to come over to my place for a bit? I could show you those clips of the old Gotham and Victoria game I was talking about."

I could have easily looked up the clips she'd mentioned on my phone. She just wanted me to come over. I smiled. "Sounds good. I'll follow you."

It wasn't a far drive, and I remembered to turn on my headlights. Her neighborhood had big, expensive-looking houses and no sidewalks. I parked behind her in a long, smooth driveway.

"This way," she said, bypassing the well-lit front door to head around the side of the house. I followed her down a small set of stairs and through a heavy door, staying close.

"My parents had the downstairs and basement turned into a separate apartment for my grandmother, but she never moved in, so I got to take it," Spiny explained, moving through the apartment, turning on lights. "Rachel is around here somewhere."

"Rachel?" A flash of fear that she meant her toxic ex.

"Ah! Here she is!" Spiny bent down behind a recliner and picked up a fluffy black cat. Thank God. "Rachel, meet Mighty. Mighty, Rachel. I adopted her when I first started derby, and I named her after Rachel Rotten, that hot Angel City jammer. I was such a dorky fangirl. Isn't that embarrassing?" She grinned, not looking remotely embarrassed.

"Pleased to meet you, Rachel." I scratched the cat behind her ears, coming closer to Spiny in the process.

She looked in my eyes again, a hint of her earlier smile clinging to her lips. When she spoke, we were close enough that her breath lightly touched on my face. "Want a drink?"

"Sure!" I said quickly, too loudly, breaking the tension.

She passed me Rachel, and I clutched the cat to me. She was warm, solid, and comforting. I stayed in the middle of the living room, squeezing Rachel, while Spiny wandered into the kitchen. The apartment was tiny and open, so I watched her go.

"Beer? Wine? Coke or Sprite? Water?" Her voice came from behind the fridge door.

Her parents let her have her own separate space, and they let her keep alcohol down here, too? My God, I couldn't imagine that sort of relationship.

"I'll have a Coke," I said quickly. The last thing I wanted to do was fall asleep and drool all over her couch like I'd done at Marie's place.

She came back in carrying two glasses of Coke with ice. I appreciated that she wasn't drinking alcohol, either. I set Rachel down and took my glass from her.

"Oh, sorry, let me move some things so we can sit down." Her couch, I realized, was completely covered in derby gear. The apartment wasn't a mess, but there was derby stuff everywhere: wheels on the coffee table, two different helmets—one green and shiny, one gray and covered with stickers—on one side of the couch, jerseys on the other side, a stack of flyers on the recliner.

She folded the jerseys and put them on top of the flyers. "I always lay them out to dry. They're too expensive to risk shrinking them."

I sat down on the empty couch cushion, and she sat next to me, only shoving the helmets over a little bit. We were within inches of each other.

I took a deep drink of my Coke. Something was going to happen. That's why I was here. It was clear, suddenly, a moment of no return. Did I want something to happen with Spiny? Of course. I mean, it was Spiny. Of course I wanted something to happen. My hands were shaky, and I gripped the glass of Coke tighter to hide it.

She reached behind me to grab a TV remote and to dim the floor lamp behind the couch. The fabric of her sweater grazed my neck as she stretched. "I'll put the game on."

The old Gotham vs. Victoria game started. Two thirty-minute halves, the timer counting down right there on the screen.

At 27:30 remaining on the clock, our upper arms were touching.

By 24:15, we were leaning against each other.

At 18:17, she said, "See, the announcer said Curly Burly is an aged-up Junior. Junior derby programs, that's how great skaters are created." And with that pronouncement, she put her arm around me.

My heart hammered. Was my inhaler in my purse? But my lungs didn't feel tight. It was just that every cell in my body felt alive, electrified. I sat stiffly at first, then slowly relaxed against her body. Her sweater was soft, her body firm underneath it.

At 14:02, Rachel hopped up on the couch and lay down across our laps. We laughed and watched the rest of the first half like that. This was nice. Comfortable. I could survive this. Oh, what a thing to think, survival. I should be excited, not terrified!

Half-time. She paused the video and set Rachel onto the ground. Then, in a swift motion, she leaned in and kissed me.

It's happening! My brain screamed. Her lips were so soft, her touch light, careful. We kept kissing. Slowly, she pulled me closer, and our arms wrapped around each other. She kissed me deeply, passionately. I was making out with Spiny! My body was flooded with electricity. I pulled myself even tighter against her, let my fingers curl into the inch of bare skin exposed at her waist. I had a brief, manic desire to text Pumpkin to tell her about this, then a moment of sadness when I remembered I shouldn't.

After a few minutes, Spiny stopped. "Do you want... to go in the bedroom?" Her forehead was pressed to mine, her voice a whisper.

My heart pounded. "Yeah," I whispered back.

"Give me one second. I just need to use the restroom." She kissed me once more on the lips, then on the neck, then scampered off across the hall.

I sat up straight, smoothed my hands over my thighs, pulled an errant strand of green hair off my T-shirt, and tucked my hair behind my ears. This was it. For real. It had been a fantasy for so long. It was hard to believe it was actually happening. I pinched the skin on my forearm, hard, and it left a satisfying red mark. This wasn't a dream.

Then, an odd gurgle in my stomach. Why did I suddenly feel like I was going to be sick? Was the Greek food not sitting right? I'd felt fine at the restaurant! What if she took me into her bedroom, got naked, and then I puked all over her? Or... worse? I'd die, I'd literally die. My stomach gurgled again.

I took a slow, deep breath, then another. I wasn't sick, I told myself. I was fine. I was about to hook up with Spiny. But my insides continued to churn.

When she stepped out of the bathroom, I jumped to my feet. "I'm so sorry, but I think I need to go. I'm suddenly not feeling well. Bad ... headache." I couldn't tell her it was my stomach; I didn't want her to picture me on the toilet.

"Oh, gosh. Okay." She looked more concerned than disappointed, which I appreciated. "Are you okay to drive? Do you need a ride home?"

"No, no, I can drive." I shook my head vigorously. "I'm really sorry for cutting things off."

"It's no problem. Rain check?"

"Of course."

She pecked me on the cheek and walked me to the door.

I drove back to my dad's apartment in a weird, messy headspace. My stomachache got weaker the farther I got from Spiny's.

The roads were emptier now, and several of the stoplights had switched to blinking yellow lights instead. I was cautious but no longer panicked like I'd been on the drive to the restaurant. I did know how to drive. The car didn't feel foreign and frightening anymore.

I wanted to tell Pumpkin about tonight so badly. What would she think? Would she be disappointed I'd had to interrupt my night with Spiny? Would she think it was kind of funny? I wondered what she was doing right now. Had she told Ben about our fight? Had she told David it was over for good?

And then Stork popped into my mind, because that was apparently what she did lately, show up in my thoughts at a million random moments. Stork would have loved hearing Spiny's thoughts about the Gotham vs. Victoria game. I bet she would have had a thousand questions. I wished she could've been there. Actually, I wished I could hang out with her right now. The night we'd played board games had been so chill, so nice in its uneventfulness.

Hanging out with Stork didn't fill my body with electricity, but it did something different, something bigger. It was as if my brain was a snow globe, so often shaken and filled with chaos, but when I was with her, the glitter settled peacefully onto the ground, leaving me steady and clear, the best version of myself.

I pulled into my dad's apartment complex, turning the steering wheel smoothly, like a pro. Maybe I could text Stork once I was inside. It was only eleven, not too late. She was probably still awake. Maybe after derby practice and going to the gym tomorrow, she'd want to hang out. We could watch that Gotham game together, and I could tell her all the things I'd learned. She could come to my dad's, or I could go to her house, if she didn't feel too weird about it.

I parked in the lot and made my way through the darkness back to my dad's building.

To get inside, I had to walk by my dad's living room window. To my surprise, every light was on. He typically was asleep by ten. There were two figures silhouetted in the window, both staring out into the darkness. My dad and—I paused. The blinds were open, so it was easy to see her.

My mom was here.

This was very bad.

CHAPTER 32

Shouting erupted as soon as I opened the door. All questions.

"Where have you been?"

"What were you doing?"

"What were you thinking?"

"Were you even thinking at all?"

I'd heard my parents shout plenty of times, but it had only been at each other. The unification of their anger took me by surprise.

"I was out with a friend!" I shouted back. "I took the car because it belongs to me, and I have a license, and I'm sick of not getting to use it!"

"You lied to me!" My dad's face was red with fury. "If I hadn't called your mother—"

"If that Pumpkin girl hadn't shown up at our house—" my mom jumped in.

"What? What about Pumpkin?" I stared at her, willing the words out of her mouth. Why had Pumpkin come over? Was it about me or somehow related to Ben?

But those weren't the details my mom cared about. She batted my question away. "I happened to be on the phone with your dad, discussing some financial matters, when she came by. She said she wanted to talk to you about something in person, and when I told your dad who was at my door—"

"You lied to me!" my dad interrupted, repeating himself. "The first thing I did, after your mom told me Pumpkin had come over, was check to see if your car was here."

"What are you hiding, Millie?" my mom asked. "What is going on?"

I stood in the entryway, feet planted firmly, hands on my hips like a superhero. "I'm not hiding anything!"

"Then why did you lie?"

"I was on a date, okay? With a girl from my derby league. And I didn't want to have my dad drop me off because it would be embarrassing. There." I flung up my hands. "That's it. That's my big secret!"

"Who is this girl? Is it that sprinter, Melanie?" my mom asked.

"Who's Melanie?" My dad's voice rose higher. He looked at my mom, directing his fury briefly to her. "Why haven't I heard about this?"

"No! Stork—Melanie—is just a friend." I blushed as I said it. "My date's name is Spineapple, or Erica, rather, but you don't have to worry about it, because we aren't going to keep dating." Why did I say this? To get them off my back? Or did I truly feel it in my gut?

"Why should we believe you?" my mom said at the same time as my dad said, "Why? What aren't you telling us? This doesn't add up."

"It's not a big deal! You want honesty? She's too old for me. That's it." That wasn't it, or at least it wasn't the only reason. But as I spoke, I knew I shouldn't keep dating Spiny. Imagining going out with her again made me feel worse than I already did.

But I shouldn't have mentioned that she was older. It was as if I'd announced she was a serial killer. My mom reached out and grabbed my dad's arm for support. "How old is this girl? This woman?"

"She's eighteen, and it's not a big deal. But it doesn't matter because I'm not going to date her! As I said!"

"Eighteen is *Ben's* age. My God. What high school does she go to?"

I answered honestly, for some reason. "She graduated early. She's doing EMT training now."

My mom clutched her head. "You stole a car to go on a date with an *adult*—"

"It's my car! I didn't steal it!" My whole body was on fire. I felt like I could shoot lightning from my hands.

She shook her head again. "You are in so much trouble. So much."

"Do you realize," my dad said, "that you could have died?"

"Spineapple is not a murderer!" I would have laughed if I weren't so angry.

My dad pressed his fingers to his temples. "I meant that you could have gotten into a car accident. And we would have had no idea where you were. What do you think that would have been like for us?"

"I know how to drive!" This was ridiculous.

"Getting your license makes you immortal, does it?" snapped my mom. "And you know you aren't insured on that car yet, right? What if you'd hit someone's car? Did you have a plan for that?"

I hadn't thought about insurance. It still seemed like they were making way too big of a deal about this, but I threw my hands in the air again, giving up. "Fine, you're right. I shouldn't have done it." I heaved a huge sigh. "I'm sorry, okay? Can we be done with this?"

My parents looked at each other and shook their heads, identical anger writ large on their faces. They normally disagreed about everything. *Now* they were uniting?

"No, we are not done with this," said my mom in a low voice.

"You think there aren't consequences for doing this, for scaring us like this?" my dad added.

No. A chill ran down my arms. I knew what they were going to say before they said it.

"You aren't going to that tournament." My dad spoke, and my mom nodded along with his words.

"But I have to!" I gasped, already starting to cry. "I need to! My team needs me."

"You should've thought of that before you pulled this stunt tonight."

"This isn't fair!"

"It wasn't fair to us to scare us like this!" my mom said, her voice suddenly tearful as well. My dad put a hand on her shoulder, supportive. It would've shocked me if I weren't so upset.

"But derby—" I lost the words, choking on my tears.

"Derby has scared me from the start," my mom continued. "This is for the best. I have never been comfortable with how dangerous it is."

"It's not dangerous!" I shouted, the words coming out mangled through my sobs.

"Millie." My dad's voice was calm. "You're over-wrought. It's time you get some sleep."

"He's right." My mom nodded. "We can talk more in the morning."

"You mean you might change your mind? About the tournament?"

They shook their heads no in unison.

"Go get some sleep, Millie."

I fled the room, not because I wanted to obey them, but because I couldn't stand to look at them a second longer.

My stomach ached, my head ached, my face was raw and puffy from crying, and I was so tired my eyes were closing on their own. But before I could sleep, I needed to message Pumpkin.

My mom said you came over tonight. I was at my dad's.

Let her be awake. Let her say everything was okay, we were friends again, our fight was forgotten. What would I do without her as my friend? I flopped on my back and set my phone on my stomach, waiting.

Waiting.

I wasn't so mad at her anymore, I realized. Hurt, yeah, but not angry. I just wanted everything to go back to the way it was before she kissed Ben, an impossibility. Was she still mad at me? Had she come over so she could yell at me more in person? Even imagining it made my stomach hurt again, an echo of the pain I'd felt in Spiny's apartment.

I looked at my phone, made sure I hadn't missed a reply. Nope. I was so tired, but I wasn't going to sleep until Pumpkin wrote.

Hey, I messaged Stork, *I watched an old Gotham/Victoria game tonight. Can't wait to tell you about it.*

Stork replied immediately. The sight of her message popping up gave my heart a pleasant little blip, a brief break from the mess of hurt and anger I was stewing in.

Hey Mighty! I'm in bed, going to sleep. Text me tomorrow? Can't wait to hear about it.

I imagined Stork in her bed, under her blue-and-white flowered blanket, in that oasis of calm and order amidst her overstuffed house. My face curved into a smile as I read her text again. She could have just waited till morning to reply. It was nice that she hadn't.

How could I tell Stork I wasn't going to the tournament? Pumpkin would probably be relieved, so she could have Ben come cheer her on without me there to make it weird. Maybe some other people on the team would be relieved, too; they wouldn't have to worry about me screwing up an important game. But Stork? I thought she'd want me there, no matter how bad my performance might be.

My phone buzzed again. Stork, still awake?

Pumpkin.

Yeah, I came over. I wanted to talk to you.

I waited for more, but that was it.

Giving up on her explaining further, I wrote back, *I'd told my parents I was with you, when I was out with Spiny. We got in a big fight when I got home.*

God, I just wanted to tell her all about everything, from the moment I'd snuck out until right now in bed.

You never told me I was your cover story. I didn't get you in trouble on purpose.

I know.

Tone was so hard to read over text. Did she think I was mad at her because I'd fought with my parents? Was she mad at me?

After a long wait, she sent one more message. *See you at practice tomorrow.*

I didn't know if I'd be allowed at practice. While my parents banned me from the tournament, they hadn't said anything about practice. I thought about explaining all this to Pumpkin, but instead just typed, *Yeah.*

No mention of what she'd wanted to say to me. I wasn't brave enough to ask. I let my phone drop from my hands and fell into a fitful sleep.

CHAPTER 33

time until Soy Anything: 27 days

My parents didn't ban me from practices, but it almost didn't matter. I was a zombie on the track, barely functioning. I may as well have stayed home. Pumpkin gave me a tight smile when I arrived but continued to carefully ignore me during drills. Stork gave me several puzzled, questioning looks. It was as if it was autumn again, my every movement wobbly and insecure. Dizziness washed over me, and I slowed to a stop and leaned against the wall. I squeezed my eyes tight to compose myself, get my balance.

Ann pulled me to the side after the third time I sloppily cut the track during a drill.

"You okay? You're having an off day."

This was the time when I would tell her I couldn't go to Soy Anything. She'd understand how upset I was, and she'd start mentally rearranging her roster assignments. Maybe she'd even pull me aside again for a heart-to-heart. I could confess how much it hurt to have to miss the tournament. She could tell me that it would be okay, there were more tournaments in my future. Maybe opening up to someone, especially someone as kind as Ann, would make me feel the tiniest bit better.

I couldn't do it.

"Sorry, Ann. Just a bad night's sleep, that's all." I skated away from her, my head ducked so no one would notice the tears leaking down my face.

After practice, Pumpkin de-geared near Toni and Luna

again, and I de-geared in a random corner; our typical corner with the Slushie stain remained empty.

Charter skaters filtered into the building as the Juniors departed. I was packing up the last of my things when arms wrapped around my waist from behind.

"Hey there, you."

I spun around. It was Spiny, looking fresh and smelling like bubblegum in a sleeveless Prairie Skate Rollers hoodie.

"Hey." I smiled, trying and, I was sure, failing to seem normal.

"You feeling better today?"

"Huh? Oh, yeah, my headache last night. No, it's fine now. Must've been some random thing."

"Glad to hear it. I've got to gear up for practice, but I wanted to pop over and say hi first." She darted her head in and planted a full kiss on my mouth, long and slow, then walked away.

Wow. She'd just kissed me in front of my whole team—only the coaches, who were in the basement putting away equipment, had missed it. Clearly my hasty departure last night hadn't repelled her.

This was the sort of thing I'd fantasized about for months. The future I'd imagined for us had never been closer to possible. The apartment we'd share in Chicago, the parties we'd throw with our teammates, the way she'd kiss me when I walked in the door—all the details were still so vivid. But so was the way my stomach had ached last night in her apartment, a stomachache that had disappeared as soon as I'd left. Even if I hadn't had to contend with my parents' objections, how could I keep dating her? Something about it just wasn't right.

I heaved my gear bag over my shoulder and glanced across the rink, and that's when I locked eyes with Stork.

I'd never seen her face like this, so drawn, so hurt. She bit her lip, then quickly looked away.

I froze. My mouth was open, wanting to call out to her, but I didn't know what to say. She walked out of the rink, her head turned to avoid my gaze and her shoulders slumped. What had I done?

My grades came in at the end of the following week, and I'd just barely scraped a 3.0. Spiny had texted a few times, her words light and flirty. I'd been running almost every day, and I could tell I was getting faster.

I had all the ingredients for happiness. I had a sort-of girlfriend! I was stronger and fitter! I even had access to my car—under extremely limited conditions for now, like running errands for my parents, but still, a car! But I kept feeling like garbage.

I knew I needed to end things with Spiny before they went any further. I knew I needed to tell Ann and Cleo that I couldn't go to the tournament. But I had no clue how to face either of those conversations.

My mom printed off my grade report and stuck it on the fridge. She clearly thought I'd be pleased. But why would I? Where would I go? Things were bad with Pumpkin, weird with Stork, and I couldn't go to Soy Anything . . . even if I'd been allowed to drive wherever I wanted, there was nowhere for me to go.

The tournament was just a few weeks away. I needed to tell the coaches I was out. It couldn't wait any longer. I sat in bed, blankets piled over my legs, and tapped out a message on my laptop.

Hey, Ann and Cleo. I have something to tell you. I'm really sorry.

I paused, unsure of how to go on, then deleted the words. Then tried again. Then deleted that attempt and shut my laptop.

I'd been crying off and on for days now, whenever I was home alone. My eyes and cheeks were puffy to the touch. My head was a mess. I kept flashing back to my conversation with Ben last December: How did you know if you were choosing the right person? How could you recognize if you were on a path that ended in mutual loathing and divorce?

More to the point: Was I doomed to screw up my love life, just like my parents had? Was there any way to unknot the tangle of feelings inside my chest? I put my face in my hands as the tears started again.

When they passed, I pulled out my phone, deciding it was time to rip the other uncomfortable-conversation Band-Aid off. I was already miserable; what was the difference if I added on one more painful thing?

Can we talk? Can you come over?

Spiny responded almost immediately.

Sure! I'll swing by on my way home from work this afternoon.

It was time to end whatever it was I had with her. Though I still wasn't sure how I'd say it, I couldn't wait any longer. I needed her to know that whatever we had was over.

If Spiny asked me why, what would I say? I couldn't even articulate it clearly to myself. Was it because the dinner had been a bit of a letdown? She hadn't asked me anything about myself, and had talked at length about her skating, her school, her skills. Or was it her age, the fact that she had an apartment and credit cards and other trappings of adulthood that were still so far away from me?

It was both of those things, but it was more, too. She simply wasn't the person I'd been envisioning, the one with whom my future self had shared a Chicago apartment. That person was a figment of my imagination.

My lie about my age popped into my mind. Spiny didn't really know the real me, either. The whole thing had been doomed from the start.

I was sitting on the porch waiting for her, my knees tucked up to my chin.

"Hey!" She smiled as she strode up the walkway, then leaned

in to kiss me. I kissed her back without enthusiasm. "What's up?"

It occurred to me, dimly, that she would not see this coming. Of the two of us, she was the amazing one—the hot, confident, sexy one, the star derby player. She wouldn't expect me to dump her.

I took a deep breath. "I think we should stop seeing each other."

"Oh." She blinked. "Wow."

"I'm sorry." I looked at my lap.

"Can I ask why?" She sat down next to me on the porch, leaving space between us.

I chose the easiest thing to understand, even though it stung to own up to what I'd done. "I lied to you. I'm not eighteen. I just turned sixteen in December. I'm only a sophomore in high school."

In my head, I'd seen what would happen next. She'd wince, and say "wow" again, and agree that we couldn't date. Then she'd wish me well and drive away.

I was unprepared for her actual reaction.

"What the hell? Are you serious?" She scooted farther away and stared at me with furious eyes.

I shrugged. "It was a mistake. I'm sorry! I just wanted you to like me. I had such a crush on you."

"Do you understand the enormity of this, Mighty?" She pushed her hands through her hair. "Jesus! I nearly slept with someone underage. Do you get that?"

I opened my mouth. Shut it again. No, I had not gotten it.

"Do you get that if we kept seeing each other and your parents found out and decided to press charges, I could have been branded a sex offender? Do you fucking get that?"

I shook my head, curled further inward on myself. My God, I'd been shockingly, breathtakingly thoughtless.

"You had a crush on me, so you thought to yourself, hey, a little crush is more important than Erica's future!"

"No," I whispered miserably. "I didn't think that."

"You only thought about yourself." Her voice was pure venom.

I started to cry. Hot, heaving sobs wracked my body as I doubled over, my head against my knees. "I didn't think at all." I choked out. The horror of what I'd done, of what could have happened, overwhelmed me. Why had this never once occurred to me?

After a few minutes with no words from Spiny and no intelligible words from me, something lightly touched my arm. I glanced up. Spiny was holding a tissue out at arm's length, her face still set in a scowl. I took it and blew my nose.

"I'm sorry," I said again, hopelessly.

She shook her head, shrugged, looked away from me. "For fuck's sake, Mighty." But the intensity had leached from her voice. "Did you think I'd be flattered or something? Like, golly gee, she likes me so much she had to trick me?"

It occurred to me that yes, maybe I'd thought that a little bit. It occurred to me that really I didn't know her at all.

"I just . . . I just didn't think. Period."

"For what it's worth," she muttered, "I'm glad you told me now, and not later. The only thing you could have done worse would have been to keep lying."

I looked at her, hoping to see a tiny bit of warmth in her face, but she was still turned away.

"I'm gonna go now. I'm gonna go home and thank God that I'm not being dragged to jail by your fucking parents." With that pronouncement, she stood up and strode away. She was gone before I could say goodbye or apologize again.

I went to bed and wept more, burrowed under my covers. When I exhausted myself, I shut my eyes, hoping for a nap to give me a break from the pain. Sleep didn't come. My bones ached with the weight of my guilt. Spiny was right to be furious. I hadn't spared a single thought for age of consent laws or sex offender lists or any of the other risks I'd put on Spiny's unknowing head when I lied to her. All that had mattered was that I wanted her, I wanted our dream life.

My impulse was to apologize again, over and over, telling her I finally knew how terrible my actions had been. But some shred of wisdom stopped me. Texting her more would only make it worse. She probably hated me, but I didn't see how I could undo that rightful consequence.

With a long, shuddering sigh, heavy with both regret and relief that things hadn't been worse, I opened my eyes and grabbed my phone. I shouldn't beg further forgiveness from Spiny. No, I knew who I actually wanted to talk to.

Maybe Stork would come over for another board game night. Maybe we could go for a jog. That would be a little ray of light in my future, a sign that I hadn't irreparably messed up my life.

Stork replied immediately, like she usually did.

No. I'm too busy.

The four-word text hit like a punch to the gut. I had destroyed my friendship with Stork, too. I started crying again.

I pictured the look on Stork's face when she'd seen Spiny kiss me at the rink. Maybe Stork was hurt that I hadn't told her I was seeing someone, because we were friends, and friends shared about that sort of thing? Or maybe she had a crush on Spiny, too, so she was jealous of that?

The third option—that it was *me* Stork wanted—felt too terrible to be true. Because if that was what I had destroyed, my loss was even bigger than I'd thought. Spiny, thank God, had escaped from my blind, naïve pursuit unscathed. But Stork . . . I knew how I felt when I was with her. I saw her clearly, as she actually was, not as some fantasy crush. How could I lose her, too?

CHAPTER 34

time until Soy Anything: 10 days

Days passed. A week, then more. I stayed in bed almost all the time. I'd told my parents I thought I might be sick, but it was clearly fiction. They must have thought I was just moping about being barred from the tournament.

Somehow, despite barely leaving my bed when I was at home, I still went to derby practices, where I did my best to pretend everything was fine. Neither Pumpkin nor Stork spoke to me unless absolutely necessary, my legs felt like lead on the track, and every time Cleo or Ann mentioned Soy Anything my heart broke further, but I kept on pretending. I still hadn't told the coaches that I wasn't going. I didn't know how.

On a break midway through an evening practice, Pay cornered me in the bathroom as I washed my hands.

"What's going on with you lately?"

I thought I'd kept up my charade of happiness, at least enough so that my teammates wouldn't notice. It seemed I'd been wrong.

I shrugged. "Oh, I'm . . . uh . . ." I couldn't lie and tell Pay I felt sick, since we weren't supposed to come to practice if we were at all under the weather. My mind was blank, fresh out of lies. My breath caught in my throat. I turned away from her, facing the bathroom wall as my shoulders heaved and tears began to fall.

Her arms immediately wrapped around me in a crushing hug. "Oh no, Mighty, are you okay?"

I couldn't speak. I cried harder.

"I mean," Pay continued, "obviously you aren't."

At this, I laughed a little through my sobs, and turned so that I could face her, hug her back. "I'm so sad, Pay! I've ruined my whole life!"

Maybe I shouldn't unburden myself to her like this. Pay was my teammate, and I liked her, but we weren't close. I wanted to stop, to pull myself together, but I didn't have the strength.

"I'm sure that's not true. Your whole life is not ruined, whatever is going on." She patted my back. "Do you want to talk about it?"

I shook my head. "It's too complicated. Family stuff and friend stuff and dating stuff and just everything."

She squeezed me tighter, then left to grab a wad of toilet paper from a stall. "Here."

I tried to clean up my face. I was so sick of crying. In the mirror, my face was red and puffy, my eyes tiny. "I don't know how I'm going to go back for the rest of practice. It's so obvious I've been crying."

"So? I'm sure most of us have cried during practice before. I cried last week when Gables snapped at me for missing the jammer during scrimmage."

"She did? You did?" I'd been oblivious.

"She apologized later. She said she was more frustrated with herself, that she'd been relying on a rookie to get things done on the track when she couldn't. Then she said I was a good skater, for a rookie. Then she said she was sorry she was acting like a dick." Pay fiddled with one of her long braids, twisting it back and forth between her fingers, not looking at me. "Typical Gables apology, not a lot of warmth. And I mean, it's fine now, I got over it. But still, it did not make me feel great about my place on the team. That's why I'd started crying."

"What do you mean?" Pay worried about her place on the team? How? Why? It seemed absurd, and my curiosity distracted me from my internal drama for a moment.

She laughed. "I'm a rookie, I'm a perfectly average blocker

with no exceptional skills, and, hmmm, I don't know if you noticed, but I'm literally the only Black girl in our entire league. And even after months of skating together, I'd still rather talk to Bee, or other rookies, than any of the vets. They intimidate me. They're mostly nice, but, well, you know. I can be a little shy."

During Skatertots, Pay and Bee had pretty much talked only to each other. I'd assumed it was because they thought they were cooler than everyone else. Now I saw it differently.

Spiny's words the other day played in my mind. *You only thought about yourself.* I'd been so focused on my own insecurity, and then on my own growth, that I hadn't truly seen Pay—a fellow teammate, a fellow rookie, a kind, shy, funny, lovely person. What else had I missed?

"God, I'm sorry, Pay. I had no idea."

She waved her hand. "It's fine. Bee and I spend every car ride after practice pouring over everything and complaining and boosting each other up. This isn't a big deal. My point was more that you don't need to hide the fact that you're crying from the team. Everyone's got issues. No one is going to judge you."

"For what it's worth, I think you're a great blocker."

She laughed. "Thanks. But like I said, it was just a crappy day, and I'm okay. Ready to head back to the track now?"

"The thing is... part of the reason I'm crying has to do with the team. Well, certain people on the team."

"I've noticed you and Pumpkin don't seem close anymore."

I nodded, left it at that. I wasn't going to mention Stork, or the tournament.

"Want me to go tell Ann that you, I don't know, have bad cramps all of a sudden, so you have to leave early?"

I smiled at her. She had a nose ring, a tiny sparkly stud that was identical to mine. I'd never noticed that before. "That would be perfect. I'll sneak out once everyone starts a drill again and is distracted, and I'll text my mom to come get me."

Late that night, long after my mom had fallen asleep, I pulled out my laptop. It was time to send a message to Cleo and Ann, to tell them my parents had barred me from playing in the tournament.

I stared at the screen. Typed "Hello." Stared longer. Shut my laptop.

Then, in a sudden burst of energy, I grabbed a notebook and a pen. My thoughts flowed, things I'd never put into words before. I had so many things I needed to say.

I love roller derby. I love my teammates: my fellow rookies— Pumpkin, Stork, Pay, Bee . . . I love Luna and Toni and everyone, even the ones who scare me, like Gables. I might not know each of them that well, but together, we're a team. I'm a part of something bigger than myself. I'm responsible to a whole group of people, and they're responsible to me. We depend on each other. There's trust.

But it's not just that. I love the sport itself. I love the way it feels when my wheels first hit the track and I start to roll. I love the way it feels to sprint on my toe stops, bursting forward. I love the rush of hearing two whistle blasts if I get called lead jammer. I love the countdown after the jam timer yells "five seconds!" I love the way it feels when I'm skating laps, leaning into the turns, thighs aching with the effort. I love the strategy, the planning, the beauty of a blocker hitting their opponent in a moment of perfectly timed offense and their jammer successfully sneaking past.

I love watching games online and studying the way the blockers line up, the way they move together like different parts of the same organism, always coming together and moving apart, amoeba-like. I love the more complex stuff that Stork has helped me understand, like bridging and passive offense—things that were incomprehensible to me just a few months ago. I love knowing that there is so much more I've yet to learn.

Look, I know I've never taken the time to explain WHY I love this sport before. I should have.

I was so lonely, for so long. I just didn't know it until I wasn't lonely anymore. These are my people. This is my world. I love it.

I took a deep breath, reread what I had so far, then kept going.

I know I really screwed up that night I took the car. I know actions have consequences. But please, please, let me go to Soy Anything. I'll happily go without the car for a month—for as long as you want!—as an alternative punishment, or whatever you want.

I just felt isolated for so long, doing online school, not having friends besides Ben, and derby means so much to me.

And it's more than that. I've changed, too. I have more confidence.

I had never realized it in these words before, but tonight it was obvious.

I'm more ME now. Less afraid, less neurotic and insecure. Braver.

I've been sad lately, but I'd still choose this sadness over the emptiness of my life before.

Please. Let me go to the tournament.

I tore the sheet of paper out of the notebook, folded it in half, and wrote both my parents' names on the outside.

I texted them both together, aware that they likely wouldn't see the message until morning.

I wrote something that means a lot to me, and I need you both to read it.

CHAPTER 35

time until Soy Anything: 1 day

We stopped at the sports center as soon as we pulled into town. It was a huge blue building right off the highway, not near anything else except our hotel.

My van, driven by Ann, arrived first. The vans driven by Cleo and by Luna's mom arrived a minute later. The vans had stayed close on the drive, and we'd made faces or held up funny signs when they passed each other. Now we all clambered out, stretching and groaning. I turned a cartwheel, gravel pressing into my palms. The drive had taken four hours. We were tired and stiff but keyed up and jittery, too.

Last week, the day after I'd written the letter, my dad came over to my mom's house for dinner. I couldn't remember the last time I'd seen my parents have dinner together like that, speaking civilly, not fuming or awkwardly avoiding conversation.

After dinner, he and my mom had spoken in private. I paced nervously in the upstairs hallway. When they called me back to the main floor, I found them sitting side by side in the living room.

They told me they'd decided to let me go to the tournament, and that yes, they were taking away car privileges for now instead. My mom said she was proud of me for expressing myself like I had. My dad said he was proud of me for how much I'd grown. They each hugged me. Then they reminded me that this didn't mean what I'd done was okay.

I stayed quiet throughout, my heart pounding like a

hummingbird's, scared of making a wrong move that might make them change their minds.

A final surprise: They told me they were going to come watch the tournament, too. My mom would come down on Saturday, my dad on Sunday. I imagined that, even though they were getting along better, a long car ride together was still too much.

Now I was finally here. The inside of the sports center smelled like rubber and sweat. We moved as a herd, clumping up in the breezeway, giggling as Gables and Pay tried to fit through a door at the same time.

Ann walked backward in front of us, like a tour leader. "Stay together so we can get signed in and get your tournament badges. Then you'll have a few minutes to explore before we check in at the hotel."

The very first person we saw in line at check-in was Simply Red, the snotty redhead who'd snubbed me during the Sauk Valley Sonics game. True to form, she gave no signs that she recognized our team.

"Are you kidding me?" I muttered to Gables.

"Don't worry about it," she whispered back. "We'll get revenge when we play them this weekend."

But when we looked at the Juniors schedule, written in bright marker on a huge sheet of poster board taped near registration, it seemed we may not play Sauk Valley, after all.

There were eight Juniors teams at the tournament, and we were separated into two groups. We were in Group A, and the Sonics were in Group B. The four teams in each group would play one another, and then, on Sunday night, the team with the best record in each group would play each other in the final game.

"I'm kind of relieved," I told Gables. "I don't want to play them again."

"Too bad, because we're going to. We'll win our group.

They'll probably win theirs. We'll face them in the final game," she said. "And then we'll destroy them."

"You really think we'll win our group?"

"There's no room for doubt, Mighty." She grinned her ferocious shark's grin.

A few self-deprecating comments sprang to mind, but then Ann's voice popped in my head, reminding me to treat myself better. So after an instant's hesitation, I grinned back at Gables. "Okay. Yes. We'll destroy them."

After we got our badges, Ann set us free for twenty minutes. I wandered on my own through the venue, awed. There were three different tracks set up, all in the same gigantic room. I paused for a few minutes and watched one of the adult charter teams warm up. The Prairie Skate charter team wasn't here, as they were at a tournament in Minnesota this weekend. I was relieved; I definitely wasn't ready to run into Spiny.

Thinking of her still hurt. I had broken down and texted her a week ago, to say she was right to have been angry, and that, again, I was so sorry. I knew I'd decided texting her was a bad idea, but I couldn't help it. I needed to acknowledge what had happened one more time, clearly own up to my mistakes instead of messily choking out an apology while sobbing, as I had at our last encounter. I regretted the lie with an intensity that made my chest ache; I regretted that I'd told her the truth so casually, without realizing what a big deal it would be.

Spiny didn't reply to my final apology, but I heard from her a few days later.

Good luck at Soy Anything to all you Juniors.

I wasn't sure if the text was just sent to me, or to a bunch of people on the Juniors team. I didn't ask. I didn't reply. This was enough.

* * *

I wandered farther inside the sports center. Vendor booths were set up alongside the derby tracks, selling every roller-derby-related item imaginable. I had decided I wouldn't buy anything right away but changed my mind immediately when I saw the official tournament merch: black shirts with Soy Anything written in red script, then, beneath the name, a cartoony drawing of a soybean wearing roller skates and holding a boombox over its head. I bought a crop top and nearly bought a hoodie as well, then decided I shouldn't spend all my cash in the first few minutes.

I meandered past a booth selling custom fanny packs, two booths selling skates, and one selling leggings and shorts covered in two-way sequins. God, I wanted to buy everything. I still hadn't spent my birthday gift certificate to Derby Warehouse; maybe I'd try on skates here and figure out what I liked.

I ran into Stork at the last booth, which did custom designs for T-shirts, printed in any color you liked. My stomach dropped at the sight of her, like I was on a roller coaster.

Stork had ridden in Cleo's van today, as had Pumpkin. Was she mad at me? Was she hurt that I'd kissed Spiny, but not actually mad? I'd been too nervous to ask her directly.

But now, with both of us next to each other in front of this booth, talking to her was unavoidable. I felt like I needed to apologize for Spiny's kiss, but how would that go? What would I say? Instead, voice shaking, I asked, "How was the trip down?"

She turned and smiled at me, though there was a reserve, a coolness, in her eyes, and she quickly looked back at the book of color samples she was holding. "I get carsick, so I got to ride shotgun. Cleo and I talked about derby the whole way down."

She'd answered, and not just in a one-word sentence to tell me to go to hell. The relief was dizzying. I knew things weren't like they had been, but at least we were speaking. This wasn't the right time for a serious talk, anyway. "I sat in the way back, squished between Pay and Luna, and we made up a theme song for our van. Ann kept playing the *Mamma Mia!*

soundtrack, so it's to the tune of 'Lay All Your Love on Me' by ABBA. Want to hear it?"

She laughed, almost like she couldn't help herself, and set down the sample book. "Sure."

We walked out together to find the others. Heart beating fast, I sang poorly, "Go, go, Annie's van of moooootion . . ."

We had arranged hotel rooms ages ago. I was sharing a room with Pumpkin, Pay, and Bee. I was scared. Pumpkin and I had been increasingly friendly at recent practices, as if the ice between us was slowly, slowly thawing, but she'd never told me why she had stopped at my house that Saturday, and I'd never asked. What would it be like, spending two nights in a hotel with her? At least Pay and Bee would be there, to ease the conversational pressure.

Our room had two double beds. Pay immediately pounced on the one by the window. "I call this one for me and Bee!"

"Why?" I asked.

"Farther from the door, in case an ax murderer breaks in."

"But closer to the window. What about vampires?" We were all kind of giddy and wound-up, plus I was trying to hide my nerves about being so close to Pumpkin.

"No, it's fine, you have to invite them in!"

While Pay and Bee showed each other what clothes they'd packed, Pumpkin touched my arm and spoke quietly. "Are you okay sharing a bed?"

"I am if you are."

"Okay."

A wave of sadness hit me. It felt like we were ex-friends, navigating our awkward friendship breakup. I shook it off, determined to act like everything was fine. "Anyone mind if I use the bathroom to shower before dinner? I smell absolutely dégoûtant."

"What nonsense are you speaking, Mighty?" Bee asked, laughing.

"It's the French word for disgusting, obviously," I said in a fake-haughty voice. My frantic studying to raise my grades so I could use the car had become a sort of habit, and school stuff was staying in my head better than it used to.

Pay threw a pillow at me, and I whipped it right back, darting into the bathroom before she could attack further. "Soy Anything!" I shouted from the shower. "Watch out! The Prairie Skate Juniors are here!"

CHAPTER 36

time until Soy Anything: 0 days

I slept poorly that night, probably because of the effort I put into lying perfectly still and not taking up too much room. Our first game was Saturday morning. Those of us skating in it had to be on the track for warm-ups by 9:00 a.m. Pumpkin wasn't skating in this one, and she was still snuggled under the covers when I left.

I rode from the hotel to the venue in Cleo's van, next to Stork. Yesterday, she'd said she sat up front because she got carsick. Today, she was sitting next to me in the middle bench seat. Maybe it didn't mean anything. Maybe it did.

When we climbed out of the car, we stretched and yawned, not saying much. Then Stork started doing her running-in-place warm-up, and Cleo grabbed me to go over today's lineup.

I'd been rostered as a blocker. Instead of feeling disappointed, eager aggressiveness began to rise inside me, my thoughts tinged with something akin to bloodlust. Yes, I still needed Gables to tell me what to do half the time when I blocked, but I couldn't wait to destroy the other team's jammers. After the sad haze of the last few weeks, I was fully awake, ready to get out there and play. I was going to enjoy this.

I needed to enjoy it, because I wasn't rostered for the afternoon game. Since there were three games, not counting the possibility of us playing in the final, most of us would play two out of the three. The best skaters, like Gables and Toni, were skating in all three. Stork was the only rookie to be rostered for all three games. I didn't feel jealous; mostly I felt bad for her, because they were still making her pivot instead of jam.

Our morning opponents were a team called the Rollerbugs. They had cute red jerseys with black spots and, judging by my covert watch of their warm-ups, a wide range of skill levels. They all seemed to be smiling and relaxed, and one of them complimented my green hair as she skated by our bench. I liked them immediately.

While sitting on the bench waiting for the game to start, I spotted Pumpkin and the other not-rostered skaters together in the audience. Her eyes met mine. We gave each other tight-lipped, awkward smiles.

I didn't have long to think about Pumpkin, though. I quickly lost myself in the game. Gables, Stork, and I often blocked together. I listened to Gables, stayed out of my head, and just played. The score was close, back and forth, back and forth. When a big Rollerbug blocker knocked me to the ground just as a jam ended, she extended her hand to help me.

"Thanks!" I said as she towed me to standing, rubbing my hip where I'd landed. "Nice hit!"

At halftime, we hustled off the track, and I spotted my mom in the audience. She was clearly texting, but glanced up from her phone just in time to catch my eye and smile. I gave her a quick wave, wondered if she'd spent the whole game staring at her phone instead of watching the action, then pushed the thought away and followed my teammates into the locker room.

The score was currently 86–75, in favor of the Rollerbugs. Ann gave us a brief speech about how proud she was of our performance, Cleo gave us a rundown of the things we could be doing better, I hurriedly ate a banana while they spoke, and then we skated back onto the track.

In the first jam of the second half, Dex, jamming for us, got stuck behind a wall of Rollerbug blockers. They whipped the jammer cover off their helmet and thrust their arm forward.

Stork was ready. She grabbed the cover and ran with it, flying out of the pack and scoring three points before the Rollerbugs' jammer could call the jam off.

"Beautiful!" I said, high-fiving her as we skated back to the bench after the jam.

She was flushed, a little sweaty. "Thanks."

The score climbed, in our favor, in their favor, in ours, in theirs. Though there weren't many people in the audience, everyone watching must have been riveted, based on the shouts and cheers and gasps we heard every time the lead changed.

It came down to a final jam that I wasn't skating in. The score was 183–180, in our favor. Those of us not on the track stood in a line in front of our bench, arms around each other's shoulders. Toni was jamming. Gables plowed down several Rollerbugs, clearing a path for her on the outside, just as she'd done for me during the Sonics game. Toni ran up the outside line on her toe stops, got declared lead, and signaled to end the jam.

We'd won!

We all rushed to the track, swarming Toni and Gables, piling on top of them. Our non-skating teammates ran in from the audience, joining the pile. As we grabbed each other, hugging and screaming, I realized Pumpkin was next to me.

"Nice job," she said, her voice quiet.

"Thanks." I looked down at my skates. "Good luck in the afternoon game."

"Thanks."

I followed the team off the track, shaking. Adrenaline from our win was still rushing through my system, but my mood had turned. Why couldn't things be normal with Pumpkin? Why did we still have to be acting so weird? She was my friend, and I needed her.

I swerved, skating as fast as I could back to the track, like it was the 27 in 5. Where had Pumpkin gone? I had to find her. I was done with this, done waiting for her to take the initiative and make things okay again.

Finally, I spotted her walking slowly away from the track in the opposite direction, partially hidden by the bleachers.

"Hey!" I grabbed her by the shoulders. "I'm really sorry. For everything."

I was scared she'd push my hands away, but she didn't. She just looked at me, and her face relaxed into a tentative smile, the ice between us melting away. "Thanks."

I paused, hoped she'd say she was sorry, too, but she didn't. Well, I guess it couldn't be that easy. "I was being selfish. You were right."

She shrugged and looked down at her combat boots, scuffing the ground with one toe. "Eh. I wasn't that great, either."

"If you want to date my brother, it's okay with me."

Her mouth thinned. "I don't need your permission."

Oh God, I didn't want things to get weird again. "I know! I just meant, I'm not gonna be unpleasant about it. I want you to know."

"Okay." She smiled. "Want to ride with me in Luna's mom's van on the way to the group lunch?"

Relief flooded me. "Absolutely. There's just one more person I need to talk to, first."

"So what'd you think?"

"I was so nervous!" My mom's eyes widened. "I was on edge the whole time, Millie."

That was all she had to say, more worries about safety? I held back a defensive response and tried to push away a wave of disappointment. "Yeah? Just nervous?"

"Of course! The score was so close! The *whole crowd* was on edge!"

Before I thought about what I was doing, I hugged her, quickly and fiercely, then backing off before she said anything about the smell of my sweaty derby gear. "I'm glad you came, Mom."

"Me, too. It was a great game. You did really well." She began walking toward the exit, and I followed her, rolling slowly in my skates. "How come you weren't a jammer?"

"It wasn't best for the team, for this game." I was high on our win, on making up with Pumpkin, on my mom being absorbed by the game. I didn't care that I hadn't jammed. "I might tomorrow, but probably not."

I'd wanted to be a jammer because I'd thought it would be a way to prove myself to the team. Now? I still wanted to jam, because when it went well, there was nothing better. But mostly, I just wanted to play.

"I texted your dad score updates every time there was a lead change." She shook out her hand. "I think my thumbs have got calluses now."

"You texted Dad?" I couldn't keep the skepticism out of my voice.

She grinned at me. "I did, yes." When was the last time I'd seen my mom grin? Her smile, when she actually smiled big like this, looked just like mine.

Something popped in my head. "Oh God, you two aren't going to get back together, are you?" The idea turned my stomach. After all this?

"*Jesus*, Millie." She shook her head. "Absolutely not. The only reason I can tolerate your father is because we don't live together anymore. Plus"—she shrugged—"it's texting. If he makes me mad, I can just mute my phone."

I shook my head, too, and skated out of the auditorium beside her.

CHAPTER 37

I chatted with my mom till it was time to go to lunch. Then, after a loud and raucous team meal that definitely caused other restaurant patrons to switch to tables farther away from us, I returned to the hotel to shower and get ready to watch the afternoon game. I wished I was playing. But it would still be fun. I'd cheer Stork and Pumpkin and everyone as loud as I could.

I rode with Ann the short distance to the venue. When we got inside, on a whim, I pulled her aside.

"Um, Ann? Can I ask you a question?"

"Of course, what's up?"

"Why do you and Cleo make Stork pivot? She's too good. She's the one who should be a jammer, not me." I had the feeling that this was more Cleo's decision than Ann's, but I never would have had the nerve to have this conversation with Cleo.

Ann regarded me with bemusement. "Stork's a pivot *because* she's so good. She has a fantastic derby brain. Pivoting is all right there in the name—you need to pivot from blocking to jamming at a moment's notice. It takes a high degree of track awareness, of pattern prediction, of mental flexibility. Most people aren't ready to pivot their rookie year. Stork is special."

"Oh." I chewed on my bottom lip. I hadn't thought of it like that. It seemed obvious now that Ann said it. "Yeah. Stork is special." I shivered a little. Stork was a hell of an athlete. A hell of a person.

Ann nodded. "She's got a real intensity to her."

I thought of our conversation at the veggie bowl restaurant, how Stork had owned up to her own intensity and said she knew it meant people might not like her. "She does. It's . . . great."

I shook myself. The point of this wasn't for me to think about how Stork was great. The point was to talk to Ann. I'd had those quick glimpses of Stork's inner thoughts, and I needed to press Ann further. "Have you told Stork this? About how you have her pivoting because you think she's so great?"

"I mean . . ." Ann looked thoughtful. "I thought it was understood. But you know what, Mighty, it wouldn't hurt for me to tell her more clearly, would it?"

I nodded my agreement, and Ann began walking away. She had to coach the game that was starting soon.

If I wanted to say anything else to her, it would have to be now. I swallowed. She was getting farther away, and I could see Gables up ahead, sure to engage her in conversation once she was closer.

"Ann! Wait!" I jogged toward her, ignoring how shaky I suddenly felt.

"What's up, Mighty?" She was too nice to hurry me, but I could sense the pull of the track, of her responsibilities for the afternoon game.

I needed to force the words out now. Right now. This was my chance. "Can I ask you one more thing? Remember my 27 in 5?"

"Of course. Why?"

"Are you sure you counted it right? I counted my laps, too, and I thought I only got twenty-six and a half, not twenty-seven and a half. I was short half a lap from passing." I couldn't look at her. I didn't think she could do anything to me at this point, but I wasn't positive.

But Ann just laughed. "I know how to count, Millie. And skaters are notoriously bad at keeping track of their own laps. Do you have unusually good attention to detail?"

"Nooo . . ." Quite the opposite.

"Then I think it's safe to trust my count."

She turned away with a smile, but I burst out one last comment, my words pushed tightly together. "Dora fell, though. That might have distracted you and made you lose count."

She gave me a knowing look. "Or maybe it distracted you?"

"Maybe." That had somehow never occurred to me. I let out an enormous breath. "All right. Thanks."

"And for what it's worth, Cleo and I have been talking, and we're going to drop that requirement for the next round of assessments. Most leagues nowadays don't require it anymore, anyway."

Before Ann could walk away, I darted forward, wrapping my arms around her. She returned my hug without question, her big arms squeezing me tight. My eyes were stinging like I might cry, but no tears fell. I was, I realized, smiling broadly.

All those months of worry, of wondering if those 26.5 laps meant something: gone. Irrelevant. I thought maybe it should have made me mad, that I'd worried so much for nothing. Instead, my steps were light as I waved goodbye to Ann and made my way to the bleachers.

Prairie Skate Juniors won our afternoon game, in another close contest. I sat in the crowd and screamed my lungs out, cheering for everyone, cheering loudest for Pumpkin and Stork. When a small group of Sauk Valley Sonics sitting to my left rolled their eyes and mimed covering their ears, I only screamed louder.

When we got back to the hotel, all chattering and cheering our victory, Ann and Cleo stood sternly in the hallway, watching us all go into our rooms. "Go to bed! Early game tomorrow! Get some sleep!" they repeated as we reluctantly went inside.

As soon as we were in the rooms, our phones started blowing up.

Pool party, Gables wrote.

Secret pool party in half an hour, Rainbow wrote.

Ann is in room 218, Cleo is in room 234, avoid their rooms, be quiet in the hall, meet downstairs in 30, Toni wrote.

We all started giggling and shrieking and then shushing each other.

"I didn't bring a bathing suit!" I gasped.

"Just swim in your underwear!" Pumpkin said.

It felt so good to have her talking to me again and being my friend, even if things weren't quite the same. "I am wearing a thong, Pumpkin. Not just a thong, but a ratty old one. No way."

"How can you wear those?" Pay shuddered dramatically. "It looks like having piano wire going up your ass."

"No, it's actually comfortable—"

"Priorities!" Bee cut me off. "We need to get ready, not stand here talking. Mighty, it's no problem. I brought two suits, so you can borrow one of mine."

I eyed the bright pink scraps of spandex she pulled out of her suitcase. "There is no way those will fit me."

In the end, I squeezed into Bee's bikini top and wore a pair of Pumpkin's black workout shorts as bottoms. My boobs were barely contained, but it was just my teammates, so who cared?

We tiptoed out of the hall cautiously, clumped together, giggling.

"Fast," Bee whispered. "Cleo or Ann could come out at any time."

"No way, they're asleep," Pay whispered back.

A door opened right behind us, and Bee shrieked. Gables stepped outside.

"Quiet, rookies!" she hissed. "You want to wake up the coaches?"

Which for some reason made us laugh even harder.

Stork was in the same room as Gables, and she stepped

into the hall a moment after her. She was in a blue one-piece swimsuit with a pair of pajama bottoms pulled over it, a towel slung over her shoulders and her water bottle in her hands. I waved at her silently and she waved back, looking away quickly. We'd been friendly all day but hadn't been alone together since that moment yesterday at the vendor booths. I wished I knew what she was thinking.

Though it was only a little after nine, it felt like the middle of the night at the pool, like no one on Earth was awake but us. Our shouts echoed, loud and free.

Toni had snuck in a bottle of watermelon pucker, and she passed it around stealthily. Some people took bold swigs, others—like myself—took tiny sips, or passed it on without judgment. Luna played dance music on a Bluetooth speaker. Gables did a cannonball, splashing everyone, which started a "coolest jump" contest. When it was my turn, I ran across the wet concrete, launched myself into the air, and twisted as I fell toward the water. I burst back out of the water feeling victorious, then realized my bikini top was around my waist when everyone started laughing.

"Chicken fight!" Gables cried a bit later, pulling Luna onto her shoulders. "Who challenges us?"

Stork was nearest to me, floating on her back and idly kicking her legs.

"What do you say?" I asked her, heart pounding.

She smiled, paused. "Maybe?"

It occurred to me that, while Stork was still, of course, more comfortable as an athlete, I was more comfortable in team social situations. "Come on," I said. "It'll be fun."

While she hesitated, Pay climbed onto Bee's shoulders and lunged for Luna. They grappled with each other, pushing and shoving, while beneath them Bee and Gables struggled to keep their balance. Eventually, Pay toppled backward into the water.

"Who's our next challenger? Who can defeat us?" Gables yelled.

I looked at Stork.

She shrugged, smiled, and blushed a little. "Let's do it."

Since she was taller, I would be on top. I grabbed her thin, wet shoulders, pushed her blonde hair to the side, and boosted myself up, slinging one leg over her shoulder, then the other. Once I was seated, I lightly touched the top of her head for balance.

She grabbed my calves tightly and tilted her head to look up at me. "Ready?"

I grinned and nodded.

"Five seconds!" someone yelled from behind us, then, "Tweet!"

Luna and I were evenly matched. We gripped each other's arms and shoved, let go and swung, smacked with open hands. Maybe one of us could have defeated the other if we weren't both laughing so hard.

Stork shifted her grip so she was grabbing both my ankles as best as she could with one hand, freeing the other. "Hang on!" she shouted to me, then used her free hand to surprise Gables, pushing her head straight down into the water. As Gables spluttered, trying to rise, Luna lost her balance. With a quick shove to her shoulders, I sent her falling backward into the water.

I hopped off Stork's shoulders, grabbed her hand, and thrust it into the air. "The winners!"

She was laughing, breathless. "I love winning!"

"Woooo!" I gave her a hug, hamming it up as if we had just won a huge derby game instead of a chicken fight. She hugged me back, cheering, too. Then something changed, shifted. Our arms still around each other, our faces wet and breathless and inches apart. This was different. I took a breath. Stork stepped back quickly, dropping her arms.

Her face was bright red.

Was something wrong? I began to panic inside.

But then she smiled at me, still red. It was a private, quick smile. Affectionate. In a flash, she swam off, going to grab a drink from her water bottle.

My stomach flipped, nervous, but not unpleasantly so. Unsure of what else to do, I climbed out of the pool and cannonballed back in.

A little bit later, a bunch of us crowded into the hot tub, limbs entangled, barely fitting. Toni climbed onto Gables's lap and settled herself there, reminding me of the old rumors about the two of them. A moment later, she twisted her upper body around so the two of them could kiss. I nudged Pumpkin with my knee, nodding toward Gables and grinning.

"Do you think we'll win in the morning?" Pay said.

"Don't doubt it," said Gables, pulling her mouth off Toni's. "We win everything, don't allow for any other thoughts."

Pay groaned. "Come on, Gables. I want a real answer, not some sort of warrior slogan. What do you actually think our chances are?"

I thought of my conversation in the bathroom with Pay, when she'd comforted me as I cried. Despite telling me that day that the vet skaters intimidated her, tonight she was giving Gables a hard time. Our eyes met across the hot tub, and we both smiled.

Luna, barely visible behind Gables and Toni, spoke up. "I think we'll win. Honest. We did really well in both our games today. We were really together."

Stork stretched her legs out in front of her. Her toes fluttered against mine. "If we want our best shot at it, we should probably get some sleep soon."

"Eh, it's not that late," Pumpkin scoffed.

"Sleep is important. I think I'm going to head back to my room in a few, even if you all don't."

Pumpkin glanced at me, rolling her eyes. "Come on, Stork," she said. "You don't need to be such a killjoy. You're only doing that 'cause your dad's a hoarder, right? This is all, like, some mental issue. So let it go, just relax, and have fun."

She said it so casually, like it was no big deal. But Stork froze, then carefully pulled herself out of the hot tub. "I—" She looked down at me. "You told her—?"

She shook her head, grabbed her things, and fled the pool room.

I felt like I was sinking. "Why did you say that?" I hissed at Pumpkin.

She shrugged. "She needed some self-awareness. This is a vacation. We can have fun."

Her tone made it clear that this wasn't a big deal to her. That she wasn't going to understand why it was.

"Stork *is* self-aware. She just cares about us doing our best." My voice rose. The rest of the people in the hot tub had fallen silent, watching Pumpkin and me with wide eyes.

"Since when do you want to defend Stork? You know what a pain she is."

"That's the thing, Pumpkin." I boosted myself out of the hot tub and sat on the edge. "She isn't a pain. She's intense, but she's also nice, and caring, and kind."

"What, are you in love with her now?" She snorted.

"So what if I was? I don't need your permission to be interested in someone." My face flushed as the words fell out of my mouth. Why had I said that? Why had I . . . well, admitted how I felt about Stork in front of half the team?

It was true, though. It was like some previously hidden door in my mind had opened, revealing contents that had been there for ages. It was a brand-new feeling, entirely different from crushes I'd had in the past.

I was absolutely crazy about Stork.

And she was surely furious with me.

I stood up. "Forget it, Pumpkin. Never mind." I grabbed a towel, wrapped it around my waist, and left. Pumpkin wasn't the one I needed to talk to.

I knocked on Stork's hotel room door off and on for five minutes. She had to be in there. She must be! But she wasn't answering.

I sighed, resting my head against the door. What had I been thinking? I never should have told Pumpkin about Stork's dad. I had regretted it as soon as I'd said it, that day in the car, but then I'd forgotten, never dreaming it would come up again.

Quiet footsteps came padding down the hall. I looked up. Stork! She had her pajama pants back on over her swimsuit, a towel pulled tight over her shoulders, and red, watery eyes.

"Hey." Her voice was flat.

"Stork, I'm so sorry!" I rushed down the hall to her. "I never should have told Pumpkin that! I'm so sorry!"

She didn't reach out for me, didn't respond, just kept walking toward her room. But when she got to her door, she paused.

"Is that what you think? That I'm an athlete, that I'm focused and driven, because I have mental health problems, it's that simple? That my whole personality is based on my dad's issues?"

"No! God, no!"

She sighed, then slid down the wall till she was sitting on the floor, knees pulled in front of her. She still wasn't looking at me, but at least she hadn't gone inside. I sat down next to her, close but not touching.

"It was an awful thing to do, and I just said it because, well . . . I was just trying to make a point to Pumpkin that you aren't some athlete robot. I wanted her to like you more. 'Cause you're awesome."

She ignored the compliment. "I don't need Pumpkin to like me."

"You're so much more well-balanced than me. I want everyone to like me." I laughed, then, noticing that my attempt to bring levity to the conversation hadn't worked, grew quiet.

We sat there in silence for a few minutes. I didn't know what to say, but if she wasn't going into her room, I wasn't leaving.

"I haven't had anyone in my house in years. I told you that." Her voice was thick with pain.

"I know. It was wrong of me. I'm so, so sorry."

"I thought I could trust you."

"You can! I swear!" I sighed. "I made a mistake, Stork. A big one. I don't blame you for being mad."

"What am I supposed to do?" She dragged a hand through her damp hair. "Anything I ever tell you, I'll have to wonder if you're sharing it with Pumpkin, someone who's always been kind of a jerk to me."

I took a minute to formulate my reply. Things needed to come together in my brain first. "Well, you don't have to worry about that anymore, because my close friendship with Pumpkin is in the past."

Stork looked over at me sharply.

I laughed a little, though everything inside hurt like hell. "She's dating my brother, and she's my teammate, so she's still going to be in my life. But before, I was clinging to her like a life preserver, and would have done anything to keep her friendship." I traced the pattern on the carpet with my eyes. It hurt to say this, to admit it. But it was true. "I think that's why I told her about your dad. I like you so much, and I wanted Pumpkin's approval." I didn't specify what I meant by "like." I let it sound as if I meant friendship.

"I'm not asking you to choose between us or something."

"I know! I just think, well, Pumpkin is fun, but she's hurt me a few times now. I'm not going to be close to her. I'm done." I turned my head to look in Stork's eyes. "And I'm sorry. You're important to me, Stork, and I really hope I haven't destroyed what we had." Hurriedly, I added, "Our friendship."

I couldn't tell her that I'd fallen for her. Not tonight. It would have felt manipulative.

"I want you to trust me. I want our—friendship to have a

good foundation. If that's possible." I hesitated. Stork said Pumpkin had always been a jerk to her. That was true. But did she realize that I'd been right there with Pumpkin initially, acting just as snarky and dismissive of her?

My heart was thumping hard. I could let this go. I didn't have to say anything. But I meant what I said about our relationship having a good foundation.

"Can I say something else?" My voice shook.

"Yeah. Okay."

"I wasn't always a good friend to you, either." I pushed the nubs of the hallway carpet back and forth with my palm, avoiding Stork's eyes. "Like, for example, I'm not sure if you heard me this one night after practice, but I said something snarky about you to Pumpkin. About how I'd made a poor life choice, agreeing to go to the gym with you. It was back in the fall. I was intimidated by your talent and your drive, and I wanted to make Pumpkin like me. And I was utterly terrified of going to the gym. But it's not an excuse. It was crappy of me. You were so good at derby, I didn't think about you as, like, being a person with your own feelings and stuff."

"Oh." She didn't tell me if she remembered that incident or not. I didn't ask.

"So, I'm sorry. I was a not-good friend on multiple occasions. And you deserve friends who are trustworthy. So if you don't want to hang out with me outside of derby, or whatever . . ."

She turned to me quickly, jerkily. Her motion caught my eye, and I looked up from the carpet. Tears were spilling down her cheeks. "I want to trust you, Millie. I'm pissed that you did this stuff *because* I want to trust you so badly."

She'd called me Millie, not Mighty.

"I can be a better friend," I said. "If you want to give me the chance, I will be. I swear."

Her big brown eyes gazed into mine, even as tears still beaded in their corners.

Time froze. I barely dared to breathe.

When she spoke, her voice was low and quiet, but firm. "Okay."

"Okay what?" I was suddenly unsure.

"Okay, I want to." She wiped her eyes with the back of her hand. "I'll give you that chance."

I took a long, gasping breath, sincere but so dramatic I couldn't help but laugh at myself a second later. "That is a relief, Stork, because I don't know anyone else I like as much as you."

She gave me a tiny smile, then climbed to her feet. "We should get some sleep. I was serious about that. I want to do well tomorrow."

"Of course!" I said it too quickly, afraid I'd been keeping her awake against her will.

She reached her hand out to pull me up. I grasped it tightly. Before letting go, she gave me a gentle, tentative hug. "Goodnight."

"Goodnight. I'm sorry."

"I know, Mighty. I know."

CHAPTER 38

I took a long hot shower, replaying that conversation with Stork over and over as I tried to get the smell of chlorine off. When I shut my eyes, I saw her face. My hand still held the memory of being clasped in hers. By the time I came out of the bathroom, the other girls were back from the pool. Pay and Bee were sound asleep. Pumpkin was sitting up in bed.

"Hey," she whispered.

"Hey," I whispered back. My heart was racing. It would've been easy to avoid this conversation forever if Pumpkin had been asleep, but here she was, and I couldn't put it off any longer. I pulled back the covers with shaking hands and climbed into bed next to her. "I have a question."

"What?"

And though I really wanted to ask why she'd said all that to Stork at the hot tub, instead what came out was, "Why did you come over to my house that one Saturday?"

"Oh." She paused. "When you had the date with Spiny? I was out driving around, and I decided to wish you luck. I was still mad, but I wanted you to have a good date."

"Oh. Well. It was all right. But things are done with Spiny. She's too old. She's . . . I don't know, but we aren't right for each other." I didn't tell her about the way Spiny had yelled at me on my porch, how foolish I'd been. I didn't ask why it had never occurred to Pumpkin, either—someone close to Spiny's age—that my lies to Spiny had been a huge mistake. It wasn't worth it.

"Seriously, that's it? After all that time obsessing about her?" she asked incredulously.

I struggled to find a way to explain it. "I think I liked the idea of Spiny more than I did the actual person. She's great, don't get me wrong! But . . . I dunno." I thought about the way the flash of a crush could distract from the fact that you didn't actually know the person. Then I thought about how the opposite could happen—how gradual friendship could turn into romantic feelings without you even realizing it.

I wished I was in the other hotel room, sharing a bed with Stork, not Pumpkin.

"Hey," Pumpkin said, her voice quiet and gentle. "Let's not worry about what happened at the pool. Neither of us needs to apologize. Let's just move on."

I took a deep breath. It was one thing to tell Stork that I wasn't going to rely on Pumpkin's friendship anymore. It was another thing to say it straight to Pumpkin. I clutched the fabric of the comforter. "I don't agree."

"What?"

"I think it was terrible that you said that stuff to Stork."

For a second, I hoped that she'd realize how wrong she'd been. But no. She just sighed. "Derby is supposed to be fun. This hardcore, bootcamp b.s. isn't fun."

I prepared a sentence in my head, arguing that it wasn't the same as goofing off all the time, and actually it was incredibly rewarding, and . . . But then I realized there was no point in saying it. That wasn't the point at all. "Even if you think that, you shouldn't have brought up her dad. That was a low blow."

"You're the one who told me to begin with, like it was no big deal."

I winced. "I know. I shouldn't have. It was a rotten thing to do, on my part, sharing personal info about her with you. But you still shouldn't have said that tonight."

"Fine." She sighed. "I shouldn't have said it. I still think she's really annoying about derby, but I shouldn't have said it."

"Okay." Where did we go from here?

"I have something I need to say, if we're having this serious talk." Pumpkin's tone was different: no longer irritable, only sad. "You really hurt me, Mighty."

"What? When?" Fences rose in my brain as I shifted instantly into defensive mode.

"With David! I was dealing with a lot, and you never once asked about the break-up, about how I was doing, about *my* life!" She took a deep breath. "And I know you apologized earlier today, after the first game, but that was just one word, and honestly, I'm still hurt."

I wanted to argue, defend myself somehow, but the heaviness building in my chest told me that at a deep level, I couldn't deny it. She was right. What I'd told Stork earlier, that Pumpkin hadn't been a good friend to me, was still true. But multiple things could be true simultaneously. Maybe neither of us had been good friends to each other.

"I'm sorry. For real." I paused, and the pause stretched out into a minute or two of silence while I tried to get my thoughts straight. "I was so wrapped up in the story of my own life—being desperate to make friends, desperate to get better at derby—that I didn't treat you like you had your own full life and needs and stuff."

I'd done it to everyone. To Stork, to Pumpkin, to Spiny, to Pay, to all my other teammates, whether they knew it or not. Even to my mother. I'd seen my mom only as my adversary and assumed anything she said had an agenda behind it. I thought of the conversation we'd had when I'd dyed my hair green. I'd been convinced she was wishing she had a different daughter. Now it seemed clear she was just awkwardly trying to connect with me.

"I've made a lot of apologies today, and you're right. I owed you one, too. I'm sorry, Pumpkin."

"It's okay." She paused. "I'm still kinda pissed at you, but it's okay."

I laughed again, a little scratchily. "Well, I'm still kinda pissed at you about the Stork's dad thing."

"At least we have something in common, being pissed at each other." One side of her mouth rose into a half-smile.

It was a tiny olive branch, her saying that, and I accepted it. "At least we have that."

After a few minutes of quiet, we both stretched out deeper under the covers. I plumped the pillows behind my head, trying to get comfortable.

"I got into U of I."

"You did?"

She nodded. "I found out last week."

"That's amazing!" I was surprised to find that I felt happy for her.

Even if things had been the same in our friendship, my relationship with Pumpkin wouldn't have been frozen in time. She'd be in Champaign; I'd be in the suburbs. She'd be in college, dating Ben. I'd be in high school, playing derby. "Are you going to go?"

"I am. I told Ben, and he says he's really happy. I know we've only been dating for a month, so it's probably ridiculous to plan so far ahead, but . . . I really like him, Mighty. I feel good about this."

"I'm glad." And I was. I had my private doubts that things would last with Ben, but that wasn't my responsibility. "The Twin City Derby Group play in Champaign. You could join."

As soon as the words came out of my mouth, I knew her response.

"I don't think—"

"I know. It's okay. You don't have to." She just didn't love it like I did.

I shut my eyes, but sleep didn't come. My thoughts wouldn't stop. I kept thinking about the pool party, and about the chicken fight. About Stork and I gazing at each other, our faces inches apart. Then, about that last moment in the hallway, when Stork and I had again gazed at each other, so much more seriously.

"Hey, Pumpkin?" I asked, slowly opening my eyes. "One more thing."

"What?"

"The thing is, you were right... I do have feelings for Stork."

She sat straight up in bed. "Seriously? You actually do? Why?"

"She's nice. She's . . ." There was a quiet, kind steadiness to Stork, and, simultaneously, a fierce competitive drive. I liked both those things, individually and in combination. I liked everything about her: the way she took notes after each practice in tiny, perfect handwriting, the way she constantly pushed her hair off her face, the way she smelled like a mixture of flowers and soap . . . everything. But probably I wouldn't be able to explain it to Pumpkin. Moreover, I didn't need to. "She's really, really nice."

"Okay . . . well, I don't really get it, but I guess it's not my place to say that."

"No." My tone was firm. "Just like it wasn't my place to say stuff about you and my brother."

"Wow." She was quiet for a moment. "Stork, huh? She likes girls, at least. I found that out on the car ride down, when we were all talking about dating. She mentioned an ex-girlfriend."

I smiled. I had thought she did, but it was good to be sure. "Thanks." Hope grew in my heart. "Okay, I'm going to sleep now. For real."

It still took a while to doze off. Stork was on my mind, of course. But more than that, some invisible tension in my shoulders and chest had eased. It was a tension I'd had inside me for a long time, maybe since sixth grade, and now my mind was exploring its absence with wonder.

I didn't need to cling to my friendship with Pumpkin anymore. Maybe things would be different one day. Maybe we'd find our way back to a new sort of friendship, something different and maybe better. Or maybe we wouldn't.

I'd told my parents, in that letter I wrote, that derby made me feel more like ME. Now, lying in the dark in this distant hotel bed, I felt something I could only describe as my spirit having the space to fill up my whole body. I was myself. I was alive. Whatever happened with Pumpkin, or with Stork, or with anything else, I'd be just fine.

CHAPTER 39

Ben was there in the morning with my dad, parked in the front row of the bleachers, his long legs kicked out in front of him. I skated up to say hi. My dad rose as I approached.

"Ready for your match?"

"It's called a game, Dad. And yeah. I feel ready." My heart was pounding and I had butterflies in my stomach, but I kept reminding myself of what Stork had said months ago, that nervousness could be reframed as excitement and anticipation.

"I'm headed to the concession stand." He started to walk away, then paused. "I'll be back before the game starts, don't worry."

"Good." Though I hadn't been worried, I appreciated that he cared enough to reassure me. I grinned and held up my hand for a high five as he passed me, and he smacked my hand in response with a satisfying thwack.

Now it was just Ben and me. "You're here to see Pumpkin, aren't you?"

He made a face. "I'm here to see you both. Don't be a dumbass."

"So, you're really dating her, huh?"

"Seems that way."

"We kind of had a falling out."

"Oh." He blinked and shook his shaggy head. "She didn't tell me that."

"It's okay between us now, I guess. Not the same, though." I peered at him. "You aren't going to break her heart, are you, like you did with that Sienna girl?"

He laughed. "I don't think so! I'm not planning on it, anyway. That okay?"

"Yeah. Good." I had no idea what would happen with Pumpkin and Ben. But I didn't need to get in the middle of it. I began to skate away, but Ben called out to me.

"Hey!"

"What?" I expected another smartass quip, like when he'd left at Christmas and given me a hard time about being bad at video games. But instead, he said, "You know I'm proud of you, right?"

I made a face. "You are?"

"God, Mils, you don't have to sound so surprised. Just take the compliment. You became an actual badass athlete."

I grinned. "I did, didn't I?"

"Go crush them out there, okay?"

"You got it."

Something weird happened in the next game, as if the universe was fulfilling Ben's request: We indeed crushed them. We completely annihilated our opponents. The final score was 301–45.

We had won all three of our games. We were undefeated. We were the winners of Group A. I couldn't believe it. It felt almost spooky. I announced to the team that since I'd worn the same pair of socks today and yesterday, I wasn't going to change them, in case they were good luck.

"Gross, Mighty," said Gables, the only response.

Cleo called me over after we'd all de-geared in the locker room. I approached her nervously, wishing I could follow everyone else as they left.

"You did well today," she said.

Well, this conversation I could handle. I smiled. "Thanks." She had put me in to jam in the second half, when we had a comfortable lead. I was lead jammer three times; I scored plenty of points. But it hadn't been about my individual strengths as a jammer, as much as I wished it was. We were clearly the stronger team, on every metric. Still, I'd heard Ben and my dad cheering, shouting my name as I'd skated my laps, and it had felt wonderful.

"You know why you did so well?"

Was this a trick question? "Because . . . they kind of sucked?"

Her mouth bent into a smile for just a second, then she pushed it away. "Because you didn't let the pressure get to you. You didn't panic, or freeze up, or just push uselessly on people's shoulders."

"All right . . ." I was getting nervous again. She was going somewhere with this.

"I'm putting you in as a blocker tonight in the final, but I'd also like you as an alternate jammer. Toni's left ankle has been giving her trouble, and we don't have a huge jammer rotation. That means I might call you to step in as a jammer sometimes when someone needs a break. Can you handle that?"

I nodded rapidly. "Yes! Of course!"

"Skate like you did today. Without thinking. Without worrying."

"I will. I've felt good on the track all weekend, and I think I'm gonna skate well tonight." I wished Ann was here to hear me say this, rather than off submitting team paperwork to the officials; I knew she'd be proud of me. "And Cleo? If you put me in as a jammer and I'm not doing well, it's okay if you just have me block after that. I won't be sad."

She looked at me wryly. "I wasn't worried about it."

The Sonics had won their three games as well. They were our opponents in the final, exactly as Gables had predicted. Just a few short hours after our big win, we were back on the track, ready to face them.

I turned away when they started their fancy choreographed

warm-up. Instead of watching and getting more nervous, I looked at my teammates. I couldn't believe we'd gotten here. Even if we lost this game, we'd done an amazing job at the tournament. Three wins in a row. God, I loved my team. I loved this sport.

Stork squeezed onto the edge of the bench next to me, drawing me out of my thoughts. "Ready for this?"

"I am." I actually felt like I was, at least as long I didn't turn around and look at the Sonics. "You?"

"Yeah."

I lowered my voice. "I'm sorry again about yesterday, about the Pumpkin thing."

"Stop." She held up a hand. "You already apologized. You don't need to do it anymore. We're okay, all right?"

I looked into her deep brown eyes. How had I ever thought she was a pain? She was amazing.

"And, uh, one more thing . . ." She paused. I had the wild thought that she was going to ask if I was still dating Spiny or not. But no. "Ann told me you talked to her about me pivoting."

"Was that okay?"

"Yeah. It was nice." She smiled at me.

I smiled back. Her eyes were focused right on mine. I leaned closer.

"I have one more thing to say, too."

"Yeah?"

Our heads were only inches apart. I could feel her breath on my face, smell the mint of her toothpaste. "I ended things with Spiny. There wasn't much going on between us to begin with, and it's over now."

Her mouth opened. "Oh." She looked happy, I thought, but just for a flash of an instant, because then heavy hands landed on both our shoulders. Gables.

"Get up, you two! It's time to kick their asses."

We got off to a good start, then clung to an increasingly small lead as the first half progressed. I blocked, working with Gables, listening to directions. I didn't get any big hits on their jammers, but I didn't let them by me easily, either. In the second-to-last jam of the first half, the score turned against us. The Sonics were winning 71–68.

Cleo tapped me on the shoulder. "Mighty, you're jamming this one. Toni's supposed to jam next, but her ankle is acting up. I want her to take it easy for a few minutes, since we're about to go in to halftime anyway."

I pulled on the helmet cover and hit the track before I could think about what I was doing. There was Simply Red, rolling back and forth behind the jam line, just like the last time I'd faced her. I didn't attempt any small talk this time.

I dropped my toe stops, got into a low stance, ready to burst. The whistle blew. I took off, aiming for the space between the hips of two Sonics blockers.

"Eugh." I made an involuntary noise as they squished me between them. Trapped. I struggled back out, behind them again, and tried to hit the inside line. A Sonics blocker beat me to it, and another one came darting over and knocked me down. I jumped back up as quickly as I could. Distantly, I heard the double whistle; Simply Red had gotten lead. I nearly screamed in frustration. I had wanted to be lead jammer so badly, to pay her back for her rudeness, to make my teammates proud, to get our team's lead back.

My fury propelled me forward, driving my shoulder into the ribs of the nearest blocker. I kept hitting, and, though they stayed in front of me, I pushed the Sonics blockers up several feet.

It wasn't enough. Simply Red was nearly behind us, about to score points on the Prairie Skate blockers. And the Sonics blockers were just too big and strong for me to part.

"Mighty!"

I raised my eyes. There was Stork. Ready.

One more desperate wish for glory flashed through my head, then was extinguished. I whipped the jammer cover off my helmet, stepped to the side, and passed it to Stork. She was gone in an instant.

Now I was a blocker, and Simply Red was my target. She hadn't been expecting it. I tried to hit her, and she narrowly scraped past me. But in the effort to dodge my hit, the wheels of her left skate went out of bounds, and she kept skating forward without realizing it.

The ref's whistle was shrill. "Orange, six-seven! Cut!"

A penalty for Simply Red! A power jam! Because of me! Following Gables's lead, we hit the Sonics blockers, clearing a path for Stork.

When the jam was over, Stork had scored sixteen points. We had gotten our lead back. I knew in my heart that I never would have scored that many points. It didn't bother me. I was so glad Stork had been there.

In the second half, I blocked. I relaxed. And like Cleo had said, I played better. I played some of the best derby I'd ever played in my life. I listened to Gables, kept my head clear, and got a few satisfyingly hard hits in on their jammers.

The score before the last jam was 161–154. We had the lead, but not a big enough lead that we could relax. Anything could happen.

Toni was jamming, Stork pivoting, me, Gables, and Pumpkin blocking. The Sonics were jamming Simply Red again. I wasn't surprised; she was their best jammer.

At the whistle blast, Simply Red ran up the inside line, dipped low to avoid a hit from Gables, and skated out in front of the rest of us. *Tweet-tweet!* She was lead. My heart sank.

Toni was struggling to get through the pack. I looked at her and thought about going back to try to hit the orange blockers to help her, but Gables shouted to get my attention.

"Get ready, Mighty! She's coming back around!"

Stork was the teammate nearest me. We came together. She braced me, I blocked, grabbing tightly onto her upper arm. When Simply Red approached, cutting to the outside of the track, I wouldn't have been fast enough to reach her on my own, but with a push from Stork, I hit her just in time. My hips slammed into Simply Red's body—a perfect, devastating hit. She flew out of bounds, sliding on her side.

I looked to Stork, ready to grin about the hit, but Stork was already behind me, skating backward so Simply Red would have to enter the track farther behind her. Ahead, I saw Toni had gotten through and was on a scoring pass.

Gables appeared next to me, breathing hard. "We're fine. Just keep holding her back, not much time left, not enough time for her to close the point difference."

While Gables played offense to help Toni, I worked with Stork and Pumpkin to keep Simply Red from getting through on another pass. There was no sense of tension or bad blood between Stork and Pumpkin, or between Pumpkin and me. The three of us were united in one goal: destroying an opposing jammer.

Time had slowed; surely the two minutes should be over. I was gasping, legs burning, heart pounding. There was no hope of Simply Red scoring enough points for them to win now—there weren't enough seconds left—but she didn't call off the jam. She was going to fight to the end. I couldn't blame her; I suspected I would have done the same.

When the whistle blew, our team erupted.

We'd done it! We won! The bench cleared, everyone rushing to us, piling together, screaming and hugging and jumping.

I grabbed my teammates tight, overflowing with love for each of them, for tough, scary, inspiring Gables, for my fellow rookies Pay and Bee, for Toni and Luna and Rainbow and Dex and every single other person. Even, despite everything, for Pumpkin. Tears blurred my vision. We'd actually done it! Cleo was howling and screaming louder than any of us, lifting Toni into the air and spinning her around. Ann was hugging each of us in turn, her eyes as teary as mine.

Stork and I had been next to each other when the whistle blew, but were immediately pulled apart by our jubilant teammates. Now, suddenly, the mass of green jerseys shifted. Stork was in front of me again, and we were wrapping our arms tight around each other.

"You were incredible!" I shouted.

"You were fantastic!" she shouted back.

And then, happening too fast to ever know which of us had initiated it, her mouth found mine, and we were kissing, deeply, crazily, fueled by our adrenaline and happiness. And then we were laughing hysterically, because . . .

"Mouthguards!" I pulled mine out and shoved it in the pocket of my leggings.

She took hers out, too, and we kissed again, tenderly, somehow simultaneously smiling, while our teammates hollered and cheered around us.

EPILOGUE

**time until the next Soy Anything:
6 months, 19 days**

The air was thick and humid. I was wearing a new pair of jeans and a cute flannel shirt, dressed for fall, even though early September always acted like summer. I was sweaty and nervous.

"What if I'm not ready for this?" I stared up at the big brick building. I was already tired, mentally and physically, and walking inside that building felt like it might be more than I could handle.

The previous weekend had exhausted me. On Saturday, we'd moved Ben back into the dorms at U of I. It was literally the first time I'd ridden in the car with both my parents without hearing them argue. The divorce had been good for them both. Pumpkin's family moved her into the dorms on the same day, and we'd all gone out to eat together afterward. Pumpkin and Ben were still dating, still crazy about each other. As for Pumpkin and me, well, we were friendly, if not exactly friends. Would things change someday? Maybe. It felt like they might. But it was also okay that they hadn't yet.

Then, yesterday morning, I'd headed to the rink, to assist Ann and Cleo with this summer's Skatertots assessment. I kept the Skatertots organized, ran a few drills, answered questions, and tried to redirect their nervous energy so they wouldn't fixate on Ann and Cleo judging them.

Juniors took a summer break, but I still couldn't get enough of derby, so I'd been helping the Skatertots all summer long.

I'd started doing it because I didn't want to go long without skating, but it had brought me joy that I hadn't anticipated. When the Skatertots mastered a new skill, finally completing a turn-around stop or gliding on one leg, I cheered them on. When the Skatertots struggled, I helped, and I reminded them that I'd been just where they were a year ago.

"How'd you get better?" a gangly, awkward girl had asked me, after tripping over her own skates and falling to her knees.

"I just kept showing up," I'd said, quoting Gables's long-ago advice to me. "And, of course, I cross-trained."

Soon, some of them would join the Juniors team, taking the spots vacated by Pumpkin, Luna, and a few other skaters who'd graduated. I hadn't been privy to Cleo and Ann's discussion of which Skatertots had passed their assessments, but I couldn't wait to find out.

Before that could happen, though, I had to face something far scarier. The brick building in front of me.

"Seriously, I might not be ready. You really are sure about this?" I asked for the thousandth time, looking up at the imposing building and the people streaming into the doors.

Stork grinned at me. "Yes, I'm still sure. It's a good school, with good teachers. We'll have fun, I promise. Maybe I can even get you to join the track team." She took my hand, squeezed it, then brought it to her mouth and kissed my knuckles lightly. "Come on. Let's get to class."

ACKNOWLEDGMENTS

Will Flux let me write an acknowledgments section that rivals the length of my actual novel? We're going to find out, because there are so many people who need acknowledging!

From the first time I spoke with Ashtyn Stann, I knew my novel had found the absolute perfect editor. She truly understands Millie, and I've felt so supported in my time working with her. I've heard other people say that their editors made their books better, and WOW do I ever get that now. Every single one of Ashtyn's notes and edit letters have made me a stronger writer. When I read her comments, they resonate on this deep level, my brain going, "Oh. Yes. THIS is how it's supposed to be." *Mighty Millie Novak* is a better book because of Ashtyn (and it's also because of her that I haven't completely botched how calendars work).

The whole Flux team has been amazing from start to finish. Meg Gaertner, Heather McDonough, Taylor Kohn—you are all wonderful.

What can I say about Allison Hellegers? My agent extraordinaire and I found each other after my bizarre semi-viral Twitter experience. Thinking of her offer of representation still gives me chills. Being repped by Alli is a dream come true. My writing, in her hands, is home. (She also understands how much I swear and how petty I am. Alli, me, you, and Tricia still need to have that glass of champagne sometime.)

My cover artist, Chloe Friedlein, is so incredibly talented! Chloe, I am so lucky to have you bring Millie's image to life. Karli Kruse, my cover designer, a huge thank-you to you as well. I am obsessed with my unique cover design!

Speaking of bringing Millie to life, Paula Carvajal, your

illustrations of Millie and her teammates on their team trading cards—SO cute. You know I love them. Thank you for every single adorable drawing. I'm still dying over how perfect Luna's hair is.

All right, time to take the track. I have so many derby players to thank!

First off, a huge thanks to Stings Like Abbie, Deus Ex Knockin' Ya, and Kim Kong, the winners of my "name a derby player" contest. I'm so glad I got to fill out the Prairie Skate roster with Bee, Dex, and Kiko.

Next, hey reader, did you appreciate all the punny derby names in this book? Well, I absolutely did NOT come up with them all myself. (In fact, I think the only one I actually get credit for is Impaylor Swift—which I am pretty proud of, to be fair.) So let me give a big shoutout to the clever people who helped me name my characters: Korfan, Glottal Attack, The Gorram Reaver, The Mean Queen, Mary Annimal, Nat Splat, Sassbot, Shelby Cobra, Slaughterhouse Thighs, Alexandra Slamilton—and a special shout out to Skullz B. Kraken, who came up with Millie's derby name!

Thank you to Wolframmer, Nat Splat, and Dark Matter for reading drafts of my novel from a derby perspective and reminding me of things like "30-minute halves, Auntie, not 60-minute halves" and "the head ref would do the ejection, not the coach" and all the other details that made sure this book was thoroughly grounded in reality.

Wolframmer: From the first time we met, when you made me grab your thigh to feel your new derby muscles, to the many, many (MANY!) snarky remarks we've traded, code words we've invented, and weird nonsense stories we've created, from Las Vegas to Berlin, you are amazing. Someday the whole world will know and love Sterling Wolverton.

Nat Splat: Our league is so lucky to have you! Thank you for looking at this manuscript with your keen jammer brain, given its writer's own immutable blocker-y-ness. (Eagle-eyed derby fans can actually find Nat herself spinning and dodging on the pages of this novel . . . well, one page, anyway.)

Dark Matter: More on you in a bit.☺

My Reservoir Dolls teammates, my Madison Roller Derby league-mates: I've got such love for you all. We are so damn lucky to get to play this sport, aren't we? As Mouse has said, we play for those who can't. Let's keep doing it forever, okay?

Calla DeWilde (Wolfie): If I move through life with a tiny fraction of your fearlessness, your bravery, your cool confidence in the face of any challenge, I will be lucky. We all miss you, love you, and will never forget you.

Rachel Rotten and Lady Trample: Thank you so much for reading my novel and letting me put your names in it! I am not too proud to admit that I am still way intimidated by you, and I squeal like a fangirl whenever you write back to me.☺

Moving along, going further back in time. How can I ever list all the people who've encouraged me as a writer? Ugh, I can't. Still, I'll continue, knowing I'm inevitably going to forget someone.

The teachers whose belief has fueled me: Mrs. Mesick, Mrs. Pleviak, Ms. Flint. I'll never forget the feedback I got on my personal essay from my journalism professor at McHenry County College: "You have something to say." Those words meant so much. (But God help me, though I will always remember your words, I cannot remember your name! That's what happens when you then switch to a physics major, I guess.)

My writing friends, going on their own journey alongside me: Thank you for keeping me calm(ish) in the face of my neurotic writing fears, and sharing your own wisdom and stories with me. The Pumpkins (my first writer Twitter chat!), the Rockets, the 2024-evers, the "bridging the gap" Discord: I love you all. Zipps, no one has better comments on my work than you (remember when you threatened to sue me after one character bought another a coffee in one of my manuscripts?). I'm so lucky to have met you, and I'm obsessed with your books.

Chris and Tasha: You are two of my favorite people. Chris, you've always believed in my career as a writer, in your unshakeable and understated way, never entertaining doubt. Tasha, you inspire me as a person in so many ways—the way you take on challenges like it's no big deal, the way you bring creativity and intelligence to all aspects of your life, and the way you live according to your values. I am honored to have you as a friend and a co-dog-mom. I hope when this novel blows up, you're both prepared for my obsessed fans to start driving by your house on an unofficial tour, since it's the scene of my Twitter blowup and my first Zoom meeting with Alli. (And if that ever actually happens, Chris, I'm confident you'll immediately find a way to monetize it.)

Amanda and Connie: Can you believe we've been friends for over twenty years? From the Trappers in the townhouse to fake names on Manor Monday, your decades of love, friendship, and support have made my life immeasurably better. Here's to decades and decades more. The Hive lives!

My family: How am I not supposed to cry while I type this, huh? I mean, let's be real, I'm definitely crying.

Katie: We're family at this point; we both know this. You and I have been partners in so many fun and ridiculous creative endeavors, ever since we were little kids. I'm so glad I found someone with an equally wild imagination, and that we found each other so early in our lives. I am honored to be Emmie's godmother. And remember, you can choose any color you want, because it's *your* makeover.

Alissa and Quinn: I won the jackpot, getting you two as (step)kids. Alissa, thank you for reading my novels and helping me make sure my teenage narrators don't sound like forty-somethings. Also thank you for being kind, hilarious, smart, and compassionate. Quinn, what a privilege it's been to get to share my passion for derby with you. Remember when you were little, doing apex jumps like Hammer Abby in our kitchen? (I hope that isn't embarrassing.) Also thank you for being my partner in chilling out in the air-conditioning on vacations (instead of walking very fast and reading every historical marker like the other half of our family).

Helen: My little sister, my podcast cohost, the one person whose sense of humor perfectly matches my own. The uncomfortable giraffe to my enthusiastic moose. Not to mention an incredible writer, scientist, and activist. I'm so lucky to have you as a sister (and I'm glad you are secretly getting thanked twice in these acknowledgments.) "You get the one, you get that other one."

Adam: You are the love of my goddamn life. I am so happy that we found each other. You're the best. (No, you are NOT Gene Parmesan, shut up.) Years and years ago (even earlier than I realized!), you read my short stories and told me how talented I was. Just a few days ago, you told me you were actively angry every time you had to set down the draft of my latest manuscript, because it was so good. Your support of me as a writer means all the more because YOU are such a fantastic writer. Hey, people reading these acknowledgments? Go look up *Modernizing Tradition: Gender and Consumerism in Interwar France and Germany.* That's him! He's so smart! Okay, now click "add to cart."

And finally, my parents. Mom and Buff, do you understand that I would not be a writer if it weren't for you two? There aren't words big enough to express my feelings here. I am so, so lucky. Mom, you wrote down my stories before I was even old enough to write ("Hey, Moon Dancer, are you pregnant? I'm pregnant!"). Buff, do you remember typing my screenplay that was going to be about me and my friends auditioning for a movie, except it was actually just the characters fighting about who got what color Popsicle? You both have modeled so many things that have made me the writer and person I am: creativity, kindness, humor, intelligence. From you both,

I learned how to lead an unconventional life that makes me happy, rather than doing society's default.

Your love has been a safety net underneath me every day of my life.

Mom, you have always been my first reader. When I sent you the very first chapter of this novel, in summer 2020, you emailed me back sixteen minutes later and said (this is a direct quote), "Oh MY GOD. Well, you had me crying at about the third paragraph in. I LOVE IT. But I keep thinking that maybe it was Mighty who miscounted? I would LOVE to read a story about her." And now you and a whole lot more people have that story. Would I have had the momentum to finish without your encouragement? Luckily, we don't have to find out. (And yes, now you know, Millie is the one who miscounted.)

Finally, to YOU, the person reading this. THANK YOU. It is seriously an honor to have you reading Millie's story. I hope it inspires you to let go of your own insecurities and live confidently and honestly. (And, okay, I also hope it makes you join a derby team.)

ABOUT THE AUTHOR

Like Millie, Elizabeth Holden is an avid roller derby player, a blocker with Madison Roller Derby since 2015. Liz's league-mates know her as Auntie Matter; her derby name is a reference to her job teaching college physics. (And, yes, she is also an aunt. Hi, William and Hugo!) When not busy writing, playing derby, or teaching, Liz is most likely leading international trips with her company, Leaping Hound Travel. Liz also cohosts an *X-Files* podcast, *We Want to Believe*, with her sister. Liz's tattoos are vibrant and numerous, her laugh is loud, and her heart belongs to her pet greyhounds. Learn more about her at elizabeth-holden.com.